Turbulence

by

Elaine Meece

Cayna,
Enjoy your
Cruise!
Elaine Meece

Turbulence – Flight for Life series - Book One.

Author -Elaine Meece

Sassafras Publishing
686 Brinsley Cove
Memphis, TN. 38017

Published May 2017

ISBN- 13:978-1546800132
ISBN- 10:1546800131

Cover Art by Valerie Tibbs Design

This book is a work of fiction. Names, characters, places, dialogue and events are products of the author's imagination are used fictitiously, and any likeness to actual person, living or dead, business establishments or locales is entirely by coincidence. References to any real people, places, groups, or organizations are intended to only provide a sense of authenticity and are fictitious in use.

Other books available by Elaine Meece include:

Eye of the Abductor	Deceitful Hearts
Under Currents	Fatally Yours
Dark Side of the Mirror	Blood Tide
When Death Calls	Love in the Shadows

Visit www.elainemeece.com

Acknowledgement

Once again I'd like to thank my husband, Geoffrey, and my daughters, Alicia, Valencia, and Franchesca, for their help and support with my writing. I want to thank Nancy Wallace for her help. Finally, I'd like to thank retired pilots, George Malone and Mike Scearce for their help.

Dedication

When I was a teacher, I took an aerospace class at the University of Memphis taught by Dr. Crabtree. He always wore a smile and listened to whatever anyone had to say. One requirement of the class was to take flight lessons. The experience was one of the highlights of my life. I was a natural at landing.

During the class, I came up with the idea for Turbulence. Dr. Crabtree was excited about the book. Unfortunately, I had other books to write before it. I'm not sure what has become of Dr. Crabtree, but I know he would be delighted that I finally wrote the book his class inspired. So this is dedicated to him.

This is me in a Cessna 172.

Chapter One

Was her mind playing tricks on her?

Cynthia Reynolds read the names of Zurtel Aerospace Corporation's recently hired employees. She squinted taking a closer look at one particular name.

Tristen Conners.

A queasy feeling twirled in her stomach.

Surely, it wasn't him.

But it said pilot. What would be the odds of there being another Tristen Conners, who just happens to be a pilot? Zero. It was him.

She marched to the secretary's desk. "Jennifer, call Human Resources and find out who hired Tristen Conners."

"Is he related to Robert Conners?"

"It's his son. Robert Conners will be retiring this year. Maybe he plans for Tristen to slide into his position. I'm almost positive Robert cornered Dad for a favor."

Cynthia returned to her office. Last she'd heard, Tristen worked for one of the larger airlines. Not that she'd kept up with him. She hadn't thought of him in years. Then she recalled the airline he'd worked for canceling its overseas flights and laying off pilots.

A minute later, the secretary poked her head through the doorway. "Your father hired him without a single evaluation or interview."

"Thanks, Jennifer." Cynthia called her father and arranged to meet for lunch. After what Tristen had done, she couldn't grasp why her father would hire him. Worst of all, she'd have to come in contact with Tristen at some point.

At the age of seventeen, she'd sworn she never wanted to see him again. If she did, she'd be tempted to run him over with her car. She wouldn't want to kill him. She'd only want to screw up his life like he had hers. While she'd believed he loved her, it had meant nothing to him but a summer conquest while he spent time with his dad in Atlanta.

Rather than break it off in person, the coward had his dad deliver a letter after he'd left for Florida where he lived with his mom.

In the letter, he'd stated their relationship had been a mistake, and he loved a girl back home. To sum it all up, he wrote it was over and not to contact him.

♦♦♦

At noon, Cynthia met her father at Mary Mac's Tea Room. She always enjoyed the quaint charm of this place that served some of the best food in Atlanta. She smiled as she walked toward the table where he sat. "Glad you could come."

"Did you drive yourself?" her father asked.

"No, I left my car in the garage. It's too hard to park here. Ellis drove me."

"So what's this about?" her father asked.

"Is it a crime to want to treat my dad to lunch?" She sat facing him.

Her father studied the menu. "I'm having the chicken and dumplings with peach cobbler."

She winked. "Better watch that waistline. The widows will stop coming around."

"They're interested in my money, not my waistline. Besides, after burying two wives, I'll never get married again."

After ordering a salad and tea, she checked her emails.

"Really? You have to do that at lunch?"

She shrugged and put her phone away. "I saw the newsletter this morning."

"Did you read my article about the Christmas bonuses?"

She hadn't. "No, I was too busy checking out Zurtel's new employees." She frowned. "You hired Tristen Conners without consulting me."

"Didn't know I needed your approval." He sipped his coffee.

"After what he did, I'm surprised you hired him. I'm assuming it was a favor to his father. Am I right?"

"You are. His father has been a loyal employee and a friend."

After divorcing Tristen's mom, Robert Conners had moved into a small house on her family's estate. He had always been at her father's beck and call.

Her dad added more sweetener to his coffee. "You're a big girl and can cope with Tristen being an employee. He needs the job. He has a six year old daughter to provide for."

"Does his wife work?"

"She died of ovarian cancer last year."

She ignored the tightness in her throat. She refused to feel sorry for him. "That's tragic."

"There's some kind of custody issue with his in-laws. He'll be going to court in March, and he needs to show employment."

"So, it's just until he goes to court, right?"

"No, he's hired permanently."

Until you retire.

"You were both seventeen. You're adults now. Let the past go."

She drew in a breath. "I've never been able to let it go. Somewhere, Tristen and I have an eleven year old daughter."

After her daughter had been taken from her, a hole had been left in her heart. For the first year after the birth, she'd had nightmares of an infant crying.

Cynthia stopped talking when the waiter brought their lunch. But the subject had destroyed her appetite. "Have you ever told Robert?"

He shook his head. "No, your mother thought it best he didn't know."

"She's not my mother. My mother died when I was nine."

Her situation was like Cinderella all over again. Except instead of sisters, she had a wicked stepmother and a twisted stepbrother. In her sick mind, Edith had hoped Cynthia and Randall would marry someday and rule the Zurtel empire together. She'd always done what she could to keep Cynthia's serious suitors away and had been successful.

Cynthia sighed. "I don't want Tristen knowing. Trust me, he's not the type who'd care."

"He was seventeen. Life has a way of beating the arrogance right out of us."

"He left that summer and never looked back. He never considered there might be consequences. I want him fired as soon as the court date is over, and I don't want him piloting any of my flights. Got it?"

"Give the guy a chance."

"No. I'd rather travel by Greyhound bus than let him pilot my jet."

Her father chuckled. "Apparently, you've never ridden a bus."

She rolled her eyes. "I didn't mean it literally."

"No, you've spent too much of your life riding in limousines. You've lived a very privileged life."

"I didn't that spring."

He grew solemn. "I know. Edith did what she thought was best."

Tears clogged Cynthia's throat. "Edith only did what was best for Edith. She didn't want it getting out I was pregnant."

"You'll never forgive her."

"Or Tristen."

Her father studied her. "Let's change the subject. You're too thin."

"I am not. But if you want to talk about weight, let's discuss the extra pounds you put on at Thanksgiving."

"Now that's playing dirty."

She sighed. "I wish you could attend the merger meeting this afternoon," she said.

"I've already delegated the majority of the power to you and Randall."

While eating, they chatted about simple things, steering away from business. Before leaving, she hugged her dad. "Enjoy your round of golf."

He blushed. "You know me too well."

After lunch, Cynthia headed for the black Cadillac XTS Coach limo. "To the office, Ellis."

"Yes, Miss Reynolds," he replied, opening the rear door for her.

As she entered the boardroom that afternoon, dread weighed heavy on her shoulders. For two weeks leading up to the vote, they had argued every day. Her stepbrother, Randall Miller, would push once again for a merger with Novik Industries. He had an overpowering personality and the charm of a snake.

So far, she'd been the only thing stopping the merger.

She'd always been leery of him. When she was twelve, he'd tried to rape her, but his mother and her father hadn't believed her. Fortunately, she'd spent a lot of time at boarding schools and hadn't been around him except for holidays and summer breaks. When home on breaks, she'd kept her door locked.

The meeting lingered on with a PowerPoint focusing on Novik. Heated arguments followed.

Cynthia glanced around the table at the board members, five men and three women. Two members hadn't made it to today's meeting. They would arrive tomorrow in time to vote.

She pinned Randall with a harsh look. "Why should we consider merging with a company who has supplied inferior products to airlines, been plagued with numerous lawsuits, and comes to us with millions in unpaid debts? Why, Randall? Without the fancy graphics and charts, explain what this merger will do for Zurtel."

He glared with hatred but remained speechless.

She smiled. "That's what I thought. The merger is off the table."

"Like hell it is," Randall snarled. "We're voting tomorrow."

"Seriously?" She faced the board members. "Our new metal will make all our products lighter from engines to fuel pumps and be ten times more cost efficient. Every airplane manufacturer in the world will want onboard. Why would we want to share this with Novik?"

"You and your winged monkeys haven't discovered shit. Every attempt to replace aluminum alloy and steel has failed. Graphene oxide will never hold up under extreme pressure, besides it's not cost efficient to produce in bulk."

"True. But we have developed a new lightweight metal, MX7 that will hold up under extreme pressure."

"If you're talking about microlattice, Boeing is already on it."

"And they haven't been able to perfect it for use yet. With our new metal, we'll jump ten steps ahead of Boeing. Like microlattice, MX7 is constructed of mostly air."

Randall rolled his eyes. "Care to share the formula for this magic compound?"

"Not just yet. It's still in the testing stage. MX7 will replace the aluminum alloy we now use."

One man raised his hand. "Explain how this new material will revolutionize the industry."

"I'll use our fuel pump as an example. Meeting all FAA CA14 standards, it will be light enough that it makes rotation from the tanks faster causing it to be more fuel efficient."

"What about contaminates?"

"Contaminate free," she replied. "The entire fuel system, including the tanks, will be almost as light as air helping with fuel consumption. The lighter material causes less deterioration on the hoses. If an airline could reduce the weight of each aircraft by seventy-percent, think of the savings from fuel alone."

"That's amazing," one of the women chimed in.

It had also impressed the others.

She tried to make eye contact with all of them. "So if we are standing on ground breaking technology that will revolutionize the aerospace industry, why share our glory and money with Novik"

“It sounds too good to be true,” Randall said. “I think this is all a smoke screen to sway tomorrow’s votes. We need more information.”

“Twice we’ve had our computers hacked and information stolen and sold. Even our Internet storage has been compromised. I’m not taking any chances with this. The formula is kept in the company vault,” she said, knowing it was a lie.

After the second hacking, she concluded someone in the company could be selling them out. She decided not to keep the formula on any computers in the lab. She had the hard drives from the lab computers destroyed and replaced.

Both attacks had been blamed on cyber thieves. This would not be handled the same as before. Instead, she’d memorized the formula. Just as a precaution, she saved it to a disc and kept it hidden. Though archaic, this method seemed to be working.

For use in the lab, the MX7 formula had been translated into an encrypted code that only the lab’s main computer could read. If anyone tried to hack the code, the algorithm sent out a series of endless undecipherable numbers.

“I’d like to see how close we are to the merger,” Randall said. “I’m conducting a mock vote.”

Cynthia studied the board members’s faces, but they remained stoic as they casted their votes and slid them to the chairman.

While he counted the votes, Cynthia fidgeted with the cuff of her sleeve. Finally, she glanced up. There would be ten votes including her and Randall’s votes. How many members had Randall bribed or threatened?

“In favor of the merger, we have five votes. Against, we have five.”

Cynthia frowned. The decision would fall on Davis and Simmons. Rather than waste time trying to sway the five people in favor of the merger, she needed to reach the two men who hadn’t been present for the mock vote.

Randall smirked. “Tomorrow, if they both vote in favor, we proceed with the merger.”

"And when it does, our stocks will drop with the momentum of a two ton iron ball off a twenty story building." Cynthia gathered her things and left.

A mere email, text, or phone call wouldn't suffice. She had to speak to both men in person tonight before they flew into Atlanta for tomorrow's vote.

Randall stopped her at the door. "You won't be running the show once we merge."

"It won't matter. If the merger is approved, the show won't be worth running." She considered hitting him with her computer bag, but didn't since board members were present.

He cocked one brow in suspicion. "Where are you running off to?"

"Christmas shopping," she lied.

Not allowing him a chance to reply, she rushed into the elevator and rode down to the parking garage on the lower level of Zurtel's twenty-nine floor office building.

She exited the elevator with a group of employees. As they entered the dimly lit garage, a black motorcycle sped toward them. People screamed and jumped out of its path. The bike's engine revved up and echoed throughout the structure.

It headed toward her.

The rider wore a black helmet concealing his face.

Cynthia dodged the motorcycle. For a moment, she froze uncertain of what to do.

He slid to a screeching halt, quickly circled around, and sped toward her. Again people screamed while others shouted at the man for almost hitting them, but it was clear she was his target.

Get to the car.

She ran toward her Mercedes-Benz convertible.

Her heart raced.

Before reaching her car, he rode past her, snatched her laptop bag, and zoomed off down the ramp, vanishing from sight.

It had happened so quickly, she couldn't react.

Someone had called 911. Sirens blared in the distance.

Cynthia drew in several long breaths to slow down her heartbeat.

She shivered all over. There wasn't a shred of doubt he'd been waiting for her. Not having time to speak with police, she climbed in her car, started the engine, backed up quickly, and left. She had to reach Simmons and Davis to persuade them to vote against the merger. Zurtel's future depended on it. As for her laptop, it was her personal computer and didn't contain anything of value.

♦♦♦

Tristen Conners stared at the custody suit documents. "Son-of-a-bitch."

"Ooo," scolded his six year old daughter. "Daddy, you said bad words."

"Yeah, I did. Sorry, Mal."

She climbed into his lap and placed her arms around his neck. "That's all right. I know you're sad about your job and Mommy."

He nodded not explaining what the papers were about.

His in-laws kept Mallory most of the time, so why seek legal custody? Did they fear he'd meet someone and eventually move away? He'd never separate Mallory from them. But this was too much to deal with. He wanted to sit down and reason with his former in-laws, but his attorney advised against it.

He'd understand it more if Mallory favored Danielle, but she didn't. His daughter had his brown eyes and hair. She resembled his mom.

If he showed up in court next month unemployed, the judge might rule in favor of the Williams. Danielle would have been disappointed in her parents.

"Daddy," Mallory said. "Did you make my snowflake?"

He sighed, knowing he hadn't remembered to buy the items needed to make it. "I'll do it tonight."

"I need it tomorrow," Mallory said. She had just turned five when she lost her mom.

"I know. We need to hurry. Grandma Rose is waiting for you." He hated leaving her with them, but he didn't have a choice.

On the drive over, Mallory said, "Sing my song."

"We're almost there."

"Sing just a little. Pleeeease."

Tristen grinned for a moment. "Okay." Though he wasn't the best singer, he sang a few verses of *Brown Eyed Girl.* He glanced back in the rearview mirror and found Mallory rocking with the beat and smiling happily.

After parking in his former in-laws' driveway, Tristen placed a hand on Mallory's knee and squeezed. "I love you, Mal. More than anything in the world. Always remember that."

She gave him a huge smile. "I know, Daddy."

"Let's go. Grandma cranky-butt is peeking through the blinds."

Mallory laughed.

"You know my nickname for her is our little secret."

Mallory pretended to zip her lips.

At the door, his daughter looked up at him. "I love you, Daddy. Don't forget to make my snowflake."

"You'll have it."

He glared at Rose. "Her school holiday program is tomorrow at 1:00. She'd like for you to come."

"We'll be there."

Actually, he wished they'd miss it, but Mallory wanted them there.

"Be good, Mallory."

She nodded and hugged him.

On his way to Zurtel's private airstrip, he stopped by a dollar store and purchased everything needed for the snowflake. Now he had to find the time to make it.

He arrived early for his first flight with Zurtel and submitted his flight plan. It'd be a straight flight to Jacksonville. His father had made a career with the company and had probably done some serious begging to convince Everett Reynolds to hire him.

At the hangar, Dwayne Black met him. "She requested your old man."

"Dad's grounded all week with the flu." Tristen tossed his leather pouch to the other shoulder. "What about the other pilot?"

"Mike's flying Randall tonight."

"Looks like she'll have to settle for me."

"You might not even see her."

"If I'm lucky."

"Trust me. She considers pilots no more than overpaid chauffeurs. We're all beneath Miss High and Mighty Cynthia Reynolds."

Tristen grinned thinking how much his uniform could pass for a chauffeur's uniform.

He didn't mention he knew Cynthia. After the summer he'd spent at the Reynolds's estate, all he could think about was a way he could spend his life with her. But at the airport, his dad gave him a letter from Cynthia. Bottom line—he wasn't good enough for her. She wrote whatever they'd shared was over. Despite the note, he tried calling to no avail. His number had been blocked.

Now he debated how to approach her. Should he casually greet her like old friends?

Cythnia, great seeing you. You're looking good, Cynthia.

An image of her firing him his first night ran through his mind, making him rethink it. Nope, this had to be business. Nothing else. If unemployed, he could lose Mallory.

At the larger airlines, a maintenance crew handled the outer preflight check. Here, each pilot or copilot conducted a preflight test both inside and out.

He walked the length of the jet, checking for fuel or oil leaks and making sure the jet had been gassed up. He didn't find any damage done to the outer skin or loose fasteners or bolts. The tires and landing gears looked good, and everything secured down.

Inside, he had to familiarize himself with the Beechjet 400. It was smaller than the 747 he'd flown. First thing, he built his nest, adjusting his seat, so he'd have some space between him and the instrument panel. Then he set the rudder to suit him. Using an iPad, he reviewed the maintenance log from the previous flight based on the Hobbs reading. Then he checked the weather report for the areas he'd be flying. Their route didn't show any problems. He conducted a standard safety check in the cockpit.

The corporation also owned and operated several Piaggio 180 II jets. From what he heard, Randall had been eyeing a Gulf Stream G450.

The outer steps vibrated as someone walked up them.

"Welcome aboard, Miss Reynolds," Annie said. The thin female attendant wore brown glasses with her hair twisted up. She had the potential to be pretty.

"How long before departure?" Cynthia asked, her voice bristling with frustration and impatience.

She didn't sound like the seventeen year old girl who had so willingly loved him.

He crossed through the galley that separated the cockpit from the cabin. In the passenger area sat four leather love seats with tables before each one. "We're waiting for the copilot. He's stuck in traffic."

When she turned around, her green eyes shot ice crystals at him. "I wasn't speaking to you."

Even her Arctic greeting didn't stop him from staring at her. She still wore her black hair long. He couldn't help but think of how many times he'd kissed her gorgeous lips. It seemed like eons ago. He couldn't deny seeing her stirred memories. But this wasn't the girl he'd fallen in love with. Though still elegant and beautiful, this woman came across as cold and hard.

He glanced past her and smiled at the flight attendant. "Please inform Miss Reynolds, our copilot is held up in traffic due to an accident."

Though appearing uncomfortable, the attendant repeated his message.

"I'm going to be late," Cynthia complained.

Tristen glanced at the attendant. "Let her know the bird doesn't fly without a copilot. It's her father's rule. I can make up the time once we're in the sky."

Cynthia huffed. "Never mind, I heard him. I requested your father."

"Dad's got the flu." Tristen grinned. "You could take a commercial flight."

She narrowed her large green eyes into slits and glared. "As soon as you have your court date, you're out of here. Got it?"

"Loud and clear."

Annie's flabbergasted expression revealed she'd probably figured out he already knew Cynthia.

He returned to the cockpit and took his seat. Just maybe he could land another job with one of the other airlines. Mallory's tuition came due in February. He couldn't afford to walk out on this job. He had to cool his attitude. He didn't like working for the ice queen. Obviously, the letter she'd written after that summer reflected her true feelings.

Once Evan joined him in the cockpit, Tristen slipped on his headphones and finished the interior preflight check, making sure all systems worked properly. He then taxied onto the private runway and checked the engines.

Unlike a class C or D airport, it didn't have a ground or tower controller to instruct him. He contacted UNICOM and made his intention to takeoff known so any aircrafts in the area would be aware of him.

Tristen sped down the runway. Once he reached a speed of 120, he pulled back on the control yoke, then increased the power, lifting into the air. Once he leveled out, he found a radio frequency and identified himself with a tower controller at ATL as he flew under their radar. He'd never get tired of the rush taking off gave him.

♦♦♦

Cynthia closed her eyes. His voice still sent shivers over her. She didn't want to feel any of her old yearnings. He had walked out on her and never looked back.

He wasn't the scrawny seventeen year old. He'd filled out nicely, and his voice had deepened.

They'd become best friends and then lovers. She had willingly given her virginity to him. It wasn't until he had returned to Florida that she realized she was pregnant.

Each night, she read his crude letter, reminding herself what a fool she'd been.

Right when she planned to tell Tristen's father about the baby, her stepmother tricked her into going to the unwed mothers's home. Friends and family believed she was studying abroad. Dumb, but everyone bought it. Giving up her daughter had left her hollow. Through the years, she thought about her daughter often especially on her birthday, April seventeenth.

"Annie, bring me a diet soda," Cynthia requested. She'd prefer something stronger but had to keep her mind sharp to deal with Davis and Simmons.

"Here's your soda," Annie said. "Anything else, Miss Reynolds?"

"No, thank you."

Cynthia recalled her father saying Tristen had a daughter. She couldn't resist the temptation to snoop. She took her phone out and looked him up on social media, then checked out his photo albums. His daughter had dark hair, brown eyes, and big dimples like her dad. Cute kid. Some pictures included his wife, Danielle.

She read his last post describing the snowflake he was making for Mallory's Christmas program at St. Mary's. It was an affluent school.

"We're approaching Jacksonville, Florida. The temperature is sixty-five and skies are clear," Tristen's dreamy voice said over the speaker.

Cynthia prepared for landing. While waiting, she tried to keep her thoughts off of Tristen both past and present.

You are so not over him

Oh, yes, I am.

♦♦♦

Tristen approached Jacksonville. "Cecil, this is November 49220, twenty miles to the northwest of Jacksonville at 4000 inbound for landing at Cecil Field."

"November 49220, standby."

Once closer to the airport, the controller came on. "November 49220, you're clear on runway 1-7, winds 150 knots."

"Cleared to runway 1-7," Tristen repeated.

Finally, he landed smoothly, then taxied into a private hangar. Once stopped and the engine shut down, Tristen jotted notes on the tablet while Evan opened the cockpit door. Tristen entered the cabin, a few minutes behind the copilot.

Tristen hadn't intended for his gaze to fall on Cynthia's glacier eyes. She lowered them and stuffed papers into her briefcase, then unfastened her seatbelt.

"Do you have anything you need help with?" Tristen asked, actually hoping to mend things between them.

"No. And I'll ask if I do. If I don't, don't offer." Cynthia stood and strutted to the door. When her purse strap caught the arm of the sofa, it jerked her back. She had her hands full and couldn't pull it free. She glared at him. "Pull that strap off."

Tristen begrudgingly removed it. "A *thank you* would be sufficient."

Annie and Evan stood flabbergasted over his boldness.

She looped it over her shoulder. "You work for me. Whatever I request is part of your job." Evan had already lowered the steps. As she stepped down, she glanced back at Tristen. "Be ready to depart at five o'clock."

After she left, Annie frowned. "You shouldn't taunt her. She'll fire you."

Evan nodded. "You wouldn't be the first."

"Employee or not, it doesn't hurt to show some manners."

Tristen filled out his flight log. Afterwards, he thought about Cynthia. What had happened to the carefree, fun girl he'd loved that summer?

♦♦♦

Cynthia spotted the small limo parked in front of the airport. The driver ran around and opened the door. While riding, she considered who had hired the man to steal her laptop. She'd like to be there when they opened her personal computer and only discovered downloaded books. If they pulled the information from the hard drive, they'd have all her Pinterest Secrets. She smiled.

She met with Davis at their Jacksonville plant. It didn't take a brain surgeon to know that Randall had already spoken with the guy.

"Let me get straight to the point, you have a lot of shares in Zurtel," she said. "Those shares will be worthless if we merge. I'm sure he failed to show Novik's downside." She pulled up the information on her company laptop and held it where he could see.

Davis studied it. "No. He didn't show this to me."

"Merging with Novik will bring Zurtel to an all time low. You'll lose your shirt. Actually, we'll all lose everything."

"Then why does he want this?"

Cynthia sighed. "That's a good question. And whatever the answer is, I'm sure you'll find it benefits Randall." She wouldn't mention her speculations on his motive. "Whatever new car or boat he's promised for your vote isn't worth what you'll lose in the long run. So, do you agree to vote against the merger?"

Finally, he nodded. "I will."

During the drive back to the airport, Cynthia considered why Randall would want the merger with a company that would destroy them. The stockholders would panic and sell. Stock prices would plummet. How could her stepbrother profit? He had as much to lose as anyone.

The owner of Novik had been listed as Quinn Adams, but no one had ever met him. They had only met his CEOs.

As the limo approached the jet, the door opened, and the steps were lowered. After telling them to be ready, she'd expected the preflight check to be completed and the engines roaring.

To her bewilderment, Tristen sat in the cabin, piecing segments of white poster board like a puzzle.

"What are you doing?" she asked.

"Mallory's Christmas program is tomorrow. I promised I'd make it tonight."

Rather than act like a bitch, she ignored him and took her seat.

"You mind if I leave this out, so I can finish it after we land in Memphis?"

She shook her head, then pulled out her company laptop, pretending to be too busy to acknowledge him.

"Thanks." He returned through the galley to the cockpit.

She waited until they were safely in the air before unfastening her seatbelt and easing over to the small table to view Tristen's work in progress.

She frowned at the mess. A chimp at the zoo could've done better. She picked up the diagram and studied it. He had all the wrong segments glued together. Fortunately, there was enough white poster board to start over. For the next forty minutes, she measured and drew off strips, cut them out, and glued them together to form the perfect snowflake. She applied the glue and sprinkled silver glitter and iridescent sparkles over it.

Cynthia smiled at her masterpiece, then frowned. He would take this the wrong way. "Annie, come here."

"Yes, Miss Reynolds. May I get you something before we land?"

"I want you to say you made this."

"But I didn't."

"I know. I'm asking you to tell a little white lie."

The attendant didn't look convinced.

"I'll do the lying. You just nod."

The attendant agreed.

After the plane landed in Memphis, Cynthia stood, dusted the glitter and iridescent sparkles from her dress.

The copilot opened the outer door and lowered the stairs. Tristen made his way to the cabin.

"You'll need to find something else to do. Annie made Mallory's snowflake. Didn't you, Annie?"

Annie nodded looking like she was standing before a firing squad.

Tristen smiled. "That's great. Thanks, Annie."

Cynthia remembered that genuine million dollar smile. She frowned. "Have this mess cleaned up by the time I return."

"Yes, Miss Reynolds," Tristen said, humbly.

♦♦♦

Tristen studied the two women. Cynthia had glitter all over her while Annie didn't have a speck on her. He waited until she left to corner the attendant. "Now Annie, I've already figured out the truth."

"Mr. Conners, please just say thank you and don't ask any more questions."

He laughed. "Thanks, Annie."

Tristen stared at the large snowflake. He glanced down at his pitiful attempt realizing he'd glued the pieces together wrong. In his defense, he hadn't read the instructions and had rushed through it.

While Cynthia was out, Tristen cleaned up the area. Afterwards, he ordered pizzas from Papa John's and had them delivered. He sat with Evan and Annie in the cabin. They shared light conversation while they ate.

"Miss Reynolds ever been married?" he bravely asked.

Evan shook his head. "Not that I know of. But you're wasting your time if you think she'd lower her standards to date a pilot. Yes, we make good money, but she's into millionaires. She was engaged to Austin Gunner, one of the richest corporate attorneys in Atlanta."

"So why didn't she marry him?"

"This is all speculation," Annie responded. "Her father planned to give full control of Zurtel to Randall once she was married. She called off the engagement and now her life revolves around the company."

"Big sacrifice. Hell, she must really love this company," Tristen commented.

"That or she hates Randall enough to give up everything just to keep his hands off it." Evan finished his soda and pushed his plate back.

Annie closed the pizza box. "That was good."

"Should we save Miss Reynolds a slice?" Tristen asked.

Evan and Annie looked at each other and laughed.

Annie shook her head. "She doesn't allow pizza on the jet. She says the aroma lingers too long."

"So what does she expect us to do? Starve?"

"Probably," Evan said. "She never slows down. Usually, she just drinks protein shakes."

Tristen considered what they said. It explained why Cynthia had the figure she had as a girl.

"Open the door. She should be back soon or at least I hope she is. I still need to pick Mallory up. She has school tomorrow."

"Don't think her highness cares," Evan quipped.

Tristen wouldn't tell anyone how well he actually knew the goddess of Zurtel. He had truly loved her with all his heart. Somewhere under the Armani suit and behind the Prada shoes and handbag, Cynthia still had a heart.

She sold herself out when she made his daughter's snowflake.

Once they'd cleaned up their dinner mess, he and Evan proceeded with the preflight check both inside and out. Though considered the copilot's job, Tristen didn't mind doing it. It went faster if they both did it.

When Cynthia returned, she climbed the steps with confidence. No sooner than she entered, she complained. "What's that smell?"

"Mr. Conners ordered pizzas," the flight attendant replied.

"Disgusting. Let's get back to Atlanta. I have a meeting first thing in the morning." She paused. "Bring me a protein shake from the fridge. See if there's a strawberry one left."

"Yes, Miss Reynolds."

Tristen stood in the doorway. "We saved you some pizza."

She crinkled her nose in disgust. "I never eat the stuff." She glanced at her watch. "It's not getting any earlier. Let's go."

"We're ready. I'll radio the tower and request to taxi out. Fasten up." He started to thank her for making the snowflake but didn't and returned to the cockpit.

Once they landed in Atlanta, Cynthia left without any comments to him or the crew. No, *have a nice evening. Thank you for a safe trip.* Nothing. Instead, she sashayed to the company limo.

Yep, she was definitely slumming the summer she slept with me.

He'd figured once that summer had ended, Cynthia realized he wasn't good enough.

That night, Tristen didn't reach his in-law's home in Duluth until midnight.

"She's asleep," Rose said. "Why not leave her here tonight?"

No doubt they'd use incidents like this in court.

"Mal has school tomorrow. It's her Christmas program."

"You told us. Did you get her costume made?"

"Yeah, I did." He sighed. "I'll leave her, but I'm driving her to school in the morning. I'll be by at seven with her clothes."

His mother-in-law frowned. "You're not being reasonable. Mallory would be better off with us. You know it. You'd get visitation rights. We could stop this nastiness and keep it out of court."

"I'll never give her up. I'm her dad. She needs me."

"But you're not around enough for her."

"Then maybe I should find her a mother," Tristen said knowing they would disapprove.

"And put some strange woman over our Mallory. Never."

He shrugged. "Then back off."

On his drive home, his phone rang. He glanced at the screen. Tanner. They had been friends long before he married Danielle, Tanner's kid sister. "Hello."

"Where are you?"

"On my way home. Why?"

"Let's meet at the Brick Store for a beer."

He'd need to wake up early to get Mallory ready, but he rarely had any down time to himself. He remembered the trendy bar they'd all frequented before Danielle and he married. "Sure. I got time for one beer."

He entered the dark pub with walls constructed of brick and waved at Tanner. He crossed the room to the bar and climbed on a barstool. After ordering a beer, he turned to Tanner. "How's the new job working out?"

He shrugged. "It's a job. What about you? You started with Zurtel today. How'd that go?"

"I survived the first day. I flew to Jacksonville then Memphis. I ended up getting back late. That's why Mallory is with your parents tonight."

"Hey, man, I never talk to them. I'm still on the outs with them."

Not wanting to talk about Rose and Kenneth, he swayed the subject towards sports and politics. Thirty minutes later, Tristen stood. "I've got to get up early."

"Oh, come on. One more beer. I'm buying."

"One more. That's it."

They talked more, and he ended up drinking a third beer. The alcohol loosened his tongue causing him to bring up Tanner's parents. "I wish they'd back off from this custody battle."

"She's all they have left of Danielle."

"Well, I won't give her up."

"That's why they'll do whatever it takes to get her."

As he stood to leave, a woman slid in the narrow space between the stools, pushing her body against his. She wore lots of makeup, but what he noticed most were her breasts rising from the corset and her very short mini skirt and long legs.

"Hey, cutie pie. I can be yours for the night. Want to take me home?" The sexy blonde leaned and swiped her tongue over his ear before he could stop her.

It'd been months since he'd been this close to a woman. Her body pressed against his, causing a partial erection.

For a split second, his eyes blinked when a light flashed. Some idiot obviously had taken a picture to post on Facebook.

"No thanks, I'm not interested." He managed to turn to the other side and slip off the stool. Tanner had vanished. Why had he left so suddenly?

Tristen made his way to his car. Before backing out, he thought about what had just happened. Then another thought occurred. How had Tanner known he wouldn't have Mallory? Why did he take off?

He recalled the woman and the blinding flash. His stomach dropped, making him ill.

As he drove, his vision blurred, and he became drowsy. Three beers wouldn't have caused this effect. Despite his condition, he made it home and crashed on the sofa.

Something about the entire evening seemed off. At the precise moment, the women had propositioned him, Tanner skedaddled out of there. Had it been a setup?

♦♦♦

Gina Ferguson couldn't constrain the next onset of tears. She couldn't believe her father was dead, and her mother was barely alive. She wiped her eyes. "I want to see my mom."

"She's in surgery. The doctor will come out when he's done," Aunt Nell said.

Gina had been spending the night with a friend when she'd been awakened from a sound sleep and informed her parents had been in a serious car crash.

Now she waited with relatives she barely knew. She didn't like Uncle Sonny and Aunt Nell, nor did she like their children, Will and Shellie. But Uncle Sonny was her dad's only brother. They had a sister in Missouri, who rarely visited. Both sets of grandparents had died, and her mother had been an only child.

Gina wanted to wake up and see her father and mother walk into her room to say goodnight. Finally, she curled up on a sofa in the ICU waiting room.

She wasn't sure how long she'd been asleep when someone nudged her.

"The doctor was here," Uncle Sonny said. "Your mom's awake and wants to see you."

Uncle Sonny walked her to the ICU to see her mom.

Gina gasped at all the machines blinking and making weird sounds connected to her mom. Bandages covered most of her head. When Gina walked to the bed, her mom managed a slight smile.

Tears cascaded down Gina's face.

Her mom lightly squeezed her hand. "I need to speak with her alone."

Uncle Sonny nodded and stepped out.

"You need to know something," her mom whispered, grimacing while speaking.

"Mom, I love you. Daddy's dead. You can't leave me."

Her mom squeezed her hand again. "I know, baby." She tried to draw in a breath. "There's a letter I had planned to give you when you were older. If I don't make it, you need to read it."

"What letter?"

"I wrote it the day we brought you home."

"Where is it?"

"It's in the back of your baby book. I keep it in my right desk drawer."

"Mom, you're going to get better and come home. You've just got to."

Her mom didn't answer. Instead, she closed her eyes.

"Mom! Wake up!"

The green zigzagging line on the machine went straight. An alarm sounded.

Nurses ran into the room. "Out of the way," one shouted.

"Get her out of here!" shouted a doctor.

Uncle Sonny stood at the door, waiting for her. "They can't work on your mom with you in there."

Gina tried to get one last glimpse before being whisked down the hall. This was all so surreal. It had to be a nightmare.

Chapter Two

Light shined through the curtain and woke Tristen. For a moment, he didn't know where he was. He sat up and wondered how he'd ended up on the sofa. Then it all came slowly back to him. He glanced at the clock, 8:00 a.m.

Son-of-a-bitch.

He'd overslept and hadn't picked Mallory up. She'd be late for school.

In less than thirty minutes, he banged on his in-law's door. Fortunately, he hadn't gotten a ticket for driving like a maniac.

Rose opened the door. She wore a sour expression. "You're late."

"I overslept." He handed her a bag. "Here's Mal's uniform. If you can get her dressed, I'll run her to school."

"We took her already. She was very upset. She didn't have her teacher's Christmas present or her snowflake."

"What'd she wear?"

"I washed and dried the uniform she wore yesterday."

"Thanks. I'll run the gift and snowflake by the school."

"You might've been on time if you hadn't been drinking and carousing with prostitutes last night."

"I was with Tanner."

"Tanner left when you solicited that hooker. It made him uncomfortable."

"For your information, I didn't solicit the hooker. I told her I wasn't interested."

For a moment, a ripple of disbelief ran through him. He couldn't believe that Tanner had been a part of this. Had he spiked his drink?

The sad part of this was he loved Danielle's family. He'd considered them his parents as well. He had always been close to Rose, especially after his mother had died. Tanner had always been like a brother.

Tristen needed to hire someone to keep Mallory. He'd always had a fixed schedule with the airlines. Problem was he didn't have a set schedule. He couldn't plan around it. His present situation would require a live-in nanny.

At the school, they called Mallory to the office.

A few minutes later, his daughter stepped inside the room, not looking pleased with him. "You forgot me."

"Mal, I'm so sorry. I overslept." He held out the teacher's gift bag and the snowflake. "At least you'll have your snowflake for the program."

She nodded but still pouted.

"Look, I'll be at that program today. You'll be the best snowflake on stage."

Finally, she smiled. "I like the snowflake."

"Well, I hate to admit this, but I didn't make it."

"Who did?"

"Cynthia Reynolds, my boss."

"Tell her thanks. It's pretty."

"I will. After the program, I'll check you out, and we can go for ice cream. Deal?"

She smiled even bigger. "Deal."

He patted the top of her head, then leaned and kissed it. "You'd better get back to class."

She nodded and left the office.

He signed out at the desk, then returned to his car. Before starting the engine, he mulled over the previous evening. He didn't think it went quite as planned. Tanner's mission had been to get him intoxicated or mentally zapped where he might fall into bed with a hooker.

Do you hear yourself?

This is Rose and Kenneth.

And Tanner's been your friend for years.

Tristen couldn't deny the entire family had turned on him. To keep Mallory in the pack, they'd turned vicious.

His phone rang. He didn't recognize the number. "Hello."

"Tristen, it's Mason. I've got some news."

"You sound happy, so it must be really good news."

"It is. Dad made me a partner in his law firm. It won't be official until after the first of the year."

"Congratulations. That's awesome." He almost choked on the words feeling slightly jealous over his best friend's success. He didn't want to be envious, but damn, it seemed like some people had all the luck. As for him, he couldn't catch a break.

"Listen, Dad's throwing me a party on New Year's Eve. I want you there. You'll receive an invitation. Just show it at the gate."

"If I'm not out of town, I'll be there."

♦♦♦

At the Christmas program, Tristen sat on the opposite side from Danielle's parents and ignored them. When the children walked on stage, he waved at Mallory. The snowflake looked fantastic.

He held his phone up and recorded the performance as they sang. Mallory did all the movements and hand gestures perfectly. Afterwards, the children paraded off the stage.

He walked to her classroom and found Rose and Kenneth at the door.

What are they up to?

"We thought we'd check Mallory out," Rose announced.

"Sorry, but I promised to take her for ice cream." He stepped into the classroom, signed the checkout list, and took Mallory.

As they walked past Rose and Kenneth, Rose grabbed her arm. "Sweetheart, wouldn't you rather come with us? We could get ice cream if that's what you'd like."

Mallory's face expressed her distain. "No, Grandma. I want to go with Daddy."

"But we love you so much," Grandma Rose said.

His phone rang. Zurtel Corporation.

No doubt someone needed to fly somewhere. Instead of replying, he cut his phone off and ignored it. "Thank your grandparents for coming and tell them goodbye."

One thing he knew, her grandparents did love her, but they had no business seeking custody. He reminded himself that even Adolph Hitler had loved someone.

While eating double chocolate sundaes, his phone signaled a text had been received. He checked it. Cynthia Reynolds needed to fly to Texas. He texted back, saying he would be there.

Too bad his father was still recovering. Then an idea hit him. Crazy, but it was the only option he had other than to drop Mallory off at her grandparents' house.

"Hey, Mal, how'd you like to go to Texas?"

She wiped chocolate from her mouth. "Grandma Rose said when you go somewhere I have to stay with her."

"I'm changing the rules. Grandma Rose has done something that's made me angry."

"Is it because she wants me to live with her?"

"Did Grandma Rose tell you that?"

Mallory nodded. "She said I could sleep in Mommy's room."

"I'd only get to see you on weekends and holidays. Is that what you want?" He held his breath waiting for her answer.

She shook her head. "No." Tears formed in her eyes. "I want to stay with you."

"And I want you to stay with me. I'm not letting anyone separate us."

She smiled. "I love you, Daddy."

He winked. "You're my girl."

He held back his anger in front of Mallory. How dare Rose bring her into this. He hadn't wanted Mallory to know about the custody suit.

Rather than leave Mallory with Rose, he'd chance taking her on the flight. She could sit in the cockpit's jump seat. Maybe the flight attendant and copilot wouldn't sell him out.

♦♦♦

Gina stood at her parents's graves. Light snow fell covering the surrounding ground. The strong scent of the flowers and the rich smell of the freshly dug earth nauseated her. Her heart was as cold as the December day. Afraid tears would freeze on her face, she wiped them. Her chest ached from her intense emotional pain.

Aunt Gwen, who had flown in from Missouri, placed an arm around her and hugged. "You poor little dear."

Gina wished she'd been in the car with her parents at the time of the crash. She wanted to be with her mom and dad. She wasn't sure what would happen to her. Who would she live with? What would happen to her home and school?

All these questions swirled in her mind making her dizzy and sick.

After the joint funeral, the family gathered for lunch at her home. Her cousin, Shellie, banged on her mother's piano. Will sat in the recliner moving it up and down.

Gina's entire world had broken in half.

Aunt Gwen sat at the table with Uncle Sonny and Aunt Nell. "I'm not going to stick around for the reading of the will. Considering I haven't spoken to him or his snooty wife in years, I doubt I'm even mentioned."

"Surely he left Sonny something," Aunt Nell said. "If he didn't, we're not raising his brat. It's not like she's blood kin. Let the state take her."

Blood kin?

The comment struck Gina as odd. What had her aunt meant?

"Don't look at me," Aunt Gwen said. "I'm not in any position to raise a kid."

Gina shuddered at the thought of not having a home. Her mother's last words came to her. While everyone was busy talking about her, she slipped into her mom's office. She opened the desk and removed her baby book.

Pictures of her at different ages filled the pages. She flipped to the back and found the sealed letter. On the outside it read, *To Gina on her eighteenth birthday.*

Mom wanted me to read this now.

She tore open the envelope and unfolded the handwritten letter.

Dear Gina,

I want you to know how much love and joy you have brought into our lives. For the last eighteen years you have given us so much happiness.

Gina let out a gasping sigh and wiped a tear. Her entire chest hurt as though it'd been crushed.

Your father and I feel it's time you know that while we will always be the parents who have loved you for all these years and will continue to love you, we are not your biological parents. I couldn't have children.

Gina's throat burned as she sensed what she was about to read.

Yes, my darling girl, we adopted you. But I couldn't have loved you more than if I had been the one to bring you into this world. I hope none of this changes how you feel about your dad and me. We will always be your parents. We felt you had a right to know.

We agreed when you were eighteen, we'd give you this letter.

As far as your birthmother, we don't know who she is. But if you ever want to find her, we'll support you. Love, Mom.

The letter went on to explain about the unwed mothers's home in North Carolina that had arranged the adoption. Then she read a section written by her father telling her how much she meant to him.

Anger flowed through Gina. She drew in another shaky breath. Why tell her now? Her real mother hadn't wanted her. Gina had no desire to ever meet the woman who'd given her life. Instead, she hated her. Then another thought occurred. Who was her father?

She tucked the note back in the envelope and replaced it in the baby book. Rather than put the book back in the desk, she took it to her bedroom and slid it under her mattress.

Now Aunt Nell's comment made sense.

Gina picked up the glass snow globe her father had given her and threw it against the wall, shattering it. Water ran down the wall. The pieces of glass lying on the floor reminded her of her own shattered life.

Later, she called her best friend, Olivia, and told her about her parents's joint funeral and her annoying relatives.

"I'm so sorry," Olivia said.

"Right now I'm in a dream, and I can't wake up."

"You're not dreaming, Gina."

"How do you know for sure?"

"Because I'm very much awake."

♦♦♦

Cynthia waited outside her house for Ellis.

Fortunately, Simmons and Davis voted against the merger. For now, it was dead. Randall hadn't been thrilled about the outcome. After his merger failed, he had taken a few days off to pout.

The police hadn't found who'd stolen her laptop. Actually, she had the impression it wasn't their top priority.

In the car, Ellis glanced in the rearview mirror. "So should I assume the dragon is off licking his wounds?"

"He's somewhere letting off steam, but he'll refuel and create a new scheme."

"When his mother came up with the marriage plan, I think he was truly in favor of making you his bride. He's always had an eye on you, if you get my meaning."

"His mother had hoped we'd form a financial dynasty." Cynthia laughed. "I wouldn't know half their schemes without you tipping me off."

"I'm just the chauffer. Guess you could say I'm the fly on the steering wheel." He chuckled. "They never considered I might repeat what's said in this car. Though there were times I should have kept my mouth shut. I didn't realize you'd cancel your wedding for the company."

"I thought Austin loved me enough to wait a couple more years. I needed enough time to secure my position at Zurtel. It wasn't your fault for telling me."

At the tarmac of Zurtel's private landing strip, Cynthia climbed from the car and made her way to the jet. Unfortunately, it would be Tristen flying her.

As she climbed the steps, Tristen was still conducting the exterior preflight check. When he came aboard, he entered the cabin. "We'll be in Dallas by six-thirty. Fasten up." He headed for the cockpit, stopped at the doorway, and turned toward her. "Mallory's snowflake was the best."

"That's nice. Be sure to thank Annie."

"I will." He disappeared into the cockpit.

Within minutes, the engine roared and shortly following Tristen had them in the sky. Cynthia preferred flying at night. It was easier to forget she was thousands of feet up in the air.

Cynthia opened her company laptop to review government regulations. Finding them boring, she searched the Internet for everything she could find on Quinn Adams. She discovered three people, but none of them owned Novik. Quinn Adams remained a mystery.

Giving up on the search, she clicked on Facebook and went to Tristen's account. He had already posted a video of his daughter wearing the snowflake. Mallory was a pretty little girl with enormous brown eyes.

Cynthia experienced a sensation of emptiness in her chest as she wondered if the daughter she and Tristen had created together would favor Mallory.

I'll never know.

She'd expected to feel shards of hate for him, but she didn't. Instead, a sentimental tug pulled on her heart when around him. She had to work on that. She didn't want to feel anything for him, not love or hate.

Cynthia made it to the Dallas banquet and socialized trying to score more points for Zurtel. It was hosted by one of their top buyers. She hated these events and all the smiling and ass kissing that went with it. Randall should have attended instead of her. He was better at it.

Several people commented they'd heard Zurtel had something that would revolutionize the aerospace industry. Cynthia avoided giving too much information about MX7. While there, she asked the guests if they'd ever met the owner of Novik, Quinn Adams, but no one had.

She made it back to the airport by nine-thirty and entered the jet, taking her usual seat. Her feet ached from her new heels. She kicked them off and massaged her feet to ease the pain.

In the air on the trip back to Atlanta, she spotted a tiny toy figurine on the floor. She walked over and picked it up. The Little Mermaid.

No one had used this jet but her. That meant this toy had to belong to one of the flight crew. Evan and Annie didn't have children. Tristen was the only one with a child. Was she on the plane?

Cynthia summoned Annie. "Where'd this come from?"

Guilt showed on the attendant's face.

"Annie, does Mr. Conners have his daughter on this jet?"

She hesitated before nodding. "He couldn't find a babysitter."

"Where is Mallory?"

"In the jump seat behind her dad."

Sitting in the jump seat couldn't be very comfortable.

"Bring her to me."

"A few minutes later, a child clutching a doll entered the cabin. She stood looking nervous and scared. Apparently, she wasn't supposed to get caught on the flight.

"Hello, Mallory. I'm Miss Reynolds. Would you like to sit with me? I'd love to have someone to talk with."

The girl timidly nodded and walked toward her. She was even prettier in person.

Mallory sat beside her. “My daddy said you’d be mad if you knew I was here. Is Daddy gonna lose his job?”

“No, but he should’ve asked. Don’t you have grandparents you stay with while your dad works?”

“Grandpa Rob is sick. And Daddy doesn’t want me staying with Grandma Rose and Grandpa Kenneth.”

“Why’s that?”

“They want me to live with them not Daddy.”

“How do you feel about it?”

Mallory twirled a piece of hair around her finger. “I want to be with Daddy.”

“I see.”

“I miss my Mommy.”

“I’m sure you do.” Cynthia empathized with the girl. “My mother died when I was young. I still miss her.”

“My mom had cancer.”

“Mine did too.”

Mallory smiled causing her dimples to pop out. “You’re pretty.”

“I was about to say the same thing about you.” She couldn’t resist quizzing the kid about Tristen. “Does your dad have a girlfriend you can stay with?”

Mallory shook her head. “Nope.”

Right now Cynthia felt as underhanded as the snake out of the *Jungle Book.*

“Why don’t your grandparents want you to live with your daddy?”

She shrugged. Finally, she sighed. “They try to make me say bad things about Daddy.”

“Like what?”

“Grandma Rose told me to tell the judge that Daddy drinks too much.”

“What else does Grandma Rose say?”

Mallory shrugged. “Just things.”

Cynthia understood why Tristen didn’t want to leave Mallory with them.

For the rest of the flight, Mallory talked about her snowflake. “Mine was the best.”

“Did your daddy make it?” she asked, wondering if Tristen had taken credit for it.

“No. His was broken.”

Broken was an understatement.

“Did he tell you Annie made it?”

She shook her head. “No. He said you made it.”

Cynthia swallowed hard. He’d known the entire time she’d made the snowflake. “What’s Santa bringing you?”

Mallory’s face grew sad. “I’d like to have my mommy back, but I know Santa can’t do that.”

Cynthia’s heart melted over the child’s comment. “You’re right, he can’t. So what did you ask him for?”

“Ballerina Barbie and a big paint set and a dollhouse with furniture.”

Again Cynthia thought of the daughter she’d never known. Was she celebrating Christmas? Being eleven, she probably didn’t do the Santa thing anymore.

“Why a ballerina doll? Do you dance?”

She shook her head. “My friends, Sophie and Isabella, take ballet.”

“You don’t take lessons?”

“Nope. Daddy said we don’t have the money.”

Surely, he had emergency savings. Then she recalled his wife had been very ill before she’d died. His savings and any other funds had probably been depleted.

Once they landed, Tristen entered the cabin. He came across as disheartened. “Sorry about bringing Mallory with me. I didn’t have a sitter.”

“You should’ve asked.” She wanted to hate him, but she couldn’t. She wanted to make him pay for what he’d done and how he’d left her. She couldn’t deny she still cared about him.

“I was afraid you’d say no.” He paused. “How’d you know?”

“She left her Little Mermaid toy behind.”

"Yeah, that would clue you in that an underage stowaway was aboard."

Rather than smile, she gave him a stern look. "I'll let this incident go, but you need to find a nanny."

"Mallory's tuition is already costing me a small fortune."

"I understand her grandparents are trying to get custody."

He nodded. "Yes, they are."

"Would it be that bad for her to live with them and you have visitation?"

He frowned. "I'd never let that happen. Mallory belongs with me. If you had a child you'd know what I'm talking about. You wouldn't let anything come between you and your kid."

A deep pain sliced through Cynthia. She wanted to tell him about the baby she'd been forced to give up—their child. With Mallory sitting nearby, Cynthia held back. "Try to find a nanny." She turned to his daughter. "Mallory, it was nice meeting you."

The little girl smiled. "I liked our visit, Miss Cynthia."

"Yes, we had a nice conversation."

"That too." Mallory's smile grew larger.

Cynthia didn't say anymore to Tristen. Her chest still burned from his remark.

Outside on the tarmac, Ellis opened the Cadillac's door. She climbed in, still feeling the pain, still wondering what her little girl looked like, and still yearning for a child she'd given up.

Ellis drove a few miles before she decided to question him.

"Do you remember the summer Tristen Conners stayed on our property?"

"Yes, what about it?"

"How much do you know?"

"Only what I overheard your dad and stepmom talking about."

"Did you know I was pregnant?"

"Yes, I was aware of it."

"They left me at an unwed mothers's home. Do you know where it was located?"

"I'm not sure exactly. I think one of the Carolinas." Ellis paused. "Why all the questions?"

She sighed. "I want to find my little girl."

"You know, Miss Reynolds, that road may lead to more heartache."

"I'm willing to chance it."

"But what about your daughter? What effect will it have on her life?"

Cynthia hadn't thought about it. "I just want to know something about her. I won't insist they tell her about me. I want to know whether she's happy and see what she looks like."

Cynthia would start her search after the holidays.

After parking in her driveway, Ellis ran around and opened the car door. "Need me to do a walkthrough of your house?"

"That won't be necessary. I left my alarm on." She pulled an envelope from her purse. "Merry Christmas."

"I received my Christmas bonus. It was very generous."

"This is from me."

"Thank you, Miss Reynolds."

From her porch, she waved Ellis off. As she started to place the key in the door, she noticed the door was slightly ajar. She turned to flag Ellis down, but he'd left. She called him. "Ellis, please turn around and come back. I'm calling 911."

Rather than go in, Cynthia waited outside. Within minutes, Ellis had returned. She climbed in the front seat with him. "The front door was open. The alarm was deactivated."

A police car arrived and parked behind the limo. The officer climbed out and walked over to them. "Are you the homeowner?"

"Yes, I'm Cynthia Reynolds. I left all my doors locked and the alarm on. When I came home, the front door was open and the alarm was off."

"You're sure you locked up and set the alarm?" the officer asked.

"Positive."

Another police car pulled up in front of the house.

Both officers entered the house, leaving them outside.

When one motioned for her to come inside, she left the car and crossed the small yard. "What'd you find?"

"You need to see this," the first officer said.

Cynthia held her breath a second as she entered her home. Her house was trashed. Drawers emptied. Papers scattered. The rest of the house didn't look any better. Even her tiny Christmas tree hadn't been spared. The copy of *Alice's Adventure in Wonderland* her mother had given her had been tossed on the floor. When the officer glanced away, she picked it up and slipped it in her coat pocket. Thank goodness it hadn't been damaged.

She assumed the Grinch who'd trashed her place was the same one who'd stolen her laptop. Apparently, he hadn't found what he was looking for.

"At first glance, do you see anything missing?" an officer inquired.

Cynthia shook her head. She didn't want to mention the MX7 formula or involve the company. "No."

The officer escorted her to the bedroom and allowed her to pack a bag. She managed to grab a blanket and pillow to take with her. Rather than go to a hotel or wake her dad, she had another idea.

In her office at the Zurtel building, Cynthia eased down on the sofa and covered with the blanket. She pulled out the book her mother had given her when she was nine. She opened it and read the inscription.

You'll find peace in the warmth of a smile. Love always, Mom.

She carefully slipped it in her purse. It was what had inspired her to hide the disc behind her mother's smile. No one would suspect it being behind her mother's photograph at her father's home. The formula was safe.

The clock on her desk ticked. The heat came on and off. Her mind twirled with questions and images of her dismantled house.

The sound of a door shutting came from outside her office.

Who would be in the building at this hour?" The cleaning crew finished up at eleven each night.

Footfalls came closer.

Hide.

Not wanting the intruder to know she was there, she stood, grabbed her belongings, then looked for somewhere to go.

Hurry, he's coming.

Chapter Three

Cynthia ran into the private bathroom connected to the office.

Her heart spit out beats as though she'd been running a marathon.

She stood in the dark, fumbling inside her purse, searching for her phone. Once she found it, she dialed 911.

"911. What's your emergency?"

"Someone has broken into the Zurtel building on Peachtree. It's near the Sun Trust Plaza."

"What's your name?"

"Cynthia Reynolds. I'm on the twenty-ninth floor. I'm hiding in the bathroom off my office. He's coming."

The footfalls pounded the floor, so she assumed the intruder was male.

"Ma'am. Don't hang up."

Afraid the phone would alert the intruder she was there, Cynthia disconnected the call, turned the sound off, and shut it down, then stood very still in the dark knowing any moment he would enter the bathroom.

On the other side of the door, a man cleared his throat. Though she couldn't see him, the sounds coming from her office helped her visualize the intruder's actions.

He opened each desk drawer, then moved to the file cabinets doing the same.

She knew exactly what he was searching for—MX7.

He walked right past the bathroom and didn't try the door. That meant he knew the layout of her office and that the room was a bathroom.

Again, the intruder cleared his throat as if he had a sinus issue. He walked straight to the small closet. Boxes and items crashed to the floor.

In the distance, sirens blared.

The intruder paused a moment before running for the door. His footfalls echoed down the outer hallway toward the emergency exit and stairs.

Relief poured through her. Cynthia finally released the pent up breath she'd held. She turned her phone back on. Immediately, it rang, so she answered it.

"Miss Reynolds, this is the 911 operator. Are you all right?"

"Yes, he's gone."

"The police are in the building. Please stay on the phone this time."

"Yes, I will." She left the bathroom and entered her office. Like her house, her office had been ransacked.

A man wearing a suit approached her. "Ms. Reynolds, I'm Detective Taylor with the APD. Did you get a look at the perpetrator?"

"No, I hid in the bathroom."

"Is there anything you can tell me about him?"

"Judging by the footsteps, I assumed it was a man, perhaps on the heavy side, but other than that, I didn't actually see him."

"Could there have been more than one perpetrator?"

"I don't think so. He never said anything."

"Here's my card," he said. "If you think of anything else, call me."

As she took it, she recalled one more fact. "He kept clearing his throat as though he had a bad sinus infection."

He jotted it down. "We've canvassed the building and discovered the rear door open. He entered the building, deactivated the alarm system, sabotaged the surveillance cameras, and went directly to your office." He paused. "Do you always work this late?"

"I'm not working. I should've told you. My house was also broken into and ransacked earlier tonight. I came here to sleep on my sofa."

Now she had his attention.

"Did you file a police report?"

"Yes, I did."

"I'll take a look at it."

"Actually, there was another incident before that." She told him about the guy on the bike in the garage.

"You think it's connected?"

She nodded. "I thought it was one of our competitors. But whoever entered tonight, not only had the security code to the alarm system, but also knew the layout of my building. It has to be an employee."

"That's what I'm led to believe."

"So I should look for a male employee with a nasty sinus infection."

He grinned. "That'd be my guess. Do you have someone you can stay with?"

She nodded. "My dad."

"I'll have you escorted there." The detective paused a moment in thought. "I'm surprised you don't have a private security company."

"We do. But they monitor several buildings in the area. It wouldn't be difficult for someone to slip by them."

"Especially someone who knows their schedule."

Before going to bed, Tristen thought about hiring a nanny. He wasn't sure he'd like someone living in the same house. But, he'd be able to be on call without worrying what to do with Mallory.

Tristen didn't have a clue how to find one.

He hadn't expected Cynthia to understand his situation with Mallory. She'd reminded him more of that seventeen year old girl he'd fallen in love with.

"Hey, Mal, what'd you and Miss Reynolds talk about?"

"What Santa's bringing me for Christmas?"

Suddenly, he remembered the packages delivered that day. After putting Mallory to bed, he started opening them. Everything he'd ordered for her Christmas had arrived except the Ballerina Barbie. Tomorrow was Christmas Eve. If Santa didn't bring it, Mallory would be greatly disappointed.

His phone rang. It was Tanner.

"Hey, man, what happened the other night?" Tristen asked.

"I couldn't stay."

"Any particular reason you shot off?"

Tanner paused. "I thought you might want to strike up a deal with that foxy lady. I didn't want to be in the way."

"I haven't been with anyone since Danielle. I don't think I'll start with a hooker. For one thing I still love Danielle, and secondly, I don't do hookers or married women."

Tanner let out a nervous chuckle. "Hell, man, chill."

For now, Tristen would let Tanner and his family believe he was dumb enough not to see what they were up to.

After Tristen disconnected, he returned to the problem at hand, the Ballerina Barbie. What should he do?

The next morning, Tristen opened his paper. The Zurtel building and Cynthia's home had been burglarized.

An overwhelming urge to protect her flowed through him. His concern went beyond her being his boss. He had to admit some of his old feelings for her had resurfaced. He reminded himself she'd turned into the corporate ice queen. Any feelings for her were a waste of time.

While Mallory slept soundly, he tracked the package containing her doll. Seeing it was held up in St. Louis, he frowned. Expected delivery was the day after Christmas. He called a local store. A clerk located one in Gainesville at the Oak Mall Store. He'd be in Florida that night. He purchased it and asked them to hold it. After disconnecting, Tristen wondered how he'd approach the ice queen about this.

While at his computer, he searched for nannies. It surprised him to see the number of agencies. He typed in his information at several sites including the living arrangements and salary. He described Mallory and what would be expected. With the pitiful amount he offered, he didn't expect to hear back from any of them.

He dropped Mallory off at her grandparents's house and headed for the private landing strip. After having some slight vibrations on the last flight, he conducted a thorough inspection of the aircraft. Zurtel's jets received regularly scheduled maintenance. When he entered the jet, Evan and Annie met him at the door with grim faces.

"She's already here. Watch out, she's not in the best mood," Evan warned.

"Did you hear about her house and office being broken into?" Tristen asked.

They nodded.

Annie's brows rose. "I don't think she's had any sleep."

"Just do our jobs and stay out of her way," Evan added.

If Tristen wanted the doll in Gainesville, he had to approach Cynthia. He entered the cabin and waited for her to glance up.

Her expression said it all.

Proceed at your own risk.

He swallowed hard and walked toward her. "I read about what happened last night. I'm sorry."

She gave the slightest nod. "I don't need your sympathy. I'm fine. Now get us in the air."

"There's something I need to ask."

"Make it quick."

"Mallory's Ballerina Barbie didn't arrive. The tracking said it's not going to arrive before Christmas."

"Is this going somewhere?"

He nodded. "They found one left, and it's in Gainesville. It's not even a fifteen minute flight from Orlando. After your appointment, can we fly there? We can still make it home by 5:00 p.m."

"Why'd you wait until the last minute to order it?"

He shrugged. "I thought I could pick one up at the store. I couldn't find one. That's when I ordered it."

"Get us to Orlando, and I'll think about it."

"Thanks." He turned and walked toward the cockpit.

"Everything looks good," Evan said.

Tristen nodded. "Thanks."

After landing in Orlando, Evan lowered the steps for Cynthia. Rather than leave, she stopped in front of Tristen. "Be ready to leave, when I get back. Make arrangements to land in Gainesville. I'm willing to wait an hour."

"Thanks. I appreciate this."

"I'm not doing it for you. I'm doing it for Mallory."

After she left, Annie and Evan stared at him with questioning eyes.

Evan swiped his hand over the back of his neck. "You've got balls, man."

Annie nodded. "I asked her if she needed anything, and she snapped my head off."

"She's more tolerant of me because of Mallory."

They ordered Chinese and had it delivered to the airport. They sat in the cabin and ate.

"Why do you think someone trashed her house and office?" Tristen asked.

"Corporate espionage," Annie said. "From what I heard she and the engineering team have some new metal that will make billions."

"I'd think Novik's behind it, because they didn't get the merger," Evan added. "Perhaps they're looking for a different way to get what they want."

"It's not like Cynthia would keep it at her house or office."

Evan's mouth dropped.

Annie's brows rose.

He realized he'd said Cynthia instead of Miss Reynolds. "My dad's been around her since she was a kid. He calls her Cynthia. Slip of the tongue."

"You'd better not slip up around her," Annie warned.

"I'll be more careful."

By the time Cynthia returned, he had the preflight check done and had contacted an airport and a taxi service in Gainesville.

Once they'd landed, he stood at the front of the cabin. "I'll hurry."

She nodded but kept working on her reports. Finally, she glanced up. "Go, I want to be home in time to attend Christmas Eve service with Dad."

Unfortunately, he wouldn't pick Mallory up until 9:00 p.m. She would attend church with her grandparents. So he had some time to kill.

Being Christmas Eve day, the taxi moved slowly. He felt like Bob Cratchit on an errand with Scrooge waiting on the jet. Finally, he arrived at the mall. "Wait for me."

"Sure. Not a problem."

Tristen ran into the store and headed to the order pick up where he joined a long line. After getting the doll, he ran back to the taxi. It'd taken slightly over an hour, but he planned to make it up once in the sky.

Evan met him at the jet's door. "Everything is done. We're ready to request taxiing to the runway."

"Thanks."

"Before he entered the cockpit, Cynthia looked up from her phone and asked, "Did you get it?"

"Yes. The doll will make Mallory's Christmas."

She nodded, then dismissed him by looking at her phone.

Back in Atlanta, he stopped Cynthia as she was leaving. "Thanks again for letting me do that. Her mom always took care of Santa shopping. I didn't realize how hectic buying toys could be."

Cynthia surprised him with a genuine smile. "Tell Mallory I said merry Christmas."

"I will. And thanks again." He thought of something else. "I placed an ad on several nanny sites. I'm not sure anyone will reply."

"Maybe I've lost my senses, but until you find someone, you can bring her with you on short flights."

"Thanks. I may take you up on it." He stood close to her, close enough he smelled her soft fragrance. He could see the glossy shine of her hair. He recalled how it had looked fanned out on a pillow.

"One more thing I've debated whether to mention."

"I'm listening." A muscle in his jaw twitched.

"It's something Mallory told me. I don't want her knowing I said anything. I wouldn't want to lose her trust."

"I won't bring it up."

"She said your mother-in-law wants her to lie about you. She wants Mallory to tell the judge you drink too much."

Anger shot through his veins. Tristen wanted to choke Rose. He drew in a deep breath to keep his cool. "Thanks for telling me."

"Remember, you promised not to tell Mallory."

"I won't."

She left first. As she descended the steps, he stared at the curve of her hips. Images of them in bed flashed in his mind. His breath hitched. He forced the memories away.

Standing on the tarmac, she stared at him for a minute before turning and lowering into the waiting car. Hopefully, she wasn't a mind reader.

"Merry Christmas," he whispered as her car drove away.

That night Tristen attended the church service where his in-laws and Mallory would be. They wouldn't know he was there. He stood in back scanning for Mallory and her grandparents and finally spotted them. He considered joining them but didn't. Instead, he moved to the far right but stayed back a few rows.

Mallory appeared so happy with her grandparents. For a split second, he considered whether she'd be better off with Rose and Kenneth. He recalled Danielle had complained her mother was too controlling. His daughter belonged with him.

As they sang a carol, Tanner walked down the aisle and joined his parents. He leaned and kissed his mom's cheek, then hugged Mallory, and shook hands with his dad.

Rose had brought up the hooker and his drinking too much, so clearly Tanner had told her about it. Since when had Tanner been on good terms with his parents?

Since setting you up.

No doubt, the snake was back in the vipers' nest.

Had their plan been to get him drunk enough he'd leave with the hooker? Tristen recalled a camera flashed when the woman edged beside him. Would a picture of him at the bar with the hooker show up in court?

During the service, Tristen's heart grew heavy as memories of past Christmases with Danielle flooded his mind. He missed her. Life had been so good. Then it suddenly turned bad. He wiped the tear that escaped, then turned and left.

Rather than drive home, he drove to the Brick Store where he'd met Tanner. He sat at the bar and waited for the bartender to come his way.

"What can I get you?" he asked.

"A beer."

When the bartender set it down, Tristen paid. "Hey, I was in here a few nights ago with this man." He held up his phone and showed a picture of Tanner. "You don't by chance remember me?"

The bartender nodded. "Yeah, I do. He kept egging you on to drink another beer."

"Do hookers normally come in here?"

"No, this isn't that kind of establishment. I'm sorry that lady bothered you."

"You saw that?"

"After she gave up on you, I had someone escort her out. Like I said, we don't allow hookers to solicit here. I'm not sure how she wandered in here."

"I think the guy with me arranged it."

"Seriously, dude?"

Tristen gave a brief rundown of what he suspected. "Would you by chance be willing to testify to a judge on my behalf if it comes down to that?"

The bartender thought for a second before answering. "Sure. Say, no more. I've been in a nasty custody battle before." He returned with a card. "Here's my information."

"Thanks big time."

Tristen had an hour before he picked Mallory up. He drove to the cemetery where Danielle had been laid to rest. He parked and buttoned up his jacket before leaving his car. Light shined on her grave from a street light. He found it hard to believe it'd been a year since her funeral. Danielle had fought so hard to have one more Christmas with them, but sadly, she died a week before.

Since her death, his daily existence had been such a struggle. If not for Mallory, he'd have given up.

"Merry Christmas, Danielle," he said. His breath turned frosty from the cold air. He told her about Mallory. He didn't mention her parents. Finally, he talked about losing his job and going to work for Zurtel. "It's about time to pick Mallory up. She'll be excited over Santa coming. We both miss you."

Tears clogged his throat.

It's been so damn hard without you.

A sharp pain ripped through his chest as he fought the urge to sob. "I'll bring Mallory out tomorrow."

A light icy mix began to fall.

He'd use that as an excuse for picking Mallory up a few minutes early.

He drove to their house, parked, ran to the door, and rang the doorbell.

Inside, he heard Mallory. "It's Daddy!"

"Please tell him you want to spend the night," Rose said.

"Not tonight, Grandma. Santa's coming."

"Your toys will still be there when you get home."

"I want to be with Daddy."

The door opened, and Mallory came out with her arms full of presents.

"Let me carry some of those for you," he offered.

"Guess what Grandma and Grandpa gave me?"

He smiled. "I don't have a clue."

"Ballerina Barbie! Now Santa can bring me something else."

"You go wait in the car," he said to Mallory. His fake smile turned to a frown. "I told you that's what Santa was bringing her."

"I don't recall that," she said with a gloating smile.

"You asked me what Santa was bringing her. You did it to spite me, but you may have ruined her Christmas? Why would you do that?"

"Why do you want to ruin her life?" Rose countered.

He didn't answer. Instead, he left angry.

It was too late to buy a different doll.

He'd have no choice but to put it out with her other toys. Once the one lost in the mail showed up, there'd be three Ballerina Barbies.

Any relationship with the Williams was lethal. It hurt to know even Tanner had turned on him.

As they say blood is thicker than water.

Until he could hire a nanny, he'd take Cynthia up on her offer and take Mallory on his flights.

At home, Mallory showed him all the presents her grandparents had given her. "Here's the Ballerina Barbie. She's so pretty."

Tristen looked at it twice. It wasn't the same doll. Rose's doll was a brunette in a turquoise tutu while his was blonde and wore pink clothes. Even the boxes were different. His doll's box was larger and came with a ballet barre and studio. Relief rolled through him. No doubt Rose thought she'd purchased the same doll.

"Now Santa can bring me something else."

"I don't think it works like that. Santa's already written it on his list. Tell you what you can do. Leave Grandma Rose's Barbie out so he can see it. Maybe he'll leave a different doll. What you can do is put out cookies and milk for him."

Mallory ran to the kitchen and climbed upon a chair to grab the cookies. "How many?"

"Three. No, make that four." He poured a glass of milk. "I think Santa might be really hungry tonight."

They set it out on the table by the window.

Afterwards, he tucked her in bed, said her prayers, kissed her forehead, and turned on the nightlight.

Tristen polished off the cookies and milk before setting out her gifts from Santa. He stood back and studied the arrangement of toys, then rearranged a few items and filled her stocking hanging over the fireplace.

Before going to bed, he checked his emails. He had a reply from one of the nanny agencies. The older lady replying had lots of experience and lived in Atlanta. He'd check her references right after Christmas.

♦♦♦

Tacky rock'n roll Christmas music played as the smell of turkey and ham filled the house. None of it appealed to Gina. She only wanted her mom and dad back.

Uncle Sonny and Aunt Nell hadn't wasted any time moving into her parents's home.

Gina had overheard Aunt Nell tell her best friend once Gina turned eighteen, they would have to move out. Aunt Nell also mentioned they planned to rent their home.

Good. They'd have somewhere to go once she kicked them out.

On another day, she'd overheard Aunt Nell and Uncle Sonny discussing ways to withdraw the money from her college fund. Fortunately, they couldn't. They also complained the monthly allowance for her care wasn't enough.

Before the car accident, her mother and father had arranged the Christmas tree with all their gifts under it. Aunt Nell had shoved their packages under there as well.

She sat on her bed going through the photo albums.

Her aunt stood at the door. "I need you to peel potatoes. All the crying in the world won't bring them back. You might as well suck it up and get on with life."

She followed her aunt to the kitchen. "What do I do?"

Aunt Nell handed her a peeler. "Peel them and put them in the bowl."

The rings her aunt wore caught her attention. A moment of anger sparked. "Those are Mom's rings. You shouldn't be wearing them."

"I will until you're old enough to take care of them."

Not only had Aunt Nell confiscated all of her mom's jewelry, she'd also taken clothing items that fit. Uncle Sonny had claimed her father's possessions including his car.

Rather than help, Will played video games while Shellie watched a silly Christmas movie with her dad.

If her parents were alive, they would have attended the candlelight service at their church tonight.

After dinner, Aunt Nell called them to the family room to open gifts.

Gina's family tradition had always been to open presents Christmas morning. Despite that, she opened the ones from her mom and dad. She received a new tablet, a karaoke machine, clothes and boots. The gifts only made her heart ache more.

After everyone had opened their gifts, only the ones her parents had purchased for one another remained under the tree.

"I see no reason not to open them," Uncle Sonny said. Then he opened the packages to her dad. One was an electric razor. Then he pulled out a new computer game."

"Wicked awesome! I speak for the game," Will shouted.

Aunt Nell held up her mother's first present. "A Fitbit. I can use it at the gym." She opened another one. "Perfume. The expensive kind," she said, spraying it on.

The scent reminded Gina of her mother. Again, a tinge of pain filled her chest. She imagined them as vultures picking the bones clean.

Aunt Nell opened the final gift. "A freaking diamond cross necklace. Maybe we can return it."

"It's mine," Gina retorted. "I want it. I'm old enough to take care of it."

"Look, missy, we've had to uproot our lives for you. And it's costing us money. So this necklace will be used to help us cover our expenses. If we hadn't agreed to move in here, you'd be handed over to the state until you're eighteen. This house and everything in it would be sold."

"I had to leave my friends," Shellie stated.

"Me too," Will complained.

Uncle Sonny added, "Gina, you're not the only one having to make adjustments."

Gina gathered her gifts and stood. "I'm going to my room."

"It's your night to clean the kitchen."

"But it's really messy. Why can't Shellie and Will help?"

"I've been going easy on you," Aunt Nell responded. "But you are pushing my buttons. Shellie will do them tomorrow night. Will's not expected to do woman's work."

Will gave her a sly grin.

Gina did the dishes and all the pots and pans. Anger whirled like a tornado through her veins, shooting her adrenaline to the roof. She wanted to throw the dishes, but they had been her mom's. Finally, she used all her bottled up energy to finish the kitchen.

An hour later, she walked in her room and found Shellie sitting on her bed.

"I like this room," Shellie said.

Gina frowned. "So do I."

"I'm older than you. I should have it. It's bigger than the one they put me in. Plus, I have to share a bathroom with Will. It's not fair you have your own."

"Not happening. Get off my bed and go to your room."

"My mom's right. You're an ungrateful little shit."

"You and your family are vultures."

Shellie glared. "I'm gonna tell Mom what you said."

"Close my door on your way out."

Gina crawled into her bed and curled into a fetal position. She tried to remember last Christmas, but the pain was still too great from losing her parents.

Christmas isn't about us. It's to honor the birth of our savior.

Her mother's voice filled her with shame for feeling sorry for herself, for making Christmas all about her and what she'd lost. She softly sang *Silent Night*.

The song painted the image of the previous Christmas Eve. She had stood with her parents, holding lit candles and singing.

As she sang, tears clogged her throat, breaking her voice.

Gina walked to her window and stared at the stars twinkling in the sky. For a moment, she sobbed over her parents and her situation. Then she thought about her birthmother. She glanced up at the sky and wondered where she lived. She placed her fingertips on the icy panes.

Mother.

Why'd you give me away?

No one answered. Her fingertips numbed from the coldness.

She left the window and pulled out the letter from under the mattress. She stared at the name of the home.

Saint Benedict's Home for Girls.

Would this place know who her real mother was?

The next morning while her cousins slept, Gina crept down the stairs. Her aunt and uncle spoke softly in the kitchen. She peeked around the corner for a second before darting behind the wall. As she was about to return upstairs, they mentioned her name, and she paused.

"With Gina adopted, I can't believe your brother left everything to her."

"We get to live in this house," her uncle replied. "The trust Scott set up covers the taxes and utilities. Shellie and Will get to attend a better school. With the money we make renting our house, we can pay it off."

"I'm not gonna want to move back to that dump after living here. Scott could've at least left you the house for taking care of his brat."

"That's seven years away. There's always a chance, she'll let us continue to live here. After all, she'll be away at college."

"If she had died in the car crash with them, who would have inherited everything?"

"That's a morbid thing to consider."

"I'm just curious."

"I suppose everything would've been divided between Gwen and me."

"I would have had enough money to open my tanning salon I've always dreamed of." Her aunt stood. "Things never go our way."

In socked feet, Gina turned and left the dining room not making a sound. Upstairs, she texted Olivia and told her the gist of what her aunt had said.

♦♦♦

Christmas Eve, Cynthia sat across from Randall and his fiancée, Kayla, at the long elegant table in her father's home in Marietta. She didn't think it fair she had called off her engagement to remain a part of Zurtel while Randall only received congratulations and slaps on the back. Her father hadn't once considered cutting Randall from the family business because he planned to marry.

It could be her father didn't expect this engagement to go anywhere. It'd be like Randall's last three. The women usually wised up and ran as far from him as possible. But Randall had her father bamboozled into thinking he was an industrial genius.

Her mother would rise from her grave if she knew Randall would take half of her father's company. When her mother passed away, Cynthia's father controlled the majority of Zurtel.

"Heard back from the police?" Randall asked.

She blotted her mouth before speaking. "Yes, I did. They didn't find anything. Whoever entered Zurtel cleared security."

"It was your imagination."

"My office was ransacked like my house." She never mentioned she was there and neither had the news media. "We need to find out which one of our employees or board members is trying to sell us out. I'm sure they also stole our last two inventions."

"The MX7 formula is kept in the vault," her father said. "So why would they look for it at your house?"

She shrugged. Apparently, whoever was behind it had already checked the vault and had discovered it wasn't there. Her first thought was Randall, but he would inherit half the company.

Would it really behoove him to sabotage and steal from Zurtel? She needed to take a look at the board members who'd voted for the merger.

"I think it's all connected to the man waiting for me in the garage." She explained about him snatching her briefcase.

"That must've been terrifying," Kayla commented.

"It had me twisted in knots," she replied.

"Why am I just now learning about this?" her father asked, looking concerned.

"The day it happened, I was in a hurry and didn't talk to the police. I spoke with them later."

"We may need to hire a new security company," Randall said as he cut up the ham on his plate. "I'll check out other companies after the holidays."

"Rob Conners will be coming back next week." her father said. "He's flying me to California. We'll be gone most of the week."

Cynthia started to argue and insist he use Tristen until she remembered his situation with Mallory.

Randall focused on her. "I'm aware you undermined me with Davis and Simmons on the merger. I traced your jet's internal GPS."

"It saved the company."

"You're suffocating it."

Kayla stared at them, looking uncomfortable.

"For Christ's sake, it's Christmas Eve," her father said. "Can't you two get along?"

Cynthia stared at Randall a moment. They had never agreed on anything.

♦♦♦

Once in bed, Cynthia flipped on the television and watched an old Christmas movie. Even after she turned the TV off, she couldn't sleep.

Her thoughts drifted to the daughter she'd never met. What kind of Christmas was she having? Did the family who adopted her celebrate Christmas?

The following morning, Cynthia attended the Sunday service with her father. She saw people she hadn't seen in years. Her Christmas wish had come true. Randall wasn't coming to the house the entire day.

She drove her car, giving Ellis the day off to be with his family.

On the drive home, her father cleared his throat. "You know I'm stepping completely away from the business. Robert Conners and I will be retiring about the same time."

"I know." She pulled out onto the road.

"The company is too big for you to run alone. That's why I want Randall to be a part of it. You two balance one another out. You're in the product development end, and he can handle daily operations and the business end."

His words made her stomach churn.

Chapter Four

"Dad, I wish you could see him for what he really is."

"What's that?"

"A weasel. He doesn't care about you. He'd throw you under a bus to get what he wants."

"He's been like a son to me."

"But he's not your son."

"He has a strong head for business."

"Like his mother, he doesn't do anything unless it benefits him."

"You've never given him a chance. I think it's because his mother replaced yours. You were so used to being an only child that you could never accept Randall as your brother."

"Trust me, he didn't see me as a sister."

"What's that supposed to mean?"

"You didn't believe me then, why would believe me now?"

"You accused him of trying to violate you. Edith convinced me you were overreacting and Randall was just clowning around."

"She also convinced you to make a will leaving him half of Mom's company. Mom wouldn't want him running Grandpa's company. He's not a part of her family." Cynthia held back what she really thought of Randall.

"The light's green," her father said.

She crossed the intersection. "Don't be surprised if Mom doesn't come back to haunt you." She dropped the conversation and concentrated on driving as she eased onto I-85.

Back at her father's house, the staff had been given the day off. After Christmas lunch, she gave her father his gift and waited for him to open it.

He gave it a baffled stare. "A magazine picture?"

"Look closely. What do you see?"

He smiled. "Golf clubs. The ones I wanted."

She reached over and squeezed his hand. "Merry Christmas. They arrive Friday."

Her father handed her a small box. "What do you give a girl with everything?"

She opened it and smiled at the diamond tennis bracelet. "It's beautiful. Thank you." She removed it from the box and held it out. "Put it on me."

Cynthia extended her wrist to admire it. "I love it."

Something her father said troubled her. He said she had everything. She didn't. Most women her age had husbands and children. She'd sacrificed her life for Zurtel. Had it been worth it?

While watching a movie, her father fell asleep.

This would be an opportunity to make sure her mother's picture hadn't been disturbed in her old bedroom. She'd left a lot of things behind such as dolls and stuffed animals. The bookcase housed her old yearbooks, awards, and trophies.

Cynthia entered the room and smiled at her mom's photo smiling back. After checking to make sure the disc remained undisturbed, she stood the frame where it always sat on the dresser.

She walked to the window and stared out at the night sky. Her thoughts returned to her daughter. She wondered what city she lived in. Was she an only child or had the parents adopted other children?

For just a moment, a sense of melancholy rushed through her. Cynthia placed her hand on the cold window pane. She wondered about the strange sensation surging through her fingers. The cold glass warmed beneath her touch.

She'd never been one to believe in telepathy, but this felt like someone reaching out from afar.

My daughter.

Cynthia dismissed the notion. She wanted to believe her daughter was well and happy. Anything short of that, and she wouldn't be able to live with herself for giving up a precious little girl.

Once her father woke up, she kissed him goodbye and headed home. She still hadn't cleaned her house. The police had given her the okay to return home, and she'd had the locks changed.

Zurtel would be closed Monday since Christmas had fallen on Sunday. She'd spend the entire day putting her house back together.

♦♦♦

Christmas Day hadn't been any better than Christmas Eve for Gina. Since all the gifts had been opened the night before, her new unwanted family piled on the sofa and recliner, watching more movies. She stood in the door going unnoticed. Uncle Sonny guffawed like a donkey. Aunt Nell sat on the sofa, clipping her toenails. Will and Shellie argued over the handheld console.

Gina realized she had seven years of putting up with them. Her mother had always called Uncle Sonny and his family low class moochers.

She decided being placed in a home until she turned eighteen would be better than this, but then she recalled what her Uncle said about the house being sold.

In the kitchen, a pile of unopened envelopes laid in the trashcan. Curious about them, Gina reached down and picked the stack up. Once in her room, she opened each one and read the expressions of sympathy sent by church members and friends.

Aunt Nell had thrown them away.

She pulled out the phone and her mom's letter. She keyed in the number listed for St. Benedict's where her birthmother had stayed. It rang and rang. Finally, an automated voice answered.

We are closed for the holidays. Please call back after January fourth.

Gina's heart sank. She texted Olivia and told her about the cards and how utterly crude her relatives were.

Olivia didn't reply.

All her friends were celebrating the holiday with their families. Sadness overwhelmed Gina. Again, she couldn't stop crying.

For the first time in her life, she looked forward to returning to school.

♦♦♦

"Daddy! Daddy! Santa's been here. Hurry! Come see what he brought me."

Tristen slipped on his robe and tied it before joining her. "What's all the commotion about?"

"He came. Santa's been here, Daddy. Look he brought me a ballerina doll. He's so smart. It's different than Grandma Rose's doll. I like it more."

"I do too. What else did he bring you?"

"An art set with an easel. I can't wait to open it." She turned. "I got my dollhouse." She pulled him over. "Look, Daddy, it has all the furniture and people."

"Wow! Santa was very generous with you. Have you checked your stocking?"

She shook her head and dashed to the fireplace. "Get it for me."

Tristen nodded, crossed the room, and removed the stocking. "Here you go. Don't eat all the candy in one sitting."

She pulled out tangerines and a chocolate moose. A Minnie Mouse watch fell out with the other stuff, and Mallory squealed with excitement.

Tristen sipped coffee and snacked on cookies while Mallory opened several gifts. He'd mainly given her clothes and a pair of boots.

The phone rang. He could guess who was calling. Grandma Rose, no doubt.

He handed his phone to Mallory. "Answer it."

"Hello."

Unlike in the past, her eyes didn't light up. Instead, she replied cautiously to anything her grandmother asked.

Mallory named off everything Santa had brought her. “No. Santa’s so smart. He gave me a different Ballerina Barbie. The one Santa gave me has blonde hair and came with a dance studio.”

Tristen smiled. He suspected the old bat had done it to agitate him. Thankfully, she hadn’t succeeded.

That afternoon, he decided to take Mallory to the cemetery and let her put flowers on her mother’s grave. Though he’d explained her mother wasn’t there and was in heaven, Mallory still liked going there.

♦♦♦

Cynthia worked all day Monday restoring her house.

While taking a break, she googled unwed mother homes in North Carolina and found two. Both had been operating eleven years ago. If she saw a picture of the buildings and grounds, maybe she’d recognize it. But neither site offered images of the property.

Needing some fresh air, she grabbed her car keys and the poinsettia someone had sent, then drove to Westview Cemetery. She hadn’t been there in so long she couldn’t remember exactly where her mother’s grave was. She drove slowly on the road that ran through the cemetery.

Ahead of her, a man and child stood by a grave. As she approached them, she recognized Tristen and Mallory. She pulled to the curb and parked.

He immediately glanced behind him. His expression revealed his surprise to see her there.

She climbed from her car and joined them. “Merry Christmas, Mallory.”

“Miss Reynolds! Did you come to see my mommy too?”

“No, I didn’t sweetheart. I came to visit my mom, but I can’t find her. I didn’t think it’d be this difficult to locate her headstone.”

“Look. We brought Mommy flowers,” Mallory said.

Cynthia smiled at the red and white flowers with candy canes in the arrangement. “Those are beautiful.” She placed her hands in her pockets to warm them and stared at the grave for a moment before looking at Tristen. "Do you come here often?"

He nodded. "Less now." He smiled. "Apparently, you don't."

"Guilty as charged."

"You can find your mom's grave online. They have a locator."

"Good. Because, I don't think I can find it on my own."

She listened to Mallory talking about the toys Santa had brought her.

"Two Ballerina Barbies? Wow!"

"Santa gave me one and Grandma Rose gave me the other one."

Tristen's face tightened into a frown. "Fortunately, they aren't the same doll. Though I think that's what her grandmother had in mind."

"That's a dreadful stunt to pull."

"What'd you get for Christmas?" Mallory asked.

She held out her wrist. The diamonds sparkled in the sun. "This. Isn't it beautiful? My daddy gave it to me."

"My daddy gave me boots and clothes."

"Did Santa bring you anything?" she playfully asked Tristen.

"Just bills."

For a moment, she regretted not including him in the company's Christmas bonuses, but he hadn't been an employee long enough to receive one. Cynthia flinched when a car pulled up. "You have company."

Tristan scowled. "That's Grandma Rose."

A short petite woman stepped from the car and marched to the headstone. "You brought another woman to Danielle's grave. Seriously?"

"Miss Reynolds, this is my mother-in-law, Rose Williams. Rose this is my boss, Miss Reynolds, who is out here today to visit her *own* mother's grave."

"I spotted Tristen and Mallory and thought I'd say merry Christmas," Cynthia responded, knowing the lady had jumped to conclusions.

The lady's tight face and narrowed eyes relaxed. "Nice to meet you, Miss Reynolds. It's just that I thought..."

"Wrong," Cynthia said interrupting her. "I don't fraternize with my employees." She glanced down at Mallory, then Tristen. "I have an upcoming trip to Salt Lake City. You'll be flying me. Be prepared to stay for three days."

"You can leave Mallory with us." Rose's eyes sparkled with delight.

Cynthia stared down on the lady. "I was about to say, she can come with us."

"Take Mallory on a plane?" Rose stammered.

Tristen smiled. "A jet to be more precise." His attention shifted to Mallory. "Would you like that, Mal?"

She nodded. "Can I bring my Barbies?"

Cynthia smiled. "Yes, you can." She turned back to Tristen. "Let's plan to leave on Wednesday." She turned to Rose. "Pleasure meeting you, Mrs.Williams."

Once in her car, she waved at Mallory and drove away.

Tristen didn't want Rose getting away with what she'd just done. "In the future before you shoot off your mouth, you may want to make sure your brain is working properly. You embarrassed Miss Reynolds."

"I like her," Mallory said. "Her mommy died from cancer too."

For a moment, guilt showed on Rose's face.

"Mal, give Mommy the flowers." A nip of pain caught in his throat as he watched his daughter ever so carefully set the bouquet down. The memory of when they'd first learned about her cancer played in his mind. They had been so positive she'd beat it.

His daughter's eyes filled with tears. "I miss her."

He lowered to one knee and held her in his arms. "I do too, sweetie."

"My Danielle loved Christmas," Rose said, waiting for him to say something comforting.

He didn't. Instead, he stood ignoring her ploy for sympathy. Rose tried to hug Mallory, but his daughter dodged her and ran to the car, opened the door, and climbed in.

"You know, Rose, you've always been a part of her life. You need to think carefully about what you're doing."

"But she's all we have left of Danielle."

"Even more reason to be careful you don't alienate her. She may be six, but she's smart enough to know when she's being manipulated. Stop telling my daughter to lie about me."

Rose's mouth dropped. "I…"

Before she had a chance to deny it, he walked away, climbed in his car, and drove away leaving her standing alone in the cold isolated cemetery.

"Grandma Rose wasn't nice to Miss Reynolds was she, Daddy?"

"Nope. She's rarely nice. This time Grandma cranky-butt messed up."

Mallory giggled.

As he drove through the cemetery, he spotted Cynthia's car in a back section. Obviously, she'd found her mother's grave.

He considered Cynthia's life. He didn't like what he saw. Her entire existence centered around Zurtel. Basically, she didn't have a life outside the company, and the new metal compound could end up getting her killed.

Tuesday morning, he received the call to be at the airstrip by 8:00 a.m. She'd moved her trip up a day. It had been scheduled for Wednesday.

Mallory packed her dolls and coloring books as though going for a sleepover. She wore a red and black dress with black leggings and her new boots.

"Remember, if Miss Reynolds is working don't bother her. Got it?"

"Yes, Daddy. I'm not a baby."

"I know, Mal, but sometimes you can be rambunctious and chatter like a squirrel."

"Oh, Daddy. That was last year. I was only five. I'm all grown up now."

"I see. Okay, let's get out of here." His phone rang. Seeing that it was Grandma Rose, he didn't answer it. "Salt Lake City here we come."

When he reached the jet, Evan and Annie had already arrived.

Evan had started the preflight check. "I found an issue you should look at."

Tristen followed him around to the side of the jet beneath the wing several fasteners had been stripped from a panel. After looking at it, he sighed. "She's not going to like this, but this needs to be fixed. Get someone over here."

Cynthia arrived. Surprisingly, she had driven herself. As she stepped out of her car, she walked toward the jet, shielding the sun from her eyes. "Is there a problem?"

"Mechanic's on the way to replace some missing fasteners."

"That couldn't wait until we're in Utah?"

Tristen shook his head. "That's a five hour trip. I didn't want to chance losing a side panel at thirty-nine thousand feet up."

"How long?" she asked.

He shrugged. "The repair shouldn't be more than an hour. What time do you need to be there?"

"No set time. I'm having dinner with the company's CEO tonight. I thought we'd fly up early and get settled. We'll all be staying at the Snowbird Resort. Jennifer made all the arrangements." She paused. "The only problem is she didn't book a room for just you and Mallory. You'll be sharing with Evan. Annie is staying with a friend in town. I thought Mallory can sleep with me at night. Is that okay?"

He nodded. "So long as she's not too far away from me. She wakes up scared and wants her mother. Then she remembers Danielle is gone, and she cries for a while."

"Where is she?"

"Already taking over your cabin. You might want to board just to claim a clear spot."

Cynthia laughed making her green eyes sparkle like emeralds.

He liked to hear her laugh. It was something she should do more often. As a teenager she'd had an amazing sense of humor and laughed over anything. Zurtel had zapped the life right out of her.

He couldn't stop gawking at her curvy hips as she made her way up the steps. For a moment, he found himself jealous that Mallory got to share Cynthia's bed. He gave himself a mental slap. Making any attempt to start something with her would be professional suicide. He'd end up fired.

This had to be kept all business. Which meant he'd never bring up anything from their past. Not unless she did.

♦♦♦

Cynthia entered the cabin and was amused. Tristen hadn't been that far off. Mallory had her dolls on two of the seats. Her coloring book and crayons covered one table.

Mallory glanced up and smiled. "Miss Reynolds. Look, I brought my new dolls."

"I see. You can call me Miss Cynthia if you'd like."

The girl processed her comment and nodded. "I liked my snowflake."

"I'm glad you liked it." Cynthia smiled. "The one your daddy made was horrible. Just don't tell him I said that."

Mallory giggled. "I'm not a tattletale like Lucy Duncan. I won't tell, Daddy." She walked over to Cynthia and wrapped her arms around her. "Thank you for making my snowflake."

Cynthia warmed all over. This little girl tugged on her heart. It made her remember the daughter she'd given up. It sent a deep pain rippling through her. "Show me your dolls."

Mallory introduced her to the Barbies including the one the wicked grandmother had given her. She shouldn't have an opinion on the woman one way or the other, but she did, and it wasn't good.

No doubt the woman was searching for some reason to deem Tristen an unfit parent. During the short time around him, Cynthia realized he loved Mallory.

Would he have loved our daughter?

While waiting for the mechanic to fix the side panel, Cynthia pulled out her laptop and searched information on how to open adoption records.

Tristen entered the cabin. "He's done. We'll be departing soon."

Mallory ran over to him. He lifted her in his arms, hugged her, and kissed her cheek before lowering her to the floor.

"I'll see she's buckled in," Annie said.

"Thanks," Tristen said.

"What about my Barbies? Can we buckle them in?"

Annie smirked. "It looks like a Barbie convention. There aren't enough seatbelts."

"Pick your favorite one to hold," Tristen suggested.

"Okay." She selected the one Santa had given her leaving Grandma Rose's doll on the cabin floor. "I'm ready. Take it up, Daddy."

Cynthia envied Tristen for having Mallory. She racked her brain wondering if there had been anything she could've done to keep her daughter. Being underage hadn't left her with many options.

Less than twenty minutes into the flight, Mallory dozed off. Her little head tilted over.

Not wanting the child to have a crick in her neck, Cynthia moved her to the sofa and eased a pillow under her head before laying a blanket over her. Without thinking, she gently brushed the hair from Mallory's face. Hearing a sound, she glanced back and found Annie staring. Cynthia returned to her seat and continued reading about adoption laws and past cases.

"Anything I can get you, Miss Reynolds?" Annie asked.

"A cup of coffee would be great. Thanks, Annie."

The woman stared at her as if she'd spouted another head on her shoulder. She realized it'd been a while since she'd said thank you.

She sipped the coffee and considered what she'd do if she located her daughter. After much debate, she decided if her daughter seemed happy not to interrupt her life. After seeing her, would she really be able to stay away?

When the jet hit turbulence, Mallory jolted awake with wide eyes.

"It's okay," Cynthia said. "It's just a speed bump in the air. Would you like to sit with me?"

Mallory nodded and hurried over, climbed in Cynthia's lap, and leaned against her.

Cynthia wrapped her arms around Mallory, comforting her.

"You smell good," Mallory whispered.

"So do you. You smell like strawberries."

"It's my Hello Kitty shampoo."

After a few minutes of silence, Mallory asked, "Do you have kids?"

"No," she said, hating the lie.

"Why not?"

"I work a lot."

Annie interrupted. "Mallory, your dolls miss you."

She sat up on Cynthia's lap and glanced at the dolls scattered everywhere. "I'd better make sure they're not scared."

After landing, they took a shuttle bus to Snowbird Resort. Cynthia chose a seat across from Mallory and Tristen. The winding mountain road had been plowed. The deep snow on the ground made everything around them glisten.

"It's an ice kingdom." Mallory kept her face against the glass, peering out. "Can we build a snowman, Daddy?"

"Maybe."

"Can we ride that?" Mallory asked pointing to a ski lift.

"Maybe."

Frustration showed on her little face. "That means no."

"No, it doesn't," Tristen said. "I'm sure we'll do something. First, I have to see what Miss Reynolds's plans are."

"Whatever you want to do while you're here is fine. You're on your own until we head back Friday. Take her skiing. I'm sure they have bunny slopes for beginners."

"Can we, Daddy?"

Tristen came across as uncomfortable. "I've never skied."

"Seriously?" She shifted her focus to the copilot. "Do you ski?"

He shrugged. "Some, but I brought my laptop. I plan to work on my book."

"Can you take me?" Mallory asked her.

"No, sweetie. I have meetings to attend."

The Snowbird Resort's lodge perched above the valley below. Large snow covered mountains rose behind the modern structure with balconies extending from the rooms. They entered the enormous lobby with a stone fireplace. A fire blazed in it. Modern furniture filled the area along with a black grand piano.

She thought of the child's request and twisted around. "If I have any time between my meetings, I'll ski with you."

"You'll teach me how?" Mallory asked.

"Yes, I'll even teach your daddy." She flashed Tristen a smile. "It's as easy as flying a plane."

"Yeah, right. I doubt that." He frowned. "I'm not sure I'm willing to secure Mal to boards and push her down a hill."

"It's almost flat, and there'll be other kids."

Evan stood with them, soaking everything in. If she wasn't careful, rumors about her and Tristen would quickly spread all over Zurtel.

"Evan, you should join us," she said. "Maybe you can help me teach them to ski."

The copilot stared as if he'd just swallowed a five pound rock. "I'll pass."

She glanced back at Tristen. "I'll let you know when I have some free time." She paused. "Bring Mallory to me at bedtime."

That night while dining with Komar's CEO in the Snowbird's Bistro, Cynthia spotted Mallory, Tristen, and Evan entering the restaurant together. They sat on the other side by the window overlooking the valley. Though dark outside, thousands of lights lit a path across the area.

Keeping her mind on business became difficult. She kept glancing toward the far corner.

"Tomorrow, we'll give you a tour of our facilities," Mr. Spencer said.

She finally turned to him. "That'd be nice. Once we receive our patent, we need a company to manufacture MX7. Our Jacksonville plant doesn't have the controlled environment to produce the large quantities needed. The final product will be shipped to Jacksonville where my people will construct and assemble the final parts."

"We only produce the finest materials. I think you'll be pleased with our cutting edge technology."

"Normally, we'd look for a factory closer to home to save on shipping, but our three structured molecule material does better in a less humid environment." She didn't mention their product was almost as light as air. Shipping shouldn't be an issue.

"I'm sure Atlanta can be quite humid in the summer."

She smiled. "Yes and hot." She paused. "Of course, the final decision will be made by Randall Miller and our board."

It irked her she couldn't make a decision without him. Until the patent was filed, she wouldn't share their formula even with Randall. Hopefully, it wouldn't be stolen like their last two break-through inventions.

When she glanced over, Mallory waved, and Cynthia waved back.

Tristen immediately scolded her. The child turned around and didn't look back.

Mr. Spencer turned to see who she was waving at. "Family?"

"No. My copilot, pilot, and his six year old daughter. My corporate jet is covered in Barbies and crayons."

He chuckled. "Not many companies would allow an employee to bring their children."

"I keep telling myself that, but he's in a bind with her being out of school for Christmas break."

When their dinners came, the conversation ceased for the most part. She'd ordered the buttered chicken and vinegar potatoes. She never liked eating with strangers, but her stomach had growled several times since being there. Surprisingly, she made fast work of her food.

Several snow bunnies sat at the table next to her employees and talked while they ate. The ladies flirted notoriously.

A hint of jealousy ran through Cynthia. Not over Evan, but Tristen.

Tristen came across as uninterested. Apparently, he still loved Danielle and mourned her loss. She recalled his dolorous demeanor at his wife's grave.

If only he could have loved me with that kind of passion.

Teenage boys aren't really capable of falling in love. Girls of any age fall in love easily. She'd fallen hard for Tristen.

After dinner, Cynthia stopped by the spa for a full body massage. She returned to her room, wearing the resort's white bathrobe with her hair wrapped in a towel.

No sooner than she'd entered her room, her cell phone rang. She recognized her lab supervisor's number. "Tom, is everything all right?"

"Actually, no. I've been trying to reach you all day."

"My phone's been off for the most part, or I was away from it. What's happened?"

"Someone tried to kill your father today."

Chapter Five

"Please tell me he's all right." Cynthia's heart squeezed while waiting for his answer.

"Yes, he's fine."

"Thank God. What happened?"

"They were parked in front of the building, waiting for the garage to open. Ellis pulled the car up right as the shot was fired. It hit behind the back passenger seat."

"Why hasn't my dad called to tell me?"

"I'm sure he doesn't want to worry you. Don't mention I called."

"I won't. I'll let him bring it up."

"I'd appreciate that."

Cynthia disconnected and called her father. "Dad, it's me. We made it safely to Utah."

"I knew you would. Tristen's a good pilot."

"His dad probably taught him everything he knows."

"Robert didn't train Tristen. He learned in the Air Force."

"Tristen was in the Air Force?"

"Just like his old man."

Hearing Tristen had served in the military surprised her. It showed how little she actually knew about him.

"Anything of interest happen today?" she asked.

He hesitated. "You know, don't you?"

"Know what? What's wrong?"

"I might as well tell you. Someone shot at the car today."

"Oh, Dad. Where?"

He repeated what Tom had said. "The shooter sped off on a motorcycle."

"Motorcycle?" she asked, remembering her experience in the garage.

"Yes, black. Ellis didn't get a good look at the guy's face."

"Let me guess, he wore a black helmet."

"That's right. How'd you know?"

"It's the same guy who stole my laptop in the garage."

"Ellis said he was a big man."

Cynthia replayed the image of the biker in her mind. "I hadn't thought of it until now. The guy seemed too large for the bike. He could have been the one who ransacked my house and office as well."

"That matches Ellis' description. I'll inform the police."

"Dad, I'm coming home. We'll leave tonight."

"No. Stay put. I don't think I'm the one in danger. Think about it. You're the one who is usually in that car. You weren't supposed to leave until Wednesday morning. I think whoever shot at me was expecting you to be in that seat. You're safer there."

"Why me?"

"I'm not sure, but I'd bet it's all connected. That formula isn't worth your life."

"Let's talk about something else."

"How's Komar looking?" he asked, changing the subject.

"So far, they've treated me to a lovely dinner. I'm touring the plant in the morning." They finished their conversation and ended the call.

As soon as Cynthia disconnected, a knock on the door made her jump. She hurried to the door and opened it leaving the security chain in place. Tristen stood in the hallway. She unlatched the chain and opened the door. She smiled at Mallory standing beside him. "I almost forgot about our slumber party."

"Are you ready for her?" He stared with interest. The intensity in his eyes made her uneasy.

"Sure. Come in." Realizing she was in the robe, heat filled her cheeks.

His daughter wore pink *My Little Pony* pajamas and carried a *Hello Kitty* suitcase. "Wow, that's a big bed."

"It's like Papa Bear's bed. I'll get lonely in it all by myself." She cringed when she thought about what she'd said. "You don't need rails do you?"

"She never rolls off the bed," Tristen said. "But she is a cuddler. So you've been warned."

"That's okay. I'm a cuddler." Again she shuddered at her remark. Did he remember that she liked to cuddle?

Stop that right now.

Before she could, an image of them in bed formed. She remembered how he looked stretched out on top of her, working his hips in perfect rhythm. Afterwards, she'd cuddle in his arms. The memories made her dizzy with desire.

"Are you all right?" Tristen asked.

"Yes," she said meekly, hoping he couldn't see the steam coming off her. She didn't want him picking up on her distress his close proximity caused. "Someone fired a shot at the company limo. Dad could've been killed."

"I'm sorry to hear that. Is he okay?"

"Yes. He insisted I finish my business here."

"Are you sure you want Mallory tonight?"

"I do. She'll keep my mind off it." She didn't mention the bullet might have been intended for her.

Mallory smiled. "Can my teddy bear come too?"

"Sure. I love teddy bears. Show me your bear."

Mallory held up a furry, gray bear wearing a deep maroon Victorian dress. The bear wore a pearl necklace and tiny black shoes. "This is Priscilla. Me and my mommy made Priscilla at Build-A-Bear."

"She's lovely. Let's put her over here." She placed the bear on the bed. "I'll put your bag over there."

"She's already brushed her teeth," Tristen said. "If you need me, call."

"I'm sure we'll be fine."

He leaned down and hugged Mallory. "Don't give Miss Reynolds any problems. I'm just down the hall. I love you."

"Love you too," Mallory said, clinging to Tristen.

Tristen straightened up and looked at Cynthia. "Thanks for letting her stay with you."

She nodded. "Goodnight."

Once he left, Cynthia looked at Mallory. "Are you sleepy?"

She shrugged. "Me and Priscilla are hungry."

Cynthia studied the room service menu. "Let's see what they have. Is there any particular thing you want?"

Mallory nodded. "Cheese pizza."

"Wouldn't you rather have yogurt or Jello?"

Mallory glanced at her bear. "Priscilla wants pizza."

"Pizza it is." Cynthia called and placed the order.

She had no intentions of eating this late, especially junk food. But when the pizza arrived, and she opened the box, her stomach growled. The aroma of the hot doughy crust filled the room. "I'll split a soda with you."

She filled two cups. The thought of Mallory wetting the bed crossed her mind.

"Aren't you going to eat?" his daughter asked.

Cynthia sighed. "I'm giving into temptation here. One slice."

She flicked on the television and found a kid's network.

Before long, they were both laughing and eating the pizza. She scolded herself for eating two slices. "What have you done over Christmas break?"

"Daddy took me to the aquarium and a movie."

Did you like the aquarium?"

"Yep. We saw a shark."

"Scary, huh?"

Mallory's eyes grew large as she nodded her head up and down.

"Have you stayed with Grandma Rose any?"

"No. Daddy calls her Grandma cranky-butt."

Cynthia laughed. "Well, she's not exactly a ray of sunshine."

After brushing their teeth again, they climbed into bed and turned off the light. The gap in the curtains allowed the snow to illuminate the room, giving enough light to see by.

"Mallory, are you warm?" she asked.

"No. Can I scoot closer?"

"Sure. Come on over."

The little girl moved so close they were almost touching.

Cynthia swallowed hard trying not to think of her daughter. But she couldn't. Again she thought of all the things they would've shared. Instead, some other woman had shared all her daughter's special times.

"Still cold?" Cynthia asked Mallory.

"Yes."

Cynthia placed an arm over the child, trying to warm her. Again her heart ached for her daughter, for the little girl she'd never known. Her stepmother had insisted she never see her baby. She'd only caught a glimpse of the dark haired newborn.

Though Tristen had never known about her pregnancy or the baby, she still resented him.

♦♦♦

Tristen couldn't stop thinking of Cynthia. For just a moment, her eyes had revealed a glimpse of the old Cynthia. The one he'd fallen in love with. Any feelings past or present could jeopardize this job. He needed it more than ever with the in-law's wanting Mallory.

Rather than think about how beautiful she looked in the bathrobe, he mulled over the issues at Zurtel. He wasn't a cop, but it didn't require skill to figure out someone wanted something and was willing to do anything for it.

Apparently, they hadn't been successful. Would they try again? If so, would it involve Cynthia?

At some point, he fell asleep.

Wednesday morning he showered, shaved, and dressed before heading down to Cynthia's room. He wondered if she got any sleep with Mallory crowding her all night.

He tapped on the door.

Cynthia opened it. She was dressed and ready to go out. "She's still asleep. Come in?"

"I hope I didn't cause you to run late."

"No, not at all. You're right on time. We ended up ordering pizza and watching cartoons after you left."

"No wonder she's still asleep." He walked to the bed and gently shook his daughter. She yawned and grumbled in her sleep trying to wake up. He gently nudged her again. "Wake up, sleepy head."

Finally, she opened her eyes. "Where's Miss Cynthia?"

"Getting ready to leave. I heard you girls had a party after I left. Why wasn't I invited?"

Mallory smiled and hopped out of bed. "Just girls, Daddy."

"Grab your stuff."

Cynthia turned. "No just leave it. She'll be back tonight."

"Let's get you dressed, so we can eat breakfast." Tristen said, enticing his daughter to hurry.

"You should take the tram up the mountain," Cynthia suggested. "You can see for miles."

"Can we?" Mallory asked. "Pleeeease."

"I don't see why not," Tristen replied.

Mallory jumped up and down. "I'm going to the top. Can we go now?"

Cynthia smiled. "You'll need to eat first, so you'll have lots of energy."

Mallory did the unexpected. She wrapped her arms around Cynthia. "Thanks for letting me stay with you."

"I enjoyed it. I'll see you later," Cynthia said.

Tristen feared Mallory would become too attached to Cynthia. He already knew when it came to choices; Cynthia would choose Zurtel over any type of relationship.

He stopped in the shop and purchased rubber boots for Mallory and a sweatshirt to wear under her coat. Two hours later, Tristen and Mallory stood in the tram riding to the top. He held her in his arms, so she could see the snow covered landscape.

"I like Miss Cynthia."

"She's really nice." Actually, he hadn't expected her to treat him so well. Of course, he knew it was because of Mallory.

"Do you like her?"

He thought for a moment. "Yeah, I do." He paused. "You do know she's my boss?"

"I know. She let me sleep next to her."

"Did you keep those icy, little feet on her?"

She nodded with a big smile. "Yep. She's really warm."

He remembered her warmth, her soft clean fragrance, and the taste of her kisses. He forced the memories away. Loving Cynthia was a one way street. She turned out to be a rich girl just getting a few thrills.

At the top, they stepped out and walked around. While Mallory stomped in the deep snow, he snapped several pictures.

Back at the hotel while eating lunch, he checked his emails. He had another reply to his nanny post. This one was much younger than the first woman who replied. "What do you think? You like her face?"

"She's okay. I like Miss Cynthia better."

"Well, Miss Cynthia is a CEO and engineer with Zurtel. She doesn't have time."

"Time for what?" Cynthia said, coming up behind him.

"To be a nanny," Tristen finished. "Mallory picked you."

Cynthia laughed. "But if I had the time, I'd love to be your nanny. You're such a little cutie."

"I could go to work with you," Mallory offered.

Cynthia had changed out of her business clothes into jeans and a shirt.

He hadn't seen her dressed like this since they were teenagers.

"You'd be bored the first day." She shifted her gaze to him. "I have the afternoon free, so I thought I'd see if you want to try skiing."

"Isn't she too young?"

"No." She smiled. "You're chicken."

"Maybe a little," he confessed.

"What are you afraid of?" she asked.

"Skiing into a tree or off the side of the mountain."

"You're a pilot. Heights shouldn't bother you."

“Flying a duel engine jet is a little different than freefalling off the side of a mountain without a parachute. It’s not the flying that scares me; it’s the landing at the bottom I’m worried about.”

“You’ll be safe enough. You can do a beginner class with Mallory.”

“Come on, Daddy. It’ll be fun. I’ll hold your hand so you don’t fall.”

“That puts my mind at ease. Let’s do it.”

♦♦♦

They took the lift to the top. At the session for novice skiers on the Chickadee slope, Tristen stood with his daughter and six other kids under the age of ten. Mallory looked precious in the rented snow suit and small skis. As for him, he felt outright stupid inching along on skis with no one over four feet tall.

Cynthia stood to the side laughing.

After an hour of instruction, he and Mallory tried their first gradual slope with only a slight slant. Cynthia skied beside them.

“You’re doing great, Mallory,” Cynthia shouted.

“What about me?” he asked.

Instead of complimenting him, she giggled. “You better hope no one captures this on their phone. Trust me, it’ll go viral.”

“How’d you learn to ski?”

“My dad owns a chalet in Breckenridge, Colorado. We spent time there each year.” She shifted her attention to Mallory. “Remember how to stop?”

“Yes, ma’am.”

“Do you know how to stop?” she asked him.

“Got it. I think.”

“Let’s try Baby Thunder,” Cynthia suggested.

“If you think we’re ready.”

“Mallory is.” She skied over to Mallory. “You’re fearless.”

The next slope offered more of a challenge. He realized they were cramping Cynthia’s style. She’d probably rather be on the big slopes.

Though he tried to keep the position, one leg went rogue and slid out from under him. Unable to control it, he landed on his back. He tried to pull himself up from the deep snow. He laid there stranded like a beetle flipped on its back.

Cynthia skied over to him and offered her gloved hand. "Need some help getting up?"

"Sure." He grabbed her hand, and she pulled hard trying to lift him. Instead, she slipped and ended up on top of him. Rather than get angry, she laughed.

Tristen gazed into her eyes. Her laughter reminded him of their summer together when they had been very much in love. "I'd forgotten how green your eyes are."

She stared a second. Her frosty breath showed her labored breathing.

For just a moment, he considered kissing her.

Before he could, she rolled into the snow and stood up. "You're on your own, flyboy."

He managed to roll over and push himself up. He grabbed a hand full of snow and threw it at Cynthia.

She screamed, then rolled a snowball and tossed it at him.

He held his hands up to surrender. "Truce."

"Agreed." She offered him a dazzling smile.

"You and Daddy are funny." Mallory glided five feet ahead of them. "I win! I didn't fall down."

Cynthia caught up with Mallory. The girls skied ahead leaving him. They waited for him at the bottom. Cynthia waved. "See you haven't gone over a mountain."

"Can we do it again?" Mallory asked.

"Mal, she may have other things to do," Tristen said.

Cynthia glanced at her watch. "I think we can squeeze in one more run down the slope. Let's head for the lift."

"I'll sit this one out. You girls will go faster without me."

Once they left, he grabbed coffee and a pastry. He thought about her father being shot at. Her father rarely used the company limo, but Cynthia did. Had the bullet been intended for her?

As Mallory and Cynthia came into range, he pulled out his phone and videoed Mallory skiing. Then he messaged it to his dad, and for spite, he sent it to Rose to show how much fun Mallory was having.

On the trip back to the lodge, Mallory dozed off.

"I wish I could fall asleep that easily," Cynthia admitted.

"She's worn out." He paused debating whether to say anything. Finally, he decided to butt into her business. "While you skied with Mallory, I thought about the shot fired at the company limo. I don't believe it was for your dad. I think you were the intended target."

"Dad has already suggested that. Personally, I think it might've been a random bullet."

"After everything that's happened, how can you dismiss the incident as random?"

"The people after the MX7 formula are thieves not assassins. My death wouldn't make it any easier to obtain the formula."

"Does your dad have enemies?"

"You don't build a company like Zurtel without making enemies, but I don't know of anyone who'd want him dead."

"Who'd benefit from his death?"

"Only Randall and myself. But we're both financially well off and run the company. Dad gave us the reins earlier this year." She grew solemn. "I can't hide from whatever this is about. If this is about MX7, I'll be safe once the patent is filed."

Tristen let the subject drop. "Thank you for today. Mallory had a great time."

She smiled. "What about you? Did you have fun?"

He grinned. "Yeah, I did. I'll probably be bruised and sore tomorrow, but it was worth it. I really enjoyed seeing Mallory so happy."

♦♦♦

That evening in the dining room, Mallory and he sat with Evan at a table overlooking the valley. While eating, he glanced around the restaurant, searching for Cynthia. Tristen wondered where she was. Had she gone to dinner with the group of business men? He figured she was safe on this mountain. It was when she returned to Atlanta that worried him.

At 9:00 p.m. he walked Mallory to Cynthia's room and knocked.

She greeted them with a smile. "There she is. The future U.S.A. Olympic ski champion."

"Are you ready for her?"

"I am." Her attention shifted to Mallory. "Hey, snow princess. Come in."

Swinging her teddy bear and a big stuffed bunny, Mallory bounced into the room. "Daddy told me not to put my icy feet on you tonight."

"Do you have our itinerary for tomorrow?" he asked, before Cynthia could comment to Mallory's foot remark.

"I have one more meeting in the morning. We'll leave for the airport right after lunch."

"I'll notify the airport and submit a flight plan." Tristen found himself wanting to stay and talk, but he needed to remember his place in the company.

♦♦♦

Friday on the jet, Cynthia read over the contract Komar Industries offered. She liked everything about them, but would she be able to convince Randall. If she acted gung-ho about the deal, he'd immediately decline the offer. She would pretend she wasn't sold on Komar and planned to visit other manufacturers.

During the flight, Mallory fell asleep on the sofa with all her Barbies. The turbulence had been rough, so Cynthia was glad his daughter had slept through it.

She smiled as her thoughts drifted to Tristen trying to ski. He'd better stick to summer sports. She recalled he had been an excellent tennis player and a good archer.

Had their daughter inherited his athletic ability?

She pulled up adoption laws again. From what she read unless there was a medical issue, no contact could be made until her daughter turned eighteen. That'd be seven more years. She wanted to know about her now.

What did she look like? What had they named her?

She continued scrolling. From what she read, it would require going to court. Even then, she might not learn anything about her daughter. She read about receiving a confidential intermediary who would mediate between the adopted parents and the biological parents. She planned to contact a family law attorney soon instead of using anyone from Zurtel's corporate firm.

For just a moment, she considered telling Tristen. Then she came to her senses.

She had let her guard down at the resort and longed for the relationship she once shared with him. If it hadn't been for Mallory, she would have never allowed herself to become so close to him. Cynthia couldn't deny the sheer joy that encompassed her while spending time with him at Snowbird.

She gave herself a mental slap. Tristen never once called to see how she was or if there had been consequences. She needed to put some space between them.

"May I get you anything, Miss Reynolds?" Annie asked.

"I'm fine. We had lunch before we left. How'd your visit with your friend go?"

Annie looked as if an avalanche headed her way. "Are you asking me?"

Cynthia glanced around. "I don't see anyone else in here other than Mallory."

The attendant blushed. "I had a great time. We hadn't seen each other in years."

"Good."

"Mallory mentioned you took her skiing," Annie said timidly.

"I did. She did really well." Cynthia lowered her voice. "But her dad sucked at it."

Annie giggled.

Cynthia had been anything but warm with her employees. The only one she ever conversed with was Ellis.

No wonder they call me a bitch behind my back.

Tristen entered the cabin. "Mallory still asleep?"

Cynthia nodded. "Think she's ill?"

"I hope not." He walked over and touched her forehead. "She is warm."

"She tossed and turned in her sleep."

"Oh, I'm sorry if she kept you awake."

"No, I was working on some reports. Once I went to sleep, I slept like a rock."

He passed by Cynthia and made his way to the restroom at the back of the jet. When he came back through, he stopped beside Annie. "In about thirty minutes, can you wake her up and buckle her in?"

She nodded. "I'd be glad to."

He returned to the cockpit.

Cynthia stared with interest as he walked by. She couldn't let anything develop between them, not even a friendship.

♦♦♦

Gina stayed in her room most of the time. She texted Olivia and told her everything that had happened.

My aunt's busy preparing for a New Year's Eve party to show off their new house. It's my house. I hate them.

She waited for a reply.

I'm sorry. I wish you could live with me.

She texted Olivia back. *Me too.*

Later that night when everyone had gone to sleep, Gina quietly made her way to her mother's office off the entry hall.

She closed the door behind her and turned on the light. The items on the desk hadn't been touched. So far, Aunt Nell spent all her time going through her parents's closets and bedroom drawers. The desk drawers creaked slightly as she opened them. She rambled through them but only found bills and office supplies.

Then Gina remembered where her mother kept important papers. Maybe she'd find information concerning her birth. She removed the framed picture from the wall and quietly set it down.

Behind it, there was a wall safe. Only her parents had known the combination.

After trying different combinations of birthdays, the safe finally opened. She removed everything and sat on the floor. A royal blue pouch caught her attention. Gina opened it and gasped. It contained stacks of hundred dollar bills. She couldn't let her aunt or uncle find the money. She stuffed the papers back inside the safe and closed it, then replaced the floral picture. The papers would have to wait until she found a place to hide the money.

In her room, Gina sat on the bed and counted out ten thousand dollars. She had never seen this much money. Her heart surged with delight. Then she frowned as she recalled how often Shellie snooped.

Gina considered possibilities of where to hide it. An idea came to her.

After placing the money in the waterproof container, she lifted the toilet lid in her bathroom and set it on the rug. It took some maneuvering to get the container under the big ball inside the tank, but she managed to slide it underneath. The lid made a loud clanking noise when she set it back in place.

A toilet flushed in the house. Who was awake?

She turned off the light and scurried to her bed. Her heart beat a little faster.

Someone walked down the hall and opened the door.

She pretended to be asleep. The person stood at the end of her bed. It had to be either her aunt or uncle. It gave her a case of the willies. Finally, whoever it was left.

Monday morning after tricking Randall into signing with Komar, Cynthia called to check on Mallory.

Stay away from Tristen. I just want to know how Mallory is.

She pulled out her phone and called him.

He answered. "I can't fly today."

"That's not why I'm calling. How's the little ski champion?"

"Sick. I took her to the doctor this morning. She has an ear infection. Of course, Grandma Rose blames it on the skiing."

"Did you tell Grandma cranky-butt she wore ear muffs?"

He chuckled. "Yeah, I did. Mallory must've shared my nickname for Rose?"

"She did." She paused a moment. "How's the search for a nanny coming?"

"I have three who responded. I'm setting up interviews with them this next week. One is in Atlanta, but the other two are from out of state."

"Are they flying here?"

"I'm not sure. If they do, they'll expect me to pay for their airline tickets."

"Before you do, check their references, and if they check out, set up a Skype interview with each one."

"That's a good idea. Thanks."

After disconnecting, she couldn't deny Tristen's voice flooded her with emotions. She found herself caring for him and Mallory more than she should. Every time she was with them, her feelings grew stronger.

Her phone rang.

"Good morning, Dad. Have you recovered from your ordeal?"

"I'm fine. It's you I'm worried about."

"Have they found the shooter?"

"No, he's still out there. And I'm positive you were his target."

Chapter Six

"Randall hired each of us a bodyguard," her father said.

"Oh, Dad. I don't want some big goon tagging along with me everywhere I go." She glanced up when Jennifer placed papers on her desk and left.

"Randall believes we need them. He signed with an agency that provides trained men. Most have a military background. It's just until we find out who's behind the burglaries and shooting."

"I'll consider it and let you know," Cynthia said.

Hopefully, the next test on MX7 would be successful. Once they had three positive simulator tests, they'd be ready to use parts constructed from MX7 in real aircraft. After they conducted a series of successful tests, she could secure a patent. So far their competitors hadn't managed to steal the formula.

Later that morning, she made an appointment to speak with a family attorney at law.

Like scattered clouds, her thoughts drifted to Tristen and Mallory. Cynthia had to distant herself from them. She would try to use another pilot. She had to back away from him. It wouldn't benefit Zurtel for the board members and the rest of the business world to know she and Tristen shared a relationship other than business. The skiing at the lodge should've never happened. The one thing it proved was she'd never stopped caring about him. She had to stay focused on Zurtel.

♦♦♦

New Year's Eve, Tristen attended Mason's party at the Atlanta Country Club in Marietta. The elite and wealthy made up most of the guest list. Mason's father hadn't spared any expense.

Mason introduced him to the available women—women who smelled like expensive perfumes and wore dresses that cost more than his monthly mortgage payment. No doubt, their daddies were rich lawyers, politicians, or doctors. He smiled and made small talk with a few of them. Within minutes, they inquired about what business he was in.

Working as a pilot for a commercial airline drew more respect than being a corporate pilot. When he'd worked for the airlines, he'd never had a problem telling what he did for a living, but not now. Cynthia Reynolds had made him feel so far beneath her. He hesitated. Finally, he said, "I'm a pilot for Zurtel."

Several of them backed away to search the pond for a bigger fish making a lot more money than he did. Social piranhas. They were here to sink their teeth into rich husbands.

He made his way to the bar, ordered a whiskey sour, downed it, and ordered another. Since he didn't have to pick Mallory up, he could let loose a little.

By the time he gulped the third one down, his self-esteem had escalated. He strolled back to the women he'd met and stopped in front of a tall ginger haired lady. "Care to dance?"

"Love to," she said.

He escorted her to the floor, embraced her, and moved slowly to the music. While dancing, he spotted Cynthia Reynolds with friends.

Her face expressed her surprise to see him. She probably thought he had crashed the party.

When he glanced back, all her friends had been asked to dance, and she sat alone. No one had asked her. Hell, the men were probably terrified to approach her. He'd seen ice sculptures that appeared more accessible.

After the dance, he returned to the bar and had one more drink for confidence before boldly walking toward Cynthia. "Miss Reynolds, how are you this evening?"

"Fine, thank you." She set her wine glass down. "You know Senator Haynes?"

"His son, Mason, and I served in the Air Force together. We've been friends ever since."

"Small world. Where's Mallory tonight?"

"With Rose. Dad had a date. It sucks when your dad's getting laid and you're not."

Cynthia smiled making her even more gorgeous. "He's seeing someone?"

"He dates several women. I'm not sure if he's serious over any of them."

"How's the search for the nanny coming?"

"I interviewed the local one. She wanted to bring four cats that still had claws. On top of that, she was grumpy. I couldn't get her out the door fast enough."

She laughed. "I'm sorry, but that's hilarious. I guess you can scratch her off your list."

They laughed.

"Where'd all your friends go?" he asked.

"Dancing."

"Why aren't you dancing?"

"I have no desire to dance."

"That's not what I see in your eyes."

A hint of fear showed on her face. "I assure you I'm not in the mood to dance."

"No one has asked you." He offered his hand. "If they see you dancing, they'll realize you're not an ice sculpture."

"Ice? You mean cold?"

"Cynthia, love, you can come across as a real bitch. I know you have a heart under the frosty façade you put up."

"Why would they think that? I haven't spoken to any of them."

"Body language and that stern expression you wear." He expected her to slap him, but instead she smiled.

"You're drunk."

"Just a buzz."

"You're way past a buzz." She stared at her friends on the dance floor, then looked back at him. "One dance."

Her highness was willing to be seen with one of her servants. That surprised him. He offered his hand and helped her from the chair.

As they strolled to the dance floor, the music changed from a fast tune to a slower song, an old tune—*Smoke Gets in Your Eyes.* He gathered her in his arms and snuggled his head next to hers. She smelled like springtime—honeysuckle and sweet clover.

"Relax. Your heart's beating fast like a nervous little rabbit. It's just a dance," he said, trying to ease her tension. "I don't bite." Before he realized what he was doing, he nibbled on her earlobe, pressing his teeth gently against her skin.

She gasped. "You said you didn't bite."

"I lied, but I've had all my shots."

She giggled. "You are so plastered."

Again her reaction left him speechless. He'd expected her wrath. Realizing she was tipsy, he grinned. Apparently, she'd had several glasses of wine.

"You're going to have a hell of a hangover tomorrow," she whispered.

He shrugged. "Thought it'd help me fit in."

"Has it?"

"Nah, I still feel like a peanut at a walnut factory."

She laughed softly. "You're not. You look nice."

"You look and smell delicious." He pulled her closer to him and let his lips brush against her cheek. "We were good together."

She tilted her head slightly, bringing her mouth near his.

He placed his lips against hers and kissed until someone tapped hard on his shoulder.

"Excuse me. I'm cutting in," a deep male voice said.

Tristen stepped aside, allowing the man to take his place. Something inside of him burned. He wanted to shove the man aside and tell him to find his own date. But Tristen still had a grain of reasoning left and resisted.

He glanced back at Cynthia. Her eyes lingered on him, until her dance partner turned her away.

For a brief moment, a sobering thought hit him. After what he'd said and how he'd drooled over Cynthia, he might not have a job in the morning.

♦♦♦

Cynthia accepted Mitchell's hand and placed her other arm on his shoulder, keeping her body a few inches from his. For the first few minutes, she couldn't stop glancing at Tristen. His kiss had awakened her heart and sent tremors of awareness through her. She could understand and deal with the sexual urges, but her heart was an entirely different matter. His kiss had left her breathless.

"I thought you needed rescuing from that guy," Mitchell said. "He seemed to be coming on rather strong."

No doubt, Mitchell had witnessed Tristen biting her ear and kissing her.

"Thanks. It was a little awkward."

"Should've called security."

"He wasn't that out of line."

"You know him?"

"Yes, he works for Zurtel."

While they danced, she searched for Tristen. He stood with Mason at the bar. The last thing he needed was another drink.

After the dance was over, she thanked Mitchell. She danced with two more men before returning to her seat. She searched the crowd for Tristen. Had he left?

She thought of his warm whiskey scented mouth on hers, causing desire to spiral through her. The sensation left her bewildered. It'd been a long time since her dormant body had responded in such a needy way.

Then she remembered he'd been intoxicated. Come morning, he'd regret the kiss.

When people started leaving, she called Ellis to pick her up. The drive wouldn't take him more than thirty minutes. Having a driver would be safer than driving herself. For one thing, Ellis kept a gun under his front seat.

She waited on the club's elegant, stately porch. When Ellis pulled around the circular drive, she waved.

"Thanks for coming after me so late." Cynthia scooted across the backseat.

"Not a problem. How was your evening?" He started down the long driveway.

"Interesting. Tristen Conners showed up. He knows Mason Haynes."

"Speaking of Mr. Conners, I believe that's his car pulled to the side."

Cynthia glanced up the long drive. "Pull over."

She left the car and walked to the driver's door.

Tristen sat with his head cocked back asleep. She tapped on the glass until she woke him. He rolled the window down. "What?"

"Why are you camped out?"

"I don't think I can drive."

She motioned for Ellis to join her. "Help me get him in his backseat."

"Stand back, Miss Reynolds. I'll move him."

Once Tristen was in the backseat of his car, she turned to Ellis. "I'll drive him home. Follow me if you don't mind. We can't leave him here. Someone could call the police."

Cynthia shouldn't care. If he were arrested for a DUI, she'd have an excuse to fire him. An image of Mallory formed. She considered how much she disliked Grandma Rose. She had no choice but to help him. She woke him up long enough to get his address. She keyed it into the GPS on her phone and proceeded down the country club driveway.

Forty minutes later, she pulled in front of his house on Danbyshire, hit his garage opener, and drove inside. She liked his house and the mature trees that surrounded it.

Ellis parked behind her, got out, and assisted her with Tristen.

"I'm fine," Tristen mumbled. "I can take it from here."

"Let Ellis help you to your room."

Once inside his house, she flipped on the lights. He kept it neat and clean. Ellis assisted Tristen down the hall to the master bedroom.

Curious about his home, she followed them. The room smelled like Tristen—a fresh citrus scent. Like the rest of the house, it appeared clean. A family picture of Tristen, Danielle, and Mallory sat on the dresser. On his nightstand stood an eight by ten portrait of Danielle. It struck Cynthia as odd that she and Danielle both had dark hair and green eyes. Other than that, they didn't look alike. Danielle had a more rounded face.

It meant her daughter and Mallory might favor a great deal.

Ellis removed Tristen's shoes and jacket before attempting to remove his dress slacks.

"Hey, you need to leave," Tristen said, his speech slurred.

Cynthia couldn't hold back a laugh. "I'm leaving."

She explored his house and first checked out Mallory's room. Someone had painted a castle mural on her wall. Her white wooden bed had a purple canopy over it and a matching comforter. It was a little girl's dream room.

After touring his home, she waited in the kitchen for Ellis.

Ellis joined her shortly. "He'll probably wonder how he got home. I doubt he'll remember."

"I'll close the garage door. We can go out the front." Cynthia made sure she locked the door before leaving.

♦♦♦

Gina listened to the loud music. People she didn't know filled the house. Some drank and smoked. Her mother never allowed anyone to smoke inside. She cringed at the profanity coming from some of the guests.

Shellie had gone to a slumber party. Her aunt had tried to push Gina into going too, but she didn't know the girl hosting the party. Her cousin didn't want her tagging along. Will had also spent the night with friends.

Her aunt didn't want her at the party, so for the most part, Gina stayed in her room with the door locked.

Later that night, Gina decided to go to the kitchen. After making it downstairs, she cut through the entry hall to the dining room and into the kitchen undetected. Dishes and glasses cluttered the counter space. On the center island, she found food arranged on her mom's silver trays. Gina filled a plate with appetizers.

When a lady stepped into the kitchen, Gina ducked behind the island until she left.

She filled a glass with soda. Something sparkled by the sink, catching her attention. Aunt Nell had left her mom's wedding ring and a diamond and sapphire ring sitting out in the open. Anyone at the party could take them or knock them into the sink.

Take them.

She hesitated. Her aunt would accuse her first.

She can't prove it. This may be my only chance.

Gina snatched both rings and shoved them in her pocket, then grabbed the plate and cup, and quietly made her way to the staircase. She didn't think anyone had seen her. Hopefully when accused, she could convince her aunt that one of their intoxicated friends had stolen both rings.

When the party ended at 2:00 a.m. her aunt and uncle went straight to bed. Gina crept to their door and listened. Both snored loudly. With her cousins gone and her aunt and uncle conked out, she could move freely around the house.

After opening the safe, she removed the papers and spread them out on her mom's desk. Not afraid of being caught, she turned on the desk lamp. She found the deed to the house along with the car titles, and finally, she came across something about her adoption.

The document contained big words she didn't recognize or understand. She read the name of the lawyer handling the adoption.

Gina wondered if she could find him. If so, would she be able to hire him to find her birthmother. She returned unimportant papers to the safe and kept the deed, car titles, and adoption papers.

When she walked into the family room, she gasped at the mess. Whiskey bottles and beer cans lay on the floor. Plates of half eaten food covered the coffee tables. The place had been trashed.

Upstairs, she considered where to hide the rings. Being so tired, she fell asleep. When sun shined through the window, she awoke.

Crap. It's almost ten.

She jumped from bed and listened to see if her aunt and uncle were up.

Silence.

She had to return her dishes downstairs and hide the rings.

On the trip to the kitchen, she considered hiding places. More than likely, her aunt would thoroughly search her room. Gina considered putting the rings back by the kitchen sink.

No. I'll never get them back again.

A door slammed.

Gina flinched.

They're awake.

She headed for the stairs. At the top, she ran to her room.

Any moment, her aunt would fly up the steps.

Gina rushed to the bathroom and hid the rings with her money.

The steps creaked. Someone came up the stairs in a hurry.

Gina dashed into her room, eased the door closed, and climbed in bed, pretending to be asleep. She had basically become a prisoner in her own home.

The door opened abruptly hitting the back wall. Aunt Nell stood with her hands resting on her hips. "Where are they?"

Gina rubbed her eyes and yawned. "Who? Shellie and Will?"

"No, you little shit. The rings."

"What rings?"

"Your mother's rings."

Her uncle joined them. "Give 'em up."

"I don't have the rings," she lied. "Why would I? You told me they'd be mine when I'm older. Besides, I stayed in my room all night."

Uncle Sonny frowned. "They have to be here somewhere. Tear her room apart."

After they dug in the bed and checked under the mattress, her aunt searched her drawers. Aunt Nell threw the contents on the floor before attacking the closet.

Gina's heartbeat surged. "Maybe one of your guests took them."

"Those are my best friends. They wouldn't…" Aunt Nell paused in thought.

Remembering her performance as Heller Keller in the *Miracle Worker* at school, Gina fired up the same strong emotional outburst. "You let your trashy friends steal my mom's rings! You promised you'd give them back when I was older. You had no business wearing them."

"I'll call everyone who was here."

Her uncle sighed. "Really think they'd admit taking them?"

"You'd better get my mom's rings back."

"Don't tell me what to do. Get downstairs and clean the house."

"It's Shellie's turn."

"Well, she's not here," her aunt retorted. Then she paused as if remembering something. "I'm late picking them up." She turned to her husband. "You pick Will up, and I'll get Shellie." She glanced back to Gina. "You get started on that mess."

Gina rolled her eyes. "I have to put my room back together."

"You can do that after the downstairs is cleaned."

While she worked on the house, memories of her parents returned. They had always gone to a movie on New Year's Day. A bucket of sadness dumped on her. She fought the tears. Then another thought came to her. How was her birthmother spending the day? Had she ever married and had kids?

It dawned on Gina that she could have brothers and sisters.

Tuesday morning, Cynthia stepped from the limousine and approached the jet. The cold air lashed against her. Tristen and Evan stood outside conducting the preflight check.

After the way her body had responded Saturday night, she found it difficult to look him in the eye. She didn't want the sensual feelings he evoked in her, even if it meant taking drastic measures.

Evan hurried around to greet her. "Good morning, Miss Reynolds."

"Good morning." She paused on the second step and directed her attention to Tristen standing behind Evan. "We need to be in Chicago by nine."

He glanced up shielding his eyes with his forearms. "You'll be there."

He checked the rudder again, then instructed one of the maintenance crew to tighten it down better.

She entered the plane, took a seat on the sofa, and buckled up before pulling papers from her briefcase.

Evan entered first followed by Tristen.

Tristen stopped before her. Uncertainty shined from his eyes, and his body language showed how uncomfortable he was. Finally, he cleared his throat. "I want to thank you and Ellis for getting me home safely." He drew in a deep breath. "I'm not remembering everything clearly, but something tells me I owe you an apology for my behavior Saturday night. Most of what I remember isn't good. I was way out of line."

"You were being honest." She smiled. "Except for the biting thing. You did bite me."

His face flamed red.

From inside the galley, Evan choked and coughed.

Standing to the side, Annie's eyes widened.

"If I hadn't been drinking, I would've never behaved so inappropriately. I know that's no excuse. I hope you don't hold it against me. I need this job."

Something about what he'd said hurt. "I believe you said you drank to fit in. Why was that so important?"

"Because you were there. I didn't want to embarrass you. After all, I'm the hired help."

"You're an employee, and I don't consort with employees." She needed to end any chance of acting on what she felt for Tristen Saturday night. "I have to put Zurtel's image first. The board members might frown on it."

Anger sparked in his eyes. "It wouldn't look good in the society column. Millionaire CEO goes slumming with pilot."

Cynthia scowled. "I'm going to overlook Saturday night, but remember your place with this company if you want to keep your job."

"You've turned into a snob, Cynthia." He turned and headed for the cockpit.

Was she a snob? Did people consider her one? He'd been right at the party. Once men saw her dancing, they came forward and asked her to dance. Had they been afraid of her? He'd said her body language and expression had given that impression. She'd learned in business people took you more seriously if you weren't overly friendly and remained stern.

The jet started down the runway. She leaned her head back and closed her eyes as the aircraft built speed and lifted upward. She hoped to put some distance between her and Tristen. This was a start. She had let her guard down. After Saturday night, she saw how easy it'd be to fall back in love with Tristen.

I never stopped loving him.

That's not true. I hated him after that summer.

Like a fool, she'd involved herself in his personal life. If she wanted to save Zurtel from Randall, she'd need to keep her heart petrified. It meant staying away from Tristen and Mallory Conners. With his daughter back in school, he wouldn't need to bring her on the flights. It'd be best if she'd request a different pilot.

♦♦♦

Once they'd landed in Chicago and Cynthia had left, Annie and Evan cornered Tristen in the cockpit.

"So, when did you bite her?" Evan asked.

"Saturday evening at a party."

Evan repeatedly shook his head. "No way, man. Are you insane?"

"No drunk."

"How?" Annie asked.

"While dancing. Someone cut in and I left. End of story."

"She danced with you?" Evan asked, his tone expressing his disbelief.

"One dance." Tristen didn't want to divulge his past relationship with Cynthia.

"She treated Mallory and him like family at Snowbird," Evan said.

"Yeah, and now she's back to being the corporate ice queen," Tristen added.

Evan's expression grew serious. "If you want to keep your job, you might want to keep your mouth shut."

The day passed slowly for Tristen while waiting for Cynthia to return. Every time Evan looked at him, the copilot started laughing.

Her limousine pulled up, and she left the car. As she approached the jet, Tristen pretended to be checking something. Once she boarded, he boarded and dashed into the cockpit—avoiding her.

Annie stopped in the doorway of the cockpit. She wore a gloomy expression. "She wants to speak with you."

He glanced at Evan. "This can't be good. Hope I can find another job." He slid from his seat and entered the cabin. "Yes, ma'am."

"We sort of bring out the worst in one another. The alcohol made you honest and up front about how you feel."

The unemployment line lurked in his near future. If only he'd skipped the party. How would he battle it out in court without any money?"

"I decided it'd be best if you don't pilot my future flights."

"You're firing me?"

"No. I just think we should avoid one another."

He nodded. “Thanks for letting me keep my job.”

She opened her briefcase as a way to dismiss him from her presence.

He returned to the cockpit.

Since they’d returned from Utah, he kept remembering his summer with Cynthia and the feelings he’d had for her. She’d let her guard down at the resort, and he’d seen a glimpse of the seventeen year old he’d fallen in love with. It didn’t help that Mallory talked about Cynthia constantly.

He’d screwed up Saturday night. Now she had her reflector shields back up. He didn’t think he’d be able to break through the ice.

♦♦♦

Gina liked being back in school. The familiar routine gave her a sense of normalcy. Her fifth grade teacher, Ms. Johnson, gave her a hug that morning. It meant the world to her.

Shellie and Will attended the junior high five miles from the elementary school. Their school started and dismissed earlier. It meant her cousins would beat her home by an hour and have a chance to snoop through her room.

Her backpack hung on the rack in back of the classroom. No one had any idea it contained two rings and ten thousand dollars. She’d placed her sweater over them.

At lunch, Gina poured her problems out to her friends. “I feel like I’m being forced to live with a troll family. They’re so gross.” She told how Aunt Nell picked her feet all the time. “She leaves behind little piles of dead skin.”

“Gross,” Sadie said.

“Disgusting,” Olivia added.

“Isn’t there anything you can do?” Tamika asked.

“Not until I turn eighteen. Then I can kick them out.” She started to confide about the money and rings but didn’t.

After school, she called Aunt Nell. “I’m going to a friend’s house to work on a book report. She said her mother will bring me home by six.”

"We eat at five."

"I'll eat at Olivia's. It's Shellie's night to do the kitchen."

"Okay. See you later."

She clicked off her phone and caught up with Olivia, who waited for her mother to pick her up. "Think your mom will give me a ride? It's not far."

"I'll ask."

"Gina, who's picking you up?" one of the teachers on car duty asked.

"Olivia's mother."

"Okay. Just checking."

When Olivia's mother pulled up, Gina climbed into the backseat with her friend.

"Hi, Gina. I'm sorry about your parents."

Unable to talk about them without crying, she nodded.

"Mom, can we drop Gina off somewhere?"

"Depends."

"I'm going to my mom's friend's house. I have some of Mom's things I want her to have," she said slightly lying.

"Sure. Where to?"

Gina gave the address.

"I know where it is." Olivia's mother drove slowly down the street. "Do you know which house?"

"The red brick one with ivy growing on it." She opened the car door. "Thanks for the ride."

"Are you sure it's okay to leave you?"

"Yes, Mrs. Coleman. My aunt knows I'm here."

After getting out, she waved them off, then made her way to the front door. She rang the doorbell. Instead of leaving, Olivia's mom remained parked in the driveway. Gina waved again, and they finally left.

The door opened. "Gina." Liz Garson knelt down and hugged her. "I've been worried about you. Come in."

The moment Gina entered the house, tears burst from her eyes. She couldn't stop sobbing.

Liz wrapped Gina in her arms and held her. “I’m so sorry you’re stuck with those dreadful people. Your mother never liked them.”

She nodded still crying.

“Let’s go sit on the sofa.” Liz directed her to the family room. They sat together. Still Gina leaned against Liz. “Do they know you’re here?”

Gina shook her head. “I lied. They think I’m with a friend. I have to be back by six.”

“That aunt of yours made it very clear at the funeral she didn’t want us stopping by.”

“She’s taken all of Mom’s things.”

“That bitch.” She sighed. “Sorry, kiddo, I shouldn’t have said that.”

“That’s okay. I’ve heard worse.”

“I wish there was something I could do.”

“There is.”

Liz sat back. “What’s that?”

“Keep some of Mom’s things for me. If they stay at my house, she’ll find them.”

“Well. Sure.”

Gina removed the plastic container and took out the pouch.

As she pulled money from the bag, Liz’s eyes grew large. “Oh, my goodness. How much is there?”

“Ten thousand. Mom and Dad had it in their safe. Aunt Nell and Uncle Sonny don’t know about it. Can you keep it for me?”

“You need a bank account.”

“I know, but I’m a kid. I’d need a parent to sign.”

Her husband, Dan, stood in the doorway. “Put it on a prepaid credit card.”

Liz turned to him. “Would that work?”

He joined them in the family room. “It should. Instead of having a checking account, some people have their tax returns and salaries put on a card. They use the same card to shop and pay bills.”

“Can she put that much money on a card?”

"I think so. We can say she's our God child, and we want her to have it for college."

"That's seven years away, and that's if I pass sixth grade."

Liz smiled. "You're smart, chickadee. Your mom always bragged on you."

"No one will be able to use it without the pin number," Dan added. "We can list our address, so any statements come here."

Gina grew solemn. "Did you know I was adopted?"

Liz nodded. "Yes, your mom confided in me."

"Do you know anything about my real mom?"

She shook her head. "Not really. Just that your mom had the impression your birthmother was from a nice family. She'd been told she was a healthy female who wasn't a drug user."

"I want to find her. I don't want to live with Uncle Sonny and Aunt Nell. I hate them, and I hate their kids." She handed Liz the information about the unwed mother's home and the attorney's number. "Can you call them? Maybe if they knew my adopted parents were killed they'd give you my real mom's name."

"I'm not so sure it works that way, but I'll try."

Gina pulled out her mom's rings. "Keep these too. Aunt Nell wears them."

"Paula would want you to have them."

"Aunt Nell said she was just keeping them for me, but I don't believe her."

"I'll put them in our safety deposit box," Liz said. "Anytime you want them back just ask. It might be a good idea to keep the prepaid card there as well."

Gina shook her head. "No, I may need it. Once they realize I have a phone, they'll take it. I'll have to buy one somehow."

"I'll buy you one. Come back Friday," Liz said.

"Can you pick me up from school? I'll walk to the corner by the flashing light and wait." Gina gave more details on a time and place.

"I'll drive you home," Liz said.

Before leaving, Gina hugged Liz and thanked Dan.

Liz dropped her off before six.

Gina entered the house and went to the kitchen. Once again Aunt Nell had trashed it. The lady never threw anything away or put anything up while cooking.

Thank goodness it was Shellie's night to clean.

She told Aunt Nell she'd eaten, but she hadn't. The smell of the roast made her stomach rumble with hunger pangs.

As usual, they ate in the family room and set their drinks on the tables without coasters. *Pigs*.

Later, Gina sat on her bed doing homework. Some of her things were out of place. Someone had left several drawers partially open. Aunt Nell had probably been searching for the rings.

Her aunt opened the door and entered the room.

"Find out who stole Mom's rings? I want them back," Gina demanded before her aunt could accuse her again.

"No, but I will. Shellie isn't feeling well. I need you to clean the kitchen."

Without arguing, she pushed her books aside and followed her aunt downstairs. It'd give her a chance to eat. "Shellie will need to do the next two nights."

"She will."

While putting the leftovers away, she made a plate of food and set it on top of the cans in the pantry.

Her aunt entered the kitchen. "Did you get your report done?"

"No, almost. Her mom said I can come back Friday to finish. It's due next Monday."

"I don't have a problem with it." Her aunt grabbed a soda and left the room.

Once Gina completed the kitchen, she took the plate and hurried to her room. She ate the food as if she hadn't eaten in years. The only thing she liked about Aunt Nell was her cooking.

At some point, she fell asleep doing her homework. She glanced at the clock. 1:00 a.m. Her unwanted relatives would be in bed. Sad to think, she had to haunt her own house at night. Downstairs, she rinsed the plate and put it away.

Gina made her way to her mom's office to see what else she could find of importance. *The green light on her mom's computer caug*ht her attention. Her mom had never fooled with a password to access it.

She sat in the desk chair and clicked the mouse. The Internet screen popped up with a list of topics someone had researched.

Top five unintentional deaths for children. Suffocation, drowning, falls, car accidents, poisoning.

Why would her aunt want to know this? A dark realization surfaced.

To kill me.

Gina's breath left her.

Chapter Seven

Friday, Gina hopped into Liz's car. "Thanks for picking me up."

"I don't mind one bit."

Once in Liz's house, Dan handed her the prepaid Visa card. "We'll call the number on back and let you change the pin number to a four digit number only you know."

"Thanks." She slipped the card in the pencil pouch inside her notebook. "Did you call the home?"

"I did," Liz said. "I was told all the records are sent to the state. I did learn your mother signed a closed adoption that means she doesn't want to be contacted, but it could've been decided by a parent, and she had no choice in the matter."

"So does that mean we can't find her?"

"It could, but the courts can assign a court mediator who will contact your biological mother and inform her you're looking for her and ask if you can contact her. There will be a charge for it."

"As long as it's not over ten thousand."

"It wouldn't be anywhere near that."

"Good. I want to do it."

"You look troubled. Want to tell me about it?" Liz asked.

Gina proceeded to explain what her aunt had been researching on her mom's computer. "I think she's wants to kill me."

"Not even she could be that bad."

"I overhead her ask Uncle Sonny who would have gotten everything if I had died with my parents."

"What'd he say?"

"He and his sister would've ended up with everything."

Liz's face grew concerned. "That doesn't sound good, not when you put it with her Internet search."

Liz stopped at a dollar store on the way back to Gina's house. "Sit here. I'll be right back." When she returned, she had a plastic package containing a cell phone. After ripping it open, she removed the phone. "I'm going to set this up for you. Keep this in your school bag. It's a prepaid cell phone. You can put minutes on it with your bank card. Only use it in case of an emergency. Use this phone to call me. I'll put my number under contacts."

"Thanks."

"You can't keep coming to my house without them becoming suspicious. Your aunt and uncle won't remember me from the funeral. I'm going to call and introduce myself as your Sunday school teacher. I'll ask if I can take you to church and bring you home on Sundays. That way, I can see you each week without all the sneaking around."

"What if she's seen this car? Won't she think it's odd you drive the same car as Olivia's mom?"

She nodded. "Good point. We'll pick you up in Dan's car."

"Don't forget to call my aunt," Gina reminded.

"I won't. Hopefully, when I see you on Sunday, I will have news from the attorney. For the time being, play it cool. Try not to rock the boat."

"I'd like to sink their boat." Gina hopped out and hurried to the front door. Wanting to put her things in her room, she headed upstairs. She stopped in her doorway, trying to figure out what had happened. The furniture remained the same, but the comforter and curtains had been changed. Her belongings had been moved. She opened the closet and discovered everything missing.

Shellie strolled into the room. "Get out of my room."

"This is my room. Where is my stuff?"

Aunt Nell joined them. "You're younger. Shellie should be the one with her own bathroom. We moved your things to the other room."

Gina's blood turned to fire. She wanted to scream and throw things. Remembering what Liz had said, she forced back her anger. "The television is mine. My mom gave it to me for my birthday. I'll be back for it."

In her new room, her belongings had been thrown onto the floor in a heap. After setting the backpack in the corner, she stormed back to her old room and claimed the television with a built in DVD player.

Adrenaline pumped through her. Despite what Liz had said, she couldn't hold back. She glared at Shellie. "Enjoy it now, because when I'm eighteen, you're out of here." She turned toward Aunt Nell. "You too."

Later that night, she walked into the bathroom she shared with Will. He'd left the toilet lid up and hadn't bothered to flush. *Gross.*

Gina decided to use the half bath downstairs off the entry hall. Shellie left for school before her. That's when she'd take a quick shower in her old bathroom.

She locked the outer hall door and the one that led to the shared bath. After putting everything in place, she sat on her bed, feeling so violated. Again, her anger soared to the level of making her insane. She wanted to hurt them. Gina thought about what her mom would do in the same situation. Her mom would pray, but Gina was too angry with God for taking her parents and leaving her in this horrible situation.

It wasn't until everyone had gone to sleep that she ventured downstairs. Too tired and hungry to cry, she finally stopped, and at her wit's end, she prayed for God to help her.

♦♦♦

Through January, Tristen hadn't needed Rose to keep Mallory. Not wanting the judge to think he wouldn't let them see her, he agreed to let Mallory spend the weekend, so she could attend church with her grandparents. Rose had offered to drive her to school on Monday. He dropped Mallory off at Grandma Rose's early

The weather forecast predicted snow. If it did, school would be canceled Monday.

Since Mallory wouldn't be home, he planned to attend a Super Bowl party with friends from the airline. Maybe he'd hear of an airline hiring and would be able to leave Zurtel. He wanted to get as far from Cynthia as possible.

Until he found a nanny, he'd arranged for Mallory to stay at an afternoon daycare. With the daycare, getting back in time to pick Mallory up hadn't been an issue. He had until 6:00 p.m. each week day. He only used the daycare when he was on a late flight. He hated making her stay somewhere late after being at school all day, but it had cut out his dependency on Rose.

Cynthia had been true to her word. All month, he'd flown Randall, her father, and other Zurtel executives but not Cynthia. She'd insisted on one of the other pilots.

No sooner than he walked in his front door, the phone rang. Zurtel. Surely, no trip would be scheduled on a Sunday. He answered it. "Hello."

Dwayne cleared his throat. "Hope you aren't planning to watch the game?"

"Yeah, I'm going to a Super Bowl party."

"Sorry, you're flying Miss Reynolds to Jacksonville, Florida. You leave in an hour."

"She made it clear she doesn't want me. You'll need to call someone else."

"They turned it down, so that leaves you—low man on the totem pole."

"Do you realize how hectic it'll be flying into Jacksonville with the Super Bowl going on?"

"I do, but she doesn't. She has an important meeting in the morning. She's afraid if the ice storm hits, our jets will be grounded Monday morning. You'll be staying overnight so pack a bag."

"There's probably not a hotel available in the entire city."

"That's not your concern. Be there." He chuckled. "Too bad you can't get a ticket to the Super Bowl since you're gonna be in town."

"I don't have that kind of money."

After he disconnected, he called his friend and bailed out of the party. Then he called Rose and asked if she'd keep Mallory Monday if school was canceled. Missing the party turned out to be a good thing since his friend had planned to fix him up with a recent divorcee.

He packed a small overnight bag and headed out.

By the time he and Evan finished the preflight check and made sure the jet had been refueled, Cynthia arrived. She didn't come across as thrilled to see him.

He approached her. "You do realize the Super Bowl is being played in Jacksonville today? There'll be a lot of private aircraft landing. We may have to circle the city waiting to land."

"I'm aware of that, but it's important I'm at the Jacksonville plant in the morning."

"And you found a place for us to stay?"

"Jennifer, my secretary, is working on it. I'm sure she'll find something."

"I wouldn't count on it. Everything in Jacksonville will be booked."

"Let me remind you that your job is to fly me without any questions. Let's go."

"You'd better fasten your seatbelt. With these winter storms, there's going to be a lot of turbulence." He chuckled. Turbulence described Cynthia.

She dismissed him with a perturbed look. When he entered the jet behind her, he stepped into the cockpit without saying another word.

Evan already sat in the copilot's seat. "Looks like it'll be just the two of us. Annie's not coming."

He grinned. "The ice queen will have to retrieve her own strawberry protein shakes and diet sodas."

"It's working out for me. I have a cousin in Jacksonville. Turns out his wife isn't feeling well, so I'm attending the Super Bowl in her place. I'm staying with him, so you'll have Miss Reynolds all to yourself."

"You lucky bastard." Tristen slipped his headset on and prepared to taxi onto the private runway.

The flight didn't take over forty minutes. As he'd predicted, they had to orbit around Cecil Field and wait for landing instructions from the tower. Zurtel had a contract with the airport for landing privileges and hangar space. They might've stood a better chance landing at HEG.

The intercom came on. "When will we land?"

"We're after Mark Wahlberg and Justin Timberlake. Shouldn't be but another twenty minutes." He sighed. "She could have waited until tomorrow."

Evan laughed. "They're testing Zurtel's new prototype."

"How do you know that?"

"I overheard her father talking. Everett Reynolds talks too much."

Finally, the tower controller gave him clearance to land. He'd never seen so many jets in one place as celebrities and the extremely elite flew in to attend the game. As he prepared to land, he reduced the power, lowered the nose, and lined up with the runway.

Once he landed, Cynthia stood and walked up front. "I called Jennifer. There'll be a car waiting for me. But there's a slight problem. She couldn't book you at the Hyatt with me. You'll share a double at the Starlight Bay Motel. It's the best Jennifer could do."

Evan smiled. "I'm staying with my cousin and going to the Super Bowl. He's meeting me out front." He slapped Tristen on the back. "Looks like you have the room to yourself. See you Monday."

Evan grabbed his gear and left.

Tristen hated being by himself for the Super Bowl.

"I can drop you off on my way into town," she said to Tristen.

He wanted to say something smart, but figured he should keep his mouth shut, so he nodded. He slipped on his bomber jacket, grabbed his overnight bag, and followed her.

When a black limo pulled up, they made their way to the car. A light sprinkle had already started falling. Cynthia shielded her head with her briefcase.

"You can sit up front with the driver," she said.

"Not a problem. The back seat is a little frosty for my taste."

She made a slight huff.

The driver waited for Cynthia to slide onto the backseat before closing the door.

Tristen climbed up front and held his bag in his lap.

Cynthia instructed the driver where to go.

On the far side of town off the beaten path, the driver pulled up to an old motel. Huge trees with Spanish moss surrounded the small place with a playground in the courtyard.

"I'll be just a minute," she said to the driver. "Let me get him registered."

The driver nodded.

Tristen looped the strap of his bag over his shoulder and climbed out. He held the motel door for Cynthia. Inside five people stood in front of them. She glanced back at her driver to make sure he was still waiting. He was. Finally, they reached the front desk. "I have a reservation for Zurtel Corporation."

The clerk smiled. "Yes, here it is. I need for you to fill out this paperwork. And I'll need to see your credit card."

After she'd filled it out and paid, the clerk handed her the key. "Room seven. At the end of the breezeway."

She handed Tristen the key. "I'll call tomorrow and let you know what time we leave."

"If Atlanta and all the surrounding airports are iced over, we may be stuck here."

"Weather forecasters are rarely right." She walked from the building like the Queen of Sheba and once again waited for the driver to run around and open the door. The limo drove off.

Tristen couldn't have been happier to get away from her. She'd been in PMS-mode since the dance. In her case it stood for prissy-moody-snob.

Inside the standard double room, he turned on the heat and television. At least the room was clean. Rather than go out, he ordered a pizza to be delivered. While waiting for it, he trekked to the vending machines and purchased several sodas and a snack cake.

A heavy rain started. This wouldn't be good for the Super Bowl. Everbank Field could end up a swamp. He envisioned an alligator grabbing the ball. The silly image made him grin.

He flicked on the weather channel. An icy mix fell over most of the south and heavy snow in the north. Cynthia had been right about flying in tonight for her meeting tomorrow. If they had waited, the conditions would've been too bad for flying. Some of the southern airports had already closed.

His phone rang, and he picked it up. *Cynthia Reynolds.*

"Miss Reynolds, what can I do for you?"

"My meeting has been postponed until next week. I want to leave within the hour. I've already checked out of my hotel, and I'll pick you up. Be ready. Call Evan and get him back to the jet."

"He's at the Super Bowl, remember?"

"I don't care. Call him."

"There's icing from the Mason-Dixon line down. I'm not flying in this."

"You will fly me home tonight, or you're fired."

She needed a straitjacket and a ride to the psyche ward.

"The airport will close before we can get there. Everything is grounded."

"If that happens, we'll land in Birmingham and rent a car."

"BHM has already grounded all planes from taking off and rerouted those landing. Let me inform you that icing is the number one cause of small jets crashing. Think about this carefully. We'll probably be able to fly out tomorrow around one or two if they get the runways cleared."

"I'm not pleased with your attitude. I think we can make it before Atlanta closes."

"You're not the pilot. It's my decision when it comes to a situation like this. You can turn around and go back to the hotel."

She disconnected.

Once his pizza arrived, Tristen got comfortable, popped the top on a drink, tossed several slices on a paper plate, and sat back on the bed to watch the Super Bowl. The aroma of the sausage and cheese filled the room. A beer would've been better, but he settled for soda.

An hour into the game, someone pounded on his door.

Forgetting he was in boxers, he opened it.

Cynthia Reynolds stood on the other side. Her wet hair hung limp on her shoulders. Tension showed on her face, and her eyes revealed pure unleashed anger. "My hotel room had already been given to someone else." She pushed past him. "I'm taking this room."

"There's not a vacancy in this city." He stepped back, allowing her to enter. "You can have the other bed."

"I can't sleep in the same room with you."

"So what do you expect me to do?"

"Sleep on the jet. The rain has almost stopped, so you'd better leave before it starts back."

"Not happening, sweetheart. It's not like we're sharing a bed."

"How would it look for me to share a room with my pilot?"

"Who's looking? No one has to know. Evan will think you were at the Hyatt."

She set her tote and purse on the dresser. Her face showed panic. "The driver left with my suitcase."

"Don't sweat it. I doubt he's your size. You can get it back tomorrow."

"But my nightgown is in it." Her gaze swept over him. "Get some clothes on and leave."

He ignored her direct order. "I have a T-shirt you can wear. Are you hungry? I have a large supreme pizza. Care for a slice?"

"Is that all you ever eat?"

"It's got all the bases covered. Got my veggies, cheese, bread, and meat."

"It's junk food. Your arteries are probably hardening as we speak."

"Suit yourself, but I don't think you'll find any five star restaurants in the area." Seeing her clothes were damp and causing her to shiver, he pulled a white T-shirt from his bag and tossed it to her. "Change before you catch a cold."

Rather than get dressed, Tristen returned to his bed and continued eating and watching the game as though she wasn't there.

Cynthia huffed, grabbed her small tote bag, and headed for the bathroom. Shortly, she returned wearing his T-shirt. She didn't wear a bra beneath it. The memory of taking her nipples in his mouth and sucking each one flashed in his mind.

Holy crap. Don't go there.

He pushed the memory aside. After tonight, he might not have a job. His dad swore general aviation was the best gig for a pilot. Well, his dad could have it. Tristen didn't like dealing with pampered, rich brats. It wasn't just Cynthia, Randall was equally as spoiled.

"As soon as you eat your pizza, you need to get dressed. I'm sure the front desk can call you a taxi."

"Lady, you'll have to call the police to get me out of this room. The jet is locked up in a hangar. No security guard is going to let me in. If you don't want to sleep in the same room with me, you can sleep in the bathtub."

Right now, he wanted to strangle her. He suspected this had more to do with what he'd said at the New Year's Eve dance. He'd been out of line, and now he was paying for it.

"If you mention this to anyone, you won't have a job."

He flashed a cocky grin. "Trust me, I have better things on us than this to brag about."

"They'd know you're a creep who lied about your feelings for me just to get me in your bed."

"No, they might realize you're not the corporate machine you give the impression of being. They'll realize you're a woman with desires, real feelings, and passion for something besides Zurtel. Now if you'll step aside, I'll finish watching the game."

Cynthia pulled the comforter back and slipped between the sheets.

When her stomach growled, he grinned.

The Patriots carried the ball into the end zone.

"Touchdown!" In a few minutes, he shouted out again, "Interception!"

During half time, he called Mallory. He'd purchased her a phone, so she could talk without Grandma Rose hovering over her.

"Daddy. Where are you?"

"Jacksonville, Florida. Are you having fun with Rose?"

She sighed. "I guess so. I miss you."

"I miss you too. With the ice storms, sounds like you'll be out of school tomorrow."

"Grandma says we'll make cookies and play board games."

"Let Grandma cranky-butt win every now and then so she doesn't get twisted out of shape."

Mallory giggled. "Okay, I will."

"Goodnight, Mal. I love you."

"Love you. Night, Daddy."

Cynthia didn't like being alone in the same room with Tristen. He affected her heart and body, and she couldn't give into her emotions. He didn't understand how important her image was.

Randall could sleep with as many women as he wanted, and they didn't see him any less of a businessman. But with her, it was different. She hated this double standard. If her stepbrother discovered she'd shared a room with Tristen, he'd turn it into something ugly and smear her image with the board members.

She considered Tristen's arrogance. Not only did he refuse to give her the room, he threatened to expose their teenage relationship. As an employer, she couldn't let him get away with it. The flyboy would need to face some negative consequences.

Sharp pangs hit causing her stomach to growl. She hadn't taken time to eat lunch or dinner. She glanced at the pizza box.

"Despite your nasty disposition, you can still have some."

Cynthia surrendered and walked to the box. She raised the lid and took several slices. She peeked in the refrigerator. It was empty. "Where are the drinks?"

He gave her a blank stare. "Drinks?" Then he grinned. "Sweetheart, this isn't the Hilton. You have to buy your drinks from the vending machine in the breezeway."

"Go get me a diet-soda."

"Not happening. You'd probably lock me out."

The thought had crossed her mind.

While microwaving the pizza, she filled a cup with water from the sink. She gobbled the first slice down, then took her time on the second one. Nothing had ever tasted better.

Tristen focused on the game. "Fumble! Hot damn! Get that ball, you idiots."

After the game, he called a friend and raved on about the Patriots winning. When the news came on, Tristen disappeared into the bathroom.

The weather girl discussed the icy conditions covering the south. Even Jacksonville had freezing temperatures. Then the male news anchor talked about the number of airports already closed and the people stranded. The first one he mentioned was Atlanta.

Cynthia hated admitting Tristen had been right. She'd taken her problems out on him. The testing facility had computer glitches and canceled the prototype testing. On top of that, a competitor claimed they were close to a new material that would revolutionize the airline industry. She had done everything she could to protect the formula. Had they found it?

They couldn't finish the tests until the computers could efficiently monitor the prototype. If someone else had the invention, it meant one thing—she had a traitor in the company. Someone very clever and dangerous, but who?

As soon as Tristen left the bathroom, she brushed her teeth and prepared for bed. Once back in bed, she couldn't sleep. Too much swirled in her head.

While watching the stock market report, she glanced toward Tristen's bed.

He'd fallen asleep. She studied his masculine face and strong jaw line. For a moment, she recalled kissing him in the heat of passion. She smiled remembering how they would kiss until their lips ached.

Finally, she dozed off.

In the middle of the night, she dreamed she was with Tristen. His body spooned hers. He had one arm draped over her, and his warm breath tickled the back of her neck. Feeling him partially hard, she pushed back causing him to become fully erect. He made a deep groan. In the dream, she placed his hand over her breast and moaned when his thumb swept across her nipple.

So good. If only he'd move his hand a little lower.

As she began to wake, she scolded herself for the dream. She opened her eyes and screamed.

Tristen sat up. "What's happening?"

"You, you son-of-a-bitch. You're in my bed. I knew I couldn't trust you."

"No, I'm not. You're in mine."

She glanced at the other bed, causing her breath to hitch. She let out a yip and climbed from his bed and jumped into hers. Then she recalled going to the bathroom in the middle of the night. Apparently, she climbed back in the wrong bed.

"See," Tristen said. "There's the problem. You want me. Just admit it."

"I wouldn't sleep with you if you were the last man on earth."

He had the gall to laugh. "That's not how I'm reading this."

"Oh, shut up and go to sleep."

"Was it as good for you as it was for me?"

The thought of doing more than she could remember left fear bubbling inside her. Had they? Maybe, they had. *No, I would've woken up.* "Nothing happened."

"You sure?"

She wasn't.

"If you remember anything, you dreamed it," she retorted.

He chuckled. "I didn't dream you moving my hand to your breast."

She swallowed hard. "I was half asleep."

"I can see the headlines in the society column," Tristen teased. "CEO admits to sleeping with pilot. Claims she did it in her sleep." He paused. "Doubt anyone will buy your defense."

She placed a pillow over her head to block him out and returned to sleep.

Later that morning, Cynthia slipped from her bed. The big lump beneath the covers in the other bed didn't move, so she assumed he was still asleep. She wanted to shower and dress before he awoke. She grabbed her clothes that had dried and tiptoed to the bathroom.

Opening the door, she gasped.

A buck naked Tristen stepped from the tub after a shower.

She stared at his body, speechless. Water beaded on his muscular chest. Before she could stop herself, she glanced lower. "I just saw you in your bed."

"There's nothing in my bed but a stack of pillows. I think you're trying to sneak a peek."

"Don't be ridiculous. I wanted to shower and get out of here before you woke up," she confessed.

His brows rose. "You're gawking. Let me remind you, you've seen it before."

Damn him.

Humiliation flooded her. "You weren't packaged like this when you were seventeen."

He grinned. "Yeah, I'm new and improved. Want to give me a test run?"

She frowned. "Don't be silly. I want you to hurry, so I can get ready."

Once in the shower, she couldn't stop thinking of Tristen. It'd been such a long time since she'd been with a man. He was definitely eye candy which surprised her with all the pizza he ate.

When she left the bathroom, Tristen had already called a taxi and left for the airport. She couldn't help but be disappointed, he hadn't waited and ridden back with her.

Cynthia arrived at the airport around ten-thirty. Tristen stood in the jet's doorway. At the top, she gave him her snooty look. "How soon can you get it up?"

He offered a sexy smile and winked. "I've never had a problem getting it up. I'm surprised you forgot."

"That's vulgar and out of line."

"You're the one who asked."

She frowned. "I was talking about the jet."

"I was teasing. You're no fun, Cynthia. You've turned into a cold, lifeless rock."

Cynthia wanted to say something equally as callous. "It's clear to me you're over your wife. Your remark wasn't that of a grieving husband."

His expression revealed his anger. "I loved my wife. I miss her. Don't ever mention her again. Now, take your seat."

The harshness of his tone caused any sexual awareness to vanish. Rather than apologize, she decided to let him remain irate over the remark.

During the flight home, she realized to sever any feelings between them, she had to make him even angrier, and she knew exactly what to do.

Chapter Eight

Monday night, Tristen knocked on his in-law's door.

From inside, Mallory shouted, "It's Daddy!"

"You think about what we talked about," Grandma Rose instructed.

Tristen frowned. The door opened, and he smiled at Mallory.

She leapt into his arms. "Daddy, I lost a tooth. And the tooth fairy gave me ten dollars."

"Wow! Ten dollars. That must've been a special tooth." Actually, it ticked him off. Rose knew he never left more than a dollar or two. Next time he left a dollar, Mallory would be disappointed it wasn't ten.

He waited until they were in the car. "Mal, I heard Grandma tell you to think about what you had talked about. What was that about?"

Guilt shined in his daughter's eyes.

"I'm not angry with you, but I need to know."

"She wants me to tell the judge I want to live with her. She said if I did, she'd pay for my ballet lessons. Grandpa promised to buy me a pony."

An uncomfortable tightness filled his chest as he recognized his daughter's excitement over ballet lessons and the chance of owning a pony.

"What'd you tell her?" His heart beat a second faster as he waited for her response.

She sighed. "I told her I'd rather live with you."

He released a sigh of relief. Every time he left her with them, Rose tried to turn her against him.

Tuesday after dropping Mallory off at school, Tristen drove to Zurtel's headquarters in downtown Atlanta. He'd been summoned. He waited in the outer lobby to be called back to see Everett Reynolds, Cynthia's father.

♦♦♦

That night Mallory stared from across the table. "What's wrong, Daddy?"

Rather than tell her he'd been demoted to copilot and received a cut in pay, he smiled. "I'm just tired."

He didn't want her slipping up and saying anything to Grandma Rose. They'd pounce on the chance to make him look like a deadbeat in court. Being demoted for any reason wouldn't look good.

The next day, Tristen received a call to assist his dad flying Cynthia Reynolds to Mexico. She was the last person he wanted to see.

"I can't believe she had me demoted," he said to his dad.

His father walked from around the jet. "You need to let it go."

"I didn't do anything wrong. You would've made the same call."

"You made the right decision, but from what her father said, you made her share a room with you."

"It sounds worse than it is." He explained everything. "There wasn't a room left in the city. As far as I knew, I wouldn't be allowed in the hangar. I didn't think I was being unreasonable."

The limo pulled up with Ellis driving.

Don't say anything. Keep my mouth shut. Silence is golden.

When Cynthia exited the car and walked up, he stood outside the jet by the steps. "Thanks for the demotion. It'll look good in court. I'll be sure to tell Grandma Rose to send you a thank you card."

He heard his dad grunt with disapproval.

She flashed him her superior look, the one he hated. "If not for Mallory, you wouldn't have a job. Count yourself lucky and don't push it."

Randall's car pulled up.

Tristen wondered what this was about. If he were lucky, Randall would make the trip in her place.

♦♦♦

Cynthia scowled as Randall parked at the private landing strip. A man left the car with him and approached her. "Can I help you, Randall? I'm about to leave for Mexico City."

"Your father and I want you to have a bodyguard. This is Douglas Holt. He's an ex-Army Ranger. You'll be safe with him."

She glanced at the big muscle bound guy. He had short sandy blonde hair and cold blue eyes. He wore a black T-shirt with some kind of emblem on it. Tattoos covered his bare arms.

"Randall, I'm going to Mexico. I doubt whoever shot at the car will follow me there."

"Just being in Mexico is dangerous," Douglas stated.

"You can't argue with a professional. This will put your dad's mind at ease. Mine too."

She sighed. "Okay, but I don't like being bothered on the jet. It's my quiet time."

"Understood," Douglas said. "You won't know I'm there."

She seriously doubted that. The man stood over six feet and had Hulk-like muscles. She preferred Tristen's physique.

"Okay, let's go," she said to the bodyguard.

Once on the jet, she introduced Douglas to the others.

"This is our pilot, Robert Conners, and our copilot, Tristen Conners."

"You related?" Douglas asked.

Tristen nodded. "Yep, he's my dad. Welcome aboard."

She expected another snide remark about the demotion, but Tristen seemed to have calmed down.

Tristen grinned at Douglas. "Don't piss her off. She'll throw you out of the plane without a parachute."

So he's still upset.

The guy's brows rose. "Warning taken."

Annie batted her eyes and smiled at Douglas like a teenage girl on her first date.

"Annie is a member of the flight crew."

Douglas didn't appear too interested in the attendant.

"Where is Evan?" Cynthia asked.

"Sick. He couldn't make it," Robert replied. "Tristen is the only copilot available."

She hadn't wanted to be anywhere near him.

Tristen pinned her with a harsh frown.

Robert Conners placed a hand on his son's shoulder. "Make your way to the cockpit before you say something you'll regret." He shifted his attention to Cynthia. "We'll be departing soon. Buckle up."

Cynthia sat in her usual seat. Douglas plopped down behind her. It made her edgy to have someone behind her. She turned toward him. "Would you mind sitting on the other side across from me?"

"No problem." He stood and moved to the other seat.

She tried to concentrate on her computer screen as she read over some of the government regulations for the production of MX7.

Once they landed, a driver drove Cynthia and Douglas to where the meeting was to be held. Her new bodyguard rode up front. Before the driver could open her door, Douglas jumped out and did it. She climbed out and walked toward the building. Again her bodyguard stepped ahead of her and held the door.

Inside, a short Mexican man greeted them. Standing beside Douglas, he looked like one of Snow White's dwarfs.

"Welcome, I'm Eduardo Hernandez. I hope you had a pleasant trip."

She thought of Tristen's angry glare. "For the most part."

Mr. Hernandez studied Douglas. "She will not need protection in the meeting. Perhaps, you'd like to relax in our lobby."

Before Douglas could object, she replied, "Take a couple of hours off. I'll be fine."

Douglas hesitated, but finally nodded and took a seat. "I'll wait here."

She followed Hernandez into the conference room. To her dismay, only a few people had shown up. She glanced at her watch. "Do I have the time wrong?"

"No, we don't fret over time like you Americans. They'll be here," Hernandez said with a thick accent.

"I'm supposed to be back at my jet in two hours. We need to get started."

"Life is short. Take time to smell the roses," Hernandez said.

"I'm afraid my rose garden has wilted. I don't have time. You're not the only company that manufactures synthetic spider web."

"You're right. But you'll have to fly to Japan."

Cynthia took a seat at the long oval conference table.

While waiting, she mused over her behavior in Jacksonville. Not only had she been angry over the test being postponed, she'd been hungry and tired. She had taken her frustrations out on Tristen. She sighed. He'd had her so turned on in the small motel room, she couldn't see straight. That had also played a role in it.

He had been right about all the flights being grounded due to the ice. The possibility of him not being able to get back to the jet made sense now.

An image of him coming from the tub after the shower formed. It heightened her senses and awakened her sensual nerve endings. She had to stifle the images and the erotic urges they caused.

Finally, everyone arrived and the negotiations began. Zurtel would probably need more material than this plant could produce. It was one of three key elements in MX7. It'd be shipped directly to the Utah factory.

Cynthia handled new products and the negotiations of raw goods. Even so, she should have let Randall negotiate this. Once her father retired, she and Randall would run things. Upon his death, she assumed he'd leave everything to the two of them.

"I thought I'd get the upper hand," Hernandez admitted. "But you are a hell of a negotiator."

She offered him a sincere smile. "You shouldn't underestimate a woman's persuasive power. It dates back to Eve."

He chuckled. "Poor, Adam. Between a serpent and a woman he didn't stand a chance." He stood. "Here we like to meet face to face and take time to get to know our customers. I thank you for coming."

"Now that we've met, any further meetings will be Skyped. We can FedEx or email any paperwork."

♦♦♦

Tristen and his dad ventured into town rather than wait at the airport. He'd picked up several gifts for Mallory. Once back at the jet, he decided to make a quick trip to the restroom before Cynthia and her supersized shadow returned. Tristen wondered about the new bodyguard. More than likely, he had been military. From the tattoos he sported, he guessed Army—maybe Special Forces.

He could kick himself for making the wisecrack to Douglas. He had to learn to keep his mouth shut. He didn't understand why she'd been so nice to Mallory and him at the resort, and now she'd turned into a fire-breathing dragon.

Coming back down the aisle, he knocked off some papers. He leaned to pick them up and froze as he read the topic—opening sealed adoption papers. He returned them to the table and made his way to the cockpit.

Why would Cynthia be interested in adoption articles?

Was Everett Reynolds not her biological father? Had she been adopted and searching for her birthmother?

When the limo pulled up, Tristen lowered the steps for Cynthia and the bodyguard. He found himself face to face with her as she boarded. Being in the awkward position, he forced himself to say something pleasant. "I'm glad you hired a bodyguard."

"I didn't hire him. Randall did. He also hired one for Dad and himself."

"With everything that's happened, it's not a bad idea."

For a moment, guilt shined through her eyes. Rather than reply, she entered the cabin with Douglas following behind her.

Tristen took the copilot's seat next to his father. He thought about his meeting with Everett Reynolds. What had Reynolds meant when he said after what you did? Was he referring to what happened in Jacksonville? Reynolds had left the comment hanging without completing it. Had Cynthia confided in her father about that summer? Tristen sighed. The old man wouldn't have hired him if he'd known he'd been boning his daughter.

They had been damn lucky she hadn't gotten pregnant.

After landing, Tristen glanced at the time. With his dad at the controls, the return flight had run behind schedule. If he had piloted the flight, they would've been back.

He had to be at the daycare by six. It had taken longer to return than he'd expected. Seeing he wouldn't make it, he called Rose. She agreed to pick Mallory up from the after school care.

♦♦♦

Shame swept over Cynthia. She wondered if her father had already hired another pilot to replace Tristen's position. A tiny pain ached for this man and what he had to be going through with his in-laws. His court date was coming up in March.

Although she hated to involve herself, she had to reinstate him as a pilot for Mallory's sake.

The bodyguard rode up front with Ellis. This one seemed to be well trained. He didn't speak unless spoken to, and for the most part, he stayed out of her way. Too bad Tristen hadn't been more like Douglas.

She pulled out her phone and called her father. She confessed her mistake.

"Does this mean you don't want to hire another pilot?"

"Yes. I behaved like a number one bitch." Admitting it made her cheeks warm.

Cynthia wouldn't say anything to Tristen yet, but she owed him an apology.

♦♦♦

Despite his attorney's advice, Tristen decided to try and reason with Rose and Kenneth. He sat in their living room waiting for Mallory to finish dinner.

"So what do you want to talk about?" Rose asked.

"You see Mallory more than most grandparents see their grandkids. Why can't you just be happy with that? If you'd like, you can keep her every other weekend."

"That wouldn't stop you from moving from Atlanta for the first job offer you receive."

"It so happens, I'm happy with my job," he lied. "I've got it made. Some weeks I only work two or three days."

"And on those days you work really long hours."

"I'm adjusting to it. Look, I don't like Mallory being torn between us. She loves you both, but I'm her father. She loves me."

"If you loved her, you'd give us custody."

He hated bringing it up. Danielle would probably haunt him tonight. "Danielle thought you were overpowering and controlling." He glanced at Kenneth. "She sure keeps you on a tight leash."

Rose's mouth dropped open. "How dare you?"

"How dare you try to turn Mallory against me?" He stood to leave. "You take this to court and I win, you'll never see her. And if you win, she'll end up hating you."

Once home, he couldn't stop the surges of extreme anger. He wanted to hit something. That something was Grandma Rose. As far as Kenneth, he was a gutless wimp who didn't have the balls to stand up to his wife.

"Daddy, you're making that face again."

"What face is that?"

"Your mean face, Daddy."

This wasn't good for Mallory. He forced himself to calm down and handed her the bag. "Hey, Mal, I picked something up for you in Mexico." He smiled. "Hope you like it."

She found the doll dressed in green and red first. "She's beautiful."

"There's more."

She pulled out the blue dress. "Can I wear it to church?"

"When it warms up. It's the kind of dress you wear with sandals."

"Thanks, Daddy." With her hands full, she managed to give him a small hug.

"Did Grandma Rose say anymore about what you told me the other day?"

Mallory grew quiet. She sighed. "Yes."

Later that night, he read *Alexander's Terrible, Horrible No Good Very Bad Day* to Mallory. He sympathized with the kid in the book. Today, nothing had gone his way.

♦♦♦

Every Sunday in February, Gina attended church with Liz and Dan. Aunt Nell had been delighted to get her out of the house each week.

Hopefully, this Sunday, there'd be some news. Things at home had only become worse. Shellie rarely did the kitchen, and when she did, she did things like shove dirty pans in the ovens rather than wash them.

When Dan and Liz pulled up, Gina hurried to the car. She climbed in the backseat. "Anything yet?"

"The attorney finally called. He petitioned the court to open your birthmother's records due to the death of your adopted parents. Sometimes due to extenuating circumstances, a judge will open the files or release information."

"How long will that take?"

"I'm afraid it could be a month or two." Liz blew out a long breath. "He said you may not be able to find out until you're eighteen. Apparently, your birthmother signed a closed adoption. She doesn't want to be identified."

"Don't let that upset you," Dan said. "Most young girls are forced to give up their babies. If they could, they would keep them."

"I understand." She paused. "What about the way Aunt Nell and Uncle Sonny are treating me? Oh! I forgot to tell you. Aunt Nell gave Shellie my phone, because I'm too young to have one. On top of that, she has my bedroom."

"That still isn't considered abuse," Liz said. "The attorney didn't think you had a case against your relatives for neglect or abuse."

"Did you mention the things my aunt said and what she pulled up on the Internet?"

"He believes it's the imagination of a very unhappy little girl."

"That's not it. You believe me, don't you?"

Liz sighed. "Actually, I do."

"Were you with your aunt and uncle when they spoke to your parents's attorney?" Dan asked.

"No, but when I turn eighteen everything is mine. I heard Aunt Nell complain. But that's a long time from now."

"Have you seen a copy of the will?" he asked.

"No."

"Obviously, they have a copy," Liz said.

"What would it look like?" Gina asked.

"It'd be a bundle of papers. It could be in a plastic covering." Liz's face filled with guilt. "I haven't mentioned this, but your mother once asked me if something happened to them could she list us as your legal guardians. I told her yes."

"That would mean your mom and dad had a new will drawn up," Dan said.

"Then why did my aunt and uncle move in?"

"More than likely they have an old copy your parents gave them when you were much younger and contacted the attorneys who'd drawn it up," Dan said.

"But wouldn't their attorney know about the new will?" Liz asked.

"Not necessarily. They might've used a different law firm or written it themselves," Dan suggested.

Liz turned to Gina. "See if you can get your mother's address book. Maybe I can find the new attorney's name."

Dan glanced at her in the rearview mirror. "Did you find a safe place to keep that card?"

"Yes, sir. They won't find it."

"Be careful with it. Don't lose it."

Gina nodded. Actually, she kept it under the insole of her shoe. She wanted it with her at all times. Though a little uncomfortable at first, she'd grown accustomed to the feel of it. Keeping it there made sense to her. Her purse would be the first place Aunt Nell or Shellie might search. At any point if she decided to run away, she'd have it with her.

"How's school coming?" Liz asked.

"Honor roll."

"Your mom and dad would be proud of you."

Gina shrugged. "My reading grade went from an A to a B."

"Considering what you're going through, that's not bad. I was truly afraid you'd bottom out."

"I like being at school, and my schoolwork keeps me from going crazy. Aunt Nell canceled my piano and ballet lessons. She said the money given from the trust each month isn't enough to cover the costs. Nor does she have the time to chauffer my ass all over town."

Liz made a face. "I can't stand that woman. Now, I see why your mom never liked her."

"In the spring, she's planning a huge yard sale with Mom and Dad's stuff. I've been hiding things that meant a lot to them. Of course, if she finds my stash, she'll sell everything."

"We have a really big attic. Think you can sneak a little out each Sunday?" Dan asked.

"I can try."

"And when you get a chance search for both the wills," Dan added.

Gina nodded. "If I find the new will, will they have to leave my house?"

Liz smiled. "Don't get your hopes up too high. Your mother never mentioned it after that day. Maybe she and your dad never made a new one."

"If it's there, I'll find it."

"You'll need to find it before your aunt and uncle get their hands on it," Dan said. "They'll destroy it."

When Gina returned home, she immediately missed the family pictures that hung in the entry hall and family room. All the framed portraits had been removed. Only the shapes of where they had been remained.

She found Nell in back with the frames stacked on the bed. Yard sale stickers had been placed on each one showing the price. "Where are the pictures that were in those frames?"

"On your bed."

Gina rushed to her room and found them. She taped several of her parents to the mirror. The others she stored in the closet along with other items she wanted to save from Aunt Nell's yard sale, including her parents's Bibles.

If only her parents had left her to Liz and Dan. Both of their sons had moved out. Of course, then the house would've been sold. She sighed. The longer her relatives lived with her, the less she cared about the house. She just wanted to get away from them. They hadn't moved there because they cared about her. Their motivation had been greed. Plain and simple.

That night once everyone had gone to bed, she searched for her parents's new will. She discovered a plastic cover with a bundle of papers inside. She stuffed it into her pants. Before leaving, she touched the mouse causing the computer screen to light up. This time her aunt had taken time to close it. A note pad beside the desk caught her attention. She read a list of items her aunt had jotted down.

Rat poison, antifreeze, cyanide, nicotine, and arsenic.

Her stomach turned at the thought of her aunt poisoning her.

Gina didn't think anyone would believe her. They'd all think what the attorney thought. She was just a desperate girl acting out for attention.

Seeing the scanner, she placed the list of poisons under the lid and hit the button. The machine made sounds as it scanned the paper.

Please don't let them hear it.

Once the paper came off the printer, she folded it up and slipped it in her pocket. If someone saw the note, maybe they'd believe her.

The entry hall light came on.

Her breath hitched.

Footfalls came closer.

She ducked down on the far side of the desk.

Someone entered the room and flipped the light on.

She assumed it was Aunt Nell but didn't dare look.

Then she remembered she'd left the note pad on the scanner.

Gina's heart pitter-pattered faster.

The lights went out and the door closed.

More than likely, her aunt had heard the scanner and came to check it out.

Once Aunt Nell left, Gina stood. Her legs ached from her crouched position. She quietly lifted the scanner lid, removed the note pad, and placed it where it had been beside the keyboard. She couldn't wait to show Liz the list. Maybe this would prove her aunt intended to murder her.

Gina patted the bundle of papers she'd slipped in her pants. If this turned out to be her parents's new will maybe her greedy aunt and uncle would be out of her life once and for all. But what if Aunt Nell killed her first?

Chapter Nine

Wednesday afternoon, Cynthia waited inside the attorney's office. He'd come highly recommended by a friend. She managed to ditch the bodyguard that morning.

Finally, the attorney entered through a side door. "Sorry, I'm late. Court ran a little longer than expected." He sat behind his desk. "So tell me what brings you here."

She dreaded pouring her pitiful story out to a stranger. She explained how her stepmother forced her to give up her infant daughter. "I'm not trying to interrupt her life. I would like to know something about her and see a picture of her."

"Once you relinquished your child and signed the papers, she was given a new birth certificate with a new name and the adopted parents listed. Was it a closed adoption?"

"I'm not positive. I was coerced by my stepmother and her attorney to sign the papers before I had a chance to read them."

"What was your maiden name?"

"Reynolds. I've never been married. I've chosen a career instead."

"May I ask why you want to know about your daughter?"

"I was seventeen and wanted to keep her. I feel like a part of me is missing. I believe if I could just see her and know that she's happy, it'd fill that void."

"Usually, it's the adoptee trying to find the birth parent. Sometimes the judge will open sealed records in what's known as 'a good cause' which is usually a medical history issue they're trying to get information about. Now if you had some genetic disease your daughter needs to be made aware of."

"I don't."

"There's a mutual consent registry that allows you to change your status. I suggest we get this submitted. I'm most certain you'll have to wait until your daughter is eighteen to learn anything about her."

"I read I can use a court appointed mediator who communicates between the two parties without revealing their identities."

"First, we have to submit a petition to the court. It all depends on if she wants to make contact with you once she's of age."

Tears clouded Cynthia's eyes. "That would be seven more years. Shouldn't a judge take into consideration I was forced to give her up?"

"Maybe during the first year, but your daughter is eleven now. It's a little late to bring up the fact it wasn't voluntary. May I ask what happened to the father?"

"Oddly enough, he's reentered my life. He works for my company. He doesn't know about any of this."

"From what you've told me, he was never made aware of his child."

"That's right. He was seventeen."

"So his rights as a father were ignored?"

"Yes, that's correct. Why?"

"Normally most biological fathers are out of luck unless paternity is established early on. There have been a couple of rare cases where the sealed adoption records were opened for a father. There's a possibility he would stand a better chance than you. As I stated, he still wouldn't receive any information until she turns eighteen." He lifted a pen from his desk and jotted something down. "You may want to tell him."

"I can't tell him. He'll never forgive me."

"Why's that?"

"He has a daughter, and he's a loving, wonderful dad. Let's just say he's not the same teenager who got me pregnant and never looked back." She paused. "Please see what you can do without involving him."

"I don't want to give you any false hopes. There's a chance her adopted parents left it open for you to contact her once she's older. I can't see any judge giving you any information on your daughter before then."

She stood and shook his hand. "I'd still like to pursue it."

Back at Zurtel that afternoon, she stopped by her father's office. Terry, the bodyguard assigned to her father, sat in a chair with headphones on. She walked past him.

A man sat across from her father. When he turned around, she recognized him. Phillip Goldman, her father's attorney.

She greeted the man. "Is everything all right?"

Her father nodded. "I'm making a few changes to my will. I called Phil last night and discussed it."

"Why change it?"

"I had a change of heart. But it's nothing for you to concern yourself with. You might say I'm making a few adjustments."

"So long as you're not leaving everything to that young housekeeper you hired."

"She's a peach, but no it doesn't involve her. We're in the middle of this. Can you stop by later?"

"It's not anything important. I'll call tonight."

♦♦♦

Tristen stared at an old photograph of Cynthia he kept in a high school memorabilia box. He recalled the article she'd been reading on opening adoption records. He'd intended to ask his father if the Reynolds had adopted Cynthia. If anyone knew, it'd be Ellis, her driver. He'd worked for the Reynolds longer than anyone.

That night at seven, he turned on his computer and connected to Skype. Sarah Cobane joined him. The third woman's references hadn't checked out, so he hoped Sarah wanted the position.

Walking through the house with the laptop's camera aimed outward, he showed the girl his house and the room she'd occupy.

Afterwards, he sat back down and talked more. He liked everything she'd said. "I've checked your references. The Milsons only had wonderful things to say about you."

"I'll miss them, but I have no desire to live in Asia," Sarah stated. "They'll be there for two years."

"The position is yours if you want it."

"I do. I'm really excited about moving to Atlanta."

After working out the details, Tristen disconnected and wondered if he was doing the right thing. His court date was a week from Friday on March sixth. Maybe, having a nanny would look good to a judge. He couldn't wait to tell Mallory. No more after school daycare. She'd be ecstatic.

♦♦♦

Thursday morning, Cynthia glanced up from her desk.

Randall stood in her doorway. "I hear you've set another testing date. "

"Yes. I'll be in Jacksonville for the tests."

He crossed the room, then slowly edged his way around the desk, and stopped next to her chair, staring down on her. "Good. Then maybe we won't need security anymore. They don't come cheap."

She preferred he stay on the other side of the desk. She didn't like him hovering over her like a drone. When he came closer, she tensed.

"You smell wonderful." Before she could stop him, he boldly leaned forward pinning her in her chair. His lips came down on hers hard in a forceful kiss. Without thinking, she shoved a knee in his crotch. "Get off me."

"Shit. Son-of-a-bitch that hurts." He stepped back. "You still believe you're a fucking princess that's too good for anyone."

She wiped her mouth. It'd been a long time since he'd tried anything with her. When she'd been twelve, she had used the same method to stop him. "You are my stepbrother."

"We're not biological siblings. I've admired you since your dad married my mother. Just think of the empire we could build if we were husband and wife."

"You're engaged. Besides marriage should be about love."

He chuckled. "Asinine idea. Hell, do you think my mother loved your dad?"

"No. Actually, I always saw her as a gold-digger trying to climb the social ladder." She paused. "I will never be interested in you. I don't need money. I'm already on top of that ladder. Don't ever touch me like that again."

He grinned sardonically. "Or what? You'll run to big daddy."

"No. You have Dad bamboozled."

An awkward silence lasted for several minutes. She kept hoping Randall would leave, but he didn't.

"Why was Goldman here?" Randall asked.

"Making sure Dad's will is in order."

If Randall thought her father was making any changes, he'd go berserk.

He frowned. "So long as he doesn't disregard Mother's wishes."

Cynthia smiled. "That's right, she finagled you into it. She's also the one who convinced Dad to write me out of the company if I married."

"That was for the good of the company."

"I'm sure any changes Dad made today will be for the good of the company also."

Randall frowned and stormed off.

Cynthia wasn't sure how her stepbrother knew about the will. Maybe he suspected her dad had done something drastic.

At one o'clock, Cynthia flew to Jacksonville. Conners senior piloted the flight. Again Douglas traveled with her.

Her thoughts centered on her conversation with the family attorney. At the time only her father, stepmother, and Ellis had known about her pregnancy and the unwed mother's home. Her stepmother had even kept it from Randall, probably afraid he'd confide in a friend, and it would spread. He had believed she was in an exchange student program in Europe. Reputation had meant everything to Edith.

In the enormous testing facility, Cynthia stood with her engineers and technicians, while they tested parts constructed out of MX7 in the simulator. They hoped it would endure the intense pressure and extreme climate changes of altitudes up to forty thousand feet it'd be subjected to.

She nervously ground her teeth, waiting for the results.

One of the techs shouted, "Break out the champagne! It survived."

Cynthia smiled and shook hands with the others. "We did it!"

Her chief engineer couldn't stop smiling. "We're almost to home plate."

"How long will it take to set up the flight tests?"

"We'll start Wednesday."

The tests would be conducted over the water as much as possible. The pilot would be equipped with a way to evacuate the aircraft at the first sign of trouble. With Jacksonville being a military town, they had plenty of young pilots willing to make the extra money despite the danger. She thought of Tristen. He needed money. His wife's cancer and funeral had probably placed him in a financial bind. Mallory's school didn't come cheap. She would offer him the job of piloting the test flights.

When Douglas and she returned to the jet, Robert Conners held a big stuffed purple hippo in a tutu with ballerina slippers. "Have you taken an interest in wildlife?" she asked him.

He smiled. "It's for Mallory. Sunday is her birthday."

"I'm sure she'll like it."

On the trip home, she thought about Mallory. Mallory would be her daughter's little sister. Cynthia woke her phone and browsed through toys and games not finding anything. She recalled Mallory wanted to take dance lessons.

That night Cynthia didn't want Douglas staying with her. She had a new sophisticated, smart security system installed which included a panic button that automatically alerted 911. The company had also installed new deadbolt locks, surveillance cameras, and an alarm system that didn't depend of phone lines. It would require someone highly skilled to undermine this system.

"I'm not going back out. I'll be safely locked in my house," she said to Douglas.

"You've got my number if you need me," he replied.

"I do, and I won't hesitate to call. Goodnight." She entered the house and locked the door behind her.

After preparing for bed, Cynthia activated the alarm using her phone. She placed the panic button on the bed beside her. The day had been a long one. Her eyelids had already grown heavy, and she fell asleep with ease.

The slightest sound alerted Cynthia, but she let herself ease back into a deep sleep. Again her brain acknowledged a sound. Finally, she woke but had a difficult time opening her eyes.

A man cleared his throat several times.

She forced her eyes open.

A dark silhouette stood over her. Immediately, a pillow came down on her face. He straddled her chest and held her down.

Her body bucked upward as she struggled against him. She tried to kick, but the cover had her legs pinned.

The pressure stifled her breath causing her lungs to burn.

Her entire body went limp.

She couldn't breathe. The air in her lungs was almost used up.

No. I don't want to die before I see my daughter. God, no.

Cynthia's right hand fumbled on the bed, searching for the panic button.

No more air left.

Blackness spread through her mind like spilled ink.

Her fingers found the button. With her last ounce of consciousness, she squeezed as hard as she could.

The alarm sounded.

The pressure on the pillow let up.

She pushed it from her face and frantically gasped for air like a fish out of water.

Finally, she managed to sit up still gasping for a breath. She glanced around for her attacker.

He had gone.

Her landline rang, and she grabbed the cordless receiver. She didn't think she could talk.

"This is 911. We received a call from this address."

"Someone tried to kill me," she forced herself to say.

"Ma'am. Stay on the line. Help is on the way."

Cynthia held the phone while the lady continued to assure her she would be all right. "The police are at your door. Go let them in."

She stood, slipped on a robe, and hurried downstairs carrying the cordless phone in her hand while remaining on the line with the 911 operator. She opened the door and two police officers entered.

"Ma'am, are you all right?" one officer asked as he looked around for the intruder.

"Someone held a pillow over my face. When the alarm sounded, he ran out." She couldn't stop trembling.

"You need to wait downstairs until we make sure the building is clear."

"Did you get a good look at him?" another officer asked.

"No. It was dark. Judging from his outline, I'd say he was a large man. He pinned me down, and I couldn't move."

Two more officers entered. One was a female officer. After being told about the intruder, the woman came up to her. "Are you all right? Did he hurt you?"

"I almost blacked out, but I'm fine now."

"You reported a burglary about a month ago. Could this be connected?"

"I think so." She sat on her sofa while they searched her house for evidence. A detective arrived and asked the same questions as the officers.

After he spoke with the first responding officers and checked the house, the detective returned downstairs. "He's not in this house. Actually, we can't find a point of entry. Nothing seems disturbed. If someone entered, he had a key, your code, and took time to lock everything when he left."

Cynthia reeled with indignation. The officer didn't believe anyone had been there. "Someone was in my house. For heaven's sake, he almost suffocated me."

"Did he use one of your pillows?" the detective asked.

"No. It couldn't have been mine. It stunk."

"He didn't leave it behind." He paused. "Are you sure you didn't dream this?"

Her mouth dropped open. "I was struggling to breathe. A few minutes more and I would have died. My alarm was…"

"Triggered by you hitting the panic button."

She nodded. "True."

"Your surveillance film doesn't show anyone entering or leaving."

"I heard noises and opened my eyes. He stood over me. I wasn't dreaming."

The detective gave the others a look of disbelief.

"I'll have my bodyguard stay tomorrow night."

"We'll keep a car out front for the next few hours," the detective said.

"There's something I forgot to mention. My intruder kept clearing his throat. So did the man who broke into my office." She explained everything that had happened leading up to this. "Detective Taylor handled it before. You may want to call him."

"I will, and from the things you've said, your life is in danger. But tonight no one entered this house. It was sealed like a fort." His demeanor and the look in his eyes indicated he still thought she'd dreamed it.

The police left.

She returned to the sofa and sat down. Being frightened and bewildered, she couldn't sleep. She figured she'd be awake when her housekeeping service arrived at eight.

In the morning, she planned to demand a refund on her new smart, security system.

One thing Cynthia knew, she hadn't dreamed it.

Chapter Ten

For a moment, fear swirled through her as she remembered not being able to breathe the previous night.

She didn't want her dad learning of her ordeal through the media. She walked to his office and entered without knocking. "I want you to hear this from me." She told him about the previous evening.

"My God. Are you all right?"

"I'm fine. The police arrived quickly."

"Where was the bodyguard?"

"I had sent him home. I figured with the new security system and locks I'd be safe."

"What'd the police find?"

"Absolutely nothing. No prints. No point of entry. The video didn't show anyone entering. They think because of the earlier issues, it was a nightmare."

"Was it?"

"No. I was awake." She explained what happened. "If I hadn't pressed the panic button, he would've killed me. I don't understand how he got in unless he hacked my security system."

Her father stood and hugged her. "Stay with me until the patent is filed."

She rubbed the back of her neck. "I might take you up on it."

"I'd feel better with you near me."

"Then they might kill us both."

"Nah, Terry's staying with me."

"I have Douglas. He looks like the Hulk."

"He's green?"

"No, just big. What about Terry?"

"Even in my prime, I wouldn't have messed with him."

Cynthia thought about these men. She wanted to know more about the security firm they worked for. How had Randall heard about it?

"What time should I expect you?" her father asked.

"I'll need to run by my place, so probably around seven."

"I'll have dinner ready."

"You plan to spoil me."

He grinned. "You, my dear, are already spoiled. I wouldn't mind seeing you gain a few pounds. Be sure you keep the bodyguard with you today."

"Trust me, I will." And she meant it.

Later Friday afternoon, Randall approached her in the hall. He placed his hands on each of her arms. "Your dad told me what happened. You could've been killed. Your privacy isn't worth your life. You need to keep Douglas with you. Am I clear?"

She nodded. It actually touched her he cared. Of course, it was only because of her value to the company.

"I'll be going to South America next week," he said.

Cynthia didn't have a clue why he was telling her. "Business or pleasure?"

"Business. I'm thinking we should open a plant there. Less taxes. Cheaper labor."

"But all our production is in Jacksonville. Plus, it would take longer and be more costly to ship material from Utah to South America."

"Depends on what kind of deal they offer. I think it's at least worth looking into," he said.

"I agree, but unless it's a major savings, we should keep the Jacksonville plant. There'd be a lot of employees losing jobs and money going over the border."

"When did you become such a humanitarian?"

She shrugged. "I like to think I've always been one."

"That's no way to run a company. That's why you need to stay in the developmental end and let me run the rest. You'd have this company bankrupt in three years."

"I'm not the one who wanted to merge with Novik. Not only would we be out of business, we would be up to our necks with legal issues."

He grinned. "Actually, you were right about them." He gave her a light hug. "Remember what I said about the bodyguard. You should never be alone." He walked away and disappeared into his office.

Something didn't seem right about his sudden concern. Maybe, he hadn't given up on the marriage plan.

♦♦♦

Tristen checked the schedule at Zurtel's landing field. He couldn't find his name on the copilots' schedule. Finally, he glanced at the pilots' schedule. His name appeared on it. He was flying Everett Reynolds to Florida.

Had this been an oversight on Dwayne's part?

He made his way to the jet.

Heather, the oldest flight attendant, greeted him as he boarded. "Morning. Where's your dad?"

"He needed a couple of days off." Tristen didn't mention his dad rented a plane and flew his latest lady friend to Las Vegas.

The copilot showed up. "See you're back in the captain's seat. That didn't last long."

"I'm astonished her royal highness has already reinstated me."

Later after they'd prepared everything for departure, Reynolds came up the steps with his bodyguard following. "Hey, boys, let's hit sunny Florida. Play a little golf."

When he realized it wasn't a business trip, Tristen grinned. It beat flying the corporate ice queen around. Remembering his court date next week, his joy deflated rapidly. Until it was behind him, he found it difficult to relax and enjoy anything.

His in-laws big play against him was the incident at the bar. They were clueless the bartender could clear him. He thought of something disturbing. What if they had convinced Mallory to lie? Would she feel pressured to make them happy?

As he flew toward Florida, his thoughts shifted to Cynthia.

Why had she reinstated him?

He considered thanking her but decided to leave it alone. He had a way of saying the wrong thing to her. If not for Mallory, Cynthia wouldn't have spoken more than a handful of words to him.

But the corporate queen wasn't the same seventeen year old he had fallen in love with. Still, he worried about her safety. He didn't like the burglaries or the shots fired at the company's limo. He still assumed Cynthia had been the target instead of Everett.

Tristen didn't know a lot about the internal operation of Zurtel. He'd never liked Randall. Would he have anything to gain if Cynthia or her father were dead? From what Tristen had heard, Everett considered Randall a son and planned to leave half the company to him. Cynthia would be his equal. Maybe he didn't want to share.

After landing at Cecil Field in Jacksonville, they found a limo waiting out front that drove them to Cimarrone Golf and Country Club.

During the rounds of golf, Tristen relaxed and enjoyed the sunshine blaring down on him. He refused to worry about his upcoming court date.

While walking on the fairway to the green, Everett cleared his throat. "Cynthia regretted what she did. She insisted on reinstating you."

Tristen nodded. "I'm glad she had a change of heart. I'll be in court next week. I'd hate to admit to a judge I had been demoted for improper conduct."

"She's very fond of your daughter."

"Well, Mallory's a charmer. She really likes Cynthia."

"Let's talk about the summer you stayed with your dad. You took advantage of my daughter."

Tristen choked on his tongue. "I loved her. She's the one who ended it. I don't understand her resentment toward me."

"Are you being serious?" Everett asked.

"Yes. She wrote a letter and made it clear I was beneath her and she never wanted to see me again."

Everett stopped walking and looked at him. "I didn't know that."

"I tried calling, but she had blocked all forms of communication with me."

Everett sighed. "I'm not so sure she wrote that letter."

"My dad gave it to me and said it was from Cynthia. If she didn't write it, who did?" Tristen asked.

"My wife, Edith. She had an unrealistic scheme to match Randall and Cynthia as a couple. I was traveling a lot. I wasn't home long enough to know what was going on. It wasn't until later I learned…" Everett drew his lips in.

What had he intended to say?

When Everett started walking, Tristen followed. "Despite being just seventeen, I was in love with your daughter."

Now it made sense why Cynthia disliked him. They needed to talk. Until he went to court, he wouldn't rock the boat and chance being demoted or fired.

♦♦♦

Sunday morning, Gina carried a small floral tote that had belonged to her mother. Inside she had her Bible and Sunday school book. Underneath them, she'd hidden the bundle of papers she assumed was the will and also the copy of Aunt Nell's poison list. Maybe now they'd see her life was in danger. This was the first chance she'd had to sneak it out.

She stood at the door, waiting for Dan's car to pull in the driveway.

Her Aunt Nell came up behind her. "Just what do you carry in that bag every week?"

Gina faced her aunt and drew a deep breath hoping to keep her voice steady. "My Bible and Sunday school book."

Her aunt cocked one brow and gave her a suspicious look. "Let me see."

Right when Gina extended the bag, Dan's horn honked from outside. She jerked the bag back. "Gotta go!"

Her aunt appeared taken back and gasped.

"I can't be late. I'm reading the scripture today." She hurried out the door and climbed in the back seat. Her heart still beat fast.

"Are you all right?" Liz asked as Dan drove toward the church.

Unable to speak, she nodded.

"Why you looked scared out of your wits," Liz added.

"Aunt Nell asked to see my bag. I think I have the will in it. Also, I have a list of poisons she'd written down. I managed to sneak it out today."

"Poisons?" Dan said.

"Yes. This time it's in her handwriting." She pulled the list from the bag and handed it to Liz. "See. Poisons."

Liz's expression changed to concern. "She's right. It is."

"I doubt it's intended for you," Dan said, as he parked at the church.

"I won't be eating or drinking anything she gives me."

"Can't say I blame you, but I agree with Dan. I don't think this has anything to do with you."

Gina's heart dropped. They didn't believe her. "I also found this bundle of papers. I think it might be my parents's will." She passed it to Liz. "I hope it is, and I hope it says I'm to live with you."

Liz removed the papers from the plastic and unfolded it. "Bingo, kiddo. You hit the jackpot. It is their will." She unfolded it and started reading the details.

Gina unfastened her seatbelt and scooted to the edge of the seat, trying to see the will. "What does it say?"

"I'm trying to get through all the legal jibber-jabber."

"What's the verdict?" Dan asked.

Liz frowned. "It's the old will. This one says if she has no grandparents still living, she goes to Uncle Sonny."

Gina's spirit plummeted. She drew in a deep breath trying to cope with the news. "I thought it was the new one."

"I was hoping it was," Liz said.

"I'd still like to read over this one and see if you have any out clauses," Dan said.

"There has to be a new will." Gina had a terrible thought. "What if Aunt Nell has already found it and burned it?"

"Let's hope not," Liz said. "Are you sure it wasn't in the safe with the cash?"

"No. It wasn't. I don't know where else to look."

Liz sighed. "I'm sorry, kiddo. Keep searching."

"Does it say they can live in the house with her until she's eighteen?" Dan asked.

"I'm afraid so. I'll speak with the attorney and tell him we think there's a newer will somewhere," Liz promised. "Until I do, you sit tight and don't give up hope. I'll keep both the will and note. It wouldn't be good for your Aunt to find them."

Once home, Gina walked in the house and left her tote bag where Aunt Nell could snoop through it.

That night at dinner, Gina only ate what the others did. She stood and poured the lemonade out and refilled her glass with water.

"Something wrong with it?" Nell asked.

"It's so sweet, I feel like gagging. I'd rather have water."

After she sat back down, Aunt Nell glanced up. "Good news, guys. Over spring break, we're renting a cabin at a Smokey Mountain resort. It has a heated indoor pool. We can hike trails. It'll give us a chance to get to know one another better."

Gina remembered one of the top five ways children accidently died was from falls. An image of Aunt Nell shoving her off a cliff flashed through her mind. Spring break was only a few weeks away.

She only hoped Liz and Dan could take her before then.

Sunday morning, Tristen recalled what Everett Reynolds had said about Cynthia liking Mallory. His daughter adored her.

He picked up his phone and hit Cynthia's number. His brain needed an adjustment for doing this.

"It's seven in the morning," she mumbled.

"Did I wake you?"

"You did. This is my one day to sleep in. This had better be important."

"Sort of. Today's Mallory's birthday. We're meeting at Laser Voyage Cafe in Duluth on Buford at two this afternoon." He gave her the address. "It'll just be Dad and a few of Mal's friends attending. She really likes you."

"The feeling is mutual."

"I know it's short notice, but I'm not good at planning these things. I know she'd be thrilled to see you there."

"Is Grandma Rose invited?"

"No. Even though they live nearby, I couldn't bring myself to ask them. Besides, parties are supposed to be fun."

She laughed softly. "I don't blame you. Will Mallory be disappointed if they don't come?"

"Lately, she seems extremely uncomfortable when she's around them."

"That's too bad. See you at two."

"Listen, you don't have to bring a gift."

"I've already bought her something. I intended to mail it and forgot."

"So now, you can bring it in person."

"I hope you don't mind, but I'll have my bodyguard with me."

"It's a birthday party on a Sunday afternoon. What can happen?"

"I haven't told many people, but someone attempted to murder me Thursday night."

"Oh my God, Cynthia. Are you all right?"

"Yes, I am now."

"Where'd it happen?"

"I was in my own bed." She gave a brief rundown of what happened. "My father made me promise to keep Douglas with me."

"You think it was business related?"

"What else could it be? I don't have much of a life outside Zurtel."

"Well, you do today. You'll be Mal's guest of honor. She'll flip out when she sees you."

At quarter after two, Tristen glanced at the door anytime someone entered the pizza place, expecting it to be Cynthia. He wondered if something had come up. Surely, she would call.

"You expecting someone else?" his father asked.

"I invited Cynthia Reynolds."

"Seriously? Why?"

He explained about her relationship with Mallory. "She reinstated me for Mallory's sake. Not the best reason, but I'll take it."

"How was the trip with Everett?"

"Good. I could get used to flying for him."

"How many rounds did you play?"

"A couple."

When the pizza came, Tristen rounded up the three girls and his daughter from the games. "Let's eat. Sooner we eat, the sooner we can light the candles on the cake and open presents."

Mallory's eyes lit up. "Miss Cynthia!" She ran to greet Zurtel's CEO. "You came to my party!"

"Yes, your dad invited me."

Mallory led her to the table and introduced her friends. "That's Sadie, Mia, and Isabella. This is Miss Cynthia. She lets me ride on her jet."

"Ooo," Mia said.

"A real jet?" Sadie's eye grew large.

Mallory nodded. "Tell 'em."

"It's a real jet."

"You're so lucky," Isabella said.

"Hey, I fly the jet," Tristen said, but the girls ignored him still enchanted by Cynthia.

Cynthia greeted his dad before glancing back at Tristen. "I'll order a salad for myself."

"They don't have salad," Tristen said. "They have chicken tenders."

"What the heck, I'll eat pizza."

After they'd had their fill of pizza, he lit the candles on the Wonder Woman cake. "Make a wish, Mal."

She closed her eyes for a moment, then blew out the candles. "I hope my wish comes true."

"What'd you wish?" his father asked.

"Grandpa Rob, I can't tell or it won't come true."

"That's right," Grandpa Rob said.

Tristen glanced to the far wall and spotted the bodyguard sitting alone watching Cynthia with the perception of a hawk. The man didn't look like someone you'd want to piss off. He stood about five inches taller than Tristen and outweighed him by about twenty pounds. Twenty pounds of pure muscle.

"Can I open my presents now?"

"Open mine first," Sadie shouted.

Mallory ripped the paper off the package and found a Barbie Art Box with markers and stickers. "I love it."

"What do you say?" Tristen reminded.

"Thank you."

Mia stuck her present under Mallory's nose. "Mine next."

Mallory grabbed Mia's gift and tore into it. Her expression grew somber. "What is it?"

Tristen had to look twice. "It's a label maker. Now you can put your name on all your toys and school supplies. Isn't that neat?"

Mallory didn't appear sold on the idea. She looked at Mia. "I'll put my name on all my pencils. Now when I drop one, Avery can't say it's his. Thank you."

Tristen couldn't imagine why someone would give a kid a label maker. Nevertheless, he smiled at Mia. "Nice gift."

"Mine next," Isabella insisted.

Mallory smiled at the snow cone machine. "Thanks, Isabella."

Thinking of the mess, Tristen frowned. "Thanks. I can't wait for her to try it out."

Cynthia smiled. "I had one when I was young. It's not too messy."

"I want to open Miss Cynthia's present next," Mallory declared. She flashed a charming smile toward his boss.

"Open the card first," Cynthia insisted.

Mallory tore it open and jerked the card out. When she opened it, a certificate slid out. His daughter lit up when the card played music. "I love it."

"That's just the card," Cynthia said. "The paper that fell out is the gift."

"Oh." Confusion masked Mallory's face.

Tristen picked up the paper and handed it to her. "What does it say, Mal?"

She stared at it. "Ballet lessons."

Cynthia smiled. "It's a year of dance lessons at the Atlanta Ballet."

Mallory's eyes bulged outward. "Dance lessons!"

"Yes, for an entire year."

Her friends squealed in delight hurting his ears.

Tristen wished she'd asked him before giving her the gift. He wouldn't have a way to get Mallory to the lessons. Then he remembered Sarah could take her.

As though she read his mind, she turned to him. "Ellis will drive her when you can't. That's part of the gift."

"Thanks, but the nanny I hired can drive her."

"So you hired someone?"

"Yes, Sarah arrives Monday."

Mallory stood and ran to Cynthia, placed her arms around her, and squeezed her tightly. "Thank you."

"There's more."

Mallory returned to her seat. She opened the box from Cynthia and discovered ballet slippers and a tutu in a ballet bag.

Tristen glanced at her. "Gee, Cynthia, that's a lot. You didn't have to."

"I wanted her to be happy."

"Well, you achieved that." Tristen thought about Grandma Rose promising Mallory dance lessons. This worked out perfectly. Now all he needed was a pony.

After Mallory opened the purple hippo ballerina from Grandpa Rob, she hugged his neck. "Thanks, Grandpa."

"Glad you like it, sweetheart," his dad said.

Finally, only his gift remained.

"One more, Mal. This one is from me." Tristen gave her the oddly shaped package. "Open it."

She laughed when she pulled out a child's tennis racket. "What is it?"

"A tennis racket."

"I don't know how to play tennis, Daddy."

"I'm going to teach you."

"Today?" Mallory asked.

"No. As soon as the weather warms up." He'd spent too much at Christmas, and this birthday party wasn't cheap. He had seen the pink racquet on clearance for five dollars.

She nodded, then talked with her friends about her gifts.

He had an idea she had categorized the tennis racket with the label maker.

"I should've asked about the dance lessons," Cynthia said.

"No. I really appreciate the gift. She has wanted dance lessons for a long time. So, thank you."

While the kids played games, and his father excused himself to the restroom, Tristen took the opportunity to say something to Cynthia. He hadn't planned to bring it up unless she did, but talking about it might clear things up between them. "You're dad and I talked about that summer I stayed here. I was blown away when he brought it up."

Her eyes became guarded. "What'd he tell you?"

"That you didn't write the dear John letter my dad handed me at the airport."

"Your dad gave me a letter also and said you had written it. The letter made it clear you were done with me. I was no more than a summer fling you regretted. You wrote you were in love with someone else."

"That's ludicrous. I didn't write it."

"I didn't write the one you received. What did it say?"

"You stated what we had was a summer fling. I wasn't good enough for you, and you didn't want to ever see me again."

"I never wrote that. But using the term 'summer fling' the same person must've written both letters."

"I tried contacting you after that, but I'd been blocked from your phone and social media, so I gave up and after high school joined the Air Force."

"I'd considered calling you, but my phone had met with a fatal accident. I lost all my contacts. Not long after you left, Edith sent me to a school out of state."

"I'm sorry I believed you had written the letter. I should've been smarter."

"We both should've been smarter," she said.

♦♦♦

Cynthia realized someone had manipulated their fates. "Why would your dad do that?"

"Everett suspected your stepmom wrote it."

"That'd mean she also wrote the one I received from you. Your Dad had to be a part of it. He delivered the letters."

His father walked toward them. "I guess I should run."

"Sit down," Cynthia said. "You're not going anywhere."

His father's expression reflected concern. "What's wrong?"

"You delivered letters to both us knowing the entire time Edith had written them. Why?"

His dad's expression not only convicted him but proved his involvement. "I was forced to do it. She told me I'd be in the unemployment line if I didn't. She also warned me I wasn't to encourage a relationship between the two of you in anyway." He paused. "I'm sorry, but I couldn't chance losing my job. You were just teenagers, so I agreed to it."

Cynthia couldn't help but wonder how differently their lives would have turned out if Edith hadn't kept them apart. "I don't blame you. I blame Edith."

After his dad left, Tristen sighed. "I'm glad it's out in the open."

"Yes. It clears up a lot of the animosity between us." She wouldn't tell him she'd cried herself to sleep several nights after he'd left.

Cynthia considered bringing up the pregnancy and telling him about the daughter neither of them had ever known. Just as she was about to speak, Mallory and her friends bounced back to the table.

The opportunity to confess passed. She considered what the attorney had said about a father possibly having more rights to open a sealed adoption record. For now, she'd see what she could accomplish without involving Tristen.

"Miss Cynthia, do you want to play games with me?" Mallory asked.

"Sure, sweetheart." She stood. "Excuse me. I have to go get beat by a six year old."

"Seven," Mallory corrected.

"That's right. You're almost grown up." She stood and followed Mallory to a row of skee ball machines. "You'll have to show me how to do it."

The girls giggled. Mallory did a demonstration. "See. Easy peasy."

As she'd expected, the little girls racked up a lot more tickets on skee ball than she did.

Once back at the table, she gathered her sweater and purse. "Well, I guess I should go. I have reports I have to read before our tests are conducted." She paused. "Are you by chance interested in using your skills as a test pilot? We start the flight testing for MX7 soon."

"What's involved?"

She explained the danger but also the large sum of money he'd make.

"I need the money. It would more than cover Mal's tuition for the next few years. But if something happened to me, Mallory would end up with Grandma Rose."

"Think about it. Let me know something tomorrow."

He nodded, but his eyes reflected his uncertainty.

Obviously, he was weighing the money against the risk. She couldn't blame him.

Cynthia's bodyguard stared intensely. The guy made her nervous. But what choice did she have? The next time someone tried to murder her, she might not be so lucky. "I'd better run. Douglas is looking a little impatient."

"I don't see how you can tell. He only has one expression—angry."

She laughed softly. "That's the look he's paid to have. I'm camping out at Dad's house. In the day time, I have him with me. Dad has one staying with him who's just as intimidating."

"Well, my grandpa always said the bigger they are, the harder they fall."

She laughed. "That is if you can get them to fall. It'd be like pushing against a Redwood." She changed the subject. "Tristen, anything Edith said about my feelings for you was a lie."

"Same here. I was devastated."

His confession warmed her heart. Cynthia couldn't believe Edith had been that manipulating and underhanded. It made her despise the woman even more. The thought of digging the old witch up and dragging her bones through the streets of Atlanta made her smile. The moment of dark humor passed.

She left the pizza place and didn't look back at Tristen or his daughter. She pushed away the 'what ifs' of the past and focused on the present. Too much had changed since they had been teenagers. She had Zurtel to run. Besides, Tristen was an employee.

On the drive home, Douglas rode up front with Ellis.

She wanted to tell Ellis about Edith, but couldn't speak openly with Goliath in the front seat.

Later that evening, Tristen called. "Did I wake you?"

"No, not this time."

"I decided to do the tests. I'll have a working parachute—right?"

"You will. You'll also wear a specially designed fireproof suit with a cord that opens a flotation device in case you bail out over water. And there will be boats stationed along the flight path.

We will monitor each flight on our computers. I'm counting on everything working as well as it did in the simulator. We'll fly to Jacksonville on Wednesday morning. We should be back late that afternoon."

"If all goes well," he said, nervously. "I have the court date on Friday."

"Not an issue. Make sure Dwayne knows to leave you off the schedule."

"I will. See you Tuesday. Thanks for coming to Mallory's party."

"I enjoyed it."

After the call, a wave of excitement filled her.

No. Stop that right now.

But he didn't walk out on me.

Zurtel is all that matters.

♦♦♦

At bedtime, Cynthia kissed her father goodnight and made her way to her childhood bedroom. She pulled a box from under the bed. Her high school memories. She first came to a picture of her as senior prom queen, several of her cheering at a game, and then she found some pictures bound together. She slid off the rubber band and thumbed through the photos she'd taken of Tristen.

At seventeen, he'd worn his hair longer, and he wasn't as filled out. She had loved him so deeply. She only had one of them together. It hadn't turned out so well with her holding the camera.

Over that summer, they had the cottage to themselves when his dad was out. They made love often. When they weren't in bed, they swam, rode horses, and played tennis.

Her father tapped on the door. "Are you still awake?"

She quickly tucked the pictures of Tristen at the bottom of her memory box. "Yes. Come in."

"I intended to mention this earlier, but it slipped my mind. I had a chance to speak with Tristen. I know you'll be angry with me, but I asked about that summer."

"I know. He told me."

Surprise reflected in her father's eyes. "He did?"

"Yes. I attended Mallory's birthday party today. He mentioned it."

"Have you told Tristen about the pregnancy?"

"No, I will when the opportunity arises."

He pulled out a chair by the desk and sat down. "I didn't come to talk about him. You should know about my will."

"You said you were making some slight changes."

"Well, I guess slight might be an understatement."

Cynthia wondered if he had cut her out of the business. "What did you do?"

Chapter Eleven

Her father sighed as if what he was about to say troubled him. “I thought about what you said. Your mom wouldn’t have wanted half the company going to Randall. I wrote him out of the company. You get it all.”

Cynthia’s breath left her. “Dad, he’s completely out?”

“No, he’ll inherit a large sum of money. He’ll also retain his position in the company.”

“Edith is probably rolling over in her grave.”

“After what she did to you and Tristen, I don’t care.”

“Does Randall know?”

“I haven’t told him.”

“Who knows besides you and your attorney?”

“You and my secretary.”

“Anyone else?”

“Terry was there, but I doubt he was paying attention to what we were doing. He had headphones on listening to music. If he happened to overhear something, why would he mention it to Randall? He’s my bodyguard.”

“Oh, Dad. Terry is not your BFF. Randall hired him.”

“You think Randall might know?”

She shrugged. “There’s a chance. He suggested we get married again. He hasn’t brought that up in a long time.”

“He’s trying to fulfill his mom’s plan.”

Cynthia thought about the attempt on her life. Though Randall could be a jackass and pervert, she couldn’t imagine him resorting to murder. “Who would inherit the company if I died?”

“Since you have no heirs, it would be Randall.”

Cynthia grew dizzy with anxiety. “Did you actually insert that into the will?”

“Yes. I’m not expecting you to die, but it’s always a possibility.”

“Especially, when someone’s trying to murder me.”

“That has nothing to do with this. I’m sure it’s about MX7.”

Cynthia wasn’t so sure, but it would make Randall a suspect.

Randall is capable of lying and cheating, but not murder. In his own sick way, he cares about me.

“I doubt he knows,” her father reminded. “Your mind is working overtime.”

“When he finds out, I don’t want to be anywhere around.”

“Me neither.” He grinned. “I don’t want him finding out until I’m six feet under.”

“That’s the coward’s way out.”

“You think I should tell him?”

Cynthia thought about Randall’s possible reaction. “No, stick with plan A.”

She shuddered to think how he’d take the news.

Her dad stood. “I’m glad you’re staying here. Once the patent is secured, I think the threats will end.”

Cynthia nodded. “I hope so.”

After her father left, she considered Novik possibly being behind the burglaries and murder attempts. She pulled out her computer and searched again for information on Novik’s owner, Quinn Adams. She followed an Internet trail of board members and past CEOs, but couldn’t come up with any information on the owner. Quinn Adams was elusive.

She turned off the tablet and set it on the table.

Her thoughts drifted to Randall and his crude marriage proposal. Even if she married him, the company would still belong to her.

He doesn’t need to marry me. All he’d need to do is kill me. Hopefully, he’s not aware of that. The temptation might be too great.

She blew off the thought as paranoia.

Monday before heading to the airport, Tristen touched bases with his attorney. The bartender had agreed to show up and testify.

He had to fly Randall to Chicago. At least he'd be back in time to get Mallory and pick Sarah up at the airport.

They took off for Chicago on time. He didn't have to be Dr. Phil to know Randall was upset. Actually, upset didn't start to describe his foul mood.

Tristen stayed in the cockpit away from Randall.

On the flight back to Atlanta, Annie repeated something she heard Randall say, something Cynthia needed to know.

Monday evening, Tristen spotted Sarah waiting along the pickup zone.

She waved and walked toward his SUV.

Mallory waved back. "I like her already. I bet she'll play Barbies with me."

"Not tonight. She's going to be tired. Don't ask her to play anything."

"I know that. After all I'm seven now. Maybe I'll ask her tomorrow."

"Give her three or four days to rest."

He jumped out and opened the trunk to put her bags in. Then he opened the front passenger door. "I hope you haven't been waiting long."

"No, I just picked up my luggage. Perfect timing." She twisted in the seat so she could look back. "Hi, Mallory. I'm Sarah."

Tristen glanced back in the rearview mirror. "Introduce yourself, Mal."

"I'm Mallory Elise Conners. I'm seven. I'm in Mrs. Henderson's first grade class. Next year, I'll be in second grade."

"Nice to meet you. I'm sure we'll get along fine."

After getting Sarah settled in her room and giving her a tour of the house, Tristen stepped into his bedroom and called Cynthia.

"I was about to call you," she said. "How's the nanny?"

"So far, so good. Mallory likes her. At least this one doesn't have cats. She'll have to get her Georgia license."

"She doesn't have to do that right away. Are you going to be able to leave on Wednesday?"

"It shouldn't be a problem. I'm not down to fly tomorrow. I thought I'd take Sarah to the school and get her on Mallory's list of people who can pick her up. I'll drive her around to the super markets and show her where everything is located."

"If you can work it in, you need to watch several training films at Zurtel. I'll set it up. You don't need an appointment. Tell them at the front desk what you're there for. Someone will assist you."

"I'll swing by there." He paused. "I wasn't calling about the nanny. I thought you should know about Randall."

"What about him?"

"I flew him to Chicago today. He left Atlanta scowling at everyone and after his meeting he looked even angrier. He also said something you should know. He said the old man will pay for this."

Silence.

"Cynthia, are you there?"

"I'm here."

"What's going on?"

"Dad changed his will. He's leaving the entire company to me. Randall will be able to keep his position and will receive a large sum of money."

"No wonder he looked like he wanted to rip someone's head off."

"There's a problem."

"What's that?"

"Randall isn't supposed to know. If he does, someone tipped him off."

"What about the bodyguard?"

“Terry wore headphones. Maybe he was listening to music, but perhaps he wasn’t.”

“There’s also a chance your offices are bugged.”

“I’ll get someone to check it out. I’ll also quiz our employees. I think I know why he was in Chicago.”

“Why’s that?”

“His best friend from college is a big-shot Chicago attorney. There’s a possibility he sought legal advice on the will. The only way to stop the new will from replacing the old one is if he can prove dad isn’t mentally stable.”

“Your dad’s mind is as sharp as a tack,” Tristen said. “Maybe that bullet had been intended for him.”

“But that was before he changed his will.”

“And if something happens to you?”

“I asked my dad the same thing. Apparently, since I don’t have a family, Randall would own Zurtel.”

“Does your dad realize he’s placed a target on your back?”

“No. He doesn’t believe Randall is capable of murder.”

“How do you feel about it?”

“I have mixed feelings.”

“Be careful around him.”

“You sound like you care,” she said softly.

“I do. I want you to be safe.”

“I will.”

♦♦♦

Tuesday morning, Cynthia hired an independent security firm to scan her office and then her father’s. To her surprise, both offices were clean. Her father informed her Terry had returned from a break right before she’d come in the day he’d changed his will. If the bodyguard wasn’t the one who told Randall, who did? It could be her father’s secretary or someone at the attorney’s office.

Randall’s anger might not have had anything to do with her father’s will. Her stepbrother had been dark and moody all his life. The least little thing ticked him off.

Later that day, she passed him in the hall. Whatever he'd been angry about on Monday seemed to have passed. He came across as jovial as he talked with a group of employees. He turned and smiled. "Good morning. Who's flying our test planes?"

"Tristen Conners agreed to do it. He'll be conducting all four flights."

"Have you explained the danger involved?"

"I did. He needs the money, so he decided to take a chance. We'll take every precaution to keep him safe."

"I thought there might be a little something between the two of you still. I must've been wrong if you're willing to let him fly off into the sunset, knowing something could go seriously wrong."

She shrugged. "I'm confident MX7 will perform as well in an actual plane as it did in the simulator." She paused. "I thought you were on your way to South America?"

"I pushed it back until next Wednesday. I plan to stay a few days."

Whatever he'd been upset over apparently hadn't involved her.

While working at her desk, she recalled Tristen's concern for her safety. It had amazed her but had also warmed a spot in her heart. She reminded herself the last time Tristen was a part of her life, she ended up pregnant. Lightning could strike twice. She needed to keep him out of her life and especially out of her heart.

♦♦♦

Gina twisted in her seat at school. She hadn't been sleeping well, and it affected her concentration. Aunt Nell had been overly nice to her. It only made Gina more suspicious of her intentions. Slipping and falling claimed the top position on the list of accidental deaths for children under twelve.

She'd already asked if she could spend spring break with a friend, but Uncle Sonny explained the trip was about being a family and insisted she go.

"Gina, I asked you a question," Mrs. Johnson, her teacher, said.

She snapped from her thoughts. "Can you repeat it?"

"Who designed the White House?"

"James Hoban. He submitted plans as part of a contest."

"Correct."

Later at recess, Mrs. Johnson pulled her aside. "Losing parents is a difficult thing to go through. I know the last couple of months have been hard on you. Would you like to sign up to see the guidance counselor?"

"Maybe, but it's more than just missing my parents."

"What else is going on in your life?"

"I found out I'm adopted. I'm trying to find my birthmother."

"I didn't know." Mrs. Johnson squeezed her hand. "How's it going with your aunt and uncle?"

"Not too well." Though she'd always liked Mrs. Johnson, she didn't mention she thought her aunt wanted to kill her. No one would believe her.

"You know, sweetie, if you find your birthmother, there is no guarantee she'll want you in her life."

Gina nodded. "I know. I still want to find her. Right now, I have no one. These people in my house aren't my family. They're only there to take everything."

"Have you considered posting a picture on Facebook?"

Gina shook her head. "No. How would that find my mom?"

"What do you know about her?"

"Nothing really. I only know the date and home where she was when she gave me up."

"That's not much, but you might try. Someone might see a family resemblance or recognize your birthday and the name of the home. It's worth a try. Do you have a Facebook account?"

"No."

"I think for this, Facebook is best."

"My mom's friend can help me."

"Sweetie, I hope you find your mom."

She hugged Mrs. Johnson before running off to play with her friends.

That afternoon rather than go home, she asked Olivia's mom to drive her to Liz's house. Gina hadn't called first, so she hoped Liz or Dan would be at home.

Liz's eyes widened. "Gina, is everything all right?"

She nodded. "My teacher told me how to find my mother."

"How's that?"

"Put a picture of me on Facebook with my birthday and where I was born. Tell them I'm looking for my birthmother."

"Gee, I don't know. You may get a lot of false leads."

"But I may find my mom."

Liz's brows rose slightly. "Does your Aunt Nell know you're here?"

"No."

"You'd better call her."

Gina did and explained she'd gone home with Olivia again to work on their homework. Her aunt didn't have a problem with it.

"I think she likes it when I'm not there," Gina said.

"Dan should be home any minute. He's the social media guru of our house. He'll need to set it up. I'll take a picture of you with my phone to post."

Gina smiled. "I feel good about this."

"Oh, kiddo, this is a long shot."

Tuesday after driving Mallory to school, Tristen drove Sarah around their neighborhood. He really hoped this worked out. So far, the nanny had been nothing but agreeable. He grinned. She wasn't bad on the eyes either.

By the time he returned home from Zurtel, Sarah had already picked Mallory up. She sat at the table with his daughter. She smiled. "We're working on her spelling words."

"Thanks. Spelling isn't her strongest area."

"I'll make a hundred this week," Mallory said, confidently.

"I guess I should've worked with you more." He picked up the mail Sarah had already brought in and thumbed through it. Bills. After seeing how much he still owed in medical and funeral charges, he realized he had to go through with the flight tests. With all that had happened at Zurtel recently, he feared someone might sabotage the tests.

Sarah offered him a sweet smile. "You relax. I'll cook dinner. It's something I enjoy doing."

Tristen wished he'd hired someone sooner. Sarah seemed to be the right fit for Mallory and him. Not only was she a beautiful strawberry blonde with freckles across her nose, she came across as intelligent with a jovial personality.

In his room, he called Cynthia. "It's me."

"You're not chickening out, are you?"

"No, but I have a question."

"What's that?"

"Are the testing planes under security surveillance 24/7?"

"Yes. The Jacksonville facility is over one hundred, twenty thousand square feet with two runways."

"If it has runways why do you land at Cecil Field?"

"We don't have a tower. They are constantly testing. They don't need the confusion of corporate jets landing and departing from there. Besides, we have other offices in town, so we're not always going to the testing facility."

"Do you use the same security firm Randall uses?"

"No, we use a different one. Are you trying to say you don't like Doug?"

"Not especially. He makes me nervous."

"That's part of his appeal. He's supposed to scare off the bad guys." She paused. "Getting back to security, no one goes into this section without a fingerprint scan. We'll need to put yours into the system."

"I guess I have a case of preflight jitters."

She laughed. "Will it make you feel better if I tell you these parts have been tested repeatedly? We've done numerous ground tests."

"And passed?"

"Yes. If it hadn't, I wouldn't be testing actual aircraft. I'm not a gambler. It has passed not one but two series of tests. Also, a flight engineer will go up with you. Feel better?"

"That helps."

"You want me to sing you a lullaby to calm your nerves?"

He chuckled nervously. "Am I behaving like a big baby?"

"A little."

"In the Air Force, I was fearless. I'm not a coward. But I witnessed Mallory's heart breaking when Danielle died. I don't want her to go through that again anytime soon."

"I understand your concern. If you want out, speak now."

He glanced at the pile of bills on the nightstand. "No, I'll do it. I need the money."

"Tomorrow will be our first air flights. We'll test with four different planes with various payloads. Run hot and cold, birds and water, and monitor the handling qualities of each aircraft. We'll measure performance including fuel consumption and cruise efficiency as well."

"Sounds like a lot."

"We have to jump through a lot of hoops to have it FFA approved. You'll provide vital input on how the aircraft handles. Feel better?"

He drew in a huge breath. "Some."

"How's the nanny working out?"

"She's awesome. Mallory seems crazy about her. Sarah insisted on cooking tonight. I have no complaints."

Later that night, he tapped on Sarah's bedroom door. Her lights were on, so he assumed she was awake.

She opened the door, staying behind it. Still, he could tell she wore her gown and robe. "I hope you weren't asleep."

"No, I spend an hour or two each night posting on all my social medias."

"I wanted to thank you for cooking. The chicken was amazing." He handed her a paper. "This is a list of contacts in the event something happens to me. My attorney's name is on that list. I made a provision that allows you to remain in this house until you can find another job."

"That's very kind of you. You're not expecting anything to happen?"

"No, but I'm piloting a series of test flights that could be considered dangerous. I wouldn't chance it, but I could really use the money."

"Let's hope everything goes well. Positive thoughts."

He wanted to tell her once you've lost someone to cancer it's hard to have positive thoughts. At the beginning of Danielle's treatments, they were optimistic she'd recover. But each time they met with the oncologist, the news was bad.

"Well, goodnight."

Once in bed, Tristen stared at the ceiling. He'd placed himself in a dangerous position that could cost him his life. It'd be ironic after all the court crap and attorneys if he died and Mallory ended up with Rose. Thank goodness he'd never told Rose she'd have to get Mallory over his dead body.

By three in the morning, he'd given up on sleep. Instead, he thumbed through his wedding album. As he looked at the pictures, he remembered how much he loved Danielle. Thinking of his own death helped put things into perspective. He wanted to live.

If he survived the tests, he planned to start living again instead of merely existing. Now he was physically and mentally ready to date. He wasn't sure if Mallory would accept it.

Mallory would be all right if I dated Cynthia.

She'd also be his first choice. He couldn't forget she was his boss. She'd made it clear she didn't socialize with employees.

♦♦♦

Gina waited until the house grew quiet to resume her search. Since hearing their might be a new will, she searched every chance she had, but so far, she hadn't found it. By now her aunt had probably gone through her mother's office. Still, it seemed the place to start.

She turned on the overhead light. Boxes sat along the back wall. After taking a closer look, she realized everything from her mother's desk had been packed. She sat on the floor beside the boxes and pulled the first one closer to her.

The first box contained tax paperwork. The second had banking records and insurance papers. She removed one of the insurance documents and slowly read it. It listed her as the beneficiary not that she knew what that meant. It listed a dollar amount of five hundred thousand. She tucked it in her pants and next Sunday would show it to Liz and Dan. She glanced at the far wall. The floral painting covering the safe had been removed and the safe exposed. Obviously, they hadn't opened it. They didn't know the combination. She smiled

After going through each box, she sighed. None of them contained the new will. What if there wasn't one? Why hadn't her parents been better prepared?

Mom wouldn't leave me with Aunt Nell.

Gina needed more time to search. Maybe she could pretend to be sick and stay home from school one day.

♦♦♦

Tristen met the technicians and engineers overseeing the tests. Knowing an engineer would be with him made him feel slightly better. He tried to conceal just how terrified he was. He would take four different planes up. The first would be a smaller jet similar to what he flew for Zurtel. The second would be a McDonnell 80 mid-sized plane, a DC-11, and the last one would be the Airbus A300, Beluga cargo plane.

Cynthia watched with the ground engineer and a group of technicians from an observation tower.

Tristan glanced up and waved as he boarded the small jet. The engineer boarded with him. The older man's presence helped calm Tristen's churning stomach.

"Relax," the engineer said. "They wouldn't run this test if they weren't damn sure about MX7."

Tristen forced a smile but couldn't speak. After building his nest and becoming accustom to the instrument panel. He slipped on the headset and conducted the usual preflight check that included the automated weather for the area, visibility, and all the gauges. He switched on all the lights and controls. He taxied to the runway and let the engines roar a few moments.

Unable to delay further, he lined up on the runway for departure, then radioed the ground engineer. "We're ready for takeoff."

Tristen started down the runway. Once he reached 120 miles per hour, he pulled back the yoke and increased the power, lifting the jet from the runway. He raised the landing gear, then waited for instructions.

"Configure to 3000 feet," the engineer requested. In a little while, the man added, "She's sounding good. Take her on up to twenty thousand. If that's good, you can take her up to thirty-five thousand feet."

Tristen pulled back on the control yoke, then adjusted the throttle to increase speed. At twenty thousand feet he pushed forward on the yoke and leveled out. "Just what's so special about MX7?" he asked the man with him.

"Well, only Miss Reynolds and our main computer know the formula. But I guess I can explain it this way. You know those little plastic 3-D toys you get at zoos out of the machines?"

"Yeah. They have a burning plastic smell."

"That's right. MX7 is sort of like that but lighter."

"Holy shit," Tristen said, feeling his stomach flip upside down. "So this material holding the fuel could melt."

"Could, but I'm not expecting it to. Our first attempts to create a 3-D light weight metal melted like ice cream on a hot July day. Then they came up with the chemical compound for MX7."

Tristen wished this man would shut the hell up.

They made a two hour flight at different altitudes and speeds, then landed safely.

Tristen had a difficult time walking. His legs had turned to rubber. He thanked God for getting him down safely. He slipped out of the specially designed fireproof flight suit that also contained a cord to pull in case he had ended up in the ocean.

One down and three to go.

Cynthia and the team of engineers ran out to greet them. She hugged him "You did great."

Her show of affection only made his knees weaker. He reminded himself it wasn't personal but about the flight.

The engineers and techs praised him for a job well done. After ten minutes of hand shaking and back slapping, Tristen beamed with pride for being a part of something so important. Though he wasn't an engineer, he recognized the breakthrough MX7 would be to the aerospace industry. Airlines would be able to cut their fuel consumption in half. No wonder someone had been trying to steal the formula.

After a twenty minute break, it was time to take the next plane up.

Taking off in the MD-80, Tristen had more confidence than before. He followed the engineer's instructions. On this flight, he was relaxed enough to evaluate the plane and give an opinion on its operation.

At thirty thousand feet, Tristen smelled something.

Burning plastic. The same scent given off by those little 3-D zoo toys.

His life flashed before him.

Chapter Twelve

Wednesday, Cynthia stood in Zurtel's observation tower. Not only did the room offer the best view, computers monitoring the flight projected data to a large screen.

Today's flights were the first in a long series of testing. Every operation parameter would need to reflect compliance with government regulations. Today would focus on the fuel pumps constructed out of MX7. They would try different size aircraft at different altitudes. If all went well, they would conduct fatigue tests using payloads of various weights next time.

When Tristen reported a burning smell, her heart dropped. She didn't want anything happening to him. "What does the computer show?"

"I'm not seeing anything wrong," a technician said.

"What about the fuselage?" she asked.

"Fuel consumption is in the norm. It seems to be functioning properly."

The ground engineer joined her. "Other than the smell, they aren't experiencing any warnings or vibrations. All their readings are good. I think they should continue."

Cynthia thought of Mallory. She sighed. "No. Bring it in."

The ground engineer spoke to them over the radio. "They're turning around."

"If they start to experience any issues, tell them to request an emergency landing at any of the Jacksonville airports."

Fifteen minutes later, she heard the plane before it came into view. "See any problems on the computer that would interfere with landing?"

"No, it looks good. It's not showing any distress," a tech replied.

The ground engineer scowled. "I think the burning smell was their imagination."

"Both the pilot and flight engineer smelled it. It's not their imagination." She realized the engineer had wanted them to finish the flight. Once they were over the bay, the boat would have tracked them. Still, she had thought of Mallory spending her life with Rose. If it had been any other pilot than Tristen, she would have completed the mission.

Cynthia glanced at the team of technicians. "Get the plane inside. The smell didn't occur until they were at thirty thousand feet. Find out why?"

"Will we continue testing?" the ground engineer asked. "The first plane had a successful flight."

"Yes, but it was the smallest of the four."

"Take the next one up. If the same thing happens, we'll take it back to the simulator. You may want to call in one of our more experienced test pilots."

Remembering how stressed Tristen appeared coming off the first plane, she smiled. "Mr. Conners is doing fine. We'll break for lunch and complete the tests afterwards."

A local restaurant delivered food.

During lunch, Cynthia sat with Tristen. "My techs are good. They'll find the problem and fix it."

"Not exactly what you want to smell thirty thousand feet up."

"No, I suppose not. We're going to take the next plane up after lunch. If you experience the same issue, we'll terminate the tests. It means we'll have to delay the patent until we fix the problem."

"It didn't cause any malfunctions. In the simulator tests, it might've produced the same smell, but unless the plane had a problem, you wouldn't have known."

"True, but it didn't happen with the first plane," she said. "There has to be something wrong."

After lunch, Cynthia stood in the observation tower watching Tristen take the next plane up. It was much larger than the last. So if the problem had anything to do with weight, they might experience the same burning smell.

The ground engineer joined her. "They're already past the point where the burning smell started. The aircraft is functioning perfectly."

"Altitude?"

"Thirty-nine thousand."

She smiled. "Good. Keep me updated."

Around four that afternoon, the Airbus landed on the private runway. Tristen hadn't had an issue using the joystick instead of a yoke. Both of the last two aircraft had flown without the smell reoccurring. Cynthia hugged her ground engineer and shook hands with the technicians.

Only one of the four planes had experienced the odd smell. The plane would be studied carefully until they found out why. Once the problem was resolved, the second phase of flight testing would begin. After the little scare, she expected Tristen to decline any more test flights. Exhaustion showed on his face.

She suggested Evan pilot the flight home, so Tristen could rest.

Back in Atlanta, she and Tristen left the company jet.

She stopped before getting in the limo. "You did really well today."

"Thanks, but I'm officially retiring from flight testing."

She smiled. "You looked like a ghost a few times. I thought you might pass out."

"I was fine until your engineer informed me MX7 is no more than a 3-D plastic. But I can see now why someone's been out to steal the formula."

"They'll have to kill me before I give it up."

His face showed concern. "Don't talk like that. Even MX7 isn't worth your life."

"That's what I keep hearing." She paused. "Tell Mallory hello for me."

"Will do. She had her first ballet lesson and loved it. Sarah is having her write you a thank you note. She's drawing a picture of herself at her first lesson."

"The nanny seems to be very responsible."

"It's been more like having Mary Poppins move in."

The thought of a twenty-one year old Mary Poppins sent a tinge of jealousy through her. To think an attractive young woman slept in the room next to Tristen. "She sounds perfect."

He grinned. "She can cook too."

"So you've mentioned once or twice." Cynthia's jealousy thermometer had shot to the top. A modern day version of Jane Eyre ran through her mind. After the way she'd responded that morning when she thought his plane could crash, she had to admit she still cared for him. This wasn't just about Mallory. Could they rekindle the love they once had? She considered confessing the feelings she had for him, but before she could, her inner evil twin reminded her Zurtel came first.

Sadly, she sighed. "I'm glad she's working out."

♦♦♦

Thursday, Gina's plan went off without a hitch. Aunt Nell believed she was sick and let her stay home. Her cousins were at school, and Uncle Sonny had already left for work.

Aunt Nell entered the room without knocking. "I hope you're better by Saturday. I've already paid for the cabin. This late we won't be able to get a refund. Hopefully, you only have a twenty-four hour bug. Are you sure you'll be all right alone?"

"I'll be okay."

"I kept Shellie's phone today. Here, take it." She handed Gina her old phone. "Call me if you need anything."

For a moment, Gina thought she'd been wrong about her aunt. She actually seemed concerned. "I will. I'll stay in bed. I don't feel like eating."

After her aunt left, she hurried to her mom's bedroom. She opened every drawer only to find Nell's belongings. What had become of all her mother's things? She searched the closet.

Right when she wanted to give up, she came across a box of papers. She snatched an envelope and glanced over it. It had belonged to her parents.

Back in her room, she sat on her bed and started sifting through the papers looking for anything like a will. The original would have been typed and kept in a plastic cover. She didn't see anything like it.

Basically, she'd wasted a school day.

After replacing the box in the closet, she couldn't resist calling Liz on the prepaid phone. "Liz, it's Gina."

"Are you at school?"

"No, I stayed home." She explained what she'd been up to.

"Did you find anything?"

"No, but that's not why I called. Has anyone responded to my picture and post?"

Liz sighed. "Not yet. It hasn't been that long. Dan keeps reposting it and encouraging everyone to share it."

♦♦♦

Friday, Tristen stood with his attorney in court before an older judge. His in-laws stood to his left with Tanner beside them. Mallory waited with Sarah in the lobby in case the judge wanted to speak with her.

"I've looked over everything your attorneys have given me," the judge said, keeping a stern expression.

"I'd also like to bring to your attention that Mr. Conners has hired a full-time nanny," his attorney said.

"She's with Mallory in the lobby," Tristen added.

The judge focused on Rose. "You're claiming Mr. Conners is unfit."

"Yes. He hasn't been there for his daughter and runs late all the time, but the real problem is his excessive drinking and sleeping with hookers. In my opinion, that makes him unfit."

Her attorney spoke up. "I submitted several pictures of an inebriated Mr. Conners at a local bar with a prostitute."

"I have looked at them." The judge shifted his attention to Tristen. "You're claiming your brother-in-law, Tanner Williams, set you up."

"That's not true," his brother-in-law said.

The judge frowned. "You need to refrain from speaking."

Tanner nodded.

Rose huffed. "But, Your Honor, like they say a picture is worth a thousand words."

"Either of you say another word before you're asked, and I'll have you removed. Am I clear?"

They nodded.

"Mr. Conners, continue."

Tristen explained everything that had taken place that evening. "I have the bartender here on my behalf."

The judge motioned the bartender forward.

"It's like he said. His brother-in-law kept insisting he drink another beer. Then a lady wearing provocative clothes came up and pushed herself on him and propositioned him. Mr. Williams left in a hurry and wasn't there to witness Mr. Conners turning her down." He paused. "Mrs. Williams may have a couple of pictures, but I have surveillance from that night. It captured the entire thing including Mr. Williams slipping something in Mr. Conner's drink."

Tristen grinned.

Rose's mouth dropped.

Tanner paled, and Kenneth just stood there.

Noticeable bewilderment overtook their attorney. "I wasn't told about the video."

"Neither were we?" Tristen's attorney added.

Rose broke down and sobbed in front of the judge. "Mallory is all we have left of our daughter. There's a chance he'll take a job away from Atlanta, and we'll lose her. I was desperate. We had to do something."

Her emotional outburst didn't faze the older judge. "So you lied?"

Rose and Tanner both nodded. "My husband didn't know."

"Tanner Williams and Rose Williams, the falsehoods you've created are despicable." He glanced at Tristen. "There are few civil remedies available for slander, but I wouldn't blame you if you refused to let them see your daughter."

At that moment, Tristen wasn't sure what he'd do or if he could forgive them.

"You deliberately misled the court," the judge said to the Williams. "Your conduct is reprehensible and disrespectful to the court. Perjury constitutes a crime. Because of the scheming to slander Mr. Conners, I will apply the court's inherent power to punish you for contempt." He focused on Tanner. "And you may face more charges for drugging Mr. Conners."

Rose cried more.

Tristen fought smiling.

The judge looked at her lawyer. "Were you aware of any of this?"

"No, Your Honor."

The judge frowned. "Mrs. Rose Williams and Tanner Williams, I'm holding you both in contempt. A hearing will be held to examine your conduct. You will be expected to pay Mr. Conner's court cost."

Rose stood speechless. Her crocodile tears had vanished.

Tristen thanked the judge, his attorney, and the bartender.

As he turned to leave, Rose grabbed his arm. "Tristen, let me explain."

"I gave you a chance to call it off, and you chose to gamble with your granddaughter. You lost." He walked off not looking back. He was thankful Mallory hadn't needed to testify.

In the lobby, he lifted Mallory in his arms. "It's over, Mallory. You're staying with me."

"Daddy! That's awesome, but what about Grandma Rose?"

"The judge isn't finished with her." He glanced at Sarah. "Let's celebrate. I'm taking you both to lunch."

They ended up at Mary Mac's. "Order what you want," he said to Sarah. "For the first time in months, I really feel relaxed." Then he glanced over a few tables and spotted Cynthia and Everett Reynolds.

So much for relaxing.

Cynthia stared at Sarah before turning her attention to Mallory. She stood from her chair and walked over to them. "How'd court go?"

"The judge got really mad at Grandma Rose," Mallory said."I hope he doesn't put Grandma in jail."

"Grandma cranky-butt is in some serious trouble," Tristen said.

Cynthia laughed. "Maybe the judge will take pity on her." She glanced at Sarah. "I'm Cynthia Reynolds, Mr. Conner's boss and friend."

Tristen didn't miss the friend added in there.

"I'm Sarah. Mallory talks about you all the time."

"Sarah put my hair in pigtails. Do you like it?"

"I like it."

"Sarah helped me with my spelling words. I made a one hundred."

"Wow! That's awesome." Cynthia focused on Tristen. "So, the custody issue is dead?"

"As dead as George Washington."

Sarah and Mallory laughed.

"You're funny, Daddy."

He tugged on her pigtail.

After a few polite comments to Sarah, Cynthia returned to her table. While eating, Tristen found Cynthia staring several times. Her face was as readable as the menu. The corporate ice queen was jealous. Did it mean she had feelings for him?

♦♦♦

That night Tristen tucked Mallory into bed and said her prayers with her. Sarah had gone to her room for the night.

While he straightened up the family room, he wondered how much trouble Rose and Tanner were in. After finishing the kitchen, he sat on the sofa and flipped on the television.

He glanced up as Sarah entered the room. She had an odd expression on her face and held her laptop in her hands.

"Is everything all right?"

"There's something I'd like to show you."

"Sure. Have a seat."

She sat beside him and clicked on her screen waking it up. "I was going through my social media accounts when I came across something that sort of knocked the breath out of me."

"Does this concern me?"

"No. Mallory. There's a girl who looks like an older Mallory. The resemblance is uncanny. It's downright freaky."

Tristen stared at the girl in the post. His breath hitched. She had Mallory's exact eyes and nose. Their hair and ears looked the same. The only difference was their lips. He studied the girl's mouth. He recognized it. Cynthia Reynolds had the same exact mouth, a mouth he'd kissed many times. He recalled the adoption articles she'd been reading.

His heart skipped a beat. "Who is she?"

"Gina Ferguson. She turned eleven last April."

April?

He did a mental math rundown of their summer whirlwind romance. Actually, it could've been March, April, or May.

Son-of-a-bitch!

"Are you all right? You look pale."

He couldn't answer. Instead, he stared at the girl's picture.

Now, the articles on adoption Cynthia had read made sense. Obviously, she wanted to find this girl. Finally, he composed himself.

"Can you share this to my page?" he asked trying to conceal the emotions swirling in his mind.

"Sure. Their resemblance is remarkable. Don't you think?"

"Yeah. I want to show this to someone."

"I can send it to their page."

"No, I'd rather be with them when they see it."

That night he checked his Facebook page. He'd received the post.

♦♦♦

Cynthia couldn't believe she'd been so jealous of Sarah. In her defense, the girl was more than pretty, she was beautiful.

Her thoughts vanished as a call came in from her chief engineer. "Dale, have you learned anything?"

"Actually, we have retested the MD80 and found not a single malfunction in the fuselage or engine. That's good news."

"So where'd the burning smell come from?"

"It wasn't the MX7. On installation of the fuselage a small plastic tab that serves no purpose but to line the part up as it goes into position seems to have broken off. Apparently it melted. We haven't found exactly where."

"We need to come up with a design that doesn't use plastic tabs."

"But it didn't cause anything to malfunction."

"If it happened once, it can happen again. If a plane is up thirty-nine thousand feet or higher with hundreds of passengers, it'd be total chaos for that to occur. A pilot would end up making an emergency landing over a plastic tab."

"I get your point. We'll start on it today. Will Mr. Conners pilot anymore of flight tests?"

"No, he took early retirement."

Thirty minutes later, her phone rang. Tristen.

"Ready for another flight test?" she asked, teasingly.

"No thanks. Where are you?"

"At work."

"On a Saturday?"

"Yes. We discovered what caused the hot wax smell." She explained it to him.

"Listen, I want to take you to lunch, and Douglas can't come."

A moment of delight ran through her until she remembered their roles at Zurtel. "Mr. Conners, if this concerns business, we can meet here in my office. I have some time around one."

"Knock off the corporate crap, Cynthia. This is personal. Cancel everything you have for the next two hours and be downstairs when I arrive."

"I'll be there." Cynthia disconnected. Whatever he wanted to speak with her about was serious. Had her father or Ellis slipped up and told him about their daughter? She called her father and then Ellis. Both denied saying anything. So if they didn't tell, who could have said something?

I'm overreacting. This probably doesn't have anything to do with her.

When Tristen's red SUV pulled up, Cynthia walked from the building and climbed in. Once her seatbelt was fastened, he pulled away from the curb and headed out. She breathed in the aroma of the fried chicken.

"How'd you get away from Douglas?"

"It wasn't easy. I insisted I'd be at the office all day. Smells good. Where are we going?"

"Back to your house."

"Seriously? What about your house?"

"Sarah's there."

"What's this about?"

"I have a Facebook post you need to see."

She laughed. "I rarely look at my page."

"I don't spend a lot of time on it."

"Then how'd you come across this post?"

"Sarah found it."

♦♦♦

Cynthia felt like Watson on a case with Sherlock Holmes. Now the mystery thickened. What would a post discovered by Tristen's nanny have to do with her? "I canceled two Skype meetings because of this. It'd better be important."

"Trust me it is."

"I can't stand the suspense. Just tell me."

"No. This is something you need to see for yourself."

She studied his face, trying to read him but couldn't. This couldn't be about their daughter or he wouldn't be able to conceal his anger.

Once at her house, he handed her the chicken. "You may want to put this in the oven until we're finished talking."

She took the chicken and stuffed the box in her oven on warm, then returned to the living room where Tristen waited on the sofa.

He patted the seat. "Join me."

A nerve twitched near her eye. This had her stressed. She sat to his right. "Okay, show me. It better not be one of those cute animal videos." While waiting for his computer to come on, she wrung her hands together. The first post he scrolled past showed his friend sporting a cast on his foot. She wondered why he wanted her to see it. She preferred the cute puppy. "That's it?"

"Nope, give me second to find it. Here it is." He lowered the lid slightly. "Sarah thought this girl looked a lot like Mallory." He turned it around. "Tell me what you think?"

Cynthia's heart stopped for a split second. She gasped on a sob. Hot tears ran down her face. She tried to wipe them away, but they kept coming.

"Is this girl our daughter?"

Unable to speak, she nodded, then wiped more tears away. She didn't think she could deal with Tristen's outburst of anger right now. Any moment, she expected him to yell and tell her how horrible she was for keeping it from him.

Tristen set the computer aside and pulled her into his arms, rubbing her back gently. "I'm so sorry I wasn't there for you."

She couldn't say anything. His reaction wasn't what she'd expected.

He continued stroking her back. "I had no idea you were pregnant. If I had known, I would've been there for you."

Finally, the tears stopped, and she sat up and reached for the computer. She stared at their daughter. "She's beautiful."

"She looks like a grown up Mallory, except for the mouth. That's your mouth."

"You're not angry with me?"

"No, not at all. I have a pretty clear picture of what went down. If I'm angry with anyone, it'd be your stepmom and my father for keeping us apart."

"Edith was evil." She brushed her fingertips over the screen. "Her name is Gina. I have wondered so many times what the people named her. It says she's looking for her birthmother. Have you contacted her?"

"No. Let's contact her together," Tristen suggested.

"It's not her page. Someone named Dan Garson posted it."

"We'll private message him."

Cynthia smiled. "You type it."

He clicked on message. When the screen came up, he began typing.

I'm Gina's birthfather. I'm writing this with her birthmother beside me. We would very much like to meet our daughter and know as much about her as possible. Please call us.

He typed out their phone numbers.

"What if he doesn't call?" she asked.

"We won't stop until we find her," he said.

"I wanted to tell you. I started to tell you at the birthday party, but Mallory and her friends were there."

"It's all right. I understand why you didn't tell me."

"I wonder if her adopted parents know she's reaching out to me."

He shook his head. "She's only eleven. Maybe they don't know. Perhaps, she figured it out on her own. I'm sure she's a smart gal like her mom." He stood and offered his hand. "Ready to eat lunch?"

She nodded." I want a copy of that picture."

"I'll do it when I get back home. Let's eat."

While they ate, Cynthia told him about the unwed mother's home and giving up Gina. "I was brokenhearted my entire stay. They had classes for us at the home, so we wouldn't miss out on the school year."

"That's good. Did all the girls give up their babies?"

"No. A lot of them planned to keep their babies. The home also trained them to be good mothers. I felt like a monster giving her up. I wanted to keep her. But Edith told me if I did, I couldn't come back home. She also said she'd make sure Dad didn't give me any money."

"Edith was the monster not you. You didn't have a choice." He grinned. "Mallory has an older sister. She's going to freak out."

"You can't tell her yet. That'd be cruel to tell her she has a sister and then learn the adopted parents won't let you visit her. It'd only confuse Mallory."

Tristen nodded. "You're right. I hope the man who posted it can arrange for us to meet her."

"I wonder how he's connected to her."

"Maybe her uncle. I'm not sure. It's someone close enough to know she's adopted."

Cynthia's heart warmed when Tristen smiled at her. She'd expected him to be outraged, but instead he had been wonderful about it. "I doubt there's any way we can get her back until she's college age."

"That's why you were checking adoption information." He grinned. "Your papers fell on the floor, so I picked them up."

She narrowed her eyes. "You were snooping."

"Maybe a little."

"Were you suspicious then?" she asked.

"No, I thought perhaps you were adopted and wanting to find your birthmother."

His phone rang. He stared at the number. "It's Dan Garson."

"Put it on speaker," she said.

"You're on speaker, so you'll be speaking with both of us."

Dan explained his connection with Gina. "Are you two married?"

"No." Cynthia said. "He works for me. She briefly explained what had happened and the circumstances. Where are you calling from?"

"Huntsville, Alabama."

Cynthia couldn't believe her daughter had been so close this entire time.

"What makes you think Gina is your daughter?"

"Hold on a minute. I'm sending you a picture of my daughter, Mallory."

They held on while Dan viewed the text. "I'm back. They look a lot alike. Gina will be excited to learn she has a little sister."

Tristen continued. "I never knew Cynthia was pregnant, but as soon as I saw Gina, I knew she had to be my daughter and Mallory's sister. Of course, we'll have a DNA test done to end any doubts. "

"You can't argue with DNA," Dan said. "Mind if I ask what you do?"

"I'm a pilot, and I work for Cynthia's company."

"You own a company?" Dan asked.

"Zurtel Aerospace Corporation. I'm an engineer, but I also stay involved in the business end of it."

"Gina's dad, Scott, worked for NASA. Strange you're also in aeronautics."

"Scott Ferguson?"

"Yes. Did you know him?"

"I attended a conference he spoke at. I can't believe I've met him before. If he's not with NASA for over ten years, where is he working?"

"He and his wife were killed in a car crash right before Christmas."

"Oh. I'm so sorry," Cynthia said. "I can't explain it, but lately, I've had this feeling that my daughter wasn't happy."

"You're a hundred percent correct."

"Tell us about Gina," she requested.

Dan cleared his throat. "She's an amazing girl."

Cynthia listened to everything that had happened to Gina since her parents's death. Her heart sank a little more with each dreadful detail about the relatives who lived with her.

"My wife believes maybe there's a new will, but Gina hasn't found it." He paused. "Gina is so unhappy with them that she's been making up stuff about the aunt wanting to kill her. Everyone we've spoken with believes she's looking for a way to get away from them."

"You don't believe her?" Cynthia asked.

"I'm afraid I don't. She produced a list of poisons her aunt had listed, but it could've been for killing moles. There's no doubt, they aren't there for Gina. It's free room and board in a big house."

"Tristen and I are flying up. We're leaving this afternoon."

"Hold up. They're out of town this week for spring break."

"Do you have any idea where they went?" Tristen asked.

"Not really. I believe they rented a cabin in Tennessee."

"In the meantime, I'll speak with my attorney and see what our legal path will be to regain custody of Gina. I was already trying to find her."

"Do you have other children?"

"Mallory is it. I lost my wife to cancer. I'm on my own with her."

"Ms. Reynolds, do you have any other children?"

"No. I've centered my life around my career. Is there any way you can get a message to Gina?" Cynthia asked. "I'm biting at the bits to meet her."

"She has one of those little prepaid phones my wife picked up, but I doubt it has coverage in the middle of the woods."

"Can I have the number?"

"I'd rather talk to Gina first. From what their will said, these relatives have legal custody of her until she's eighteen. That might trump your birthmother card."

"It could, but you said they don't care about Gina. That means they'll be easily bought off."

They exchanged contact information with Dan.

"Gina is going to be so thrilled. I'll get back with you." He disconnected.

Cynthia couldn't have been happier. She considered what was said about the aunt wanting to kill Gina. What if it wasn't Gina's imagination? Cynthia's motherly instinct kicked in. She wanted to protect her daughter.

"Tristen, I'm worried about her."

"Dan didn't believe she was in any real danger. I'm sure she'll be fine. A week from today, we'll be in Huntsville. I don't plan to leave without our daughter."

"Me either. I'd sell every share of Zurtel stock to have her."

He grinned. "If these people are anything like I imagine, they'll probably give her up for a hundred thousand." He winked. "Hell, they may settle for a new car."

Cynthia didn't think it'd be quite that easy. She didn't want to underestimate the situation, so she would first speak with the family law attorney again.

♦♦♦

Gina trudged toward the rustic cabin with a heavy heart. She'd done her best at feigning an illness, so they'd cancel the trip. Though she begged to stay home, her aunt insisted she go. She had an entire week of being crammed in the small cabin with them.

In the cabin, she had to share a room with Shellie. The room had two twin beds. Her cousin wasted little time putting her clothes away. "I left you that chest and some of the dresser drawers."

"Thanks." If she felt threatened in anyway, Gina planned to run away. She decided to leave her clothes in her backpack and small suitcase. If she could make it to the highway, she could find a ride home.

She thought of the social media post. Had anyone recognized her? Maybe by the time they returned, she'd know who her mother was.

Rather than participate in games, Gina continued to claim she was sick and stayed in the small room curled up in bed.

Aunt Nell entered the room. She placed her hand on Gina's forehead. "You don't have fever. That's good. I brought soup for you in case you're too sick to eat heavy food."

Confusion twirled through Gina's mind. Aunt Nell had actually been really nice the last couple of days. Something had to be up.

While the others ate, she tried to use the prepaid phone. Nothing. Gina couldn't pick up a signal. She returned the phone to the front pocket of her backpack. Hearing laughter outside the window, she stood and peeked out.

Uncle Sonny had set up a badminton net. They swatted the rackets around trying to hit the birdie. They almost could pass for normal. Almost.

She stayed in the cabin. The dark room smelled like pine. It wasn't until the aroma of grilled steaks overpowered her senses that she left the room.

"Look who's feeling better," Aunt Nell said. "Nothing like food to bring you around."

Uncle Sonny frowned. "I didn't fix her a steak."

"I'll share mine," Aunt Nell said. "This steak is more than I can eat."

"Thanks. I'm tired of soup."

"You think you can keep it down?"

Gina nodded and sat beside Will. "Who won?"

Finally Shellie spoke up, "Me and Will did."

Will and I.

Gina didn't correct her. "I've gone to tennis camp every summer, so I'm pretty good at anything with a racket. Maybe, I'll play next time."

"I speak for Gina as my partner," Will announced.

Aunt Nell's gleeful expression faded, and her eyes grew distant. "There won't be any tennis camp this summer. Your days of being a pampered little rich girl are over. You're one of us now. We're just plain people. And you won't be doing anything Will and Shellie can't do. Since you're feeling better, you can clean the kitchen tonight."

The real Aunt Nell is back.

Gina's stomach tightened. Suddenly, the soup sounded better than Aunt Nell's steak. She remembered the Internet search listing the most common accidents leading to the death of kids.

Chapter Thirteen

Monday morning Cynthia met with the attorney. Unfortunately, getting legal custody of Gina might be more difficult than she thought. She hadn't realized how hard a will was to break. And if she couldn't take her daughter legally, she'd buy the damn relatives off. While there, she had a new will drawn up leaving everything to Gina with the exception of a generous college fund for Mallory.

She stopped by a mall and purchased everything to redo one of the bedrooms for Gina. She selected what she thought an eleven year old girl would like. She wanted it to be perfect.

Douglas actually came in handy getting everything to her car. Finding a place to put it in her small car presented a problem.

Later that afternoon, she stopped by her father's office.

He glanced up when she walked in. "I wasn't expecting a visit from you. Actually, I was about to leave. Anything important?"

"I found her. Actually, Tristen did."

"Who?"

"Our daughter. Her name is Gina. She's been living in Huntsville."

She told him everything Dan said.

"You plan to get custody?"

"You bet. By this time next week, I'll have her back."

♦♦♦

Tristen invited Cynthia in.

Immediately, Mallory ran and hugged her. "Miss Cynthia, did you come to play with me and Sarah?"

"No, I actually have a story I want to tell you."

Mallory lit up. "I love stories. Does it have a witch in it?"

Cynthia glanced at Tristen. "Actually, it does. Her name is Edith."

Tristen grinned. "You might want to start at the beginning."

"Okay. Once upon a time, there was a princess who lived in a fine castle, but she had a wicked stepmother who was the queen."

"And two stepsisters," Mallory added.

"No. She had an evil, weird stepbrother. Her name was Princess Cynthia."

"That's your name," Mallory said.

"Yes, this is a story about me."

Mallory clapped with delight. "What happens?"

"One summer a handsome man stayed near the castle, and the princess and the man fell in love. But the wicked queen didn't think he was good enough to marry a princess and made him think the princess didn't love him."

"What was his name?"

"Tristen."

Mallory cut her eyes to him.

"Yes, it's me."

"So what happened?"

"Because they loved each other so much, they made a baby together. But Tristen never knew about the baby."

"Because the queen sent him away," Mallory said.

"That's right. And that queen wouldn't let Princess Cynthia keep this precious baby girl. She made the princess give her daughter away."

"What's her name?"

"Gina."

"What happened to Gina?"

"We found her, and now we want to finally bring her home."

"I'm her daddy."

"And you're my daddy too." Confusion showed on Mallory's little face. "Am I still your little girl?"

"Of course you are. I'll always love you, but Gina needs a home and needs to be loved."

Mallory gave a questioning look. "What about Mommy?"

"This story took place a long time before I met Mommy and had you."

Mallory nodded. "Are you and Miss Cynthia getting married?"

Cynthia blushed. "No."

Tristen's mouth dropped. "Miss Cynthia has her company to run."

"If you can't marry, Miss Cynthia, will you marry Sarah?"

Tristen choked. "No, I'm not. And Gina will live with Miss Cynthia, but she'll get to visit us each week."

"I don't want her here."

Tristen sighed. Mallory wasn't making this easy. He'd never expected her to be jealous. "Gina is your older sister." He glanced at Cynthia, then back to Mallory. "Mal, you've had me your entire life. Gina hasn't. So don't you think it's only fair that you share me with her?"

Mallory's expression revealed her reluctance. She shrugged. "I guess so."

'Guess what?" Cynthia said.

"What?" she asked on a gloomy sigh.

"Gina looks like you." Cynthia held up the picture on her phone.

Mallory studied the picture. "She sort of looks like me."

"You're sisters," Cynthia said. "We're bringing Gina home soon. She's going to need your dad and my love, but she needs your love also. The people she thought were her mommy and daddy just died. She doesn't have anyone."

Mallory nodded. "Think she'll play Barbies with me?"

Cynthia laughed. "I know she will."

After Mallory left the room, he blew out a breath in frustration. "I thought she'd love having a sister."

Cynthia laughed. “She’s had you to herself for a long time. She’ll come around.” She paused. “Gina will be returning on Saturday. Sunday, I thought we’d fly over and meet her.”

“I should be back by then,” Tristen said.

“Back from where?”

“I’m supposed to fly Randall to Brazil. He’s expecting to be there a few days and told me to pack a bag.”

“I have to be in Jacksonville on Friday. We’re running the second phase of test flights. This time with varied payloads.” Cynthia hugged him. “Thank you for being so wonderful about Gina.”

Tristen hugged Cynthia for a moment. It was like holding her as a seventeen year old. His heart warmed. He wanted to kiss her, but he didn’t. He had to remember his place in the company.

♦♦♦

Monday night, Gina sat on the cabin’s front porch swing. It was dark and slightly chilly, but she didn’t care. She liked having a moment to herself. No one knew she was outside. They probably assumed she’d gone to bed.

The room behind the window lit up revealing Aunt Nell and Will’s silhouettes. Gina recalled the small room was Will’s.

“We’ve got to talk,” Nell said to Will.

“Can’t it wait,” he replied. “I’m tired.”

“No. This is about Gina.”

“What about her?”

“When she turns eighteen, she’ll throw us out into the street. She hates us. If she had died with her parents, everything Uncle Scott owned would have been ours.”

“But she didn’t.”

Gina’s heart rate rose slightly.

“No. But if she dies now, everything will be ours. I wouldn’t need to worry day and night about what’s going to happen to us when she kicks us out. If she were to have an accident before then, I wouldn’t cry myself to sleep at night.”

“Why does it involve me?”

"We're going to hike a steep trail tomorrow. I want you to hike a little ahead of us. Encourage her to go with you. Then push her over and claim it was an accident."

"That's murder?"

"No, it's protecting what should've been ours in the first place. She's adopted. She's not even family."

Gina's breath became shallow as she waited for his answer.

"No, I won't do it. I can't."

Gina decided she'd misjudged Will.

"It has to be done tomorrow," Aunt Nell said.

Gina shivered. If she went on the trail tomorrow, she would die.

♦♦♦

Tuesday, Cynthia reached her office at ten.

Jennifer, her secretary, popped in the door. "Randall called. He's trying to reach you."

After Jennifer left, she called Randall.

"It took you long enough to call back," he complained. "I have the damn flu."

"Then you'd better call and cancel."

"I can't. They've already left to meet me."

"Surely, they have phones."

"No coverage until they reach Belem."

"What do you want me to do about it?"

"Go in my place."

"To Brazil? You're delusional. We're running the second phase of tests on Friday."

"You'll be back late Thursday. This will give you a chance to see the property before I strike a deal."

"I don't know."

"Look these guys are old school. They'll take it as an insult if no one shows up."

"They'll be more insulted if you send a woman in your place."

"Wilkes is going, but it's not the same as family."

"What time do I need to be at the landing strip?"

"You've got an hour. Ravelo has old fashioned ways. You may want to wear dresses or skirts."

"Seriously? Is the man still living in the dark ages?"

"The times I've visited I've never seen a woman in pants."

"I can't see trekking through the jungle in a dress."

"You'll be in a jeep when he takes you out to see the property. Don't forget it'll be hot and humid."

"If I do this, you'll owe me."

"Thanks. I won't forget it. Even though Ravelo has his own army it might be wise to take Douglas."

"I will."

Remembering Tristen was piloting the jet, she smiled like a giddy school girl. She couldn't deny the thought of being with him excited her.

After notifying Douglas to meet her at Zurtel's landing strip, Cynthia called Ellis to pick her up. "I need to run by my house and grab a few things."

"Yes ma'am."

Cynthia smiled. "I found my daughter." She told him all about Gina.

At her house, she slipped out of the heels and into a pair of sandals but remained in the silky dress she wore. She packed several dresses, one skirt and blouse set and her hygiene items and left.

♦♦♦

Tuesday morning, Gina stared out the window at the heavy rain coming down. She couldn't have been happier. Her aunt's hiking expedition had been snuffed out by the sudden bad weather. In the early morning hours, Gina had attempted to run away before her relatives woke up. She'd made it as far as the front porch when the storm started. It had rained ever since.

Just in case Tuesday turned out to be sunny, she'd keep her belongings packed. Somehow, she'd try to make it to Liz's house and hope her aunt and uncle would be delighted she was gone and wouldn't bother searching for her. They could have the house. She didn't care anymore.

♦♦♦

At the landing strip, Cynthia entered the jet behind Mr. Wilkes.

A hint of surprise filled Tristen's eyes when he saw her. "I was expecting Randall."

"He's sick. I'm going in his place. We'll come back late Thursday. I have to be in Jacksonville on Friday. How's Mallory?"

"Ever since she learned about Gina, she's been needy and clingy."

"Once she meets her older sister, she'll change her mind."

"Hope so. Buckle up. We'll depart soon."

"Douglas isn't here yet?"

Tristen glanced at his watch. "If you need to be there by 4:00, we need to leave now. Have you called him?"

"Yes, it went straight to voicemail. We'll give him ten more minutes." She called the bodyguard once more, but this time his voicemail was full. Finally, she gave Tristen the okay to leave.

Douglas had always been dependable. She wasn't sure what had happened.

While in flight, she called her father to tell him where she was going.

He wasn't pleased. "You have no business stomping through a jungle with these people. Do you have Douglas with you?"

"No. I'm not sure what happened. He didn't show up. Don't worry about me. Randall said Ravelo has his own military to deal with rebels."

Surprisingly, the long flight was uneventful with only a small amount of turbulence.

Tristen made a smooth landing in Belem.

A sleek black limousine awaited them. A handsome middle-aged man stepped from the back of the car and walked toward the jet.

Tristen and Evan stood at the door. "Watch your step, Miss Reynolds. Mr. Wilkes."

The South American, smiling like a two bit gigolo, immediately approached her. "Senorita Reynolds. What a pleasure to have you. Your brother just called to inform me there'd been a change of plans, but he didn't tell me how beautiful you are."

"Thank you. I'm glad you speak English so well."

"Most here speak Portuguese. Spanish is also spoken. I'm fluent in both as well as English."

Cynthia liked his thick accent. She smiled. "I speak neither."

"We'll communicate just fine." He took her hand and kissed the back of it. "Welcome to Brazil."

"Thank you."

"I hope you enjoy your stay."

"I'm sure we will." Cynthia tried to relax, but couldn't. She couldn't stop wondering if Randall had really been sick.

Maybe he wanted me out of the office.

The merger with Novik was dead. She couldn't think of any other agenda where he'd want her out of his way.

Tristen stood watching this middle-aged Casanova charm Cynthia.

Finally, Ravelo turned to him and the other man. "You are?"

"Mr. Pruitt Wilkes. I'm Zurtel's head accountant." Wilkes shook hands with Ravelo.

"Mr. Wilkes is Randall's right hand man," Cynthia said, trying to make them think Randall sent someone important with her.

Ravelo shifted his attention to her. "I'm sure Randall sent you to close the deal. He calls you the piranha of the business world."

She choked. "He gives me more credit than I deserve."

Their host glanced at Tristen. "The pilot I assume."

"Yes." He introduced the rest of the flight crew.

Tristen pushed his shades up on his head. "Miss Reynolds, we need instructions."

She stared at him for a few moments. Fear danced in her eyes. "You're coming with me of course. This might take a couple of days. I can't leave you here."

Ravelo interrupted, "Arrangements have been made. They will be fine at the hotel."

"If they choose to go, will that be a problem?" she asked.

"No, I can make arrangements. Tonight we'll stay in the city and head out in the morning."

"How far is your plantation?" Cynthia asked.

"About one hundred and sixty kilometers up the Xingu River. Miss Reynolds, I'll show you parts of Brazil tourists never see. We'll travel for a short time down the Amazon to the Iriri that branches into the Xingu. It's called the River of Despair."

Cynthia paled slightly.

Tristen wasn't sure what this trip was about, but he sure the hell didn't trust this man. She'd been edgy since boarding in Atlanta. He glanced at the copilot and attendant. "Let's grab our things. Looks like we'll be taking in some scenery."

"I can see all the scenery I want in Belem," Evan said. "I plan to stay here."

"Me too," Annie said. "I have no desire to travel down the Amazon."

Cynthia focused on Tristen. "If you want to stay, Mr. Wilkes and I can go alone?"

While she said one thing, her eyes expressed something different. They reflected apprehension.

"I'm going with you. Might be fun."

The tension left Cynthia's face.

Relief eased across Mr. Wilkes face. He also had reservations of venturing off into the Brazilian jungles.

"Let's go," Ravelo said. "We have dinner reservations."

Once Tristen approached the limo, the driver relieved him of his bags and placed them in the trunk. Mr. Wilkes climbed in first, then Cynthia beside him. Evan and Annie sat across from them.

"Sit here beside me," Cynthia requested.

Tristen gave her a nod and slid beside her, leaving Ravelo no choice but to sit by Evan. During the long ride, their thighs pushed against one another. He glanced at Cynthia's shapely legs. An image of sliding her dress up played in his mind.

Thoughts like that will get me in trouble.

The limousine came to a stop in front of a large, ritzy hotel. Ravelo spoke up, "The Equatorial Palace—the best hotel in Belem."

"It's beautiful," Cynthia commented.

Ravelo checked them into the hotel. "We meet downstairs in two hours. You'll find Brazil has the best food in the world."

Tristen's room was next door to Cynthia's. The others were on the floor above. Six rooms in this joint had to cost a small fortune. Still, it was nice having his own room rather than sharing with Evan.

At the door, Tristen paused. "You don't feel safe, do you?"

Cynthia shook her head. "No, I don't. Something doesn't seem right about this."

"Mind me asking why you're here?"

"No." She explained about the new manufacturing plant Randall wanted to build. "But why build so far out where it'd be impossible to transport our products?"

Tristen shrugged. "Doesn't make any sense. So what do you think this is about?"

"A wild goose chase. Apparently, he wants me out of the office this week. I'm sure he has something up his sleeve."

"We can fly back in the morning."

She sighed. "No. I have no evidence. The merger is off the table, so I have no idea what he's up to. He mentioned this trip several times over the last few weeks. I'm being paranoid. If you prefer, you can stay in Belem. Mr. Wilkes and I will be fine."

"I'm going. I'm not letting you sail off without me."

Her expression showed her gratitude. "You have Mallory to put first."

"I know. But Gina needs us both. I'm taking that into consideration."

Cynthia gave a longing sigh. "I can't wait to meet her."

"Me either." He swiped the key card. "See you downstairs."

After she disappeared into her room, he entered his room. "Hot damn."

Now he was jealous of the others spending most of the week in this gorgeous hotel with resort sized pools.

He showered and dressed in clean clothes before returning downstairs to meet the others in the extravagant lobby. Unsure of what to expect, he wore a white dress shirt, jeans, and cowboy boots. He removed the small .22 from his leather pouch and shoved it in his right boot.

When he spotted the group waiting in the center of the lobby, Tristen couldn't take his eyes off Cynthia. She wore a dark blue dress that fit like a second skin and stopped just above her knees. Her hair flowed on her shoulders in silky curls.

"Put your tongue back in your mouth," Evan whispered.

"What are you talking about?"

"You're drooling. You look like the Big Bad Wolf." Evan chuckled.

"It's your imagination."

"Ladies and gentlemen, shall we leave?" Ravelo asked.

Tristen tensed when Ravelo placed his hand on the small of Cynthia's back as their host escorted her to the car. This time in the limo, Ravelo scooted in beside her. There wasn't anything to do but sit across from them.

When he glanced over, her gaze locked with his, and she smiled. "Is Mallory with Sarah?"

"Yes, I'm glad I hired her."

"Are you ever going to let Grandma Rose see her?"

"Eventually."

"How many children do you have, Mr. Conners?" Ravelo asked.

Unsure if Cynthia had told anyone about Gina, he wouldn't include her. "One."

People wearing colorful costumes crowded the narrow street while festive music filled the air.

Cynthia leaned her head slightly to get a better look. "Is this the parade for de Cirio de Nazare`?"

"No, that's in October. It is our Carnival celebrating Lent." Ravelo lowered the automatic windows on both sides allowing a rush of warm air to enter the vehicle, bringing with it a blend of tantalizing aromas. Her mouth watered. She was relieved no one noticed her stomach growling. Everyone stared out the windows, too engrossed in the music and parade.

The limousine bobbled over cobblestones as they approached a long line of beautifully dressed people carrying lit candles through the streets. Voices singing hymns were faded out by African music playing nearby.

"I like the music," Tristen commented. "It sounds African with a Spanish rhythm."

"That's called Carimbo`. It originated from the music of Bantu slaves who were brought here from Angola."

"I've never been to Brazil," Cynthia stated.

"Too bad you don't have time to visit Basilica de Nazare`. It's a church turned art museum. A lovely place with lots of marble and gold."

"I might return for a vacation."

He smiled at her. "Well worth the time."

When the car stopped at a light, a girl selling roses stood outside Tristen's window. She offered him a flower.

Not having any Brazilian currency, he pulled out an American five dollar bill and handed it to the girl. "Keep the change."

No doubt, the girl had heard it before because her eyes lit up. "Valeu."

He assumed she'd said thank you.

As the car drove on, he sniffed the red rose and stared at Cynthia. His heart skipped a beat. He handed it to her. "You look radiant tonight."

She blushed. "Thank you, Mr. Conners."

♦♦♦

Cynthia stared out the car window not wanting her eyes to reflect how flattered she was with Tristen's gesture.

Beautiful colored lanterns dangled around an enclosed courtyard where people danced. She couldn't help recalling the evening she'd danced with Tristen.

"Mr. Conners, have you always worked for Zurtel?" Ravelo asked.

"No, I flew for one of the major airlines. They had to cut back, so I was left without a job. My father has flown for Zurtel just about his entire career."

"I'd like to learn to fly. I acquired a plane. No more than a crop duster."

"Flying is simple. Probably easier than driving a car."

"Second nature to you, but I'm sure it's more complicated than you say," Ravelo added.

"No, he's right," Evan stated.

"The difficult part is when you have a problem and have to cope with it. Your decision might determine whether you and your passengers live or die," Tristen admitted.

"Maybe you can take me up in my plane," Ravelo said.

"I'm not too fond of single engine planes. What is it?"

"Cessna 172. It's an older model."

"I'll take a look at it," Tristen promised.

Cynthia didn't want Tristen taking up the small plane that probably hadn't been serviced in years. Like he'd said earlier, Gina needed them both.

At *Pomba de Dourado*, Tristen exited first and waited to assist Cynthia. When she placed her hands in his, sensual sparks traveled up her arm. "Thanks."

She tried to appear unaffected. She wondered if he felt it also.

Tristen followed the others into the elegant restaurant. A man greeted them and offered Tristen and Evan a dinner jacket and tie. Both dark coats and plaid ties were the same making them look like Twinkies.

A man seated them immediately at a table positioned near a small dance floor. A candle burned in the center of the white table cloth. Their host pulled Cynthia's chair out, and she thanked him.

Cynthia observed Tristen's behavior with interest. Each time the South American touched her or allowed his eyes to linger on her, Tristen's expression showed concern. Though his reaction could be mistaken for jealousy, she assured herself he was just being protective.

She glanced across at Annie. "Latin men are always so charming with women."

Annie giggled. "I agree."

Ravelo sat on her right. She had hoped a member of her flight crew might sit there first. He lifted the menu and studied the choices.

"What does *Pomba de Dourado* mean?" she asked.

"The Golden Dove."

"That's beautiful. What do you recommend?"

He glanced up. "May I suggest the Pato no tucupi. It's a very lean duck dish."

Tristen grinned. "Don't think I could eat Donald or Daffy. What else is on the menu?"

Mr. Wilkes and Cynthia laughed. The joke flew right over Ravelo's head.

"They have excellent seafood." Ravleo said. "You may want to try filhote, a very delicious fish."

"That sounds good," Tristen said.

"Any chicken dishes?" Mr. Wilkes asked.

"Frango churrasco. It's served with rice and beans."

After ordering, they listened to Ravelo rattle off facts about the city. When the band started to play, their host offered his hand to Cynthia. "Let's dance while we wait for our food."

She remained reluctant for a moment before surrendering and standing. She flashed Tristen a look hoping he'd intervene.

Ravelo caressed her hand in his and escorted her to the dance floor. His touch didn't affect her.

As Cynthia walked to the dance floor with Ravelo, Tristen turned his chair, so he could see them.

"I need to find the gentleman's room," Mr. Wilkes announced, then walked away.

"I don't think Ravelo wants us tagging along," Evan said.

"I think you're right, but that won't stop me. I'm going."

"I won't pretend I like her," Evan said. "She's not my favorite person."

Tristen turned back and flashed the copilot a hostile look.

"Don't look at me like that. She's not as friendly with us."

"She's not so bad if you can pick your way through the ice."

"You're involved with her," Evan said. "We all know it."

"I'm not an ice climber. I don't have time to chisel my way into her life."

"Then why go with her? You've got a daughter to think about," Annie said.

"She'll have Wilkes with her," Evan reminded.

"Yeah, but that's like sending Sheldon Cooper. She'd end up having to defend him if anything goes wrong." Tristen stood. "Excuse me." He walked between the couples dancing and tapped Ravelo on the shoulder. "I'm cutting in."

"Si, Mr. Conners. She's all yours."

Tristen quickly moved in taking Cynthia in his arms. "You all right?"

"I am now."

"Did he get out of line?"

"Yes."

"Something he said or did?"

"Both."

Tristen left it at that. But he knew he couldn't let Ravelo take Cynthia off with just Mr. Wilkes to protect her. "That's why I'm not leaving you."

She tilted her head just enough so that their gazes met. "I think you should stay with Evan and Annie. Because if something happens to me, you don't only have Mallory to think of, now you have Gina."

"I'm not letting you leave with Casanova and his quick hands. I'm going with you."

Then she placed her head on his shoulder as they moved with the music. "You dance very well."

"When I'm not drunk."

She laughed softly. "Who taught you?"

"Danielle and I took ballroom dancing before our wedding. We enjoyed it."

"I took dance lessons most my life," she shared.

When the music changed to a spicy fast tune, she started to walk away, but Tristen jerked her back. "Food's not there yet. Do you really want to be stuck listening to Ravelo talk about how wonderful Brazil is?"

She laughed. "No. Do you know how to Samba?"

"Some. I think we'll manage." Facing one another, Tristen placed his hands on her waist as they stepped back and forth, swinging their hips to the rhythmic beat.

"You're not so bad for a flyboy," she confessed. "You're better at this than skiing."

His hands slid to her hips and pulled her closer until their bodies touched. Sensual heat consumed him. He wanted to take her to his bed and forget the damn fish and rice.

♦♦♦

Cynthia should've refused to do the sensual dance. With each twirl, her hair flew up. The heat pulsing through her grew in intensity as their bodies touched. Her nipples pearled beneath the stretchy material of her dress.

She glanced up at his face to see whether he'd noticed. He had. Lust sizzled in his eyes.

Desire spiraled through her, awaking a dormant body. An erotic fire raged through her causing her inner core to burn with a needy ache.

She urged herself to pull away, but the tingling sensations from pressing against his solid erection held her prisoner.

He feels so good.

Her legs weakened, and she feared passing out.

The music stopped. Rather than let her go, he held her. Then boldly, he lowered his lips to hers and kissed parting them with his tongue. He tasted like wine and chocolate mints. He smelled even better. He wore some type of citrus scent, probably shaving cream or an aftershave that mingled with a strong virile scent. As the passionate kiss grew in intensity, the patrons cheered. When he finally released her, she realized they had been the main attraction.

Oh, sweet Heaven.

"Sorry, I got a little carried away," he admitted. "Are you all right?"

She couldn't answer. As she turned to walk back to the table, she observed Mr. Wilkes, Annie, and Evan's stupefied expressions. Ravelo looked extremely perturbed.

More heat blossomed in her neck and cheeks. She probably looked like a boiled lobster.

Tristen had sent shockwaves through her that rocked her world. She walked like someone intoxicated as she stumbled weakly to the table. When he pulled the chair back, she lowered her body, missing it completely and landed on the floor.

Immediately, Tristen helped her up. "Cynthia, I'm so sorry."

She tried to speak, but only a squeak came out. The man had her unraveled at the seams. This time, Tristen guided her into the chair. When she noticed the men gawking, her cheeks burned. She reached for her glass of wine but knocked it over.

"Miss Reynolds, are you all right?" Ravelo asked.

She grabbed her water, swigged it down like chugging beer, then looked at him. "I think the heat and twirling around on the dance floor made me dizzy. That's all."

Tristen flashed a confident grin. "It was damn hot out there." He winked at her. "The heat was even too much for me."

She tried to ignore his innuendo he implied and hoped the others would as well. Suddenly, she realized what Tristen was doing. It didn't reveal the way he truly felt about her. This was a show for Ravelo's benefit. Now, she felt outright foolish, because Tristen had her overheating and ready to fall into bed with him.

Tristen smiled. "Least I didn't bite your ear this time."

"That was considerate of you," she said. Hopefully, the suave South American wouldn't try touching her rear again. Not to mention the vulgarity he'd uttered in her ear. If this wasn't important to the company, she'd be on her jet within the hour. If Randall wanted to close the Jacksonville plant and open one here, she needed to see exactly where this place was.

When she glanced up, Evan and Annie were dancing. It struck her as odd to see them together.

The waiter cleaned up the spilled wine and poured her another glass. Then before anything else could be said, another waiter served their dinners. Annie and Evan returned to the table.

"Mr. Wilkes will be with us," Ravelo mentioned to Tristen. "Are you still determined to come?"

"Yes. It beats hanging around a hotel room all day."

"I'll call ahead and make sure they have a room ready for you."

"Put me with Cynthia. We've shared accommodations before." He winked at her. "Haven't we?"

She choked on her duck. When she started to deny his comment, he kicked her foot.

"I can't imagine being that close with someone under my employment." Ravelo gave Tristen a snide grin. "She is your boss. That would make you an employee with special benefits."

Anger flickered in Tristen's eyes.

"Mr. Conners may be my pilot, but we travel in the same social circles. He has a lot of friends in high places. Trust me, there's a big difference in what he earns and what my chauffeur is paid."

"I see."

Hopefully, Ravelo would give up on the idea of anything happening between them other than business negotiations. She would set Mr. Wilkes and the others straight concerning Tristen's charade once they headed home.

Ravelo grinned. "I think you've misunderstood my intentions. I am a married man."

She offered a polite smile. "That's good to know, Mr. Ravelo. Your wife must be an understanding woman if she puts up with you groping other women and whispering nasty remarks in their ears."

Ravelo paled.

That evening at the hotel, Cynthia walked out on the balcony and stood against the rail, staring at the city. The sky illuminated with brightly colored fireworks. She breathed in the night air. The enticing aromas of the Brazilian food had faded—replaced by the salty scent of the ocean air.

Her hair danced about wildly in the tropical breeze. Each time her gown blew above her thighs, she pushed it down.

When she glanced toward the next balcony, Tristen stood watching her. He wore the white hotel robe. She assumed he just stepped from the shower.

She remembered the dance and the feel of him against her.

Suddenly her body became hot. Desire taunted her unmercifully tearing apart her ability to reason. She wanted Tristen Conners. She stared in his direction. A gush of wind lashed across her, and she deliberately let her gown rise above her thighs.

It was an invitation.

Would he take it?

Chapter Fourteen

Tristen had never seen a lovelier sight than Cynthia Reynolds standing on the balcony. Her invitation had been clear. But if he slept with her, it could jeopardize his job. And even though the court case was over, he still needed his job especially now that he had hired Sarah.

He debated on whether to go tap on her door. He'd already pushed the boundaries of employer and employee relationship on the dance floor. He hadn't planned on kissing her. Temptation taunted him. He should take a cold shower and forget her invitation.

His libido overpowered his common sense.

After tapping on her door, Tristen wondered if he'd have a job after this. He admitted he had wanted her since she'd stepped on the jet his first day. As far as Danielle, he loved her, always would, but his heart, body, and soul were ready to move on.

Cynthia opened the door and immediately wrapped her arms around him, rose on her tiptoes, and kissed him. While returning the kiss, he backed her into the room and let the door close behind him.

One kiss led to another. They indulged in a long kiss. Once they became breathless, she leaned her head against him to catch her breath. When she glanced up, her eyes revealed her desire.

She took his hand and guided him to the enormous king-sized bed. With the balcony doors opened wide, moonlight painted them in blue light, and a cool breeze blew across their heated bodies. Bright colors flashed in the sky from fireworks nearby.

Standing by the bed, he gathered Cynthia in his arms and kissed her passionately. "I've wanted to do this since my first day on the job."

"I haven't been able to stop thinking about our summer together."

He lowered her to the bed and joined her. He kissed her shoulders, then up her neck, causing her to gasp. Being with Cynthia felt so natural. While kissing her, he let his hands explore her body, touching her in all the special places he'd touched before.

She moaned softly. "Do that some more."

His thumb rubbed over her sensitive spot making her squirm. He leaned and kissed her breasts before kissing a path down her stomach. As he started to kiss lower, she stopped him. "I can't wait. I want you now. Please."

Tristen was hard and definitely ready.

He leaned her back and kissed her deeply while positioning his body over hers.

She parted her legs opening herself to him and arched her hips.

Without hesitation, he slid into her and began working his hips slowly. "You feel so good," he whispered. "We were always good together."

He rose up supporting himself on his arms and stared down on her while stroking her in a steady rhythm. "You're beautiful."

She smiled, then arched her body to bring him deeper inside her.

He lowered himself pressing her breasts beneath him. Again they kissed in long slow intervals. He placed a hand on each side under her bottom and lifted her slightly. She moaned as he stroked deeper.

Unable to control the sexual heat building, he fought the urge to explode.

The intensity of their kisses grew as he worked his pelvis and hips, driving himself against her until they both cried out. Her entire body shook in pleasure.

So good. So damn good.

He collapsed on top of her a moment recuperating. Finally, he rolled over on his back.

She cuddled against him, draping her arm over him.

After resting, he whispered, "If I had known about Gina, I would've found a way for us to get married."

"Thanks for telling me."

"It wouldn't have been just about the pregnancy, I loved you very much." He wanted to tell her he still loved her but didn't. He wasn't sure how far she wanted to take this. He couldn't see her giving up Zurtel for him.

"I loved you too. That letter broke my heart."

Not wanting to bring up Edith, Tristen leaned and kissed her forehead before he lay back on the bed.

Her hand lightly rubbed his chest, then slowly lowered beneath his waist. The moment she touched him he grew hard again. He moaned as she lightly squeezed.

♦♦♦

Cynthia wanted him again. Uncertain of what the future held for either of them made her want him even more. He was fully erect again, and she planned to take advantage of it. This time they'd take their time and make it last.

As though reading her mind, Tristen leaned over and sucked each nipple while his fingers touched her in all the right places, making her insane with desire.

Each little touch sent erotic shimmers through her. When he raised his head from her breasts, she kissed him. Their tongues twirled in a ritual dance while their bodies heated once again.

Since they had been an item before, it made this more enjoyable. They didn't have the awkwardness of a new couple. It was as if fate was giving them a second chance. A chance to recapture what they'd lost.

For the next hour, they took turns driving one another to the edge of ecstasy, then pulling back. And when they couldn't wait any longer, she straddled him. She moved up and down on him in a slow sensual rhythm. Her breasts jiggled as her body slammed down on him. He closed his eyes and grimaced in pleasure. Witnessing it turned her on even more.

He placed a hand on each of her hips and helped her move faster until they both cried out.

Rather than lay back in his arms, she stood and walked to the mini-bar and fixed them a drink. She handed him one. "I have a confession."

He grinned. "I can't wait to hear it."

"I wanted this in the Jacksonville motel room. And the dream only made it worse. I think it's why I became so angry and had you demoted. I did it to keep this from happening."

"I wanted you too, but I was afraid to cross the line. Actually, when I was on the balcony, I kept hoping you'd invite me over."

"I didn't think you were coming, but I'm glad you did."

It wasn't long before they fell back into the heat of passion. This time they became bolder and indulged in foreplay before he ended up behind her.

Afterwards, they fell back on the mattress. She panted lightly to catch her breath. This time, she stayed on the far side of the bed. One of them had to be the bigger person and put an end to this or neither of them would get any sleep. They'd be exhausted tomorrow.

She gathered the sheet around her and rolled over facing him.

Tristen stared at the ceiling, his expression and eyes appearing so distant.

"Are you thinking of Danielle?" she asked.

He nodded. "Yep."

"Feeling guilty?"

"A little. I haven't been with anyone since she died. I've known for a while I was ready to move on. But this is different. You were my first love."

"And you were mine. You still look troubled. Anything else bothering you?"

"We didn't use protection."

"I had a period last week. I think we're safe."

She tried to read between the lines. If he didn't want her being pregnant, did that mean he had no intentions of taking their relationship farther than the bedroom?

"You should return to your room and try to get some sleep," she whispered.

He nodded, sat up, and kissed her before leaving the bed.

♦♦♦

Wednesday, Gina hoped it would still be raining, but instead, the sun shined through the curtains. She sat up in bed. Voices came from the other side of the door. Aunt Nell and Uncle Sonny were already up. She had missed her opportunity to run away. She climbed from bed and entered the main room that had a kitchen to one side. Her aunt stood at the stove. "Oatmeal?"

Remembering the night before, she shook her head. "I'm not hungry."

That wasn't true. Her stomach growled. If she made it through spring break, she decided to tell Mrs. Johnson about Aunt Nell.

Her uncle came in through the door. "It's muddy as hell out there. Those steep rocky trails are too slippery today. One of us could break our fool neck."

Aunt Nell frowned. "I don't want to spend another day in the stuffy cabin. Let's at least try to hike. If the trails are too bad we'll turn around."

"We can't chance it." Uncle Sonny sighed. "Let's drive into the nearest town and see a movie."

"We could've gone to the movie theater at home."

"Then let's take advantage of the indoor pool."

Aunt Nell sighed. "I guess so."

Gina actually enjoyed being in the pool. They played water volleyball. Aunt Nell couldn't swim, so she stayed in the shallow end. At least she didn't have to worry about her aunt drowning her.

Back at the cabin while Aunt Nell showered, and the others sat on the porch, Gina pillaged the refrigerator. Since she had refused breakfast and lunch, hunger pangs drilled her stomach. She made a ham sandwich and gobbled it down like a starving pup. Knowing she had to run away that night, she grabbed snack cakes and bags of chips and stuffed them in her backpack. Seeing the flashlight on the table, she hid it under her bed.

By tomorrow, the trails would be dry enough to hike. There was no doubt Aunt Nell planned to push her off a cliff first opportunity she had.

♦♦♦

Tristen woke Wednesday morning and felt like hell. He hadn't returned to his bed until 2:00 a.m. At 6:00 a.m. someone banged on his door.

"This is a wakeup call, Mr. Conners," he heard Ravelo say.

"I'm awake," he shouted.

"Be down in thirty minutes if you plan to join us."

Rather than a limo, a city taxi waited downstairs.

Ravelo sat between Cynthia and him in the backseat. He wondered if she regretted what they'd done. Would it affect their working relationship? Or his job?

At the dock, he had a few minutes alone with her while they waited to board the boat.

Her expression wasn't that of a happy woman.

He wondered if the previous night impacted her mood. "Something wrong?"

It took a few moments, but she finally faced him, her expression still grim. "Have you taken a good look at the boat we're going on?"

"No, which one is it?"

"The old dingy one with all the rust. I saw them carry our bags aboard. After the limousine and exquisite hotel last night, this boat comes as a shock."

"I expected something nicer," he admitted.

"Tristen, I need some time to think about last night. I don't regret it. I'm just not sure it should continue."

"Afraid I'll file a sexual harassment suit against you?"

She shrugged."That crossed my mind."

"Are you serious?"

"As your boss, I was out of line."

"No, you weren't."

"But I initiated it."

Tristen grinned. "Yes, you did, but I wanted you. I came willingly. I have no grounds to claim harassment."

"You weren't playing fair when we danced."

"Look, I get it. You had your night of passion and now you're done. Don't worry, I won't file a grievance against you. If you'd like I'll sign a contract giving you permission to use me anytime it suits you."

Her mouth dropped open. "I can't believe you said that."

"I can't believe you think I'd really stoop so low as to exploit what we did."

She'd already reclaimed her position as the corporate ice queen. He tried to hide his anger from the others. He turned to leave.

"Tristen, wait."

He didn't; instead, he crossed the dilapidated dock to the boat. Once across, he turned and waited for the others. Mr. Wilkes followed behind him. With Ravelo's help, Cynthia crossed over last.

Tristen didn't like the man putting his hands on her.

Workers stopped their tasks and stared at Cynthia.

"Mr. Conners, I don't like the way those men are looking at Miss Reynolds," Mr. Wilkes commented.

"Maybe she can work out a business deal with them," he replied, still angry.

Tristen glared at the crew. The diverse group made up of different ethnicities devoured Cynthia with their eyes.

She hurried to where he stood. "Put your arm around me. Do something to let them know we're a couple."

He winked. "Just explain that you're corporate, and if they raped you, it wouldn't look good for your image."

"Smartass."

Tristen laughed. "Stay beside me. Don't wander anywhere on this boat alone. Got it?"

She nodded. “Thanks.”

Once the journey was underway, Cynthia and Tristen joined Ravelo at the stern of the boat.

“You’re carrying a lot of cargo back,” Tristen stated.

“Si. It requires a lot of supplies and groceries to run such a big plantation.”

Tristen studied a stack of long wooden crates and figured they contained rifles. He smiled at Ravelo, pretending to believe him. Was Ravelo a plantation owner or a gun runner? Who would he sell guns to?

Maybe the rebels who’d caused issues in Manaus.

Rather than appear too interested in the cargo, Tristen stared at the brown water extending as far as he could see. Small islands with heavy vegetation dotted the river.

Cynthia turned to her host. “Is this the Amazon?”

“Si. We won’t be on it for long. We will enter the Iriri and then the Xingu where the compound is located.”

Compound?

Tristen’s stomach twisted in knots.

Since when had it become a compound rather than a plantation?

Cynthia’s brows rose slightly. No doubt, she had noticed, but Wilkes remained clueless.

Tristen preferred it being called a plantation. Compound brought to mind machine guns and war hungry rebels. He recalled the long gun crates they’d loaded.

“Why would Randall want a factory in a location so difficult to reach?” Cynthia asked.

“Actually, it’s not,” Ravelo stated. “It’s close to Manaus. From this city, you can drive to the compound.”

“Then why didn’t we meet there?”

“As I said at dinner, there are rebels causing problems there. Also, your brother expressed a desire to travel on the Amazon.”

“He didn’t mention it to me,” Cynthia said.

"By the time he realized you would be coming in his place, I'd already left. As you can well imagine, phones don't work in this thick jungle."

Cynthia nodded but didn't seem pleased. After the South American left them alone, she turned to Tristen. "I know what this is all about."

"What's that?"

"By the time I return to Atlanta, Randall will have pulled a fast one. I bet he called an emergency board meeting the minute I left. He better not be putting the Novik merger back on the table. When I return, he'll regret everything he's done behind my back."

I hope we get back.

Something seemed off about this entire trip. Tristen recalled how angry Randall had been on the Chicago flight. Then he considered Douglas not showing up.

He thought of Mallory and then Gina. He regretted his decision to escort Cynthia into this Godforsaken jungle. Hopefully, he was just being paranoid.

♦♦♦

Cynthia hadn't been able to look Tristen in the eyes after the accusation she'd made that morning. What had come over her? Why was she pushing him away?

She stared ahead at the wide river as boats maneuvered around larger boats in their paths. River traffic consisted of everything from rafts hauling bananas to dugouts carrying entire families. The mother in one held a red and yellow striped umbrella shielding them from the sun.

As the day passed, fewer shanties dotted the river bank. Instead, a towering wall of green forest bordered each side of the river. Pollen and floating seeds filled the earthy scented air. On occasions, a fish would leap from the water.

Cynthia turned to Tristen. "I need a cup of coffee. Will you walk me to the galley?"

"That's not in my job description."

She sighed knowing he was upset with her. "I know, but I'd appreciate you going with me."

He stood. "I could use a cup of coffee too. Maybe we can scrounge up a doughnut somewhere. I'm hungry."

"Me too. This isn't quite the experience I expected after having the red carpet rolled out yesterday." After standing and stretching, she walked down the side of the deck to the companionway that led downstairs to the galley.

Tristen stayed right behind her. They passed Mr. Wilkes sitting under the boat's canopy.

Downstairs, a group of men sat at a table, drinking coffee. They glanced up when she entered the galley. Immediately, she grew uncomfortable.

After pouring the coffee, Cynthia found an empty table and sat.

Tristen joined her and took one of the cups. "No doughnuts."

"Why does that not surprise me?" She sipped the strong Brazilian coffee, then figured the time was right to apologize. "I'm sorry about what I said this morning. I can't explain what came over me. I just need time to think about us."

"Take all the time you want."

"You're still angry."

"Yeah. You took a night that was magical and ruined it with all your sexual harassment bullshit."

"Guilty as charged." She added cream to the coffee. "You didn't want to come on this excursion, did you?"

"Not especially."

"So why didn't you remain behind with Evan and Annie?"

"I think you know the answer to that."

"Chivalry."

"More like stupidity."

She observed the fortress of trees on each side of the river. "Something about this doesn't add up."

"Agreed, but there's no way off this boat. Not only does this river have crocodiles, it has electric eels, anacondas, and piranhas."

"So much for jumping ship," she said.

"Play along, and hope we're both wrong. Has Randall ever been here?"

"Yes. He fell in love with this land, but relocating our manufacturing here would be a bad move for our business, and Randall's not stupid. It makes me wonder what this is really about."

For a moment, she recalled her father's new will leaving her the entire company. If she died, Randall would own Zurtel. She pushed the thought away knowing it meant she'd never see Gina if something happened. Was her daughter enjoying her spring break? She wondered if the Garsons had spoken with her yet.

She sipped the rich coffee. "If you had stayed in Belem, what did you have planned?" she asked.

"Just hang out at that resort pool and tan a little."

"I'm sorry I got you into this. Like you said it's not your job to escort me."

"I made the decision not because you're my boss, but because I care about you. On top of that, you're the mother of my oldest daughter." He stood and took her empty cup. "Let's go top side."

Cynthia picked up on his anger. She'd deliberately ruined what they'd shared the previous night. Why? What was she so afraid of? She wasn't sure Tristen would forgive her.

He scowled. "I wish I was in a position to tell you to take your job and shove it, but I'm not. I need this job. Without it, I'd probably lose everything."

Above, they joined Mr. Wilkes at the stern. They sat in plastic lawn chairs allowing them to view the scenery. The noise from the forest deafened her. Howler monkeys cried the loudest. The birds made every kind of noise imaginable.

"How well does Randall know this man?" Wilkes asked.

"I'm not sure," she replied. "I think this was a setup to get me away, so he could pull something underhanded. Surely, Randall's still not wanting to merge with Novik. I can't believe he ever suggested it in the first place." She didn't mention her father's will or any of the dark thoughts she'd had about her stepbrother.

Guilt washed over Mr. Wilkes's face. "There's a reason Randall wanted the merger?"

"What possible reason could Randall have for wanting it?"

Mr. Wilkes sighed. "I accidently came across this. He doesn't know I know. When Novik's stocks bottomed out after settling a law suit, Randall refinanced everything he had and purchased as many shares as he could."

"How many?"

He shrugged. "I'm not sure. Think about this. If Novik and Zurtel had merged under the Zurtel name and brand, Novik stocks would have skyrocketed. Then he'd sell them off and make a fortune. This is just speculation on my part."

"Or the opposite effect. Zurtel's stocks could have plummeted," Cynthia said.

"Not with MX7. Randall was counting on it to shoot the value of our stocks through the roof."

Cynthia considered something else. "Or perhaps have enough stocks that he could take over Zurtel and Novik. I wonder if Quinn Adams, who owns Novik is aware of it. Randall might be deceiving both companies."

The day passed with them talking. The sun had dropped, and the long shadows of the trees fell across the river. The boat slowed, and the engine shut off. They stood and walked to the bow to see what was happening.

Ravelo appeared seemingly from nowhere. "We have arrived at the compound. You will stay the night at my house. My wife has dinner waiting. We have about a thirty minute ride. I'd like to make it before nightfall." He looked at Cynthia. "I hope you'll be discreet."

"Wouldn't think of upsetting your marriage."

Once off the boat, they were hustled into a van and driven from the village. The pavement ended, and the vehicle drove over gravel into thick jungle. Just as the sun was setting, they entered a wide clearing. An old Victorian house stood in a clearing as well as other buildings.

"I'll have your luggage taken to your rooms. Mr. Conners and Mr. Wilkes will share a room. Ms. Reynolds, you'll be just

...wn the hall in my daughter's room. She'll sleep with her sister tonight. You can shower and change before dinner."

As they entered the house, Cynthia relaxed a bit. The house was beautifully decorated. Mary welcomed them to her home and introduced them to their four children—two boys and two girls. Her accent was more difficult to understand than Ravelo's.

She smiled. "The children have eaten. So they are going to bed." She glanced at the children and motioned for them to go. They said their goodnights and left. "Dinner is being served in the dining room."

"Thank you," Cynthia said and followed their hostess.

Being so hungry, she had a difficult time eating slowly and not gobbling the food down.

"How was your trip?" Mary asked in English.

"Not bad. I don't mind a little adventure."

Ravelo smiled. "If you like adventure, you won't mind the supper."

"The chicken is really good," she said.

He grinned. "It's iguana."

It required a few moments for what he said to process. "I'm eating a giant lizard?"

Ravelo poured a glass of wine. "Yes. He's an iguana who visited our garden one time too many."

Cynthia finally swallowed the bite of the chicken imposter.

♦♦♦

Tristen wanted to laugh as Cynthia's face paled. "It's good. Actually it's better than chicken."

Ravelo turned to him. "I agree. Anytime someone here orders chicken more than likely they are eating iguana."

"I'll be sure I order fish," Cynthia stated.

Ravelo chuckled, then grew serious. "I think you'll like the land Randall has selected. Once I've taken you to see it, we'll talk."

"You realize the road from town to here would need to widened and asphalted," she said. "You'd lose a lot of your privacy."

"I understand that." Ravelo turned to Tristen. "Perhaps after looking at my plane, Mr. Conners will take us up. Then you'll be able to get an aerial view of the property."

Tristen didn't like single engine planes, but he didn't want to seem uncooperative. "I'll consider it if your plane checks out."

"Too bad you'll only be here a few days. I'd be willing to pay for flight lessons."

"Maybe another time."

"This is such a lovely home, Mary," Cynthia commented.

"We enjoy it," she replied. "Though I hate Senor Randall couldn't come. The kids adore him, especially little Marie. I'm glad I had the opportunity to meet you."

"Me too. How far are you from the nearest town?" Cynthia asked.

Mary smiled."Only forty kilometers. We drive to Manaus. It's closest."

Tristen glanced at Ravelo. "Will we return to Belem by boat?"

He came across as unprepared for the question. "No, I'll take you to Manaus, then you can fly back to Belem."

"I can call Evan Green, our copilot, and have him fly the jet to Manaus."

"That would work, but unfortunately, you can't use your phone from here."

Tristen reviewed everything said earlier about Randall. Maybe Ravelo was on the up and up about the land.

"First thing in the morning, we'll drive out to the property," Ravelo said. "You'll need to get a good night's rest."

"What about the threat of rebels in this area?" Mr. Wilkes asked.

"There are rebels hiding in the mountains, but they rarely bother me or anyone on my property. We have an understanding. I leave them alone, and they return the courtesy."

ɪristen knew exactly why the rebels left him alone. He'd noticed men taking the gun crates inside a large storage shed. Tristen assumed the smaller crates contained ammo.

After dinner, Ravelo escorted them to their rooms. "The bed linens are clean."

"Thank you for your hospitality. I'm so tired I could sleep on a bed of thorns," Cynthia said. "Goodnight."

Tristen knew exactly why she was tired. They had spent last night coiled together like two horny snakes. It had taken its toll on him as well.

He and Mr. Wilkes thanked their host.

Before going to bed, he walked to Cynthia's room and tapped on the door. "It's me."

"What do you want?" she asked as she opened the door.

"We need to talk." He informed her about the guns and ammo. "I think Ravelo is involved in more than raising sugarcane and tobacco. I'm not feeling good about any of this."

"If Ravelo wanted to get rid of us, he'd have thrown us overboard. No one would have ever found our bodies. I think at most he's detaining me for Randall. I have no idea what my stepbrother is up to."

"Well, goodnight," he said to her.

"Night."

Whatever magic they'd shared the previous night was gone. Maybe like him, she'd gotten caught up in the romantic atmosphere of Belem.

By noon on Thursday, Tristen felt more at ease than the previous day. As Ravelo had promised, his plantation and home surpassed their expectations. Even though things seemed legit, Tristen remained by Cynthia's side. He truly cared about her and doubted he'd stay angry for long. Today, she looked radiant in the sheer, floral dress. Good thing she wore a slip beneath it.

As they were walking out, Tristen grabbed his jacket and pouch.

Cynthia smiled. “I didn’t bring a purse, but since you did can you hang on to my passport?”

He frowned. “It’s not a purse.”

She examined it. “Hmm. It has a strap you drape over your shoulder, and it’s made of leather. Looks like a purse to me.”

He stuck her passport with his and snapped the pouch shut.

“It even snaps like a purse.”

“It’s a pouch. There’s a difference.”

She giggled. “If you say so.”

They rode with Ravelo to the hangar a few miles from the house. He opened the double doors and stepped inside. They entered behind him. A white and royal blue Cessna set in the center. “What do you think, Mr. Conners?”

Tristen walked around the plane and rubbed his hand over the skin of the plane, looking for any damage caused from impacts or cracks. He checked the flaps and ailerons to see if they were secure. He didn’t find any loose fasteners or bolts on the outer surface. Then he proceeded to examine the wings, wheel chock, elevators, and rudders.

He didn’t find any fuel or lubricant leaks around the engine. The plane had a full tank of gas. After checking the wheels, he checked the spinner for obstructions. “Your tires need replacing. They could probably land a few more time without it being a problem.”

“You may want to order new ones,” Cynthia said.

“I will soon.”

Tristen opened the door and closed it several times.

“What are you doing?” Ravelo asked.

Cynthia smiled. “He’s making sure the frame is in line.”

“Your frame is in good shape.” Tristen glanced inside the Cessna. “Where’d you get it?”

“Won it in a poker game. Start it up. The key should be in the ignition. I keep the battery charged. I had planned to teach myself to fly by watching Youtube videos.”

Cynthia laughed. “Not a good idea. I know a lot about aircraft, yet I wouldn’t attempt flying one without proper training.” She glanced back at Tristen. “Are the seats secured?”

Yep.” Tristen climbed in the pilot’s seat and adjusted the seat. He made sure the ignition switch was off before turning the master switch on to check the gauges. He listened to the equipment powering on. All the flight controls checked out. Finally, he pulled the choke out, then turned the key. The single engine turned over after several tries. After gunning the engine, he shut it down and climbed down. “It probably needs some basic maintenance, but for the most part, it’s in good shape.”

“It hasn’t been started in a very long time. I had the forest cut to make a runway. I even had lights installed so it could land at night.”

“Now all you need is a pilot.”

“And here you are. So let’s go.”

Tristen shook his head. “Not so fast. I’d need to go over it more thoroughly.”

“Thanks for looking at it.” Ravelo offered Tristen his hand and shook.

After they returned to the house, Mary had breakfast ready. Mr. Wilkes joined them.

Ravelo turned to Cynthia. “Before you woke this morning, I explained the easement to the property to Mr. Wilkes.”

“Easement?”

“You’ll have to cut across my land to reach yours.”

“What’s to keep you from going up on your price each year?”

“I’m a man of my word.”

“What if you die, who will uphold your agreement then? I’d feel better buying the easement outright.”

“Randall is correct. You are a piranha.”

“I can be. The easement is a deal breaker. Unless you will sell us that strip of land, I’m done here. We’re not buying land that depends on an easement to enter and leave.”

Ravelo’s concern showed. “Look at the land and see what you think. Then we’ll talk about the easement. I’m sure we can work it out.”

At the jeep, Mr. Wilkes sat behind the driver. That left two seats. Cynthia climbed in back with the accountant. "I'm not sure there's room for all of us."

Tristen frowned. "You're not going without me."

"Sit," the driver said to Tristen.

"Where is Ravelo?" she asked. Her uneasiness returned.

"How do you say, he has other business. Call me Marco. I drive you," he announced in broken English. Once they left the paved road, Marco grinned. "Hold tight."

No sooner than he'd said it, they hit a huge bump that jarred them from their seats. A small scream escaped from Cynthia as she bounced up. Mud spattered the sides of the vehicle.

They drove through fields of sugar cane and tobacco plants, then down a muddy path through dense jungle. How had Randall ever found this land?

Ahead in the road, a truck parked sideways blocking them. Men with automatic weapons stepped around the vehicle. They aimed their guns at them.

"Rebels." He stopped the jeep and argued with the men.

The man shouted at Marco as he glared at them taking each one of them into account. "Americanos?"

"Si. Amigos of Senor Ravelo."

The man in charge motioned for them to step out.

Chapter Fifteen

Tristen considered pulling the .22 from his boot, but after looking at the number of automatic weapons aimed at them, he decided against it.

As Marco reached for his gun, the headman fired a bullet through his head. The man slumped over the steering wheel.

Cynthia screamed.

Tristen flinched, and his heart went into overdrive.

Mr. Wilkes gasped in horror.

The scent of gun powder filled the air, and the piercing sound from it made his ears ring.

"Tristen, do something," she whispered.

"Not happening. I'm slightly outnumbered. Do what they say."

"Gringos, out!"

Tristen's stomach knotted. He had no choice but to step from the jeep with Mr.Wilkes crouching behind him. They found his pouch and leather jacket. The man smiled admiring the items and kept them. The pouch contained their passports and his phone.

Cynthia climbed out of the front seat. Their abductors eyed her with lustful glares. Finally, one reached out to touch her.

Tristen sidestepped over and blocked the man.

The crude man jammed the butt of his automatic rifle into Tristen's stomach.

He doubled over and gasped for breath waiting for the pain to ease. That's what he got for his heroic efforts.

When the same man touched her again, Cynthia slapped him.

Rather than punch her, he laughed and turned to the others boasting.

For several moments, Tristen couldn't breathe and remained hunched over.

Cynthia placed a hand on his shoulder. "You shouldn't have done that."

Tristen rose slowly and glared at the man who'd punched him. "You keep your damn hands off of my wife."

The man jabbed Tristen with a hard right to the jaw and knocked him over, then pulled Cynthia into his arms and pawed all over her. The others laughed and shouted egging him on.

Wilkes shook like a leaf and was no help whatsoever.

Then a man dressed in a camouflage uniform stepped forward and shouted at the others.

Still, the man continued to grope her.

The uniformed man jerked him back and spouted off what seemed to be a warning.

The man cowered and backed away.

She dashed into Tristen's arms. Her entire body trembled with fear. "I shouldn't have come here. I'm afraid we won't make it back, and I'll never see Gina."

"We'll be fine. I'm sure they plan to ransom us for U.S. currency," he whispered, wanting to calm her down.

"I wonder how long it'll take Ravelo to realize something's wrong. Maybe he'll come after us," she said softly. "Hopefully, he'll know how to deal with these animals."

"I'm counting on it."

"The man in the blue shirt was on the boat," Mr. Wilkes said. "I'm certain of it."

Immediately, the man yelled to silence them.

If the guy in the blue shirt had been on the boat perhaps that's how the rebels had known they were coming. Tristen scanned the men, trying to see if any looked familiar.

The men escorted them to the back of a truck and tossed them inside.

If Ravelo couldn't work out a deal with these land pirates, there'd be no telling how long it'd take to negotiate with Zurtel.

Tristen wondered if the company carried abduction insurance. If they didn't, he was screwed. No doubt Everett would pay any amount for Cynthia. Wilkes might be included as well, but buying Tristen's way out of this Godforsaken country might fall on his dad's shoulders. He'd hate to see him deplete his retirement funds to save his ass.

What would happen to Mallory? Would his in-laws take advantage of the situation and seek custody once they learned he was missing? Probably. Then he worried about Gina.

A guard toting an automatic machine gun sat in the back with them. After bouncing over clear-cut meadows and driving through shallow rivers, the truck started up an incline that grew steeper with each mile—the road no more than a wide path. To one side, a wall of trees and vines formed a natural fortress. Monkeys dangled from branches, and brightly colored birds fluttered between trees. As far as he could see, mountains and even thicker jungles lay before him.

The truck stopped where the road ended.

"Where are they taking us?" Cynthia asked.

The man didn't understand and nudged her forward.

"Looks like from here we're going on foot," Mr. Wilkes said.

Tristen glanced at Cynthia's delicate little sandals and knew they wouldn't last over the rough terrain. As they entered the jungle, he glanced back wanting to remember the landscape.

Thursday morning, Gina's second attempt to runaway had failed. Unfortunately, her uncle had caught her about to sneak out. Nor could she play the sick card any longer. The March morning turned out to be perfect for hiking.

Gina trekked behind her relatives. She didn't want to stand too close to any of them. Had her aunt asked Shellie to push her off the cliff? Or maybe, Will had changed his mind. The trail gradually grew steeper totally shaded by thick woods to the right of them. She swatted tree branches out of her face as she walked. The scent of honeysuckle filled the air.

They finally stopped for a break and sat on large rocks. Gina removed her water bottle and gulped down a fourth of it. For the first time, she had a chance to look at her surroundings. She found the Tennessee landscape breathtaking.

"This is more work than I remember," Aunt Nell said. She glanced back at Gina. "Why don't you take the lead?"

Gina shook her head. "I like walking in the back."

"I'd rather you stay closer to me. If you slipped, there'd be no one back there to grab you."

Uncle Sonny smiled. "She can walk with me."

She offered him a 'thank you' smile.

She doubted her uncle was aware of his wife's plan. Nor did she believe he'd go along with it.

The trail grew even steeper.

"My legs hurt," Shellie complained. "I want to go back."

"The trail loops around," Uncle Sonny said.

Despite the day being cool, sweat rolled down Gina's face. Hearing birds overhead, she glanced skyward. A hawk soared effortlessly. She smiled. When she looked back at the trail, she realized her aunt had moved behind her uncle. With the others in front, her aunt could push her over the side without them seeing her, then pretend it had been an accident.

Will would know the truth, but why would he say anything against his mom?

They stopped at an overlook with a wooden platform extending from the rock. It had massive wooden rails around it to prevent anyone from falling.

Her aunt walked out on it. "Come see this view."

Will, Shellie, and Uncle Sonny joined her.

"You coming, dear?" Aunt Nell asked. "You're missing out."

Gina studied the platform. There wouldn't be any way her aunt could push her off. She bravely walked out on the overlook and glanced at the land below.

"I want to go swimming when we get back," Will said. "I'm hot."

"Me too," Shellie echoed. "This is boring."

"Let's head out," Uncle Sonny said.

Gina didn't like the position she'd ended up in.

Aunt Nell walked behind her with Shellie in front of her. Uncle Sonny and Will had walked ahead of them.

Once again, the trail narrowed along a steep incline.

Rocks shuffled behind her.

Hands clamped down on her shoulders.

Gina's breath hitched.

Her aunt pushed her toward the edge.

Gina dug her heels into the dirt and tried to scream, but it came out as a squeal.

As her feet neared the edge, she grabbed a low hanging branch dangling over the trail and gripped it with all her strength hoping it wouldn't snap.

She broke free of Nell's grip, causing her aunt to fall back.

Aunt Nell's arms flailed about as if trying to fly. Her feet slid in the loose rock at the edge. She screamed as she went over the side.

Uncle Sonny and Will ran back and stood on the edge looking down.

"Mom!" Shellie screamed.

"Hang on!" Uncle Sonny shouted. "We'll get help!"

Gina's heart pounded harder than a bass drum. Finally, she forced herself to look over the side.

Aunt Nell had landed on a narrow rocky ledge protruding from the mountain. A scrawny tree growing from the rock had prevented her from falling to the bottom.

"Do something?" Shellie shouted, her voice reflecting her fear.

"I can't reach her," Uncle Sonny replied. He turned to Will. "Go for help. Find a ranger or anyone and tell them there's been an accident. Hurry."

Will left in a flash.

Her uncle leaned over the side. "Hang on, Nell."

Aunt Nell didn't respond.

Shellie's face tightened in anger. "It wasn't an accident. She pushed Mom over."

"I did not. She was trying to push me. I would have gone over if I hadn't grabbed the branch."

"You, liar," Shellie accused.

"You pushed her?" Uncle Sonny asked. "Why?"

"No, I didn't. I told you she pushed me. That's why I didn't want to hike today. I heard her ask Will if he'd do it, and he refused."

Her father turned and stared down at his wife. "I don't believe you. Nell wouldn't do something like that."

Gina had never been a mean person, but right now she was very disappointed Aunt Nell hadn't hit the bottom. She planned to tell anyone who'd listen about this. Even if it meant living in a foster home or orphanage, she wanted to get away from these people.

Shortly, Will returned with several rangers toting rescue equipment.

Her uncle and cousins stood at the edge of the rocky cliff watching the men repel down. Gina stood back waiting for them to bring Aunt Nell up.

Once the men had her up, one of them turned to them. "She's alive. We know her right femur is broken, and she has a nasty laceration to the head. We've already requested a chopper."

"She'll be airlifted to the nearest hospital," another ranger said.

"Can you tell us what happened?" a ranger asked.

Shellie pointed at her. "She pushed my mom."

The man focused on Gina.

"I didn't. She slipped when she tried to push me over."

The man's face grew concerned. "I need to call the sheriff on this."

"Good," Gina said. "I've been trying to tell everyone my aunt planned to kill me, but nobody will listen." She looked at Will. "He knows."

Will frowned. "I don't know what you're talking about."

Uncle Sonny wore a somber expression. "Gina, why in God's name would you do such a thing?"

The approaching helicopter drew everyone's attention.

An image of her being handcuffed and taken to jail formed in her mind.

Panic set in making Gina want to flee. While everyone focused on Aunt Nell, she shot off down the trail. By the time they reached the cabin, she'd be gone. She had no idea where she'd go or how she'd get there. She recalled the park had bears and glanced around her.

Gina found the cabin locked. She raised the front window and crawled through. In her room, she stuffed one change of clothes and filled the rest with food and water. The water made her backpack hard to carry. She ended up removing four of the bottles. She slipped the phone Liz had given her into her pocket. Once she had reception, she'd try to call Liz and Dan and explain what had happened. She also wondered if anyone had replied to the post about her birthmother.

As she left the cabin, she looked both ways before heading out. She expected them back any time. Rather than walk directly on the road, she skirted through the campgrounds and park section. Kids played and ran all around her. The smell of food cooking on grills made her stomach growl. She didn't have time to think about food.

Who would believe her over her aunt, uncle, and cousins? Anyone they asked would mention how much she hated them. Everyone would believe she was guilty.

Now, she'd be wanted by the police. She was on the run.

♦♦♦

Light seeped through the canopy as Tristen stepped over small boulders and shrubs. He tried to stay behind Cynthia. Her dress revealed way too much. He feared one of the men would eventually rape her. He wondered why in the hell she'd worn a dress.

After trudging a few miles through the jungle, Cynthia's sandal strap popped. Her shoe flopped up and down, slowing her down. One of the guards stopped to see what the holdup was. Their abductors discussed the situation. One man walked over with duct tape and wrapped it around her shoe and foot.

Tristen considered escaping now. His conscience wouldn't let him leave Cynthia, but then he thought of Mallory and Gina. He had two daughters who needed him.

Large raindrops pounded them. Soon the rain came down in solid sheets. It didn't take long for rivulets of mud to flow beneath them. When Cynthia slipped he managed to catch her. Then his feet slid out from under him. He grabbed a branch, only to have a thorn stick him. "Damn it."

The blanket of rain washed away the blood from his cut. When the rain stopped, the muggy humidity and heat returned.

He glanced at Cynthia. Her long wet hair hung in clumps. Her dress had ripped up the side and had tears from where it had caught on branches.

After several hours of walking, they stopped. The guards secured them to a large tree with prop roots that extended out across the ground. The bark scratched his hands. The fragrance of wildflowers choked him.

Tristen's parched throat ached as he watched their captors swig down water letting it run down their chins and necks.

Finally, one man stepped forward with a canteen. He held it to Cynthia's mouth first. After several swallows, he jerked it away and offered it to Mr. Wilkes. Finally, he put it to Tristen's mouth. He managed a couple of good gulps before the man pulled it away. Tristen's stomach growled loudly. Right when he thought he couldn't be more miserable, he felt something bite him, then a second one and yet a third one. He yipped in pain.

Cynthia and Mr. Wilkes cried out also.

"Son-of-a-bitch," Tristen shouted. "Ants!"

They squirmed trying to pull away from the tree they were tied to. Their captors laughed.

A woman stepped forward, dressed in the same green and brown camouflage uniform as the commander. She scolded the men, then released them from the tree. But it did little good since ants had crawled beneath their clothes.

Tristen couldn't hold back. He cried out and dropped to the ground and rolled around hoping to crush the vicious insects. Mr. Wilkes and Cynthia danced around.

The men laughed harder than they had at first. When the uniformed man came forward, they stopped laughing and helped Tristen up.

"Aguentar os a para rio," the commander ordered in Portuguese.

"Sim," the man helping him said as he nodded.

They escorted them to a nearby river. Tristen wasted little time jumping in to drown the ants still biting him. He glanced at Cynthia. She had to be in pain as well. Her black eyeliner had smeared from the rain. Her dress had ripped even more.

Again thoughts of escaping crossed his mind. If he could reach the plantation, he'd return with Ravelo.

These fools planned to cross the river. In the middle of it, white rapids ran over the boulders. Though relatively shallow, how would they cross without being swept away?

One of the men stepped into the water and lifted a rope from the white foam and motioned for the others to follow. Each soldier held to the rope as they worked their way through the powerful rapids.

Tristen studied the land around him, so if he escaped he could find his way back to the plantation.

A man helped him across with one hand on the rope and one on him. What would happen if they lost their grip? He'd be swept away. The thought held appeal. If his head didn't slam into a boulder, it could be an easy means of escape. He'd wait for a better opportunity.

Once his feet reached the far side of the river, he sighed with relief. He looked back in time to see Cynthia stepping from the river while men still escorted Mr. Wilkes across. At least the water had eased the pain from the ant bites. The wound from where the thorn pricked him hurt like hell.

Despite the sun sinking beneath the horizon, they still trudged up the side of the mountain. A huge waterfall cascaded down from three different levels of rock. When the sun disappeared, they trekked in the dark, using flashlights to light the path. After what seemed an eternity, Tristen heard dogs barking, and a flickering campfire came into view.

Once the dogs stopped barking, children's voices could be heard laughing as they played. Tristen caught a whiff of marijuana mingled in with the scent of cooked beef. More than likely, everyone in this village was higher than kites.

A huge bonfire roared in the center. Among the several crudely constructed buildings stood fifteen to twenty military tents. Every muscle in Tristen's body ached, and his head throbbed. All he could think of was lying down and sleeping.

"How are you holding up?" he asked Cynthia.

"I'm not. My feet are raw from these sandals. I'm about to collapse."

"Ravelo will come after us tomorrow." Tristen hoped Ravelo would be able to work a deal with the rebels. Maybe swap those rifles and ammo for them.

Ahead, stood what looked like a dog kennel. The cages had plywood on top to block the rain. He figured they weren't intended for the dogs. He hoped they'd keep them together?

The men shoved Mr. Wilkes into the end cage. They placed Tristen and Cynthia together in the cage on the far end from the accountant. Apparently, the men believed they were married.

The straw did little good to prevent the mud from oozing up from the ground. Tristen motioned for Cynthia to join him.

"This smells awful," she said. "It's wet."

"Lay on top of me. At least you'll stay dry."

"What about you?"

"I'll manage."

He pushed some straw behind his head, then opened his arms to her. "Let's see if this works."

She lay on her stomach on top of him with her face resting against his shoulder. "This isn't fair."

"If you want it to be fair, tomorrow I'll sleep on top of you."

"That's not what I was referring to. Randall should be here instead of us. I hate I let him talk me into doing this. I was so close to finding Gina, and now I'm not sure I'll ever see her."

Tristen patted her back gently. "If Ravelo doesn't show tomorrow, I'm going to escape and try to make it back to the plantation."

"Take me with you?"

"There's no way you can make it in those shoes. I can travel faster without you."

"You're right. You'll come back for me?"

"Seriously, Cynthia, you really have to ask?"

"No, I know you will. I'm just tired and scared, and I'm so mad at Randall."

"Keep that attitude. It'll help you survive."

Wet mud dampened the back of his shirt, but still he was too exhausted to care. He rubbed his hands over her back trying to assure her they'd be all right.

"Thank you, Tristen," she said as her voice faded off, her breathing heavy and labored.

Sleep didn't come as quickly for Tristen as it had for Cynthia. Instead of sleeping, he listened to the men obviously getting drunk and stoned as they talked around the campfire. In the distance, a jaguar screamed.

Though the cage had a padlock on the door, the chicken wire could probably be ripped away from one of the panels. And this would be the time to disappear, when everyone was kicked back having a good time. But in the darkness, he'd never make it.

Surprisingly, they'd never searched them for weapons. His .22 was still in his boot. After being drenched in the river, he wasn't sure it'd work.

The following morning, Cynthia sat to the side slapping at mosquitoes. Her hair appeared tangled and wild. Mud covered her shredded dress. She had huge whelps on her arms and back.

He sat up. "I see I wasn't dreaming. We're still here."

"That we are, and there's still no sign of Ravelo."

The soldier who'd taken his jacket and bag brought three bowls of mush.

Tristen wasn't sure what it was—watered down rice or grits. It'd be the first nourishment since Mary's homemade cinnamon rolls the previous morning.

Cynthia stared at the mush.

Another man poured water into a large bucket as though watering animals. The water immediately clouded up from the dirt on the bottom.

"What is this?" she asked Tristen.

"Food. Eat it."

"But mine has worms in it."

He glanced at her bowl. "Maggots."

She set it down. "I can't eat it."

"Trade with me. Mine looks fine."

"You've already sacrificed your comfort last night for mine. If you escape, you'll need energy."

"You also need to keep up your strength." He grinned. "Maggots are protein."

"You're not kidding are you?"

"Nope. Pass it over."

They traded bowls.

♦♦♦

Tristen had eaten worse. All he cared about was keeping up his strength.

Cynthia grimaced as he ate the mush never giving the wriggling worms a second thought. "Remind me to never kiss you again."

She stared at the white mixture of meal and water, then finally ate it.

Tristen dipped his empty bowl into the water bucket, waited a few minutes for the dirt to settle, then drank it. He turned to her. "Drink. You don't want to become dehydrated."

"It's dirty."

"The dirt will settle to the bottom."

"I can't take much more of this," Mr. Wilkes shouted from his cage.

Tristen tried pushing on the wire, but it didn't stretch as he'd hoped. He searched for another way out.

"There's no way out. We're gonna die," Mr. Wilkes whined.

"When they're not watching us, start digging under the backside of your cage," he said to her. "Cover it with straw when they come over."

"What about the dogs?" Cynthia asked.

"I'll take care of them."

"They're mixed pit bulls," she said. "Good luck with that."

"Last night when the men settled down to share a few joints, the dogs did too."

"I need a pair of shoes," Cynthia whispered to Tristen.

"That's a problem."

As the sun blared down on the clearing, the heat inside the small cage became unbearable. Sweat ran down Cynthia's back. She peeled out of what was left of her dress, leaving her in a slip.

Despite the dirt, she found herself scooping water from the bucket and drinking it.

They were taken for bathroom breaks. She had sweated so much she rarely had to go, but she went anyway just for a chance to leave the cage and stretch her legs.

Instead of dwelling on how miserable she was, she thought about Gina. When they didn't call or show up, Gina would think she had been discarded again. She'd be too young to understand. As for Mallory, she'd end up with Rose.

Zurtel didn't seem important. She had something to live for—Gina. Hopefully, it'd be enough to help her survive.

She swatted flies from the cage. "Ravelo didn't come today. You've got to escape and find help."

"In the early morning before anyone wakes up, I'll try to leave. That way I'll have enough light to see where I'm going. Might not be as many predators about."

"The only animals you need to worry about are the ones holding guns."

As the sun began to set, women cooked over open fires. The smell of well-cooked meat and spicy sauces made her mouth water.

People sat around the larger fire, enjoying the feast. Cynthia finally realized they didn't plan to feed them again until morning. More than likely, it'd be another bowl of mush.

A few feet away from them, a dog gnawed on a bone. If she could find away to drag it into the cage, she'd eat it. Right now even roasted iguana sounded wonderful.

This was hell.

Again that night, she slept partially on top of Tristen.

In the early morning hours, he woke her. "I'm going to crawl under the wire. I dug out a section under it." He pulled back all the hay, stretched out on his belly, and began trying to climb under it. His shirt caught and ripped. Soon, he stopped unable to go farther. "This isn't working. I'm too large to go through."

"I might fit," she suggested.

"How far would you get without shoes?"

"Not far."

"So much for escaping," he mumbled.

The next morning, she passed her bowl of mush to him. "Take it. You can have mine."

"No, eat."

"I want you to eat mine too," she replied. "And when there's a chance to escape I want you to leave without me. I don't want you stopping until you make it home. Don't come back for me. You have to make it back for Mallory and Gina."

"Do you know what they'll do to you?"

"If they're determined to rape me, you won't be able to stop them. It was honorable of you to tell them I'm your wife, but I doubt they care. I'll help you dig. Leave me your shirt when you go. Wearing this slip is asking for trouble, and I'm cold at night.

She didn't tell him she planned to escape right behind him and use his shirt to hopefully plant his scent in the opposite direction. It might buy him some time. The dogs would find her instead.

They'd tear her to shreds, but it beat being raped by every son-of-a-bitch in the camp. One thing she knew, Tristen would find Gina and raise her with Mallory.

♦♦♦

Everett Reynolds paced back and forth in his office. When his stepson entered, he stopped and faced him. "Any word?"

Randall sighed. "Ravelo has men searching for them." He lowered his head. "This is my fault. She wouldn't be there if not for me."

"Don't blame yourself. What about Evan and Annie?"

"I saw no reason for them to stay. Mark took a commercial flight down to fly them back."

"I just want to know why her bodyguard never showed up."

Terry removed his headphones. "He's not to blame."

"How come?" Everett asked.

"He was involved in a serious wreck. He's okay now, but he wasn't in any condition to notify anyone," Terry said.

"Well, I'm sorry to hear that. I'm glad he's okay." He looked back at Randall. "Do we have insurance for this?"

"We did. But when we were looking for ways to cut back, I dropped it. Hell, we rarely traveled anywhere dangerous." Randall sat on the edge of Everett's desk. "I have a friend who's had some experience at this. He said we'll probably receive a ransom demand in the next few days."

"I want experts brought in. And I'll pay any amount to get Cynthia back alive."

"My friend said they'll take a lot less then they demand. You'd be a fool to pay what they ask without bargaining. They expect you to bargain."

"There will be no negotiating with her life. I will pay what they demand so long as she's returned alive and unharmed. Am I clear?"

"Yes. We'll get her back, Dad. What about Mr. Wilkes and Tristen Conners?"

"Negotiate a deal for them. No more than five hundred thousand each." He paused for a moment. "But before I send a dime, I want proof of life."

♦♦♦

When they were pulled from the wire cages, Tristen had a difficult time standing up. After he steadied himself, he took Cynthia's hand in his. They were forced to sit in three side by side chairs. They shoved a newspaper showing the date in his hands. A girl snapped pictures of them.

Tristen assumed Everett had been contacted, and this was a proof of life picture. One good thing, the picture included the three of them not just Cynthia. Someone was willing to put up money for him as well. They were returned to the cages. With this new development, he'd put his plan to escape on hold.

That afternoon the dogs woke suddenly and barked as a large group of armed men hiked into the center of the camp. Ravelo led them.

"Cynthia, it's Ravelo! He's here!" Tristen said, waking her.

She sat up and brushed the straw from her matted hair. "My prayers have been answered. I want to get out of this country as fast as we can. I'm never returning."

Ravelo and the commander glanced their way and talked.

Relief ran through Tristen when the men shook hands. But then, Ravelo offered the man a cigar. They lit up, turned, and walked away.

Chapter Sixteen

The men sat under the enormous trees and talked. Cigar smoke drifted above their heads.

Finally, Ravelo and the commander stood and walked toward them.

As they approached, Tristen rose to his knees and leaned back on his haunches, eager to be freed. Cynthia had already moved to the gate.

"Mr. Ravelo, we knew you'd come," she said, her voice full of relief.

The two men laughed as though a joke had passed between them.

Cynthia's smile faded.

Ravelo grinned. "Bet you'd be willing to fuck me now for a slice of bread."

"You bastard. You planned this," she screamed.

"You are worth more than the land deal with Randall. I couldn't resist." He glowered at her. "Your father is willing to meet our price of ten million dollars." He glanced over at Tristen, then Mr. Wilkes. "But I'm afraid you two aren't as lucky. Senor Randall said he will only pay for his sister."

"Then what do you plan to do to us?" Wilkes asked.

"You're a liability. We have no choice but to kill you."

"Please, don't kill them!" Cynthia pleaded. "I'll pay their ransom."

Tristen hated seeing a successful, savvy businesswoman like Cynthia Reynolds reduced to begging these shitheads for mercy.

"How do you plan to pay me when you're a hostage too?"

"Release me. I promise I'll send the money back."

"Sorry, love. I have my orders to kill them. They're excess baggage."

Tristen's throat tightened. He needed to give them a reason to keep him alive in this tropic hellhole. "You said you need a pilot. I'll work for you."

Ravelo contemplated a moment. "What about your daughter in the states?"

"Her grandparents will raise her. She'll probably be better off without me."

"This deal is just for you, correct?"

"That's right."

Hate radiated from Cynthia's eyes. "You're cutting a deal for yourself?"

"You catch on fast. Sorry, but my plans don't include you. You've been a real bitch since I started working for you," he said trying to come across as believable.

"But at the hotel, you seemed to be in love," Ravelo reminded.

"That was just about getting laid." He grinned slyly. "And it worked." He had to convince his captors that he didn't give a damn about her. It was the only way to save them both.

"I hate you." Cynthia glared at him.

"This is my only chance. You don't need to worry. There's ten million dollars coming on your behalf. I don't see your rich daddy sending anything for me."

As far as Mr. Wilkes, there was nothing Tristen could do to save him.

The two men conversed in Portuguese obviously about Tristen's offer. Ravelo turned back to him. "I do need a pilot, but my friend asked what's to keep you from flying away with my plane."

"Like you, I'm a man of my word."

They laughed.

Ravelo tossed his half-smoked cigar in the dirt and ground it with his boot. "I came up with another solution."

"I'm listening?"

"The first time you decide to make a run for it, I'll order a hit on your daughter and her grandparents."

Tristen nodded. "Deal, but I still expect to be paid a salary. If a time comes when you trust me, I'd like to kidnap my daughter and bring her to Brazil," he lied.

Ravelo grinned and nodded. "I'm starting to like you. As a Christmas bonus, I'll put a hit on the grandparents. Your daughter could even grow up and marry one of my sons."

Not happening in this life time.

"My wife will cash in our investments," Mr. Wilkes pleaded.

Ravelo laughed. "My source informed me your wife has been screwin' around on you for years. She wishes you'd die. This is her lucky day." He glanced at the men aiming AK-47s at them. "Mator o contactor," he ordered. The men fired.

Bullets penetrated Wilkes's body, causing it to convulse in jerky motions. The accountant dropped to the ground.

Cynthia turned to Ravelo. "Rot in hell, you bastard!"

"He wasn't needed. You, my dear, are money in the bank."

How had Ravelo known about Wilkes's wife being unfaithful? How much does he know about me? And who the hell is he working for?

Tristen's heart moved into his throat, waiting for Ravelo's order to kill him. Sweat beaded on his forehead.

"Let's move," Ravelo commanded.

"You're taking me with you?" Tristen asked.

"If I wasn't you'd already be dead."

The men started to haul Wilkes away.

"Wait," Tristen insisted. "She needs his boots if we're traveling very far. Her sandals will only slow you down."

"It's not like he needs them. Make it quick," Ravelo said.

Though the boots would be slightly big on her, they'd be better than her flimsy sandals. If a chance for them to escape presented itself, she'd need good shoes for trekking through the rainforest.

Tristen removed Wilkes's boots and socks. The old man's feet were still warm. He offered them to Cynthia. "Put these on."

She jerked them from his hands. "You could have saved him, but instead, you made the deal for yourself."

"Too bad big daddy didn't include Mr. Wilkes and me in that deal." He turned to Ravelo. "Mind if I get my jacket and pouch back?" He didn't mention he had both their passports in the bag.

"For a man who barely escaped death, you are pushy. Where is this jacket and pouch?"

He pointed to the man who took it, and Ravelo ordered to see the pouch. After removing the phone and their passports, he handed it to Tristen. Without their passports, it'd be difficult to leave Brazil.

"Thank you." Tristen didn't dare look at Cynthia for fear his eyes would reflect how much he cared for her.

"Where are you taking us?" Cynthia asked.

"To the home of my boss. He arrives today."

"You're not the boss?" Tristen wondered who the puppet master actually was.

"No, I'm what you call the middle man. Even the deal between us will need his approval."

"We leave for our main camp, Lair do Leao A Parte, soon."

Tristen didn't plan to wait around for the head honcho if a chance to escape arose. Then he remembered the threat made. Until he could find a way to contact Sarah and Rose and tell them to leave town with Mallory, he was stuck.

"I can see there is no love lost between you two." Ravelo chuckled.

As they walked away, Cynthia glanced back at the dead man, her eyes beaming with tears.

Fear not remorse controlled Tristen's emotions. These men wouldn't hesitate to execute Cynthia or him if things went south. His top priority was getting them both out of there and making it back to Mallory and Gina.

Thank God, Ravelo needs a pilot.

If he hadn't struck a deal with the devil, he'd be laying sprawled out with a bullet in his head like Mr. Wilkes.

He hated he didn't feel more. Should he? He hadn't really known the man.

Crude slurs and comments sputtered from the men's mouths as Cynthia walked by. She wore only her slip and under garments. She ripped her dress to pieces and stuffed some of it in Mr. Wilkes's boots to make them fit better. But now her apparel left nothing to the imagination.

"Want my jacket?"

She refused to take it or even look at him.

Large trucks and cars zipped by Gina as she walked down the busy highway. They passed so quickly she doubted they had time to see her. The fumes and heat from the trucks nauseated her. Her stomach ached for something to eat, but there'd be no stopping on the highway. She'd wait for somewhere safer.

The sun blared down on her. Her legs ached and cramped from being on her feet too long.

Finally, she came to a rest area. Picnic tables dotted the outer lawn. She walked faster almost running. She slowed down afraid running might draw attention to her.

At the rest area, Gina chose a table under a shady tree. She sat, opened her backpack, and pulled out a bottle of water. She guzzled it down. Before leaving, she'd refill it with water. Then she ate a banana and a snack cake.

She pulled out the phone.

Please let it work.

She called Liz. Relief ran through her when it rang.

Please pick up.

"Hello," Liz said.

"Liz, it's Gina."

"Oh, honey, we've been trying to reach you."

"This phone doesn't work in the park."

"Where are you?"

“I’m at a rest area somewhere in Tennessee.” Gina didn’t want to say anything yet. She’d let Liz believe she was with her aunt and uncle. Right now, she didn’t trust any adults.

“I have good news. Dan and I wanted to tell you together, but he’s not here. I don’t want to wait.”

“You found my mom!”

“Yes, she and your father contacted us.”

“They’re married?”

“No. I believe Dan said he works for her.”

“What’s her name?”

“Cynthia Reynolds. She owns Zurtel Corporation. She’s already been trying to find you. She told Dan she had been forced to give you up.”

Joy exploded through Gina. Despite her situation, she couldn’t stop smiling. “Where does she live?”

“Atlanta, Georgia. Dan told them you wouldn’t be back until today. They should be calling us back soon.”

Gina couldn’t bring herself to tell Liz she was wanted by the police. “Do you have her phone number?”

“No. Dan does.”

“I’ll call back when I can. Thanks, Liz.” She disconnected the call.

Seeing a police car pull into the parking lot, Gina moved behind a tree. Once it left, she made her way to the restroom. She splashed water on her face and body, filled her drink bottle, and headed out. Destination—Atlanta.

Humiliation and embarrassment consumed Cynthia as she paraded before these men in only her slip and undergarments. After the first hour of walking, she concluded they had orders not to touch her.

Tristen actually had a gun. But with men toting M-16s and other automatic weapons, pulling the small gun would be suicide. He was no match for the opposition. Then she remembered his deal with Ravelo, the deal that saved him and not Wilkes.

At the far edge of the forest, four jeeps were lined up along the dirt road.

One of the guards shouted at them. Though they couldn't understand him, it was clearly an order to head for the vehicles.

While she was hoisted into the first one, Tristen had been shoved into the one behind her.

Though she despised him, she didn't want to be separated from him.

When Ravelo climbed in the jeep beside the driver, he signaled the man to leave. As the jeep jerked into gear, she gripped the armrest.

Hopefully, the boss would agree for Tristen to be Ravelo's pilot. She couldn't believe they had asked for such a large ransom. It meant they had done their homework. Nor could she believe her father had refused to pay anything for Wilkes or Tristen.

The jeep spiraled around a mountain, crashing through streams and dense vegetation that had overtaken the dirt road. At the base of the mountain, a fortress stood in a clearing. At the entrance, cement lions painted in gold stood on each side. Stones formed the outer wall of the house while red terracotta tiles adorned the roof. An outer wall made of the same stone enclosed the estate in a secure cocoon.

"Where are we?" she asked when they stopped.

"Lair do Leao A Parte. It means the Lion's Lair," Ravelo stated.

"Who lives here?" she continued to pry.

"It's more of a vacation home. The boss uses it to escape when he feels overly pressured."

When the other jeep pulled in behind them, she sighed with relief to see Tristen unharmed. She'd had time to consider his deal with Ravelo. Tristen was alive due to his wit. If he hadn't made the deal, he would have been shot and buried in a shallow grave with Mr. Wilkes in this hellacious country of endless jungle. Nothing could have saved the accountant.

Obviously, Ravelo had taken Tristen's offer seriously. She'd play her role as the jilted bitch.

"I assume the boss is scheduled to arrive," Cynthia said.

"Si, very soon now."

When the men from the second jeep joined them, Ravelo started toward the front door. A man and girl approached him, and he paused.

The man spoke in Portuguese and was probably a local farmer. He motioned with his hand toward a very young girl. The girl was probably about the same age as Gina. Her dark hair had been washed and braided. She wore a simple but provocative dress for such a young age. Her bare shoulders showed and the front revealed her small amount of cleavage.

It was clear the man wanted money.

The girl was being sold to Ravelo. Why? They had women at the camp. Once the man received his money, he left. One of the guards escorted the young girl into the house. Cynthia cringed when she realized the child's fate. Some pervert planned to molest her.

She glanced at Tristen. Anger brewed in his eyes. No doubt he'd come to the same conclusion.

Inside, they were taken to the kitchen where a fat jolly woman who they called Bonita offered them each a plate of food. Neither wasted any time choking down the pork dish—a casserole of sorts with rice and vegetables.

Cynthia considered licking the plate. Tristen grabbed a roll from the basket, tore off a piece, and rubbed it over his plate. She did the same.

She didn't want to think about what would happen if 'the boss' wouldn't allow Tristen to work for Ravelo. Would they kill him immediately like they had Mr. Wilkes?

Probably.

When Bonita turned away, Tristen stuffed a couple of rolls in his pocket. Smart move. She did the same since she wasn't sure when they'd eat again.

She couldn't quite read Tristen expression, but his eyes expressed endearment. God, she didn't deserve it.

"I won't leave without you," he whispered.

"Why chance it," she whispered glancing back to see if anyone was listening. Bonita stood at the sink, and a man guarded the back door. “Once I’m released, I’ll pay a hefty ransom to get you back. I’ll make it large enough they can’t refuse it.”

“Do you really think they plan to let you walk out of here?”

“You don’t?”

“No, I don’t. They’ll have their money. What guarantee is there they’ll fulfill their end of the bargain?”

“What do you have in mind?”

“Somehow, we have to make it back to the hangar at Ravelo’s plantation.”

When Bonita returned to the table, they stopped talking. She wasn’t sure if this woman understood English.

Once Bonita removed their plates, the guard motioned them toward the rear door. They went without a word. The tropical sun funneled down through the canopy. The humidity in the air made breathing difficult.

♦♦♦

Tristen didn’t share Cynthia’s faith in their abductors. Of course, no one had put up ten million for him. If this mystery man didn’t like the idea of him working for Ravelo, he’d get a bullet in the forehead. But then a horrible thought crossed his mind. What if they let him live and murdered Cynthia after getting the ransom money?

No, he wouldn’t go there. Surely, there’d be an opportunity to escape before the ransom money arrived. Security had slacked off since arriving at Lair do Leao A Parte. Why should they worry with a garrison of armed men guarding the joint?

He had made a point of studying each position where a guard was posted. Did the guards take breaks? Would someone be there during the night?

Behind the house, steps led down to a basement. The guard unlocked the door and shoved them through it. Another man entered behind them. They couldn’t understand what the men said, but Cynthia’s breath hitched at the mention of a man’s name.

“Are you okay?”

She shook her head.

"You look like you've seen a ghost."

"I have."

The men warned them to be quiet.

He tried to think of the name he'd heard the men say. They'd said it so fast, he couldn't remember. Apparently, Cynthia recognized it.

It required several minutes for Tristen's eyes to adjust to the dimly lit room. Chains and cuffs dangled at different positions from the stone wall. On a table lay several whips. This was some kind of torture chamber. What did they have in store for them?

He thought about pulling his pistol and firing on the two soldiers. But then what? It was daytime, and the noise would bring every rebel down on them like a swarm of killer bees. He could only hope another chance presented itself.

They shoved Cynthia down and yanked her hands above her head, securing her wrist in the cuffs. They placed him beside her and cuffed him as well. The men left locking the door behind them. Faded bloodstains covered the floor where they sat. He didn't have a clue how to get out of this.

"I think I know what this is about. And Randall will be walking into a trap."

"What kind of trap?"

"The guard mentioned Quinn Adams."

"Who's that?"

"The owner of Novik, the company that wanted the merger. That means this is about something bigger than the ten million."

"MX7?"

"Right. I think they'll threaten to kill Randall if I don't give them the formula."

"So what will your decision be?"

"How can I refuse when he's risking his life coming after me?"

"That's called stuck between a rock and a hard place. You'll have to hand over the formula."

"Like you said, if I give it to them, I doubt they'll let any of us live. Tristen, I'm scared."

"Me too," he admitted.

"At least we're still together. Why would they feed us if they planned on killing us?"

"Ever hear of the last supper? So how'd they know about Wilkes's wife being unfaithful?" he asked.

"There's a spy at Zurtel selling information."

He studied the small room. He hated the dim lights. The scent of flesh and blood made his skin crawl. "This Quinn Adams has to be a sadistic son-of-a-bitch."

During a silent moment, Tristen thought of Mallory. Had they told her yet? His mother-in-law would rejoice over his death. She'd finally have Mallory.

"Tristen, I'm sorry I doubted you. I realize you had no choice but to make a deal with him. There's no way you could have saved Wilkes."

He smiled. "Those things I said about you weren't true."

"I know."

♦♦♦

Cynthia awoke suddenly. She wondered how long she'd been asleep. When she started to speak to Tristen, she heard him breathing heavily. She wanted to wake him but didn't.

It started softly. No more than a soft whimpering. A child. It had to be the little girl who'd been sold to Ravelo.

Empathy for this child caused tears to fill Cynthia's eyes. When the girl screamed out, Cynthia gasped.

"What's wrong?" Tristen asked as he came out of his sleep.

"I'm assuming it's the child we saw. Men like that should be castrated. If I get my hands on Ravelo, I'll kill him," she added.

"I doubt it's him. He likes women not kids."

"So it's Quinn Adams. I could kill him and never lose a minute of sleep."

Finally, the screaming stopped.

When Ravelo entered, Cynthia frowned. "Who's the sick bastard abusing the child?"

"My boss."

"Quinn Adams," she said.

"Oh, so I see you learned his name. This is not something he does often. Only when the predator in him surfaces does he seek out innocent prey."

Cynthia's temper raged.

"Will we meet 'the boss' any time soon?" Tristen asked.

"I'm afraid the boss is undecided about you, Mr. Conners."

"So when will you know something?" Tristen asked.

Ravelo shrugged. "Right now your chances aren't looking so good. He doesn't think you can be trusted."

Cynthia didn't want to sit back and see Tristen murdered like Mr. Wilkes. Maybe if she could meet 'the boss' she could reason with him and convince him to let her buy Tristen's freedom. And she knew exactly what it would cost her to save him—MX7.

She figured Quinn Adams would take it. If he was any kind of businessman, he'd jump at her offer.

A guard entered and freed them. He motioned at the table.

Bonita entered carrying a large tray covered with a cloth. "Venha comer."

Using her hands, Cynthia brushed her hair from her face. Once she sat at the table, the woman placed a plate of bacon, eggs, potatoes, and biscuits before her. "Thank you."

"Since this could be my last meal, I've lost my appetite." Tristen stared at the plate.

Bonita poured two glasses of juice.

"I hope we make it back. Someone has to stop Adams."

"Out here, he's above the law."

Bonita stared at them.

Cynthia wondered if the woman hid the fact she could speak English.

"Do you speak English?"

The woman looked frightened and motioned so-so with her hands. "Little."

"What will happen to the girl?"

"There have been many girls. I send to Sister Anna. She heals them." Bonita spoke better English than she let on.

"Does Adams know?"

She shook her head.

"But if he found out?" Cynthia asked.

The lady moved her index finger across her neck and made a sound as though her throat was being slit.

Cynthia's eyes widened.

"How do you say, Senor Adams is a…" Bonita searched for the correct English word. "Monster."

"Well said," Cynthia said.

Tristen stared up at the woman. "If you help us escape, we'll see that he's arrested for what he does."

"And I will donate money to the church to care for the girls he's used in the past," she added.

Fright showed on the woman face as she looked toward the door to see if the guard had heard anything. She didn't give them an answer. Instead, she gathered her things and left.

Cynthia sighed. "She's too terrified to help us."

She hated giving up MX7. It had the potential to make billions. She should be able to use it to bargain for Tristen and Randall. But if she could only save one, she'd choose Tristen, the father of her child.

♦♦♦

Late Sunday night, Gina stared out the window of the semi-truck. The man who'd given her a ride from a truck stop had purchased her a burger and fries. She wadded up the paper. "Do you have a trash can?"

"Just toss it in back."

She did and wiped her hands on her jeans. "Thanks for letting me ride with you."

"You're mighty welcome. I couldn't leave a little one like you walking alone. Just where are you going?"

"Atlanta."

"What's in Atlanta?"

"My birthmother." She spent the next hour telling him her story. "So you see, I should have told you I'm on the run."

He grinned. "Well, Chattanooga is as far as I'm going. You got plans once we're there."

She shrugged. "Buy a bus ticket. Do you think you can drop me off at a bus terminal?"

"I reckon I can. I'd much rather see you on a bus than hitchhiking. Does your mom know you're coming?"

"No, I'm going to surprise her. Don't worry. She's been looking for me." At some point, she dozed off.

When the truck driver woke her up, she sat up and glanced around her. "Is this Chattanooga?"

"Yes ma'am. You got the money for a ticket?"

"I'll manage." She grabbed her backpack. "Thanks for the ride."

"Wait up, apple dumpling." He held something out for her. "Take my card. You get in trouble, you call me."

"Thanks."

Once she closed the door, he drove off.

She stood outside the bus terminal in the dark. The building had lights on, so she opened the door and hurried inside. She stared at the counter. Would they sell her a ticket without a parent?

Seeing an ATM machine, she decided it was time to try the card. After removing it from her shoe, she slid it in the machine and followed the instructions. Gina shoved the money into her backpack before replacing the card in her shoe.

Sweet. That was easy.

Now, she had to figure out how to buy a ticket.

Chapter Seventeen

Cynthia didn't think she could take much more of this.

Ravelo chuckled as he walked to the door. He paused and glanced at Tristen. "I might as well tell you now. He has rejected your offer. Looks like you won't be a part of our little family."

Fear shined in Tristen's eyes.

Ravelo turned to her. "Your brother, Randall has arrived with the money. He didn't want anything going wrong, and he came very well armed with some impressive looking men. He didn't trust us. Imagine that."

While Ravelo was distracted by a guard, she looked at Tristen. "Don't worry. I'll be back with enough money to buy your way out of this."

"Don't plan too far ahead, Cynthia. You're not out of this yet."

She wondered what would keep them from holding them all hostage, Randall included. Though, she truly despised her stepbrother, she owed him a lot for coming after her. This proved he didn't know her father's will had been changed.

"When can I leave?" she asked.

"That's being decided."

"I have more to offer than the ten million, but it includes both of us walking out of here alive." She turned to Tristen. "I got you into this mess, I'll get you out."

"You won't hear me objecting," Tristen said. "Rotting in a shallow grave doesn't appeal to me."

Ravelo chuckled and left.

Hours passed without food, water, or knowing whether Randall had arranged for their release.

"What's taking so long?"

The door opened and Ravelo stepped into the room. A guard followed. "Your brother is waiting outside."

"Thank you, Jesus," she said. "Tristen too?"

"Yes, he is coming."

As she left the basement, Cynthia straightened the mud stained slip and tried to groom her hair with her hands. She looked and smelled terrible, but she didn't care. It took a moment for her eyes to adjust to the brightness.

Men with guns encircled the area.

She scanned the courtyard looking for Randall.

He stood in the center. Douglas and Randall's bodyguard along with two more men with guns flanked him.

"Randall!" She ran toward him. "Thank God you're here."

"You look like hell," Randall said. "Have they harmed you?"

"No, they haven't. They murdered Wilkes. Quinn Adams is behind this. I'm surprised he didn't demand the formula."

"So you know about Quinn Adams?"

"I heard his name mentioned. I was afraid you were walking into a trap. I figured he intended to abduct you when you came to look at the land, then hold you hostage until I gave him the MX7 formula." She noticed two large black rectangular bags and assumed they were empty. "They have the money so let's go."

"No, I still have it." He opened both cases. "Ten million—five in each bag."

Cynthia gasped. "Give it to Adams and let's get the hell out of here."

"Like you said, Adams is more interested in the formula."

"I won't give it to him until we're all out of here and safe."

One of Randall's bodyguards cleared his throat several times. A sinking feeling eased into her stomach. He'd been the man who'd tried to murder her.

A soldier walked up behind Randall. "Mr. Adams. The girl has been taken care of."

Cynthia's head swam with total confusion. She glanced around to see if the man had been speaking to anyone besides

Randall. The light flashed on in her brain, bringing with it a sickening sensation. "You're Adams?"

Randall, Ravelo, and all the men laughed.

As she recognized their predicament, her stomach knotted.

Tristen's expression showed sheer disbelief followed by disappointment. Obviously, he also sensed their pending doom.

Randall grinned. "At home I'm your loving brother, but here I'm Quinn Adams, a man who is feared by many. I have formed a new identity using the name."

"No wonder I couldn't find anything on Adams."

"You've been the only thing standing in my way from building my own empire. How convenient your father made it. If you die, everything goes to me."

Cynthia realized he'd known about the will the entire time. "Who tipped you off about his will?"

"Your dad's secretary has been quite informative."

Cynthia knew if she made if back the secretary would be fired.

"I thought I had this all worked out. Everett would think the rebels killed you and kept the money. He'd never suspect I arranged it and kept the ten million and the million sent for Wilkes and Conners. Your dad would be so devastated he'd die of a massive heart attack. I'd own Zurtel and have MX7 as a bonus. Perfect plan. Until…"

Cynthia held her breath. Surely, he didn't know.

"I discovered I'm an uncle. I believe her name is Gina. Douglas informed me you were preparing for a young girl to come live with you. When I mentioned it to Ellis, he assumed you'd told me about her and congratulated me on being an uncle. I didn't believe it until I had your computer and phones hacked. She's young and innocent. Just the way I like them."

Her instinct as a mother to protect her child replaced her fear. Fire shot through her veins. "You stay away from Gina, or I will kill you."

Randall and the others laughed.

She glowered at Douglas. "You're a part of this."

He nodded with a sly grin.

She turned to Randall's bodyguard, the man with the sinus condition. He had been the one behind the thefts and burglaries. "It was you in my house that night."

"One more minute, and you would have died."

"They all work for me," Randall said.

Cynthia didn't see Terry. Was he with her father? "You're one sick son-of-a-bitch, and I mean that literally. Your mom was a bitch."

He slapped her hard.

Tristen jumped forward, but Douglas pointed his gun at him.

She held her cheek. "If I give you the formula, you won't need Zurtel. There'd be no reason to harm Gina. Novik will have MX7."

"But Mom wanted me to own Zurtel. It was her dream."

"If you're going to kill us all anyway, I'm not giving you the formula. I'll take it to my grave."

Randall ordered his men to hold Tristen. "Lower him to his knees."

"Cynthia, don't give it to them," Tristen said.

Her stepbrother pulled a gun and forced it in Tristen's mouth. "I'll blow his fucking head off if you don't give me what I want."

♦♦♦

Tristen's heart pounded as he gagged on the cold metal pressed against the back of his throat. Any minute he expected Randall to pull the trigger. The only thing he could think of was Mallory growing up without him and never knowing Gina.

"The formula or he dies. You have one minute to decide."

It was the longest minute of Tristen's life. Sweat beaded on his forehead and ran down his back. His entire body shook.

"Wait! Release him, and I'll give you the formula."

Randall removed the gun.

Tristen fell face down on the ground. His body still shook. Finally, he managed to stand.

Cynthia wrote the formula down without hesitation.

"Now if this isn't right, Terry will shoot your dad."

Cynthia nodded and continued writing.

After Randall tucked it in his billfold, he grinned. "You idiot. You know I can't let any of you live."

"We had a deal."

"Well, I just broke it. See if you'd just married me like Mom had wanted."

"I'd never marry you. I realized years ago what a pervert you are."

"Now, sis, that's not nice. Tell you what; I'm going to give you a sneak preview how things will work tomorrow." He made a gesture to all the men. "After I've had my fun with you. They get to take turns with you." He looked at Tristen. "And you get to watch before I kill you."

The men laughed and slapped each other on the back.

Randall grinned. "And I'll take care of Gina." He looked at the men. "Put them back in the cellar."

Cynthia lunged for him but was blocked.

For just a moment, Tristen held Cynthia. "You gave up the formula for me."

"Of course, I did. You're Gina's father."

"For a minute, I thought you were going to say you loved me more than Zurtel."

♦♦♦

Gina had ended up spending the night in the bus terminal restroom. She entered the main terminal area and looked for someone who might help her.

A young attractive woman with blond hair counted her money. She wore jeans and a black T-shirt. After counting it, she became despondent.

She stopped in front of the woman. Two bags sat on the floor beside her. "Where are you going?"

The lady shrugged. "Looks like I'm headin' nowhere."

"Where were you trying to go?"

"Anywhere but here."

"How 'bout Atlanta?"

"That'd work."

"If you'll pretend I'm your kid, I'll buy both our tickets."

"I'm not old enough to be your mom."

"Then tell them I'm your sister."

"Sure why not. Give me the money."

"How much are two tickets to Atlanta?"

The woman studied the board. "Around two hundred twenty."

Gina handed her three hundred. "You're not going to run out on me, are you?"

"Are you always this suspicious?"

"I have been lately."

"You can come with me up there. What's your name?"

"Gina. What's yours?"

"Sierra."

After purchasing the tickets, they waited for the bus to be called.

"Why are you going to Atlanta?"

"Meet my mom." Gina shared her situation with her new friend.

The bus was called, and they made their way to it.

Outside the man took Sierra's suitcase. He looked at Gina. "Do you want to check your backpack?"

"No, I'll hold it."

Once on the bus, Sierra motioned to the seat beside her. "Better stay with me until we reach Atlanta. Thanks for buying my ticket."

Gina smiled. "Thanks for helping me."

As the bus pulled out, she wondered how Aunt Nell was. Had she lived? Were the police still looking for her?

♦♦♦

Cynthia and Tristen sat in the basement. This time, the guard hadn't chained them to the wall as before. She rested in his arms. "Do you still have that gun?"

"It's not enough to shoot our way out of this. At best, we might bring one or two men down before they cut us down."

"I just want to kill Randall. He wouldn't see it coming. Then Gina would be safe."

"It wouldn't save your dad. He's with Terry."

That evening the door opened, and Bonita entered with a tray and a basket looped around her arm. The guard held the door for her. She said something to him and offered him a muffin.

The man grabbed four or five from the basket and returned to his post.

She set the tray on the small table. "Eat."

Cynthia stood slowly and joined Tristen at the table. While drinking the juice, she eyed the muffins. As she reached for one, Bonita scolded her and pulled the basket away. "Those are only for the guards. Now eat the food on your plate."

"The food is good," Tristen said, appearing unconcerned it could be their last meal.

She forced herself to eat the roast and potatoes.

While placing everything on the tray, Bonita refused to look at them.

Cynthia had to try once more. "Mr. Adams will keep raping these little girls until someone stops him. Help us escape, and we will stop him."

The lady stopped in the doorway and stared a moment before nodding. The door closed behind her.

"Do you think she'll go through with it?" she asked.

Tristen sighed. "She'd better make it fast."

They sat side by side against the wall. Neither spoke. She prayed silently for a miracle. A miracle that revolved around Bonita.

During the night, Cynthia awoke to the sound of the door opening. Bonita and a man entered. She woke Tristen.

"I'm Felipe. We're getting you out of here. Come quickly before the guards wake up."

Tristen stood and helped her up. He grabbed his jacket and leather pouch. He removed the .22 pistol from his boot.

The man handed him a .40 semi automatic Glock. "This might work better."

Tristen stuffed the larger gun in the back of his jeans."Thanks."

"Give me your gun," Cynthia said.

He handed it over. "Don't shoot yourself."

"I can handle a gun."

Felipe handed them their passports. "Bonita managed to steal these back."

"What about our phones?"

"Sorry, but no. I will guide you part of the way. We have five hours to reach the pickup point," Felipe said. He spoke very good English with a pleasant accent. He toted a camouflaged backpack and carried a canteen. A sheath for a machete hung from his belt.

Bonita spoke to him in her native tongue.

"She said be sure to bring back people to arrest Senor Adams."

"I'll do better than that if I get close enough," Cynthia said.

Bonita hugged them, said a small prayer, and made the sign of the cross. She handed them each a canteen. "Go now."

At the door, the guard who had eaten the muffins was slumped over.

"Is he dead?" she asked.

"No, drugged," Felipe said. "Magic muffins."

As they moved through the compound, Cynthia noticed other guards slumped over. Apparently, Bonita's muffins had hit the spot.

"Will she get in trouble?"

"No. The guard by the door will be in so much trouble for falling asleep, none of the others will want to admit they had fallen asleep too."

"What about the dogs?" Tristen asked.

"I locked them up," Felipe said. "But when they find you missing, they'll turn them loose and give them your scent."

Cynthia realized she'd left her torn up dress behind. She cursed herself for being so careless.

Felipe jogged toward the forest. The darkness didn't slow him down.

She hoped she could keep up with the fast pace. Their feet pounded the ground. Thank goodness Tristen had been smart enough to keep Wilkes's boots. Sweat ran down her back making her glad she only wore the slip.

Her side hurt, and her legs cramped, but finding Gina before Randall and saving her father motivated her to continue.

Bats fluttered above their heads, but she kept jogging. In the distance, the howler monkeys screamed cacophonous calls.

"The male monkeys howl right before sunrise," Felipe said. "We must run faster."

Tristen stayed behind her.

Her heavy breathing and heartbeat pounding in her ears blocked the jungle sounds. Her lungs burned as though breathing liquid fire.

At the edge of the forest, Felipe stopped. "How are you holding up?"

Tristen nodded. "I'm okay." He turned to her. "The boots working out?"

Cynthia held her side and panted. "Yes."

"Drink now. It will be your last opportunity for a while."

After several swigs, she capped the canteen and draped the strap back over her shoulder. The sun shone on the horizon. It wouldn't be long before they were discovered missing.

Inside the rainforest, her eyes adjusted allowing her to see.

She inhaled a couple of deep breaths to calm her nerves. The earthy scent of the forest filled her lungs.

Tristen grinned. "Aren't you the one who said you liked a little adventure?"

"This isn't what I had in mind."

When they came to a stream, Felipe ran down the middle of it. She followed having a difficult time running over the slick moss covered rocks. She assumed he did it to throw the dogs off.

Finally, he ran back up on the other side of the stream.

Sweat drenched her entire body and burned her eyes. She didn't have anything to wipe them with. All she could do was follow blindly.

Felipe stopped, giving her time to catch her breath. "The dogs will only be fooled for a short time with the stream. They'll pick the scent up again."

They moved at a quick pace—almost jogging.

When Felipe came to an enormous tree, he stopped. "One more trick to confuse the dogs."

"What's that?" She expected him to cover them in mud like she'd seen in movies.

"Climb the tree."

She glanced up wondering how they'd get up it.

"We're hiding in a tree?" Tristen asked.

Felipe grinned. "No, you'll see my plan."

Tristen and Felipe helped her climb upon the first limb. Once on the strong limb, she climbed higher without any help. After going up higher than she felt comfortable with, Felipe pulled out the wicked machete. He hacked on a thick vine until he'd cut through it, then offered it to her. "Hold this."

He cut one for Tristen and finally himself. "See that path through the trees?"

Cynthia's heart dropped. "Path? All I see are trees."

He pointed to the narrow clearing. "See it now?"

She gasped. "You expect us to swing through that?"

"Yes and now."

"I'll go first." Tristen pushed out and swung far out before letting go and dropping to the ground. He had passed right through the opening between the trees.

"Now you," Felipe said. "Push off and aim where he landed."

"I will. Give me a moment."

He grinned. "No time to think."

Before she knew what was happening, he grabbed her, pulled her back, and pushed her off the limb.

Cynthia held the vine for dear life. She couldn't stop screaming as it twisted and spun her around. Any second she expected to slam into a tree.

When she swung above Tristen, he shouted, "Drop now!"

She let go and hit the ground with a thud. For a moment, she couldn't move. Her heart beat uncontrollably. "You could have caught me."

Tristen grinned. "It's not in my job description."

She huffed, but still took his hand, letting him help her to her feet.

Felipe swung out and joined them. "Sorry, I pushed you. But now the dogs will lose your scent at the tree."

Tristen glanced at her and chuckled.

"What's so funny?"

"You swinging from that tree. You screamed louder than the monkeys."

"It's not funny. I was terrified."

Sunlight filtered through the canopy shining beams through the forest.

In the distance, dogs barked.

Felipe paused. "They're coming. The hunt is on, my friends. Let's move."

Chapter Eighteen

Tuesday morning, Gina and Sierra sat in a coffee shop around the corner from the Greyhound station.

Monday evening they had stayed at the bus station until it closed. Then they walked down Forsyth to Memorial Drive. They tried the front doors on the Believer's House Church but found them locked. They checked in back and discovered an unlocked door. In the church's sanctuary, they slept on the wooden pews.

That morning, they left through the door they had entered and looked for somewhere to eat.

"Thanks for breakfast," Gina said to Sierra.

"You paid for the tickets."

"Mind if I ask how old you are?" Gina said.

Sierra smiled. "Twenty. How old are you?"

"Eleven."

"Not to hurt your feelings but you stink."

Gina glanced up from her pancakes. "I do?"

"Yes. Why don't we get a motel room? That way you can clean up before you meet your mother."

Gina considered Sierra's suggestion. The police would be looking for one girl. It might help if she stayed with Sierra. "I'd like that. And I'll buy dinner."

Sierra smiled. "Deal." She studied Gina's backpack. "Do you have any other clothes with you?"

"I have a clean pair of shorts and a shirt."

"Too bad you don't have a pretty dress."

"I could buy one. Can you help me?"

"Sure. We'll find the closest mall, but first we need to find a place to stay, so we can clean up."

The waitress instructed them on how to take MARTA and where to find a hotel and mall. By noon, they had checked in to a room with double beds. Gina showered and changed into her extra set of clothes. It felt so good being clean again.

That night after returning from dinner and shopping, Sierra stopped at a guest computer in the lobby. "I need to find a job and somewhere to live."

"My mom owns a company. Maybe she'll give you a job."

"Do you know the name of it?"

Gina nodded. "Zurtel."

Sierra typed in Zurtel. She clicked on the site. It showed a high rise office building over twenty stories tall.

"I wonder which floor it's on?" Gina asked.

Sierra's eyes grew large. "They own the entire building."

Gina's mouth dropped. "For real? That's awesome."

"Good thing you bought a dress. You can't go into a place like this looking homeless." Sierra copied the address down and handed it to Gina. "This is where you'll need to go."

"I'm afraid. Can you come with me?"

Sierra sighed. "Maybe. Do you have her phone number?"

"No, but I know someone who does."

Gina pulled her phone out and called Liz and Dan.

"Gina, we've so worried about you. The police came here asking questions."

"Did Aunt Nell die?"

"No. She broke her leg and hit her head. She's fine."

"She pushed me, but when I pulled away, she lost her balance and fell. They blamed me."

"Your aunt cleared that up."

"Did she admit she pushed me?"

"No, but she told them she slipped. They're not blaming you. They've been searching everywhere for you."

Gina changed the subject. "Has my mom called back?"

Liz hesitated. "No, I'm surprised she hasn't. I've tried calling her, but no one answers. Where are you, Gina?"

"Atlanta."

"Oh dear Lord, how did you get there?"

Gina described her journey. “Don’t worry God has sent angels to help me.” She glanced at Sierra and smiled. “Can you give me my mom’s phone number?”

“Yes.”

Gina wrote the numbers for her parents down. “I’ll keep in touch.”

♦♦♦

Cynthia jumped over fallen trees and small streams.

The dogs barked and howled for a long period, then stopped. Obviously, they’d lost their scent. It meant they were at the first creek. It didn’t take long for the dogs to start back. After thirty minutes, another silence fell over the area. They had to be at the tree they’d climbed. How long would it take them to pick up the scent?

Felipe kept going. “We need to reach the river. Hurry!”

Cynthia’s side hurt. They’d been going like this since before daybreak. Leaves and branches continually slapped her face, and scratched her arms.

It took about forty minutes before the dogs howled.

Suddenly, the bottom dropped out of the sky. Rain came down in sheets.

Running became difficult, and they slowed down.

“Will this wash our scent away?” she asked Felipe.

“No, if anything it makes it easier to track.”

Finally, they came to the wide river they had crossed before. Since the heavy rain had just fallen, the rapids raged cascading over the boulders.

“The dogs won’t cross the rapids.”

Unlike before, there wasn’t a hidden rope. They left the cover of the rainforest and walked over the rocks to the river.

“It’s important we stay together.” Felipe removed a rope from the burlap sack tied to his belt. “I’m tying us together.”

“We’ll drown together,” she said.

"Not if you keep your head above the rapids. As it sweeps us downstream, we will work our way to the other side. Hopefully, we will not go too far."

"Give me the pistol," Tristen said. She handed him the .22, and he placed it and the larger gun in his pouch. Then he stuffed his beloved jacket between him and the rope before draping his pouch around him.

Cynthia had nothing but the canteen to carry.

They edged their way into the river. As they neared the middle, the rapids and current grew stronger. In a flash they were overpowered and swept away.

Cynthia's head dipped under the water for a moment. She bobbed up to the top like a cork, gasping for a breath. Her arms flailed wildly as the water swept her away. A tug on her waist pulled her in the right direction. Despite the water rushing around them, Tristen and Felipe kept them moving toward the opposite bank.

Finally, they were out of the current's grip. They untied the rope and stood in the shallow water. Her wet slip and undergarments were transparent. She shivered from being wet.

Tristen offered his jacket. "Wear this."

Though damp, the jacket eased her chills. As far as modesty, at this point she didn't care. She only wanted to survive this green hell and return to her daughter and father.

Tristen removed the gun from the pouch and stuck it in back of his jeans, then handed her the smaller one.

"Aren't you afraid of shooting your butt off?"

"I could keep it in front, but I'd rather shoot my butt off than my…"

"I get the picture." She pushed the gun in her bra, then took in her environment. Overhead, birds flew between the canopies.

When the dogs started barking, Felipe headed toward the forest. "Let's move out of the open. Several men will stay with the dogs, so we won't have as many to deal with."

"Good," Tristen said.

"What's not so good is the water carried us away from our destination. Now we have to work our way back up stream." His eyes reflected his concern. "If they crossed ahead of us, they might be closer to us. They could even come out ahead."

Cynthia hoped the men hunting them would be swept even farther downstream.

Once again, they entered the forest and forged through the undergrowth. The boots had rubbed blisters on her feet, and her muscles ached severely. She reminded herself what was at stake. Everything she loved. Not Zurtel but the people in her life. They were all that mattered.

The dogs barked from a stationary spot.

"They've reached the river."

When she lagged behind, Tristen waited. She slipped from his jacket and gave it to him. "The jacket is too hot. Just leave it."

"It's the last thing my mom gave me." Rather than carry it, he slipped it on.

She knew before long he would regret wearing it.

Felipe stopped suddenly. "Listen."

Her hearing ability wasn't nearly as keen as Felipe's.

She only heard the birds and her stomach growling.

"Men. At least three or four men are coming. Let's hide."

They pushed between the tall plants and undergrowth. Tristen positioned her behind him. Felipe motioned for silence.

Cynthia crouched in the tall vegetation and prayed they wouldn't be found.

Soon the men came close enough she could hear them.

She recognized Douglas's voice speaking to Randal's body guard. The man constantly cleared his throat. Several of Ravelo's men accompanied them.

Just as they passed, Cynthia detected a slight movement to her left moving through the leaves. She turned to get a better look and gasped. A wicked looking snake moved toward her.

Tristen glanced back. "Fer de lance. Don't move."

At the same time, bullets whizzed past them.

Tristen whipped his gun from behind him, shot the snake, and turned back shooting at the men

With bullets flying everywhere, she ducked lower finding herself staring at the dead snake. Her heartbeat surged as she feared Tristen or Felipe would get shot.

As the battle continued, Cynthia prayed.

She heard movement coming through the undergrowth. She removed the small gun. She imagined another snake slithering her way, but instead, Douglas pushed his way through the tall brush. This snake stood on two feet. He had doubled back and crept in behind them.

He didn't see her crouching low to the ground among the plants. He aimed his gun at Tristen.

Without a second thought, she aimed and fired.

♦♦♦

Panic hit Tristen when he heard the shot behind him. He glanced back. Douglas wore a look of disbelief. Despite the shot to the chest, the bodyguard tried to raise his AK-47.

Another bullet fired and hit Douglas in the forehead, and he crumpled to the ground.

Tristen glanced down.

Cynthia crouched near the ground, the small gun crutched tightly in her hand.

Tristen turned back around and fired several times at the men shooting at them. He heard a painful cry as a man dropped to the ground.

Felipe hit another one.

Ravelo's men fled into the forest.

"They'll be back with reinforcements." Felipe stared at Douglas, then shifted his attention to Cynthia. "You did good."

Tristen helped Cynthia to her feet. She still shook from the ordeal.

"He would've killed us if you hadn't killed him first."

Though looking disheartened, she nodded. "I know."

Tristen grabbed Douglas's AK-47 and the ammo belt.

Shortly after resuming their trek, light shined ahead of them. At the edge of the rainforest down a steep slope, a van waited.

"Don't worry. It's a friend," Felipe said.

They slid down the embankment, then ran toward the van.

Felipe opened the back of the vehicle and rolled a small motorcycle out of it. "From here, the good sister will drive you to the hangar."

Cynthia hugged him. "Thank you for risking your life."

"I have my reasons. My sister is one of the girls he ruined."

Tristen shook his hand and thanked him. "You'd make one hell of a personal trainer."

They laughed.

"Let me return your gun."

"You may still need it. Also keep the AK-47. You'd better go. They'll know you're trying to make it to the hangar."

"Get in," ordered the nun sitting behind the wheel. She wore one of the modern habits.

"Sister Anna?" Cynthia asked as they climbed in.

"Yes, and you're the one who has promised to stop the monster."

"That's the plan. Wipe out the snake pit."

"Bonita said he was angry when you escaped and even angrier when his money came up missing."

"It wouldn't surprise me if Ravelo stole it."

Looking into the rearview mirror, Tristen caught the nun smiling.

"Actually, Bonita stole it. The bags are behind you. We're returning your money." She pulled onto the road.

Tristen grinned. "I bet he's majorly pissed." He paused. "Excuse me, sister."

Again she smiled. "Pissed is an understatement."

"Tell me what you do to help the girls he abuses," Cynthia said.

"It is a very long healing process. We try to continue their education, so they can have a decent life."

"Bonita said no one knows the girls come to you."

"That's correct. Senor Adams believes they are dead. He has no idea the girls are sent to me. In first Peter, chapter five, it says to be sober, be vigilant: because your adversary the devil, as a roaring lion walketh about, seeking whom he may devour. That is Senor Adams."

Tristen couldn't have agreed more. Randall was evil.

He remembered the bumpy road they traveled before. It was the road the rebels had first stopped them on. After a short distance, he spotted the hangar. He hoped Ravelo and Randall wouldn't show up before they could steal the plane.

Sister Anna pulled over to the side. "This is as far as I can go. You'll be in the open, so you'll need to hurry. Don't forget your money."

Cynthia and Tristen climbed out. He pulled the bags of money over. "Now you can give it back to your dad."

"Dad's getting most of it back." She opened one and pulled out stacks of money. "Put this in your pouch." She looked at the nun. "Sister Anna, I'm not sure how much is left in the bag. Use it to help the abused girls and your church. Split one stack between Bonita and Felipe."

"But this is a fortune."

"I'm a little behind on my tithing."

The nun smiled. "The church and I thank you. Now go."

Tristen carried the other heavy bag of money.

After Sister Anna drove away, they hurried across the open space that seemed the distance of two football fields. The ground squished beneath their feet. The air smelled like burnt wood where someone had been clearing land. Any minute he expected bullets to whiz toward them.

Opening the hangar, he prayed the key would still be there. There wouldn't be time to check everything. They'd be flying on faith. Hopefully, God was looking out for them.

After helping Cynthia in and loading the money and AK-47 inside, he climbed in the pilot's seat. The key was in the ignition. He switched the master switch on, the lights, and radio, then made sure the flaps were down. "Let's see if this bug smasher can fly." He pulled the choke and turned the key. "Start, damn it."

After several tries, the single engine roared. He glanced at the gauges, checking the oil pressure and fuel. “It’s gassed up. You’d better start praying because I’m not sure this plane is safe. It’s been sitting here for a long time. Talk about your wing and a prayer.”

She buckled up.

Tristen taxied out onto the runway.

♦♦♦

Cynthia assumed they’d never make it out of Brazil on foot. This plane had been their salvation. As soon as they were safe, she had to find a way to warn her father.

“Son-of-a-bitch!”

“What?”

“Look up the road.”

Four jeeps headed their way.

“What are you waiting for? Take us up.”

“Come out of the seat belt. Grab the AK-47 behind you.”

Cynthia did as he instructed. “What now?”

“Push the window open.”

“It won’t open all the way.”

“Cessna’s have a brace. Damn it. See if you can point that barrel out the window. Try to aim it down. Don’t get the straps hung on the yoke.”

Again she followed his directions and twisted around in the seat, half sprawled in the floor to position the gun.

“Try to put it against your left shoulder. Pull the trigger.”

When the gun fired, it jolted her hard. The heavy weapon was almost more than she could hold.

“What are they doing?” he asked.

“Hiding behind the jeeps.”

“Keep shooting.”

She braced herself and fired again.

Someone shot off a round.

“They’ll go for the fuselage. Hang on.”

As Tristen pulled back on the throttle and increased the power, she couldn't angle the gun out the window, so she returned it to the backseat, sat back, and fastened her seatbelt.

The jeeps drove behind the plane with the men firing on them.

"Can you do some aerial stunts to dodge the bullets?"

"Not in a Cessna. It'd damage the frame. We're out of their range."

"How is it doing?"

He glanced at the gauges. "So far so good. Hopefully, the worst we'll have is a little turbulence."

"Our lives have been nothing but turbulence since arriving in Brazil."

He pushed forward on the yoke, then leveled out the plane. "I bet Ravelo had a tantrum as he watched his plane fly away."

"Can we fly home?"

He grinned. "No. Right now we're flying off the grid. There's a chance they'll report us to the authorities and claim we hijacked their plane. We'll be listed as armed and dangerous. If our fuel holds out, I'd like to make it to San Jose, Costa Rica."

"We need to reach Dad."

"And Rose or Sarah."

"As soon as this is over, I want to fly to Huntsville and get Gina." She glanced out the window as they flew over the jungle. From such a high altitude, it looked like the top of broccoli stalks.

"We'll take a commercial flight home. Before we do, we'll need to shower and find you some clothes. I can't see you walking into an airport in those boots and your dirty slip.

"I have a better idea?"

"What's that?"

"Let's buy a jet."

"You can't just drive down to Jets R-Us and pick one up. When we land, it'll be late. We'll find a place to stay. Tomorrow, we'll catch the first direct flight to Atlanta. It beats trying to buy one."

"I'm too tired to argue. It sounds like a plan. Let's do it."

♦♦♦

Gina sighed. "No one answers. I left a message."

"Let's call her company and ask to speak with her," Sierra suggested.

She nodded. "You do it. I sound like a kid."

Sierra took the paper she'd written the number on. "Give me the phone."

Gina turned up the volume so she could hear. "Take it."

Sierra keyed in the numbers. "It's ringing."

A prerecorded voice answered.

If you know your party's extension, please dial it now or wait for an operator to assist you.

"Zurtel Aerospace Corporation, how may I direct your call?"

"I'd like to speak with Cynthia Reynolds."

Gina nodded in approval.

"May I ask who is calling?"

"Gina Ferguson," Sierra said.

"I'll transfer you. Hold please."

Gina's heart beat fast. Any moment she'd hear her mother's voice.

"Miss Reynolds's office."

"I'd like to speak with Miss Reynolds," Sierra said.

Gina smiled.

"I'm sorry she's out of the country at present. I'm not sure when she'll return. Can I take a message?"

Gina took the phone. "Tell her Gina called, and I'm in town."

"Does she know you?"

"I'm her daughter."

The lady laughed. "She doesn't have a daughter. Waste someone else's time."

After the lady hung up, Gina blew out a long breath. "That didn't go over very well."

"I don't think your mother has told anyone about you. If you go there, I'm not sure they'll believe you."

She held her hands up. "Then what am I supposed to do?"

"Seems your mom is out of the country. Maybe she doesn't have phone reception where she is. Give it a couple of days and call back."

"Surely, there's someone who knows about me."

"Like a grandparent or an aunt or uncle."

Gina held her hands over her ears. "I never want to hear the words aunt and uncle again."

Sierra laughed. "Least you've got people who care about you."

Gina grew serious. She'd been so busy thinking of herself, she hadn't considered Sierra. All their conversations had centered on her. "Why did you leave home?"

"My dad is an alcoholic. Do you know what that is?"

She made a face. "Duh. Of course, I do. I'm eleven. I'm not stupid. What about your mom?"

"She left him and never looked back."

Gina listened to Sierra describe her life. It made her realize she wasn't the only one with problems.

♦♦♦

Everett Reynolds wiped the tears from his eyes. He didn't want his secretary see him cry.

Randall called. His news wasn't good. The rebels had taken the money and refused to release his daughter.

The odds of getting her back remained slim. Wilkes and Conners were dead. He needed to call Robert Conners. He couldn't bring himself to tell Robert about Tristen. Evan and Annie had made it back safely.

As for Randall, he'd barely escaped with his life. Douglas and the other bodyguard had been killed trying to rescue her.

Terry would be meeting him at the house. He considered telling the bodyguard he wanted to be alone. All he'd been able to think about was Cynthia.

Everett stepped into the elevator as Jennifer, Cynthia's secretary entered.

"Have you heard when Miss Reynolds is returning?" Jennifer asked.

He swallowed hard. "No."

"The engineers at the Jacksonville facility have delayed the final test. They're waiting to hear from her. They're starting to get edgy."

He couldn't answer.

"Is everything all right?"

"Fine." He had made the decision to keep Cynthia's situation from everyone until he knew the outcome. Needing advice, he had confided in Austin Gunner, who had been engaged to Cynthia.

Jennifer laughed. "I had a very odd call today."

He sighed. "Odd in what sense?"

"It was a kid who asked to speak with Miss Reynolds. She said she was Cynthia's daughter, Gina, and was in town."

"Did you get a return number or find out where she's staying?"

"Well, no. I told her Miss Reynolds didn't have a daughter and to stop wasting my time."

"If she calls back, put her through to me."

"It's just some kid playing phone games."

"Put the call through to me," he said firmly.

"Who is she?"

"Cynthia's daughter. Don't mention this to anyone. Do you understand?"

Jennifer appeared shocked for a moment. "I'm sorry, Mr. Reynolds. I didn't know. How old is she?"

"Ten or eleven."

Everett didn't know where to start to find Gina. Once Randall returned, maybe he'd know how to find her.

Chapter Nineteen

Cynthia wanted to celebrate when they flew out of Columbia and into Panama, entering Central America. Though she didn't think Ravelo's connections went beyond Brazil, it was good to be out of South America.

The plane had only experienced turbulence while flying over the mountains. More buildings blotted the land beneath them. Instead of flying inland, Tristen banked right and flew over the open ocean, descended to a low altitude, and leveled out.

"What are you doing?"

"Staying out of PTY's air space? We'll stay about twelve miles out. If I stay low enough, we'll go undetected."

"Why can't you request landing there?"

He chuckled. "Where do I start? First of all, I don't have a flight plan. No paperwork on this plane. No certificate. No proof of insurance. Not to mention, we happened to have three weapons—two that are automatic. They frown on that in Panama."

"So what's your plan?"

"I still want to make it to Costa Rica. If I can find a class G airport, they might not be so particular."

"Can we just explain what happened to us?"

"Yes, then you may be detained for several days while they investigate. Look on the bright side. At least it's not hurricane season."

Flying not even two hundred feet above the water's surface, she glanced out at the beautiful ocean. The sun rested just above the horizon. "Tristen, it's getting late."

"I know. Thirty more minutes."

Voices came over the radio, but didn't speak directly to them. She knew Tristen didn't want to make any radio contact.

"We're over Costa Rica," Tristen announced. Then his expression grew grim. "We're almost out of fuel. We've got to land."

"What's the closest airport?"

"Some privately owned charter aircraft landing strips around Tortuguero."

The airplane engine choked.

Her heart dropped to her stomach. "Please tell me we're not out of gas?"

"I'd be lying. Make sure you're strapped in well. I'm making an emergency landing."

Cynthia's breath left her a moment. "Where?"

"On the beach. Barra Airport in Scotland uses the beach as a runway. Of course, it's listed in the top ten most dangerous runways."

"I doubt they land when the tide is coming in. We'll be swept out to sea."

"We'll have to chance it. I have a long stretch of beach ahead of me. Thousands of feet of runway. Be positive."

As he lined up with the beach, Cynthia prayed. Thank goodness, they had continued at a low altitude. Still, even a crash from an altitude of two or three hundred feet could be fatal.

"Pull my pouch and the money bag up front. Once we land, we'll jump from the plane. Those waves will pound it."

"They're heavy." Cynthia managed to drag the heavy black bag and Tristen's leather pouch to the front. As the plane glided down toward the beach, she braced for impact. The plane made ground contact with a thud and jerked them forward. Water splashed on the plane's windows. As he rolled down the pristine beach, its inertia kept it moving and from being swept away. As he braked and slowed down, a wave crashed against the Cessna, jarring it. She gasped.

The huge waves rolling in and crashing on the shore could tear the plane apart.

"When the next wave goes out, jump out and run toward the tree line. Give me my pouch and your bag. I'm on the side away from the water."

"How do I know you won't run off with the money and let me drown?"

He laughed. "Because I love you, and you know it."

Cynthia's heart warmed. It had been a stupid question, and she regretted asking it. She opened the door and mentally prepared to jump. As the wave drew back to the ocean, she jumped and landed in the wet sand. An enormous wave headed toward her. She scampered to her feet and sprinted for higher ground. Water rushed up around her ankles, but wasn't enough to drag her back.

Tristen met her half way up the beach, and they ran beneath the tree line. They turned and watched as the wave crashed against the plane and pulled it out to the sea. After several more waves, the plane slowly sank into the sea.

She sighed. "There goes any evidence."

He removed his jacket and handed it to her. "You might want to wear it. That dirty slip will make you stand out like an orange in an apple tree."

She laughed at his analogy. "What now?"

"There's a small town just ahead, but we'll have to find someone to take us across the river."

They found a water taxi to transport them across the canal to Tortuguero. They were his only passengers, so he talked as he steered his boat. "Nice resorts. This is off season, so you may find a vacancy."

"What about an airport?" she asked.

"SANSA and Nature Air do chartered flights around Costa Rica. To get back to the states, charter a plane to San Jose."

"I hope we'll be able to get a direct flight to Atlanta." She looked back at the driver. "What about telephones? I need to call the states."

"There's a small shop that sells calling cards. Then you can use the resort's phone."

Not having anything smaller, they paid him with a hundred dollar bill and told him to keep the change.

"Wait," he said. "I have a friend at Pachira Lodge. It's nice. Go there and tell him Pasca sent you. They'll find a place for you."

In the quaint town, they entered a small drug store just as it was closing. The shop owner allowed them to shop. Cynthia filled a handheld basket with hygiene products, a flimsy little pair of sandals, two T-shirts with turtles on them, two pairs of one-size-fits-all shorts and a diet soda. Tristen tossed a phone card into the basket and several candy bars.

Fortunately, the shop owner had change for a hundred.

Being late, they couldn't find anyone to drive them to the resort. The drug store owner saw them standing outside. "Where are you going?"

"Pachira Lodge."

"I'll drive you."

"Should we point out we're dirty and stink?" Cynthia asked.

Tristen grinned. "I think she knows."

At the resort, they climbed out and thanked the lady. Cynthia offered her money, but the store owner refused it and wished them luck.

As they entered the lodge, everyone stared as if they were looking at Amelia Earhart returning from her flight. Cynthia realized they looked like something that had crawled out of the swamps. She wore a slip, men's boots, and a leather bomber jacket.

The manager greeted them with a cautious, unfriendly look. "We have no vacancies."

"Pasca sent us. He said you would find us a room. It's just for one night."

The man looked hesitant. As he studied them his eyes softened. "One night?"

"Yes, we're flying home tomorrow."

After filling out the paperwork under phony names and paying cash for the night, Tristen met the manager's scrutinizing stare. "Do you do room service?"

"Yes, we do, and we have a very romantic restaurant."

"We better stick to room service. We'll come back and dine here on our honeymoon." He winked at her.

"We have honeymoon bungalows with hot tubs."

Cynthia looked bewildered. She made a hand gesture toward their clothes. "We need to clean up and change clothes." She knew before she did anything, she'd call her father.

"There is a menu in your room. Also, we have a small gift shop across the way there." He gave them their keys. "Room Twenty-three. The steps are just outside to the right."

The room had a light airy feel to it. Two bamboo beds with floral bedspreads stood in the center, a nightstand between them. Seeing the telephone, Cynthia rushed to it and sat on the edge of the bed. She opened the card. "How many minutes?"

"Two hours worth. It should be plenty."

She called her father's house and let the phone ring. She tried his cell to no avail.

After her third failed attempt, Tristen took the phone and called Rose.

"Hello."

"It's Tristen."

"Oh sweet Lord, you're alive. I was informed you were being held by South American rebels for ransom. We've been on pins and needles waiting to hear. We've had you on our church's prayer list." She held the phone. "Go wake Mallory up."

While waiting for his daughter, he explained that he'd escaped. He heard Mallory coming to the phone.

"Daddy, where are you? Why didn't you come home?"

"Honey, it's a long story. Some really bad people wouldn't let me. But I'll be back soon. Promise. Now let me speak to Rose."

Rose returned to the phone.

"Is Sarah still at the house?" he asked.

"No, she returned to the previous family she'd worked for. We took Mallory when we found out you had been abducted. I hope that was okay."

"Yes, thank you. But you need to take Mallory and go stay somewhere. There were threats made against her. Can you do that?"

"No. She has her spring program at school tomorrow and then dance class. But we won't let her out of our sight. I'll be sure to notify the school. We'll keep the doors locked. Kenneth will keep the gun somewhere handy."

"That's not good enough. Promise me you'll go to a hotel or stay with Tanner until I return."

"I promise. We'll go now."

"Thanks, Rose. Tell Mallory, I love her."

Everett Reynolds was on the line with Randall when another call beeped in. He ignored it. "You think they'll keep their word this time? I've already given them a small fortune. It's time to call the FBI. I should have contacted them from the start."

"That'll mean certain death to her. I screwed up before, but I think another five million will clinch the deal. I'll get her out of there. Dad, I promise."

"What's to keep them from taking the money and not releasing her again? I want proof of life again." He sighed. "I've got something else I need help with."

"What's that?"

He explained about Cynthia having a daughter with Tristen Conners. "The girl called wanting to speak to Cynthia."

"Where from?"

"Here in Atlanta. But Jennifer didn't find out where she's staying. I figured you might know how to have the call traced."

"Who's she with?"

"I'm not sure. I got the impression she ran away."

"I'll certainly do what I can to help. I'd really like to get to know my little niece."

Tristen placed a hand on Cynthia's shoulder. He knew she was worried about her dad. "Did you try his cell?"

"He's not answering it either. I hope Terry hasn't harmed him."

"You're tired and dirty. Let's shower and put clean clothes on. We can order dinner and then try to call him again after we eat."

She sighed. "Randall could be back by now. He probably had a jet on standby in Manaus."

"Calling over and over isn't accomplishing anything."

Finally, she surrendered with a nod.

While Cynthia showered, he tried calling his dad with no luck. He didn't know if his father was on a flight or just on a date.

When Cynthia came out, her hair was wrapped in a towel. She wore the shorts and T-shirt. She didn't wear a bra. "I picked the one with the baby turtles."

"Feel better?"

"Much. My feet have blisters."

"Mine too." He stood. "I tried calling my dad. He didn't answer."

"Clean up. I'll order us something. Anything particular?"

"Hot food and a beer works for me."

After he showered and their food had been delivered, they ate in silence. So much had happened, and now it seemed surreal, almost like a bad dream or something that had happened to someone else. "What's in the box?"

"Two slices of key lime pie." She smiled. "I think our jungle workout this morning entitles us to indulge on desserts."

"You don't have to convince me. I don't worry about calories."

She smiled. "Yeah, I've noticed." Her expression changed. "I need to call the Garsons and explain why we've been out of touch. I wonder if Gina enjoyed her spring break camping trip."

"She's a kid. Kids love camping. It's the adults who do all the work."

Once he set the dishes outside the door, he turned around and faced her. "Try calling again."

♦♦♦

Everett sat at his desk, debating whether to send more money. He glanced at Terry. "What would you do?"

"She's your daughter. You've got to try."

"Four people Zurtel sent down there are dead. I regret your coworkers were killed."

"Shit happens. It's one of the hazards of our job."

The phone rang. He thought about letting it ring. He glanced at the number. It was one he didn't recognize. Then he realized it was from out of the country. Thinking it could be news about Cynthia or the abductor directly demanding more money, he answered it.

"Hello."

"Dad, it's me. Don't say anything. Don't tell anyone it's me. Just listen. Are you alone?"

"No, I'm not."

"Is Terry with you?"

"Yes, that's right."

"Dad, he's probably going to kill you. All Randall's bodyguards were hired mercenaries. Terry is one also."

"That's good to know."

"Randall orchestrated my abduction. Then he planned to kill me and keep the money. You'd think the rebels were behind it, and he'd get off scot free."

"So what are you up to tonight?" he asked, not wanting Terry to piece it together.

"We're in Central America. Tristen and I are safe."

"I thought that part of the program had been eliminated."

"No. They killed Mr. Wilkes. Apparently, he knew too much about Randall. Wilkes was close to figuring out Randall was Adams and owned Novik."

Everett was dumfounded but tried not to let it show.

"Randall forced me to give him the formula, but I left out part of it. He wants Zurtel."

"Why want it if he has his own company?"

"He's trying to fulfill his mom's dreams." Cynthia paused. "He knows about Gina." She explained about Randall and the abused girls. "He promised to do the same thing to her."

"She's in Atlanta looking for you. He knows she's here."

"Dad, you've got to get away from Terry and find her first."

Terry stood and moved closer. He concealed something in his hand.

Everett eased his left hand into the drawer and removed his .38 Smith and Wesson and kept it under his desk. "I will do my best."

As Terry inched closer, he recognized he had a syringe in his hand. Everett was sure it was something that would make his death appear to be from natural causes.

"Dad, call the police and tell them what Randall has done."

"I think Terry plans to do me in now."

"Who are you talking to?" Terry asked.

"Someone who's going to hang up and call the police now." He hung up the phone and tightly gripped the pistol.

♦♦♦

Cynthia's stomach twisted. "He hung up. It's Terry. He's trying to murder dad. He wants me to call the police, but I don't know how to reach Atlanta Police Department. It's not like I can dial 911." She grimaced as if about to cry. "I feel so helpless."

Tristen took the phone and called his dad. "Pick up." He covered the phone. "He's answering."

"Dad, it's Tristen. We're safe. Listen. I need you to hang up and call the police. Everett's bodyguard is trying to murder him as we speak. Do it now."

After Tristen disconnected, he held Cynthia in his arms. "He's contacting the police. Once he reaches them, he's going over to the house."

"I hope they reach Dad in time," she whispered.

Rather than guarantee her it'd be all right, he hugged her closer and gently rubbed her back.

After not hearing anything for twenty minutes, Tristen called his dad back. “Are the police there?”

“Yes, but I’m not sure they got here in time. When I was beating on the door, I heard three shots fired. They won’t let me in to see. An ambulance just pulled up.”

Chapter Twenty

Tristen read the fear in Cynthia's eyes. He held the line while his father reported the unfolding scene.

She put it on speaker phone. "I want to hear what your dad says."

"They're bringing someone out in a body bag," Tristen's dad said.

"Oh God, no," Cynthia cried as she sat on the edge of the bed. "Please no."

Tristen wrapped his arm around her and gently pulled her closer. "Dad, give the phone to a policeman. Tell them it's Cynthia Reynolds, Everett Reynolds's daughter."

Tristen handed her the phone. "Speak to the officer."

The officer responded. "Please verify who you are and your relationship with Mr. Reynolds."

"This is Cynthia Reynolds, his daughter. Is my father dead?" She squeezed Tristen's hand while waiting for an answer.

"Your father is fine."

"Then who was shot?"

"Terry Britt, the bodyguard. Your father shot him dead."

"Are you arresting my dad?"

"I won't know until a full investigation is done."

"It was self-defense."

"We'll know more tomorrow."

After the call, Tristen hung the phone up. "We'll fly out in the morning. We should be in Atlanta by tomorrow evening."

"It's not Dad I'm worried about. It's Gina. She's in Atlanta, and Randall knows it. Apparently, he's back. As soon as we arrive, we need to speak with Detective Taylor. We have to find Gina."

Tristen wanted to kill Randall, but he knew he'd have to get in line behind Cynthia.

"Once we arrive in San Jose tomorrow, we'll purchase new smart phones. You'll be able to locate Taylor's number then. As for tonight, we need to sleep."

"I don't know if I can."

"Drink another glass of wine. That should do the trick."

"I've already had two." She climbed in the bed closest to the bathroom.

Tristen pulled the cover back and crawled into the other one. It cushioned his body like a cloud. After sleeping on the ground and concrete, he considered this heaven.

A few minutes later, Cynthia left her bed. It surprised him when she climbed into bed with him.

Rather than say anything, he turned on his side and embraced her.

"I want to be near you," she whispered.

He kissed the crown of her head. He loved her. Once back, he planned to take her to dinner at Aria's and propose.

♦♦♦

Tristen slid his new cell phone into his pocket. Normally, he kept it in his pouch, but it was still full of cash.

Before boarding in San Jose, Cynthia contacted Detective Taylor and informed him of everything that happened in South America and gave him their new numbers. He promised to search for Gina and contact Brazilian authorities concerning Ravelo's gun running business. An APB had been issued on Randall.

She had also called the Garsons and told them if they spoke with Gina to tell her to stay away from Uncle Randall. Dan said Gina had been ignoring their calls."

On the flight to Atlanta, Tristen glanced at Cynthia. She slept like a baby. He let her sleep knowing she'd only worry herself sick if awake. The seatbelt light came on. They'd arrive within the next twenty or thirty minutes. The attendants moved down the aisle gathering the trash.

"Cynthia, wake up. We're landing."

She yawned and stretched, then pulled the money bag from under her seat.

They still wore their turtle T-shirts and shorts. Anyone looking at their apparel and tans would think they'd been on a pleasant, restful vacation.

After landing, they headed for the exit. As they walked past security, he spotted Everett. His father stood with him, and a man he didn't recognize. Then he zoned in on Rose and Kenneth with Mallory.

He hadn't expected a welcoming party. This wasn't exactly the precautions he'd asked them to take with his daughter.

"Daddy! Daddy!"

"Mal, give me a hug." He lifted his daughter and spun around with her in his arms just in time to see the strange man embrace Cynthia and kiss her. Not a simple greeting kiss, but one full of passion.

His heart sank. It was as though the bottom had fallen out from under him.

Rose and Kenneth hugged him. His dad joined them. "Glad your back, son."

"I didn't think we'd make it back." He focused on Cynthia.

The tall attractive man backed away allowing her father to hug her.

"Dad, who's the man with Cynthia?"

"Austin Gunner, big shot attorney."

Tristen recalled the name. Cynthia had been engaged to him.

He squeezed Mallory close to prevent his raw emotions from showing. The part that hurt the most was she had returned the kiss.

He planned to resign. Knowing Cynthia was with another man, he couldn't work around her. They'd share Gina.

Right now, he had to focus on finding his missing daughter.

♦♦♦

Gina tried calling her mom. It rang and rang as before. Hopefully, Liz had given her the right number.

Someone answered. "Hello."

It was a man. Maybe her mother had a boyfriend.

"May I speak to Cynthia Reynolds?"

"Is this Gina?"

"Yes, who's this?"

"I'm your Uncle Randall."

"Where's my mom?"

"The secretary mentioned you were in town. I'm not sure when Cynthia will be back, but I promised to look after you. I can pick you up and drive you to your grandfather's house. That way you'll be there when she returns."

"If she's out of town, why do you have her phone?"

"She thought you'd call. There's no reception where she is. Why don't you tell me where you are?"

"How do I know you're really my uncle and not some pervert who found my mom's phone?"

"Didn't you call Zurtel and speak with your mom's secretary?"

"Yes."

"If I'm not your uncle, how would I know that?"

Gina considered what he said. It made sense, but still there was something she didn't like about his voice. "I'll wait until she returns."

"Are you at a hotel?"

"Yes. But I'm not telling you where."

"Paying for a room is silly when you could stay at her house. Do you have the address?"

"No."

"Get some paper. I'll give it to you."

"Just a minute." Gina grabbed a pen and paper. "Okay, what is it?"

"555 Ridgewood Circle. That's in the Buckman area. She hides a key in the flowerpot on the porch. There's food in her fridge. Make yourself at home. I know she'd want you to stay there."

"My room is paid up for a few days. I might after that. I've got to go." She disconnected and turned to Sierra. "He said he's my uncle, but he sounded creepy."

"What did he say about your mom?"

She repeated what he'd said.

"What about your dad?"

"I have his phone number."

"Call it."

Gina keyed it in and let it ring.

Someone answered. "Hello, young lady."

She disconnected the call.

"What's wrong?" Sierra asked.

"It was my creepy uncle."

Sierra frowned. "Well, I'm not the smartest thumbtack on the bulletin board, but if you ask me, something's wrong."

"It made sense him having mom's phone, but no way would he have my dad's phone too?" She smiled. "But now I have my mom's address." She flopped back and stared at the ceiling. "Maybe we'll go there Friday."

Sierra sighed. "I don't know. What if your uncle is there?"

"Why would he be? It's my mom's house. I don't plan to call and tell him I'm there."

♦♦♦

Cynthia stood in the waiting area at the Atlanta Police Department on Spring Street. She glanced at her watch. When the door opened, she glanced up.

Tristen entered the precinct and joined her. He came across as withdrawn and grim. "Sorry I'm late. Sarah resigned and returned to her previous family. Rose has Mallory today."

"I hate to hear that. I noticed Rose at the airport. She actually seemed thrilled to see you."

He shrugged. "Maybe. You had your own greeting party."

"Yes, I was surprised. I'd expected Ellis to pick us up. Certainly not Austin and Dad."

"Looks like you picked up where you left off."

She had to think about his remark. Then she remembered the kiss. This was her chance to cool things with Tristen. Now that she was back in her world maybe it was the right thing to do. With Randall gone, Zurtel would need her full attention.

"He took Dad and me to dinner at Aria's."

Tristen paled.

"Are you all right?"

Before he could answer, Detective Taylor called them back.

They sat beside one another and focused on Taylor.

"Have you located Randall?" she asked.

"No. The pilot who flew him back doesn't know where he went. We have a BOLO out on him. We'll get him."

"He tried to get more money out of my dad. I don't think he's aware that we made it out of Brazil alive. He made threats against our daughter, Gina. It's imperative we find her before he does."

"Why would he want her dead?"

"She's the only obstacle standing between him and Zurtel."

"From what you said, Randall Miller had orchestrated the perfect crime. Your Dad would believe you and Tristen were murdered by South American rebels, and Randall would walk away with the ransom money."

"Ingenious plan," Tristen admitted.

"After he murdered Dad, Randall would've been the sole owner of Zurtel," Cynthia added. "Then he learned I have a daughter who would inherit most of the company." She fought being emotional. She had to keep a level head. "Any leads on Gina?"

"We contacted authorities in Tennessee. They were able to pull video from the Chattanooga bus terminal. They're not sure how she got there from the Smokey Mountains."

"They sold a ticket to a minor?"

"The video showed her with a female companion. We're approximating her age at twenty. She found someone old enough to help. Smart kid."

"Where would she get the money?" she asked.

"Some family friends admitted Gina has ten thousand on a Visa card. She picked up five hundred at the terminal's ATM."

"From what my father said, she's somewhere in Atlanta."

"We're checking the video from the Greyhound station on Forsyth. We've had officers patrolling every street in that vicinity from I-20 to the South downtown district. I'm assuming Randall is in South Georgia where Novik is located or headed back to South America where he thinks he's above the law," Taylor said. "Once Gina realizes you're back in town, she'll come to you."

Cynthia sensed the danger her daughter was in. The area near the terminal wasn't the best place for young girls. There was a detention center nearby. She concentrated on where two girls might hangout in Atlanta. "Maybe you should shift your search to the Peachtree Center. There are hotels in the area along with the mall and food court."

Taylor grinned. "Pricey area for kids."

"You said she has ten thousand dollars," Tristen reminded.

The detective paused as if about to deliver bad news. "She'll be returned to her family in Huntsville."

"I don't think so. My attorney called. Seems the Ferguson's attorney had me sign the adoption papers a month before Gina was born. My stepmom went along with it. They are not supposed to be signed until after the delivery. If I had known, I could have gotten Gina back years ago or at least worked out something with the adopted parents for updates on her. This will still have to go before a judge."

Tristen stood. "Thank you for your time. Keep us updated on any new developments."

Sensing the detective was ready for them to leave, Cynthia stood and thanked him. She expected Tristen to walk her out. She wanted to run a few things by him, but instead, he left ahead of her and didn't bother to wait or hold the door. He'd been cold to her. Obviously, he was brooding over Austin's kiss.

She recalled in the plane Tristen telling her he loved her and his comment at the Costa Rican lodge about returning on their honeymoon. Their passionate night in Belem flashed through her mind. It shouldn't have happened.

When she checked her calls, Austin wanted to take her to dinner again, but this time without her dad. She thought of the millionaire attorney and his powerful connections and social standing in Atlanta.

He was better for Zurtel than Tristen.

I love Tristen.

Cynthia couldn't let her heart control her.

She called Austin and turned down his dinner invitation. Nothing was more important than finding Gina. Right now, she planned to search for her daughter. She'd start with all the hotels around the Peachtree Center. Surely, someone would recognize her.

Ellis jumped out and ran around opening the door for her. "Mr. Conners handed me this when he first arrived." He gave her an envelope. "He asked me to give it to you."

Once in the car, she opened it and stared at his resignation.

For some reason, it hit her with a wall of emotions. She inhaled several deep breaths fighting the urge to find him and tell him she loved him. After a few moments, she spoke to Ellis. "Drive down Peachtree near the center."

Gina and Sierra stopped at an ATM near the hotel and removed five hundred more dollars before returning to the front desk. Gina's phone rang. It was Liz.

She wants me to turn myself in.

Rather than answer, she clicked her phone off.

Sierra stepped up to the desk clerk. "We would like to extend our stay for another three days."

The clerk checked on the computer. "I'm sorry but your room is booked from Friday through Monday."

"Can you give us another room?"

"Sorry, we're booked solid. There's a lot going on in town this weekend."

Sierra turned to Gina. "Should we look for another hotel?"

"Let's go to my mother's house. We know where the key is, and maybe she'll show up while we're there."

They packed their few belongings and left for the MARTA station.

♦♦♦

Ellis waited out front while Cynthia ran into the elegant hotels that connected to the food court, but she came up short. By that afternoon, she'd already been to ten hotels in the area and no one remembered them. She approached the desk clerk at The Inn at Peachtree and held up Gina's picture. "Have you seen this girl?"

"Sure, she's been staying here with her sister, Sierra."

Joy rushed through Cynthia. "What room?"

"She left about an hour ago. We didn't have any vacancies this weekend."

"Do you know where they were going?"

"I overheard her say something about going to her mom's house. She mentioned having a key."

Cynthia frowned. "She doesn't have a key to my house. Has their room been cleaned?"

He checked. "No. Not yet."

"Please may I take a look to see if she left any clues to where they might be going?"

"Sure." He gave her a key card. "Just drop that off when you leave."

She nodded. "Thanks."

Upstairs, Cynthia stared at the two partially made beds. The girls had straightened up the room before leaving. She picked up the trash can and thumbed through the empty food containers and drink cans. A sheet from a hotel pad lay at the bottom. She picked it up.

Cynthia recognized the numbers on the slip of paper. They were their old cell phone numbers. The numbers Tristen and she had given the Garsons.

A terrible dread fell over her. Randall had their cell phones. Had Gina called the numbers and spoken to him?

Where would he send them?

Would he be bold enough to meet them at his house?

The possibilities terrified Cynthia.

Before leaving, she contacted Detective Taylor.

"I was about to call you," Taylor said. "You were right. She withdrew five hundred this morning from an ATM near the center."

"She's been staying at the Inn at Peachtree not far from there." She told him what she'd discovered at the hotel. "I think she's been in contact with Randall."

"We notified our patrols in that area to watch for them."

"Do you have people watching Randall's house?"

"Patrols drive by regularly and some have stopped and knocked on the door. No one's been there."

After disconnecting, she called the one person she could count on.

"Tristen, it's Cynthia." She explained everything. "She's with a girl named Sierra. There's no way she could have a key to my house. Meet me at Randall's house now." She gave him the address.

"I'll be there."

After disconnecting the call, she climbed in the car. "Ellis, drive to Randall's house as fast as you can."

♦♦♦

That afternoon, Gina and Sierra watched the taxi drive away before walking up the driveway of her mother's house. "It's beautiful."

"It's big," Sierra replied. "Think she's home?"

Gina shrugged. "Let's find out."

They walked up the side steps leading to the big federal style home.

Just as she'd been told, she found a key in the flowerpot. "Guess I should knock first."

"Ring the bell."

She pushed the button and chimes played. "Cool."

They tried several more times and then knocked.

Gina slipped the key in the door. “Here goes nothing.”

After she unlocked the door, she returned the key to the flowerpot. They cautiously entered the enormous house.

“Sort of cold looking. All the furniture is chrome and glass. Nothing’s out of place,” Sierra said. “Maybe we should leave.”

“We’re in the right place.”

They explored the two-story home. It smelled like furniture polish and oranges.

“I’ve never been in a house this big,” Sierra remarked.

They returned to the kitchen. All the appliances were stainless steel. A long wide island ran down the center. Gina opened the refrigerator. “This is the biggest refrigerator I’ve ever seen. Let’s check it out.”

Sierra peered inside it. “It’s filled with food. I’m hungry. Let’s eat.”

They pulled out ham and cheese. Sierra searched through the cabinets until she found the bread and condiments.

“I need a knife or spoon,” Gina said. “Check that drawer.”

Sierra opened a drawer stuffed with mail. She pulled it out. “We’re in the wrong house. This says Quinn Adams lives here.”

Gina’s heart surged. “He must be the man I spoke with. He tricked us. This isn’t my mom’s house.”

Sierra threw everything back in the refrigerator. Let’s get out of here.”

Gina nodded.

They rushed to the living room.

As she grabbed her backpack, a car pulled into the driveway. She walked to the window. A man left a fancy car and walked toward the front door. Gina’s stomach rolled over. “It’s got to be the creepy man who said he’s my uncle.”

The girls grabbed their things and ran back to the kitchen. They tried opening a back door.

Sierra frowned. “It won’t open.” She played with the lock, but it still remained locked. “You have your phone. Call 911.”

The sound of someone walking through the house sent panic through Gina.

"He's coming!" Sierra darted into a small room off the kitchen.

Gina froze.

Sierra motioned for her to follow.

Instead, Gina squatted beneath the quartz countertop extending from the rectangular island. She drew her knees to her chest, hoping he wouldn't notice her.

"Do I have company," called the sinister man. "Gina, I know you're here. Come out, come out, wherever you are."

He sounded so evil.

Along with his steps, Gina heard a clicking sound. It sounded like a retractable pen. He clicked it five or six times and stopped a moment.

"Ladies, I know you're here. I saw you on my surveillance system from my phone. I also locked all the doors, so you have no way out."

Click, Click, Click.

As he came closer, Sierra motioned again for Gina to join her.

Knowing they'd be cornered in the small room, Gina shook her head.

Click, Click, Click, Click.

As he came closer, Gina drew in a breath. She patted the phone in her pocket. There was no way she could call now without him hearing.

When he stepped in front of where she crouched, her heart pounded in her chest. If he looked beneath the counter, he'd see her.

When he took another step, Gina crawled around the end of the island and down the opposite side.

"I love playing hide and seek. I'm very good at it."

Her heart beat faster.

He entered the room where Sierra had hidden. Gina figured he'd find her. He walked back out and stood nervously clicking the pen. Click. Click. Click. Click.

Where had Sierra gone? There had to be another way out through that room.

He left the kitchen and stealthily walked through the house searching for them.

She stood and rushed into the little room off the kitchen. A small window above the laundry room sink had been raised. Sierra had left her.

Gina climbed upon the countertop surrounding the sink and started through the window. Once she was outside and safe, she'd call 911.

"Going somewhere?"

Two strong hands gripped her ankles and jerked her back.

She screamed and tried holding the window.

♦♦♦

Tristen waited outside Randall's house with Cynthia.

The police walked out.

"Anything?" she asked.

"Nothing. No one's been here."

Cynthia turned to him, looking as if she wanted to be comforted.

Tristen ignored her. She'd made her position clear at the airport. Whatever had happened in Belem hadn't meant anything to her. They'd both been drinking and caught up in the romantic atmosphere.

Standing to the side, he remembered Gina had a burner phone. He called Dan and got Gina's phone number. Afterwards, he joined Cynthia. "Ride with me."

She didn't question him.

In his SUV, he handed her Gina's number. Dan Garson just gave it to me. He said she hasn't been taking their calls. Call her. Maybe, she'll pick up. Ask where she is."

Cynthia keyed in the number. "It's turned off."

"Keep trying."

Gina struggled against the man's grip. When his arm came near her mouth, she bit it.

"Shit! That hurt." He slammed her down on a bar stool. He grabbed her hair and jerked her head back, then slapped her hard. "You're a feisty little bitch." He held her face, his fingers digging into her skin. "You hurt me. I hurt you back. It doesn't have to be this way. I have a nice little trip to South America planned for us. You get to join your lovely parents after I'm done with you."

Suddenly, Sierra ran out of the laundry room and jumped on his back. "Run, Gina!"

Gina sprinted to the front door, but it wouldn't budge. She turned and looked for a place to hide. Not seeing anywhere, she ran upstairs, darted into a bedroom, and locked the door behind her.

It'd only be minutes before he found her.

Remembering her phone, she pulled it out and turned it on. As she went to call 911, it rang.

She answered it. "Hello."

"I know you're still in my house."

She gasped. "I called the police," she lied. "They're on their way."

He disconnected the call. Within minutes, he banged on the door. "I'll kill your friend if you don't open this fucking door."

As Gina started toward the door, her phone rang again.

She answered it. "Hello."

"Gina, it's Mom! Where are you?"

She couldn't stop the tears. "I'm in a house, and there's a man trying to hurt me."

"Sweetie, do you remember the address?"

He rammed against the door. It sounded like the door would come off its hinges.

"He's coming!"

"Think hard. What's the address he gave you?"

"It's on Ridgeway Circle. I don't remember the address. It has lions on each side of the driveway. I put the key back in the flowerpot on the porch."

"I know that house. Hang on. I'm on my way."

He slammed against the door, then kicked it in.

Gina screamed as the door crashed open.

"We have a plane to catch." He grabbed her wrist and dragged her through the house. "We're leaving."

Gina kicked the front of his leg.

"You little bitch." He jerked her back. "It's going to be exciting breaking you in. You're full of fight."

As he dragged her down the stairs, the front door opened. A man and woman stood there.

"Randall, let her go!"

Gina recognized the woman's voice from the call. Her mother.

"Thought you were dead," Randall said.

"Ravelo lied."

Randall pulled a gun and held it at Gina's head. "I'll kill her. You know I don't bluff. Now get the hell out of my way."

"It's over, Randall," the man with her mother said. "The police are right behind us." He shifted his attention to her. "Gina, I'm your father."

Tears clogged her throat.

He smiled. "We're not letting him take you."

Her mother pulled a small gun from her pocket and aimed it at Randall.

Her father flashed a stern look her way. "Gina drop!"

Gina let her body go limp and dropped from Randall's grasp.

In the same second, the gun fired hitting Randall. He crumpled to the floor.

Her mom stood with the gun still in her hand.

Gina's ears rang from the shot, and the room smelled of sulfur. Her heart still raced, making breathing difficult.

Sirens blared in the near distance.

♦♦♦

Cynthia walked over to Randall. He was still alive. She glanced back at Tristen. "Take Gina outside. I need to speak with my stepbrother."

Tristen hugged her. "Come on, Gina. Let's go outside."

"Sierra," Gina whimpered. "He said he would kill her."

"Take her out and send help back for the girl," Cynthia said, thinking Sierra could be dead. If that were the case, she didn't want Gina seeing her.

"Call me an ambulance," Randall said.

As the police cars pulled into the driveway, she turned back to Randall. "You won't need one. I plan to kill you."

"You won't do it," he taunted.

"I told you in Brazil, if you went near my daughter, I'd kill you."

Randall started to raise his gun.

She pulled the trigger. This time she hit the center of his forehead.

Randall's eyes remained open, but it was evident he was dead.

Cynthia quickly removed her phone and took a picture. She planned to send it to Sister Anna. Now her promise to them was fulfilled.

Detective Taylor and three officers plowed through the front door. Immediately, the detective took her gun. The others rushed to the kitchen to find Sierra.

Tristen entered behind them. "Are you all right?"

"I'm fine. I can't say the same for Quinn Adams." She motioned to the gun still clutched in Randall's hand. "It was self-defense."

A policeman yelled from the kitchen. "Get an ambulance. We have a young white female suffering from head contusions."

"Where's Gina?" she asked Tristen.

"She's outside waiting for you." He offered his hand. "Let's go see our daughter."

Gina stood to the side telling another detective what had happened.

Cynthia made her way through the people. She held her arms out, and Gina ran toward her. They embraced and cried as they held one another. An overpowering sense of fulfillment and warmth surged through Cynthia, bringing more tears to her eyes.

"My dear sweet, little girl, I love you, and I've been trying to find you."

Gina squeezed her harder. "I know. The Garsons told me. They said you were forced to give me up."

"I was, but I thought of you everyday especially on your birthday. We have so much to catch up on."

The EMTs pushed a young, pretty blonde woman out on a gurney.

"Sierra!" Gina shouted. She ran over to her friend. "Your face."

"I told them I'm okay, but they insist on taking me to the hospital. That bastard just about knocked my teeth out when he punched me. I must've hit my head because that's all I remember until the policeman woke me."

"It's my fault. I thought you'd gone out the window."

Sierra took Gina's hand. "You silly nilly. I can't fit through that window. I wanted him to think I escaped. But when I heard you screaming, I had to leave my hiding place."

Cynthia stood by the gurney "We'll be at the hospital once I get this mess cleared up. You won't be alone."

Gina smiled. "She needs a job."

"Sounds to me like she needs a home."

The EMTs placed Sierra in the ambulance and drove off.

Gina nodded. "Do I have to go back to Huntsville?"

Cynthia placed an arm around her and squeezed. "Not if I can help it."

Detective Taylor joined them. "It's clear to me it was self-defense." He looked at Gina. "Your family in Huntsville is worried sick."

"I ran away, because my aunt tried to kill me, but no one believed me."

The detective's expression revealed his concern. "Tell me about it."

They listened as Gina explained. Afterwards, she appeared uncertain. "Do I have to go back?"

"No, you're mine," Cynthia said. "There's just a little red tape I'll have to take care of." Cynthia frowned. "I plan to deal with Aunt Nell in person."

Gina hugged her. "You believe me?"

"You bet I do."

Gina peeked around at Tristen. "You're really my dad?"

He nodded. "Yeah, I am."

Cynthia looked at Tristen. "Sunday night. Six o'clock at my house for dinner."

"What's wrong with tomorrow?"

"Gina and I are flying to Huntsville. And one more thing," she handed him his letter of resignation. "I'm not accepting it."

"Why not?"

"Because I don't want to be married to a trophy husband."

Tristen grinned. "Is that a proposal?"

She nodded. "I guess it is."

"What about Austin Gunner?"

"I don't love him. I love you."

Tristen pulled her into his arms and kissed her. "I love you. I always have. And my answer is yes."

"Yes, you're coming back to work, or yes, you'll marry me."

"Both." He kissed her again. "Someone's got to keep you in line."

Gina beamed with happiness. "I'm getting a mom and a dad."

"And a little sister," Tristen said.

"Sweet. I've always wanted a sister. I can't wait to meet her."

♦♦♦

Cynthia and Gina stood at the door of Gina's house in Huntsville on Bramble Wood Drive. It thrilled her to think her daughter had grown up in this lovely home. Her adoptive parents had been wonderful people.

The door opened, and a short, dumpy woman answered. She wore a cast on her leg. "Gina, you're home. Oh, we've been worried sick about you." She shouted through the house. "Guys, Gina's back."

An older boy and girl ran down the stairs and glowered at them. They didn't look pleased to see Gina.

"Cut the crap," Cynthia said.

"Who are you?" Aunt Nell asked.

"She's my mother," Gina said proudly.

Aunt Nell flashed a confident look. "We have legal custody of Gina."

"Not for long. My attorneys found a loophole in the original adoption. Gina isn't returning to you. Furthermore, you have five hours to pack your personal things and move out."

"You can't make us leave. We have rights. I'm calling the police."

"You do, and I'll make sure they arrest you for attempted murder. You can be evicted or convicted. Your choice."

Aunt Nell's face paled. Shellie and Will stood dumfounded.

"And be sure you only take what you came with."

Gina offered Aunt Nell a sweet smile beaming with delight. "By the way, I have Mom's rings."

Her aunt's face tightened, and her eyes narrowed. "Why you little…"

Cynthia gently nudged her daughter aside and got up close and personal with Aunt Nell. "You call her an ugly name, and you'll need a cast for your other leg as well. I'm I clear?"

Nell paled and nodded.

Later that day, Cynthia and Gina found the house vacated. She gave her daughter time to pack what she wanted to keep and then arranged for a company to move it to Atlanta. The house and anything left inside would be sold and the money placed in a trust for Gina.

Before leaving Sunday morning, they stopped by the Garsons to collect Gina's belongings and to thank them. Gina said her goodbyes and promised to stay in touch.

Sunday on the midday flight home, Gina reached over and clasped Cynthia's hand in hers. "May I call you mom?"

"I'd like that." Tears of joy filled Cynthia's eyes. She had her daughter, the little dark haired infant she'd only seen briefly. "I can't believe it. You're finally mine."

♦♦♦

Tristen called Mallory into the den. "Sit by me. There's something I need to tell you."

She placed her dolls down beside her. "They want to hear too."

He nodded. "Remember the story we told you about the princess finding her baby?"

She nodded.

"Do you remember the part about how the princess and prince loved each other?"

She sighed looking bored, then nodded. "Is this about that girl?"

"No. This is about Miss Cynthia and me."

Her eyes flickered with interest, and she sat straighter and listened more keenly.

"I loved your mom, so much. You know that, don't you?"

She nodded. "But you used to love Miss Cynthia."

"That's right. Well, we've discovered we still love one another. What I'm trying to say is, Miss Cynthia and I are getting married. And you get to be in the wedding."

Mallory asked, "What about that other girl?"

"Gina—your sister?"

"Hmmm, yeah her. Will she be in the wedding?"

"Probably."

"Will I call Miss Cynthia, mom?"

"Not until you're comfortable with it."

She sighed and stared off for a moment.

"So are you good with it?"

She appeared in thought a moment before nodding. “It’s what I wished for on my birthday. Can I wear a pink dress in the wedding? Do I get to throw flower petals?”

“Of course.” Tristen sighed with relief. Though he still would’ve married Cynthia, Mallory’s blessing made it even more special.

♦♦♦

Sunday night, Tristen rang the doorbell at Cynthia’s house on Marann Drive. “Be nice.”

Mallory stood beside him holding a bag full of Barbies. “What if I don’t like Gina?”

“You will. Remember she’s just recently lost the only mother she’s known. You know how much that hurts.”

“If you marry Miss Cynthia, will we live here?”

“Probably, since it’s twice as large as our house.” Tristen knew there would be too many memories of Danielle in his home.

Cynthia opened the door. “Come in, you two. Dinner is almost ready.”

“You look beautiful,” he said and kissed her lightly. Tristen had been nervous about the kiss. It was the first time Mallory had witnessed any form of intimacy between Cynthia and him other than the incident at Snowbird. His daughter stared with interest, but didn’t question the simple kiss.

Cynthia hugged Mallory. “There’s someone who wants to meet you.”

Gina entered the room and froze the moment she saw Mallory. “Wow. We do look alike. Cool.”

Cynthia introduced the girls. “You’re half-sisters.”

Gina smiled. “I always wanted a sister. I never had anyone to play with.”

Mallory held up the bag. “Will you play Barbies with me?”

“Sure. Show me your dolls.”

Mallory smiled. “I got Ballerina Barbie for Christmas. She’s my favorite. I take ballet.”

“I dance too.”

The two girls ran off to the family room, chattering like two monkeys."

"See, I told you they'd hit it off," Cynthia said.

Tristen pulled Cynthia into his arms and kissed her deeply—a kiss of passion and love. He had melted the ice around her heart and reclaimed the love he'd once lost.

Now if only he could convince her to spend less time at Zurtel. With Gina and Mallory in her life, he didn't think that would be a problem.

For once life had gone his way. He was thankful.

After dinner, Cynthia glanced at the girls sprawled over the living room furniture. Mallory leaned against Gina. It was as if they'd been born into the same family and raised together. Sierra sat across from them. She'd been instructed to take it easy for the next week. Cynthia had arranged for Sierra to live with them and help with the girls while attending college.

Tristen came up and placed his arm around her. "Think you can handle being a mom of two girls and run the company?"

She smiled. "I'm hiring someone to take over for me. I'll still be involved in the development, but I won't have to work nearly as many hours."

"You'll make a wonderful mom." He pulled her into his arms and kissed her deeply. "I'm glad you've learned there's more to life than Zurtel."

"I want time to smell the roses." She turned her attention to Mallory, who was repeating the story they had told her.

"And the prince and princess found their baby," Mallory said. "But now she wasn't a baby. And they took their little girl home to meet her sister, Mallory, a ballerina. And they lived happily ever after. The end."

Epilogue

Sister Anna held the phone up where Bonita could see the picture. "Miss Cynthia kept her promise."

Bonita smiled. "The monster is dead."

"And Ravelo will spend many years in prison for selling guns to the rebels."

"Tonight, we celebrate."

♦♦♦

Pete Wilson opened his mail and thought he was hallucinating. There was a check from Zurtel Aerospace Corporation for one hundred thousand dollars and a letter from Gina, the girl he'd given a ride to. Reading that she'd found her mother, he smiled. At the bottom of her letter, her mom had written one line. *Thank you for being my daughter's guardian angel. Cynthia Conners.*

♦♦♦

Kayla stood at Randall's grave, holding back the tears.

Cynthia Reynolds approached her. Being the one who killed him, the lady had her nerve attending his funeral. She hadn't seen the wealthy CEO since the Christmas Eve dinner at Randall's stepfather's home.

"Kayla, I'm truly sorry about Randall," Cynthia said.

"You didn't have to kill him."

"I'm afraid I did. He aimed his gun at me. It was him or me. You didn't know him like I did. He would've never married you. You're better off without him."

She laughed softly. "We were married at the courthouse right after he returned from Brazil. I'm Mrs. Randall Miller. "

Cynthia appeared surprised.

"I own Novik now. I intend to make it the most successful company in the industry."

"Good luck with that," Cynthia said, sarcastically.

Kayla smiled. The Reynolds couldn't stay on top forever.

Cynthia and Tristen walked through the doors of Parchira Lodge in Tortuguero, Costa Rica. She wore a lovely Oscar De La Renta dress and Espadrille sandals. Tristen wore Armani pants and shirt.

The manager glanced up. He stared as if trying to place them.

"Remember us," Cynthia said. "Pasca sent us. We stayed just one night."

The man's mouth dropped as he studied their appearance. "Si, I remember you."

Tristen grinned. "I told you that we'd come back for our honeymoon."

The manager smiled. "You clean up well."

That night, they dined in the lovely restaurant with the high ceiling supported by wooden beams. Soft island music played giving off a romantic ambience. She couldn't wait to retire to their bungalow.

After they ordered dinner, she sipped on a tropical drink garnished with fruit slices. "Let's toast to Zurtel's patent on MX7."

"You promised no business talk. Let's toast to us and our children." He raised his bourbon and Coke and clinked her glass lightly. "To us and our beautiful daughters."

Cynthia smiled. "I'll drink to that."

Tristen glanced around. "Too bad they don't have a dance floor."

"I danced enough at our reception." She smiled. "I'm glad Annie caught my bouquet."

"She was really excited." He chuckled. "Evan didn't look too pleased. I've always thought she had a thing for him." He sighed. "I'm afraid Mallory will be sick from eating too much cake."

"Gina too. Think Sierra can handle things?" she asked.

"I'm certain she can. Rose said she'd check on them. You're not getting out of ziplining or rafting."

"No, I'm looking forward to it." She paused. "I'm surprised Rose and Kenneth came to the wedding. She was extremely nice to Gina and me. It has to be bittersweet for her."

"She's just really happy you're rooted in Atlanta."

"I'm a genuine southern belle."

He grinned. "Yep. Headstrong and gorgeous."

Later in their room, Tristen held her in his arms. "You look gorgeous tonight. I'm the luckiest man in the world."

"You're about to get luckier." Cynthia guided him to the king-sized bed in the honeymoon bungalow. She pushed him back on the bed, then leaned over and kissed him with more passion than she'd ever kissed anyone.

He patted the bed. "Lie beside me." She did. He leaned over her and stared down with love in his eyes. "I love you, Cynthia Conners. We were always destined to be together."

Overwhelming joy filled her heart, and she fought the tears.

For the next three hours, they made hot steamy love beneath the tropical moonlight shining through the window. Island music played nearby.

Afterwards, Cynthia rested in his arms.

She had put her life into perspective. Life was short. She wanted to spend all of that time with Tristen and the girls. This time, the flyboy wouldn't leave her. There'd be no turbulence, just blue skies from here to eternity.

The End.

Thank you for reading.

If you enjoyed Turbulence, please leave a review with Amazon. It really helps Indie published authors like myself to reach new readers and helps me obtain advertising on promotional book sites. It also affects the way my books are ranked.

Coming Next

Grounded

Book Two of the Flight for Life Series

Zurtel's new CEO, Brice Jordan, finds himself thrown into a whirlwind of espionage along with a mission to rescue Annie's sister from a Phoenix based religious cult. Hoping to reconnect with his ex-wife, he fights falling in love with the quiet, reserved flight attendant.

About the Author

Elaine Meece writes romantic suspense novels. She is an active member of Romance Writers of America, River City Romance Writers, Music City Romance Writers, and Malice of Memphis. She has been a finalist and won many RWA chapter contests for best romantic suspense.

She resides in Bartlett, Tennessee with her husband, Geoffrey. Elaine is a former elementary school teacher. Besides writing, she loves hiking, kayaking, inner tubing, and whitewater rafting.

She is a member of the Memphis Scottish Society and Bartlett United Methodist Church. She also sings with the Rhodes Master Singers, who perform with Memphis Symphony Orchestra.

Join her Facebook page: author Elaine Meece or follow her on Twitter or visit www.elainemeece.com to sign up for her newsletter.

74949778R00177

Made in the USA
Columbia, SC
09 August 2017